SPOOK CITY

PETER ATKINS
CLIVE BARKER
RAMSEY CAMPBELL

EDITED BY
ANGUS MACKENZIE
INTRODUCTION BY
DOUG BRADLEY

Encyclopocalypse Publications
www.encyclopocalypse.com

CONTENTS

FOREWORD

ANGUS MACKENZIE

This book of horror stories was conceived in Amsterdam, realized in Los Angeles, Nottingham and London and exists solely because of another city: Liverpool.

That city, spreading from the deep cut that is the river Mersey, was, for the dreaming Carl Jung, *the pool of life,* and if this city dreams unto itself, then not all of its dreams are easy. The collective unconscious of its people is as much marked with a dark filigree as the city is itself marked by the dark waters of the Mersey.

From its leafy Georgian avenues, oppressive terraced streets, and now-pulled-down developments has come an overwhelming tidal force of talent: cutting humor in a procession of comedians, passion in the energy of footballers, music that has 'shook the world', captivation in the disguise of actors on worn wooden stages and smoke stained screens and fear and dread, anxiety and panic, horror and dark, dark wonder in the form of Peter Atkins, Clive Barker and Ramsey Campbell. Along with Doug Bradley, they make up The Ceno-Beatles; four lads who 'spooked the world'.

A horror writer, just like everyone, must come from somewhere and that somewhere will leave its mark on you if you see enough sunsets there. This, in itself, is probably not worthy of much remark when everyone is formed by an incalculable number of factors of which environment is but one. So, if a writer of horror fiction could be conceived anywhere, then why not in a river city at the end of a railway line in the North West of England? What is a little remarkable however is that from this city we have not one horror writer, nor two, but three; all born within the space of ten years of each other and as many miles.

Everyone comes from somewhere and these writers come from Liverpool (all, in fact, from the same southern suburb of Wavertree) and each has in turn written about their city: Peter Atkins in *Morningstar* (1992) and *Big Thunder* (1997); Clive Barker in *Weaveworld* (1987) and *Everville* (1994) and Ramsey Campbell—well Ramsey, who still looks out at the Mersey from the windows of his haunted house, has, from *The Doll Who Ate his Mother* (1976) through to *The Creatures of the Pool* (2008) brought human madness, supernatural malevolence and such a saturating fog of horror down onto the place that there is barely a visible corner of it left untouched by the cold hand of his imagination.

This book brings together for the first time the work of all three of these writers and those of their stories specifically set in or inspired by Liverpool. Some are familiar modern classics; some have been written specifically for this collection; and, in the case of 'Coming to Liverpool', we have Ramsey Campbell's new non-fiction companion piece to 'At the Back of My Mind: A Guided Tour'. As that piece, published as the introduction to the restored edition of *The Face That Must Die* (1983), dealt with brutal honesty about the traumas of his childhood and the subsequent death of his parents, this new work covers the early happier life of his family in Liverpool and is all the more poignant and melancholic as a foreshadow of the disintegration that was to come.

I too, like the writers and like Doug Bradley (the actor

who portrayed the iconic character of Pinhead in the Hellraiser movies and who provides the introduction to this book), was born in Liverpool and spent my formative years there. I knew the streets that John Horridge, the blade wielding sociopath from Ramsey Campbell's *The Face That Must Die* (1979), limped down. The Scourge from Clive Barker's *Weaveworld* (1987) was hit head-on by a train on a railway line that I took journeys on. The bowdlerizing protagonist from Peter Atkins' *Here Comes a Candle* (1988) meets his end in a house Pete told me was much like the one that Ramsey lives in overlooking the river. The horror in these stories was therefore personal to me and occurring in the very place in which I was living. In the same way that Strawberry Fields and Penny Lane— evocatively known throughout the world through the music of The Beatles—were just locations in Liverpool that I knew from living there, so too was the work of these writers familiar to me in a way that it could only be to someone from Liverpool. Only through meeting people from other faraway places did I come to realize the magic and significance of the Beatles' music to so many people and that not everyone can take for granted such an artistically explored hometown.

For me, as a fan of the horror genre growing up in Liverpool, it had another greater significance in that I also grew up knowing the people that created this work, as this shared passion invariably brings you to the same dusty bookshops, film societies and circle of friends.

In Ramsey we have a prodigiously gifted writer who has given his creative life to the horror genre. In a career that now casts a very long shadow he has learnt how to precision engineer selected words into sentences that have been meticulously designed to achieve disquiet. And yet he is such a cheery chappie, with a mischievous sense of humor, garrulous laugh and neat line in offensive t-shirts. Even in the most innocuous of settings, though, I've seen him quietly take out his notebook and scribble something onto the page in his quick and fluid handwriting. These notes can become elements of stories that have won him more awards than anyone else working in the field.

The movies *Hellraiser II: Hellbound* and *Hellraiser III: Hell on Earth* were written in the back room of a terraced house in Wavertree (which had a big imposing black front door) and which some critics thought came from a sick mind. Peter Atkins doesn't live in this house anymore (and it now has a nice white glass front door) and I wonder what the current owners would think if they knew what horrors of desire and rendered flesh were hammered out from a manual typewriter in their back room (it was only after the success of *Hellbound* that Pete could afford to buy a computer). It was during the filming of *Hellraiser III* in North Carolina that Pete, strolling past the outdoor pool and wearing shades, glanced down to see Doug Bradley swimming in the warm sunlit water wearing shades. They both realized that they were a long way away from their days in Liverpool and burst out laughing at the absurdity of it.

Given that Clive began to achieve significant success with a series of sometimes autoptical stories in *The Books of Blood* (1984), he was never that comfortable with the ol' claret stuff in Liverpool, nigh on fainting in the cinema at the sight of it spurting one memorable time. He also had a bad episode after giving blood once and was saved from falling out of a window by a quick thinking nurse who pulled him back after he opened a window to get some fresh air after feeling faint at the sight of the coagulating glue sitting in bowls under the donors' beds. He subsequently—in the company of a similarly overwhelmed Pete Atkins— was to feel a little unsteady on his feet browsing through the pages of forensic pathology books in a medical bookstore, and it is therefore only to his credit that he could produce such harrowing, visceral horror in such beautifully executed prose.

As I mentioned, this book exists because of Liverpool: the introduction was written by an actor whose performances as the Pinhead Cenobite from the Hellraiser series have given this character an unquestionable iconic status in the history of horror cinema; the stories, written over the course of four decades, come from writers who have all breathed its air, walked its beautiful and frightening streets and slept under its night skies. They know their way around this place and if you are ready to go with them they'll be happy to show you around.

Angus Mackenzie, Amsterdam, August 2008
(revised for this edition in May 2024)

INTRODUCTION

DOUG BRADLEY

Wonsuponatime[1] on the banks of a dirty great river, there was a small fishing village where not a lot happened. There were some monks with a boat, but not much else. But the people ate so much fish from the dirty great river[2] that they grew and grew and the King was forced to give them a city which grew and grew and became dirty and great like the river.

People dreamed dreams in and of this city. Some said it was the pool of life and calculated that it was the center of the known or unknown universe: others had more disturbing dreams about the deep dark mud on the shores of its river.

Dirty great ships sailed up and down the dirty great river to and from far away places with strange sounding names like New Brighton and New York. Many people sailed away from the city to lead new lives in New Worlds. Some were forced to leave and it made them very sad. Many people sailed into the city to lead new lives in Old Worlds. Some were forced to come and sold for money which made some people very rich and it makes us sad to think about it.

---

1. *Deliberately and shamelessly nicked: don't write in.*
2. *Which was probably quite clean back then, but don't write in.*

Lots of things came into the city on the ships, like cotton and spices and tea, which made more people very rich. Other things arrived by accident. Rats, probably, but also strange new musics which made people in caverns tap their feet and rock and roll. Lots of rock was dug out of the ground, too. Much of it from a quarry near where John met Paul and Eleanor was laid to rest, and it was used to build dirty great buildings, including a cathedral. In fact, the city got two of those, and three graces, too.

Occasionally, strange things happened in this city. Sometimes people fell out of the sky, sometimes on flaming pies, and that made some people do extraordinary things. One of them was called Clive and he wrote plays and stories and painted pictures and made films with puppets and people. I met him, and he became my friend. Inspired by him, I tried to write and draw things, too, but that wasn't how my brain worked. I spoke a lot of his words instead in far away places with strange sounding names like Redditch and Spokane and Cricklewood.

And we had a friend called Sue who had a brother called Graham who had a mate called Peter. And Graham said to Peter: you should meet my sister's friend, Clive. And, in a library, they did, and that made Peter write things too, and I spoke lots of his words, too, in far away places with strange sounding names like Pinewood and Hollywood and High Point. And all this time there was a Proper Writer called Ramsey and he met Clive and they became friends and I spoke some of his words too, about a ghost train in New Brighton, in the basement of a radio station in another dirty great city on the banks of a different dirty great river.

I've lived in the other dirty great city for more than thirty years now. I regard London as my home, but the old adage about taking the boy out of a place but not the place out of the boy has always been true. Liverpool is in the marrow of my bones and, while I can't imagine myself ever living there again, I don't ever expect it to—or want it to—let me go. Between the twin loyalties of family and Liverpool Football Club, there has not been a single year in those thirty when I haven't returned at least a couple of times.

It's changed dramatically in that time, of course. Probably the most obvious is that now, like Paul McCartney's granddad in *A Hard Day's Night*, it is 'very clean'. It's difficult to remember it, but the photographs confirm it: where now St George's Hall and the Liver Buildings, along with Liverpool's other civic buildings (and few cities can boast better), positively gleam in the sunshine, they used to wear a dark black coat of soot.

Football crowds seem to have undergone the same transformation over time. On my first visit to Anfield in 1964, the Kop appeared to be a mass of disembodied pink faces, floating on a black sea. Fast forward to today and the Kop is a mass of replica shirts and the whole scene is awash with color, including many of the faces, but in the forty year old snapshots in my memory even the grass and the players' shirts are rendered in black and white. No doubt this apparent monochromatic perception, coupled with a child's focus on a big city, goes a long way to inform my feelings about Liverpool four decades ago. I'm sure factors as mundane as improved street lighting play their part, too, but that city in my head seems an altogether more forbidding, grander, darker and more dangerous place than does the city that lies at the end of the M62 motorway today.

Now, for example, the Albert Dock is a beautiful sight, even if it has been reduced to yet another playground for the modern human whose life seems to revolve entirely around shopping and eating (and, I hope, a visit to the Tate or one of its museums), but it was not like that when I was growing up. Rumors always swirled about its fate (demolition, University halls of residence, hotel etc.) but it remained defiantly empty and enticing, filled with seafaring and laboring ghosts and

Mersey mud. I seem to recall a bunch of us on a winter's night (who knows when? 1970 would be some kind of marker) down at the Pier Head, rain and wind whipping in off the river, gazing towards its mournfully elegant, deserted warehouses with Clive in full imaginative flow, spinning fantasies through its dereliction. I have, I should warn you, learned not to trust my memories over time and distance, but I'm so sure about this one that as I write I have a vague sense of annoyance that, to the best of my knowledge, Clive never featured Liverpool's abandoned docks in any of his fiction.

The travails and woes that afflicted Liverpool through the seventies and eighties have been too often chronicled for me to wade through them again. Suffice to say that the sense of abandonment and decay that afflicted the Albert Dock seemed at times to be a microcosm of the whole city. I have no intention of suggesting any psycho/socio/politico/economico/any-otherico basis for the dark fires that burn in these pages (and Clive for one would probably never speak to me again if I were to try), but it might also be invidious not to see some connection. Liverpool's *genii loci* are a varied bunch, it seems to me, and while those detailed to look after Wit and Sheer Downright Determination To Have A Good Time No Matter What are clearly pulling 24/7 shifts, there are darker gods moving among them whose voices will be heard. So, while Lennon & McCartney brought a psychedelic whimsy to the Liverpool of their childhoods, and writers such as Willy Russell and Alan Bleasdale chronicled in harsh and humorous detail the realities of life in the city at that time, Messrs. Atkins, Barker & Campbell—the ABC of Liverpool horror writers (can I copyright that?)—while no less faithful to the city they lived in, found the landscape of their city as mythological as it was real.

Take a walk through the Spector Street Estate with Clive and you will have no doubt that you are in a real, decaying urban landscape. While I was still at school and Clive was at

Liverpool University, I recall him talking about going on long lunchtime walks that took him into Gerrard Gardens, the Bullring: tenement flats built in the 1930s to replace 'slums' and hailed in their day as Art Deco gems and the face of The City Of The Future but condemned as slums in their turn by the time Clive was visiting and finally falling foul of the wrecker's ball in the late 1980s (the flats, not Clive). Had Clive chosen to merely chronicle the urban environment he found himself in (he, like me, was a child of the suburbs of South Liverpool and so brought the eye of the proverbial 'anthropologist on Mars' to these places) I have no doubt he would have done so memorably. In fact, he did exactly that. And had it stopped there, his writing might have been admired by a small circle of interested souls. But Clive did a great deal more than that. Here he encountered, in his head if not in fact, the figure of The Candyman, who fired one of the most powerful stories in his *Books Of Blood* anthology and who has (albeit relocated from Inner-City Liverpool to South Side Chicago), through the medium of cinema and the person of actor Tony Todd, touched people in every corner of the globe.

The dark gods prowled the leafy, well-heeled suburbs as well. I recently revisited the path along the side of Woolton's disused quarry— the 'Bogey-Walk' of Clive's *Coming To Grief* —for the first time in more than thirty years. It is a far more managed and manicured place than it used to be—and I had the benefit of a perfect summer morning of warm sun and dazzlingly clear light rather than the wintry wind and rain of Miriam's re-encounter—but I was surprised by how it still retained its powerful and unsettling atmosphere. There are no gaps in crumbling brick walls giving way to dizzying prospects of the rubbish and rainwater-filled quarry below these days. A high, solidly maintained breeze-block wall surmounted by an impressive array of twisted, barbed metalwork keeps the vertigo at bay and ensures that no latter-day equivalents of Marjorie Elliot's widower could step off the path to an inevitable fate below, but that same wall promotes a sense of claustrophobia and ensured that on my visit the path remained in deep, cool shade: the ferns rooting themselves in the sandstone testimony to that.

It's a place of baffling Escheresque geometry. You leave a broad suburban street, make your way along the path and emerge onto a broad suburban street having apparently travelled on the level. You could be forgiven for being unaware that for a considerable part of your journey, there was a drop of some one hundred feet to one side of you. That becomes evident when you walk around and enter the site of the quarry itself. Not that it serves as a rubbish dump anymore (I recall it being a tire dump: on one memorable occasion, a fire started and a thick, black, acrid pall of smoke hung over the area): now It's a small estate of proudly and neatly kept houses. Like any other modern suburban street were it not for the sheer slabs of ancient sea—or river—bed rising high above the roof tops: still a distinctly atmospheric place. An ideal setting for another sequel to Stephen Spielberg's *Poltergeist*, perhaps, or maybe, just maybe, still a place of 'a dozen rumored atrocities' or where 'tales of hook-handed men and secret lovers slaughtered in the act of love' might still be whispered on cold, dark nights halfway along the Bogey-Walk.

Sandstone is everywhere in this part of Liverpool. Its walls ring Sefton Park, the setting for Michael's fateful encounter with Carol on his late night walk home. I was amused to see that Liverpool City Council are currently undertaking 'improvements' in the park which include draining and clearing the old boating lake. I just hope that they won't have disturbed things better left untouched among the prams and shopping trolleys.

I'm afraid It's time for me to state the obvious. I've been trying to find some way to avoid it, but in vain. Liverpool is a city of spooks. There it is. I found a website that tells me so. At 44 Penny Lane there's a recurring manifestation of footsteps pacing in the house. At 82 Wimborne Road in Huyton, a family were terrified by the shade of an old lady with a shriveled skull for a head, bent over a walking stick. 'George' has been seen standing by beds on the fifth floor of the Adelphi Hotel on many occasions. Shoppers in Bold Street have at various times reported finding themselves briefly back in the 1940s. A phantom peers through the windows of parked cars on the corner of Argyle and Canning Streets. The Sixth Earl of Sefton is keen on visiting the tea-room at Croxteth Hall. An ill-advised hitch-hiker, hit by a car in the Mersey Tunnel, is apparently still trying to get out. Etcetera. And so on.

That's not the obvious bit. The obvious bit is that this makes Liverpool no different to any other city, town or village anywhere else in the country or, indeed, the world. I could, for example, tell you about Spring-Heeled Jack, the extraordinary diabolic gentleman possessed of a supernatural ability to leap prodigious heights, sometimes breathing flames as he went, who terrified inhabitants of the Everton area of Liverpool in the nineteenth century. The trouble is that if I did, I'd have to also tell you how he similarly troubled the good citizenry of Sheffield and London, the Midlands and Scotland. And I wouldn't bet against discovering Jack—or someone very like him—turning up in other countries as well.

I could take more time to share the specific places referenced in these pages: the bus stops and journeys in *Eternal Delight*, perhaps. I could take you on a tour through Ramsey's *Calling Card*, but by the time we'd made the walk from Lark Lane to Otterspool Prom, taken the ferry 'cross the Mersey from the Pier Head to Woodside and taken in the aquarium and the museum, you'd be fairly exhausted and possibly not much the wiser, depending on my abilities as a guide.

Because the *really* obvious bit is that these stories are, as I think somebody else once put it, tales of mystery and imagination, of human fears and terrors. They are therefore universal: here to be enjoyed whether you've lived your whole life in Liverpool or have never—and are unlikely ever to—set foot in the place. There, I did it.

But—at the risk of contradicting myself—these are also very much stories rooted in a relatively small number of square miles of land to be found at the end of the M62 motorway. So I'm going to leave you now in the most excellent company of Messrs. Atkins, Barker and Campbell and invite them to lead you into the dark heart of Spook City.

Actually, I'm jealous. Do you mind if I tag along?

-Doug Bradley

For my mother, Johanna

"You know what some people are calling Liverpool these days?"
"No."
"Spook City."
"Spook City?"
"And with good reason, believe me."

—Clive Barker, *Weaveworld*

SPOOK CITY

PETER ATKINS

...was born in Liverpool in 1955. He was educated at Heygreen Road County Primary, the Liverpool Bluecoat School, and Liverpool University. In 1974, between grammar school and university, he joined a Liverpool theatre collective that would eventually be known as The Dog Company and which included Clive Barker and Doug Bradley. Over the next several years they performed in many Liverpool venues including the Everyman and the Eleanor Rathbone theatres and the parking lots of council estates. Alan Bleasdale did them out of a grant for a mime oratorio to be performed in the Anglican Cathedral by describing the proposed work as 'a prime candidate for Pseud's Corner'. He was doubtless right but they still think he's a twat. In 1980, Atkins founded the pop/rock band The Chase with whom he played most of the much-missed venues of the early

'eighties such as The Warehouse, The Masonic, *and* Brady's *and the group achieved the dizzy heights of hearing two tracks from their cassette EP played on Janice Long's show on Radio Merseyside while driving back from a gig in New Brighton. Their final performance was at a lunchtime show at The Cavern. Atkins newest book is the story collection* All Our Hearts Are Ghosts. *His previous collection,* Rumours of the Marvelous, *was a finalist for the British Fantasy Award. He is the author of the novels* Morningstar, Big Thunder *and* Moontown *and the screenplays* Hellraiser II, Hellraiser III, Hellraiser IV *and* Wishmaster. *He can be found on Facebook under his own name and on Twitter and Instagram as @limeybastard55.*

ETERNAL DELIGHT

PETER ATKINS

> *Energy is eternal delight.*
> —William Blake

> *A Wop Bop a Loo Bop a Lop Bam Boom!*
> —Little Richard

Liverpool, 1985

It was only when all his friends had betrayed him that David Holloway became an unusual person.

The signs of this collective betrayal had been various but invariably vicious, had been sometimes subtle but mostly ruthlessly overt: Andy selling his guitar; Paul's conversation turning inexorably from boxing and blowjobs to babies and bathroom extensions; Tracy marrying a confectionery representative; Maurice—a man obsessed with style from the age of fourteen—allowing his *girlfriend* to take over the cutting of his hair; and so on, and so on.

What happened in the face of all this sociological reconstruction was that David too found his life remade.

What happened was that he saw such visions and did such things that, had he lived in less civilized times, he would have been hung by the neck until he was dead.

What happened was this.

1.
MYSTERY TRAIN

The plate shattered.

David blamed the fancy washing up liquid. He was accustomed to cheaper brands but there'd been a special at the Tesco's on Picton Road, so he'd indulged. And now look. Fucking stuff was so slick that the dishes had needed a good tight grip, much tighter than he was used to, and his Elvis Presley commemorative plate had slid out from his fingers, cracked against the side of the sink, fallen to the floor, and smashed into five pieces.

"Shit," said David. The King had only been dead seven and a half years. This was disrespectful. He slapped at the detergent bottle to teach it some manners and, gathering the broken pieces of the plate, turned to the pedal bin at his side.

The bin, the fragments, and David himself were in the relatively large kitchen of the relatively small Housing Association flat that took up half of the ground floor of an early 20th century terrace house at the Smithdown Road end of Wavertree.

The flat had been home to David for the last three years, ever since he dropped out of the Poly. Well, not dropped out so much as just stopped fucking going and not bothering to tell anyone. The combination of his DHSS rent allowance and the occasional income from his freelance journalism (of which the DHSS were ignorant) would actually have allowed him to find a slightly larger living space by now, but his position here at the back of the ground floor gave him access to what amounted to a private garden—theoretically, his fellow tenants could knock on his flat door and ask to be allowed through to the garden but fortunately no one was that much of a knobhead—and, in the summer months at least, he found this sufficient compensation for having dominion over only a bed-sitting room and a kitchen.

But this was not summer. David was into the autumn of his twenty-third year, in the literal sense, and, in the metaphoric, deep into the autumn of his youth. His perception of his life as something for which ripeness was a memory colored his perception of everything else around him: The view through his kitchen window of the garden in the afternoon light seemed to him neither mellow nor fruitful but merely dull and brown, a conscious entropic insult by a nature grown not merely senile but malicious with it; the fragments in his hand seemed evidence not of a simple domestic accident, but of a continuing campaign to confirm the willful transience of life and its pleasures.

David shook his head to free it from the gathering of depression and, at a touch from his left foot on the pedal, the lid of the bin flew back. Without bothering to bend down, David dropped the shards of Elvis onto the yielding mass of yesterday's excess prawn curry.

"There you go, mate," he said. "One more for the mystery train."

And then he froze, standing very still as a small and speedy rush of fear jetted through his system, leaving his arms and legs tingling and paralyzed.

Something had slithered.

Something was in the bin.

It had been the tiniest of movements and David couldn't be sure what he had seen exactly—indeed, couldn't be sure that he had actually *seen* anything. Perhaps, in fact, had seen effect only, not cause at all; just the rising and subsiding of the trash as something unseen had probed and retreated. But the path of that rise and fall had nevertheless managed to suggest a shape, and a quite specific one. Something long and thin and pliable. Something like a tail. Something like a rat's tail. Jesus Christ, there was a rat in his fucking bin!

With an involuntary cry of terror and disgust, David threw himself back towards his kitchen door as the lid of the bin snapped shut. For a long and bowel-loosening five seconds, David simply stood quite still by his door and stared at the stained steel tube of his bin. If you'd asked him what he was waiting for, he might have said that he was waiting for a rattle or squeak or some other sound from within the bin to confirm the problem. Or he might have said that he was waiting for inspiration as to how to deal with the matter. But the truth is that he wasn't waiting for either of those things. He was simply waiting for it not to be true anymore.

And after these five seconds, after this silence and this immobility, the notion of a rat actually being in there—though not empirically proven to be untrue—nevertheless began to seem farfetched enough for David to feel he could perhaps try a little test or two. He seized the long-handled brush which rested against the fridge and, from the safety of the other end of its four foot length, he struck it against the side of the bin.

Irritatingly, the dull thud of wood on metal awoke his ears not just to any new aural evidence of an unwanted inhabitant of the bin but to the entire sonic life of the kitchen, which he had previously managed to tune out. The rhythmic dripping of water from the tap, the low humming of the fridge, the high-pitched keening of the wind in the ventilator above the cooker; across the entire range of his hearing swelled an orchestra of conspiracy that almost succeeded in blocking out the other noise he'd heard. Thought he'd heard. Wondered if he'd heard. Knew damn well he'd heard.

Tiny, ungraspable, a third-generation analog recording of an echo of a whisper, but there it had been.

And there, therefore, it was.

Something in the bin.

This time David acted on instinct and slapped the far end of the brush onto the closed lid of the bin. A rat *in* a bin was considerably better, in the confines of David Holloway's kitchen, then a rat being given the opportunity to get *out* of a bin should it so desire and circumstance permit. Indeed, a monster contained is almost pleasurable. David remembered pressing his nine-year-old palm against the thick museum glass that had, by an all-important quarter of an inch, separated his flesh from that of a very black, very hairy, and very large bird-eating spider.

The sensation had been, if not exactly nice, then not exactly nasty. The fear had been there inside him, granted, but he'd been the one in control of the fear. Like the times he had used the electric-shock slot machines that you no longer saw in the seaside towns, he was his own torturer. His was the decision as to how many volts of electricity or terror he would allow inside his body before letting go. But today's quota had been made, thank you very much, and, if it was all the same to the great arcade proprietor in the sky, he was getting off this particular machine right the fuck now.

He had a plan. Not a complicated plan. A very do-able plan. He was going to pick up the bin, holding the lid tightly shut, and he was going to walk into the back garden. There, he was going to fling the bin and its contents as far away from himself as he possibly could. And if curry, cigarette butts, Elvis Presley, or a very confused rat landed in anyone else's garden, then sorry mate but tough shit.

It was a good plan, and the first two or three stages of its execution went exactly as they should. David picked the bin up. He held the lid tightly shut. He began walking to the back door that would let him into the garden. He was eight feet from it. Then he was six feet from it. Then he was two feet from it. And then something landed on his foot.

It was at this point that David wasn't in control anymore.

First, he lost control of his fear which, grateful for the opportunity, swept through his body in a triumphant tingling wave, roaring in his ears, clouding his sight in a yellow and black haze, and stopping his lungs. Then he lost control of his voice, which celebrated its escape in a wordless song of rising pitch. Almost simultaneously he lost control of his arms, which demonstrated their independence by losing control of the bin. And, finally, he lost control of his life—though this last was not to be made fully apparent for another five or six seconds.

In the first of those seconds, David looked down at his foot. What had landed on it was an empty tin can. In the second second, David realized that this meant there must be a hole in the bottom of his bin. In the third second, he looked back over his shoulder to where the bin had been. There was a small hole in his kitchen floor and, protruding from it, there was a tiny pink wriggling thing standing upright like a worm making claims on evolution.

In the fourth second, David found time to realize several things; whatever this was, it was not a rat's tail; whatever this was, it seemed to sense that he was looking at it; whatever this was, there was a lot more of it than he could at that point see, because—for a diameter of several feet around the hole— his kitchen floor was pulsing upwards and throbbing like a pustule about to burst.

There were also several things David didn't realize; he didn't hear himself moan, he didn't see himself shake, he didn't feel the sudden pool of saliva that cascaded from his shock-slackened jaw to run over his chin.

In the fifth second, David's kitchen floor exploded. And in the sixth second—in what all his upbringing led him to assume was in fact his last second on earth—David saw rushing toward him through the dust and debris with all the malevolence of inevitability, an absolute fucking absurdity.

It was big and it was round and, in a last and unwilled piece of analogy drawing, David thought of it as an enormously large golf ball with all the hard white casing ripped off to reveal not rubber bands but an infernal knot of tightly packed and intertwined worms, all wriggling feverishly in a collective rage to escape collectivism. Its pinkness was the pinkness of newly flayed flesh and in those few areas of its surface not covered by its squirming appendages there shone a gray and glistening mucus.

It moved astonishingly swiftly but nevertheless, in the fraction of a second it took to reach him, David saw several of the thousands of twitching wormlike miniature limbs extend and stiffen, each of them growing impossibly—and impossibly quickly—to a threatening length of several feet.

The sight of this was David's last sight of all. Three of these extended limbs rammed into his face, one slipping into his mouth and down his throat and the second and third through each of his eyes and into his brain. At the same time, another tentacular explorer crept between his legs and rammed itself into his gut via his anus, bursting cloth, flesh, blood vessels, and intestinal walls easily and indiscriminately, like a first-time sodomite, charmingly over-eager but hideously over-endowed.

As if some kind of decision had been reached, the other probes withdrew and, instantly, the entire mass of the creature catapulted itself after its scouting limb and began to squeeze itself inward, forcing its enormous mass into David's body, contorting itself, twisting and stretching to ease its passage.

The holes made in David's face, along with his other remaining natural orifices, allowed for the exit of his body's former contents with surprisingly little damage to their fleshy container. Of course, as it was leaving under fairly severe pressure through fairly small holes, the thick liquor that consisted of pulped organ, powdered bone, and plain blood did add quite considerably to the aesthetic disaster that the kitchen had become, jetting out like streams of tomato puree from a pressurized tube and decorating the walls and ceiling like a meeting of the minds between Jackson Pollock and Charles Manson.

When it had completed its occupation, when what was left of David's innards did nothing else but slither and steam, the creature, like a fussy customer in the shop of a ready-to-wear tailor, proceeded to the fine fitting, to the adjustments and the alterations. One by one the body's flaccid fingers were filled, one by one the toes. Only one tip—that of the second finger of the right hand—had burst and later, when it had learned to use needle and thread, the creature would repair that. The scrotum, the penis, the nose, the ears—carefully and gradually all the nooks and crannies, all the highways and byways, of the creature's new property were explored, exploited, and inflated.

All things considered, it really didn't take very long. Two or three minutes and a lot of wriggling and rippling later, a quick glance would have led you to believe that David Holloway was standing in the middle of his kitchen floor. A second look, one which took in the fact that his Sergeant Bilko T-shirt and his Levi 501s were completely covered in blood, would have led you inevitably to a third and to the sickening realization that what appeared to be a small worm was hanging out of each eye-socket. You'd probably not have needed any more prompting than that to leave the flat rapidly, call the Police, and thus save several lives but, as you weren't there, that isn't what happened.

What *did* happen was that the creature—having spent some time and considerable concentration on getting the fit just right—decided in a moment of pique that it found the entire style unsuitable and sprang back instantly to its globular appearance, stretching its new flesh with it. It began to bounce rapidly around the kitchen and then into the bed-sitting room adjoining it, where it hurled itself from wall to wall and between ceiling and floor for an energetic few minutes until it finally settled, wobbling slightly, on David's bed.

Whatever else the creature was, however, it wasn't stupid. It realized that most of the pleasures of this world came with triggers designed for the human frame and the human finger and so, having taken these moments to reassure itself of its independent nature, it resumed its David shape, a little more quickly this time, and set about learning what to do with it.

As if some genetic memory in the borrowed skin aided the creature's learning curve, walking was a problem soon overcome, the manipulation of the taps in the sink of the wrecked kitchen a lesson soon mastered. The elasticity of the T shirt and jeans had proven less accommodating than that of human flesh and so the shredded clothes were now simply part of the debris that the David thing had stepped delicately over on its way to the sink, and it was an already naked body that carefully washed all the blood off itself and out of its hair before returning to the other room to dress itself.

Apart from the bed—which, covered by day in cushions of varied shapes and sizes, also served as the main sitting or slouching area—the bed-sitting room contained one deckchair of wood and bright red canvas, one large beanbag, one wardrobe, one chest of drawers, one desk plus stool, and a wall of entertainment—a complicated and jerry-rigged shelf unit providing homes for various stereo components, a TV, a VCR, hundreds of LPs, and a few dozen books. Ashtrays, magazines, and an acoustic guitar lived on the floor.

On top of the chest of drawers was a line of toiletries; talcum powders, colognes, aftershaves, and antiperspirants. The David-thing tried them all, spraying, rolling, splashing, and patting its clean new body with a heady cocktail of scents before selecting, from an extensive range of clothes, the only actual suit in David's wardrobe, a jet-black narrow-lapelled two-piece which David had bought to wear at a '60s theme party a year or so earlier, claiming variously to have come as a CIA operative or as an R'n'B musician, depending upon the sensibilities of the person to whom he was talking at the time.

Finding the necessary white shirt and thin black tie in the chest of drawers, the David-thing dressed itself, adding a pair of black suede winkle-pickers it found in the bottom of the wardrobe and completing the look by donning the Ray-ban sunglasses which had perched stylishly on the polystyrene nose of a milliner's bust atop the shelf unit. This last was an entirely aesthetic decision but it did have the concomitant advantage of not revealing that those were worms which were his eyes.

The sharp looking figure in the black suit lowered itself casually into the red canvas deckchair and picked up the various remotes that were scattered on the floor about the base of the chair. It hit several buttons and brought several machines to life. Music filled the air and images flickered to life on the screen. Eddie Cochran's *Something Else* segued into Elvis Costello's *Stranger in the House* while Mister Ed got the better of Wilbur once again. Had the creature learned how to smile yet, it would have done so.

The thing veiled in David's flesh spent the ensuing thirty-six hours watching TV shows and videos, listening to records and tapes, and reading books and magazines, more often than not all at the same time. Finally, at 3:00 o'clock in the morning of the day after the day after the day it had arrived, it decided to have a word.

"David," it said, in a pleasantly resonant Mid-Atlantic voice.

"David," it repeated in a guttural Scouse twang.

"David," it growled, like Pazuzu from *The Exorcist*.

"David," it giggled, like *Laugh-In* period Goldie Hawn getting availably playful.

From somewhere deep inside itself, the creature sensed an answering groan.

"Ah, David. Splendid." Donald Pleasance.

Oh, God. Where...

"Where are you?" The creature said. "Where you've always been, I suppose. Somewhere inside. It's just that you're not alone anymore."

But I... Oh God. Oh God.

"David, please. You've had a very traumatic experience. That's why I let you sleep so long. Try not to get excited."

Who are you?

"Me? Oh, I don't know. What do you think? The Monster from the Id, maybe? The Lump of Goo from Outer Space? The Innocent Young Virus Mutated by Chemical Pollutants? The Devil? Take your pick, David. Whatever floats your boat, mate. I don't give a shit."

Who am I?

"Who are you? You're David. Just as you've always been. You're still here."

Yes. But—

"You're still here, and you're starting to get boring."

But I—

"Do you want to go back to sleep?"

No.

"Good. Now—"

Where do I go when I ... sleep?

"Where do you go? How the fuck do *I* know where you go? You go where Larry Talbot goes when the wolfbane blooms. You go where Billy Batson goes when the Thunder speaks. Where do you go? Who knows? Who gives a damn? Frankly, my dear, I'm a little disappointed by this consistently selfish way of looking at the interesting situation in which we currently find ourselves. Where am *I*? Who am *I*? Where do *I* go? Come on, David. We're in this thing together. Try and think of yourself as part of a team."

Who are we?

"Ah, now that's a *much* more interesting question."

The David-thing got up from the deckchair, stretched itself, and laughed. The laugh was deep, rich, and attractive.

"Who are we?" it said. "We're the Bruise Brothers, my man. And we're gonna boogie."

2.
LOVE IS STRANGE

Lisette Connaught was having a bad night. She lay, naked and alone, beneath the lime green and shocking pink duvet. It was her first night on her own since she'd married Charles six months earlier and the first night ever that she had been alone in this house.

Both she and Charles had realized that his latest promotion, while giving with one hand the wherewithal to buy this, their first home, would with the other take away occasional nights together in a kind of modern-day *droit de seigneur*, requiring Charles's presence at the odd course or conference while his wife welcomed loneliness and silence into her bed. They had realized it—but that didn't mean she had to like it.

"If you're going to join the rat race, Mister Connaught," she had joked when he first joined the company eighteen months earlier, "just make damn sure you're the fastest rat." And their laughter had dissolved into lovemaking and her worries had dissolved into warmth. But now she was beginning to wonder if the undeniable speed that Charles had since demonstrated really did compensate for all the other trappings of an upwardly mobile urban rodent.

It wasn't as if she actually *missed* life amongst the educated unemployed. It wasn't as if she yearned for mac and cheese three nights out of every seven or dwelled nostalgically on the days of one movie a month and a show every six. She would *kill* rather than ever have to share a bathroom again. It was just that if the hypocrisy, paranoia, and mask-wearing that seemed to be an inescapable part of Charles's new life ("*Our* new life," she heard him automatically correct her) were to fly from her tomorrow, then she wouldn't actually miss *them* either.

But she would miss the house. And the car. And the central heating. And the big new bed, and the money.

"Shit," she said aloud, as she changed position for the thirty-fourth time that night. Not a wink so far. She looked up at the radio alarm clock on the unit next to Charles's side of the bed. The warm green figures of the LCD told her it was 3:55.

"Three fifty-five. Three fifty-five. That's five to fucking *four!*" she told the room.

"Oh, Christ!" Lisette slammed her hands petulantly against the mattress and then, the little explosion of anger having diffused some of her tension, she folded her arms behind her head and breathed out slowly, enjoying the relaxation of her body. She even managed a passable imitation of a languorous stretch, and suddenly she was amused rather than angry at her inability to sleep—'cause, Jesus, it wasn't like she had anything to actually *do* now that Charles had transformed himself into such a convincing likeness of Mister Happy Breadwinner with a Semi-Detached in Mossley Hill, so who cared how late she fell asleep or how late she got up? She pushed the duvet down to her waist in order to let her body feel cooler and lighter.

Idly, she toyed with her dark brown hair, long and newly

permed. "It makes you look younger," Charles had said in a tone that suggested, astonishingly, that this was not perhaps altogether a good thing. Lisette liked it, though. It reminded her of the Pre-Raphaelite paintings that she had always, in their student days, guiltily preferred to the abstract and kinetics that had won the approval of her peers (and the *affection*? she had often wondered—but never out loud).

She dropped her hair over her not insignificant breasts, (now, to her relief, prominently back in fashion) and slowly pulled it back, brushing it gently over her nipples which, happily asleep unlike their mistress, were at first slow to rise but after a few more hairy caresses were fully alert and eager for activity.

"Oh," said Lisette. "That was a bit bloody silly."

She started to giggle but then paused, attentive to the eager pulse of their silent argument.

"Well, what do you think?" She asked the room. "Should I have a wank, or what?"

"That won't be necessary," said a voice from behind the bedroom door.

Lisette shot up in bed, clutching the duvet to her body, her eyes wide in shock and fear. But the scream conceived as she watched the door handle turn was stillborn because, as the door was flung open and the main bedroom lights switched on, the grinning figure revealed in the doorway was familiar to her.

"Surprise," it said.

Lisette's lungs grabbed gratefully at the mouthful of air she drew in as she allowed herself to breathe again. She held the breath less than a second, though, before exhaling it in a shouted torrent composed half of anger and half of relief.

"David! Jesus fucking Christ! Do you have any idea what… I … My God… I nearly *died*, you fucking prick! What is this?"

"This? What is this? This is this," said the tall figure in the black suit and shades. The voice was a pretty perfect Robert De Niro and Lisette was about to congratulate David on a heretofore unrevealed talent when he continued, in a pretty perfect David Holloway. "And this is *this*."

Lisette froze.

The intruder had pulled a gun from his pants pocket and was aiming it at her.

"Now do as you're told, and maybe you won't get hurt," he said, as he crossed the room to the bed and, keeping the gun trained on her with his right hand, threw the duvet onto the floor with his left.

"David, what are you—"

"Quiet!" he said, and unzipped his pants. "Got a little job for you. Make this hard in ten seconds or I'll decorate the walls with your brains."

Lisette bent her face forward towards his groin and succeeded within the appointed time limit, the cold firm pressure of the gun barrel against her temple helping to make easy the necessary moist slackness of her mouth. She fell back onto the bed, staring silently up at the impassive set of his mouth, the implacable blackness of his shades,

"That was very good, Lisette," he said. "Very good. You're a talented girl. Now—what do you want me to do with this?" He gestured at the fully engorged cock.

Lisette swallowed, bit her lip, and spoke. Her voice was a hollow whisper. "Oh, God," she said. "Please don't do this."

"What do you want me to do with this?" he said again.

"I... I..."

"Tell me!"

"I want you to..."

"Go on."

"...to fuck me."

"Properly," he said. "Say it properly."

"I want you to fuck me," she said, in a very small voice.

"Well," he said. "Seeing that you ask so nicely, I'd be delighted to oblige."

He dropped his pants and clambered out of them and the black suede winkle-pickers. He kept his jacket on. He mounted Lisette swiftly and brutally, placing the back of her knees against his shoulders and pressing down on her. For two minutes, he moved in silence, the gun held constantly at her head, and then he spoke again.

"In ten seconds," he said, "I'm going to pull this trigger."

At Lisette's answering gasp, he began to thrust into her more rapidly and more violently, counting down as he did so.

"Ten, nine, eight, seven—"

Lisette stared up at the face of her husband's friend, at the unfamiliar black glasses.

"Six, five, four, three—"

He dropped his face to hers and kissed her. His tongue felt swollen and invasive in her mouth.

"Two, one—"

The gun found the precise center of her temple.

"Zero," he said. And pulled the trigger.

They came together, explosively, the click of the gun's empty chamber lost to both of them in the mutual orgasmic roar.

They clutched at each other for a few more seconds, sweating and slick, before her visitor in the sunglasses rolled sideways and away, laughing with pleasure as he lay on his back on the cool side of the bed, a few inches separating him from Lisette's warm body.

Lisette lay silent for a little longer and then turned her head toward him, a small smile playing about her lips.

"The shades were a nice touch," she said. "Bit of variety." Her tone was relaxed and sated, and she snuggled in closer to him, laying her head on his shoulder and leaning her arm across his chest. "You still play that really well. Was that Robert de Niro you were doing? You know, the accent bit?"

"I couldn't find the gun at first," he said, ignoring her question. "I was wandering around downstairs for at least five minutes. Surprised you didn't hear me. I was looking everywhere. Began to think you'd thrown it away, now that you're a respectable married woman and everything."

She laughed.

"But the *worst* bit," her lover continued, "the worst bit was when I started the countdown. I suddenly realized I hadn't checked the gun and I thought, what if Charles has started taking home security seriously? What if this fucking thing's *loaded*?"

This time, they laughed together. Lisette raised herself on one elbow and looked down at the grinning face beneath her. She tried for a stern expression.

"Never mind laughing," she said. "I'm very annoyed with you. First of all, you nearly gave me a bloody heart attack. I didn't know you knew Charles was away—I thought somebody else had got inside somehow. I was terrified."

The face below her smirked upwards as if to say it all added to the fun, but Lisette ignored it and carried on. "And, secondly, I told you this would all have to stop when I got married, didn't I?"

Her visitor's grin didn't waver. Lisette paused for a moment and then spoke in a different tone; relaxed, inquisitive. "Anyway, how *did* you get in?"

"Love laughs at locksmiths."

"Fuck off. How'd you get in?"

"Through the letterbox."

"Bit of a tight squeeze, wasn't it?"

"Yeah, it was. But then I'm good at squeezing into tight places, aren't I?"

They laughed together again. But Lisette had the sense

that somehow the joke was twice as funny for him as it was for her. She shook her head at him, sighed in an exasperation that was only half playful and, turning the light off from the secondary switch by her side of the bed, wriggled in close again, so that they could lay together in the warmth of post-coital silence.

It was about five o'clock in the morning, and Lisette was just beginning to drift into sleep, when she heard David's voice in the dark.

"Isn't it scary?" he said. "Being in a big house all on your own?"

"You're here," she murmured, snuggling deeper against him, reluctant to be pulled back into the world of words.

"Yeah, yeah," he said. "But what if I *wasn't*? Could you sleep alright on your own? I mean, you were awake when I got here."

"Yes, I was awake," she said. "But that was... other stuff. I was just thinking. I wasn't scared. I don't have bad dreams or anything. I haven't had bad dreams since I was a kid."

He shifted position, apparently interested. "What was the worst dream you ever had?" he asked.

Lisette knew he'd won, now. His interest was infectious, and she liked telling this story anyway.

"The worst?" she said. "No question about it. It was a long time ago now. I was still a little girl. About six, I think... maybe seven... I don't know. Anyway, it started in a big room in a house I'd never seen..."

She raised her head towards David's, her storytelling tone suddenly replaced by an explanatory one. "Well, in the dream it was *my* house, of course. What I mean is that it wasn't a house I knew in real li—"

He interrupted her. "Tell it," he said. "Just tell it. Straight through."

Lisette smiled. She nodded and shifted position slightly so that they were both lying on their backs, staring upwards. On the ceiling, the light from a moon very low in the sky threw a distorted black and blue reflection of the half-closed Venetian blinds. As clouds drifted over the distant moon, diffusing its light, the clarity of this image would wax and wane. Lisette found herself focusing on these small and slowly shifting patterns of precision as she narrated her nightmare.

"There were four or five of us," she said, "all gathered in this one room. I think they were all adults apart from me. I knew that they were family or close friends, though I didn't know their faces at all.

"We were all grouped around a big black-and-white telly in the corner of the room, two or three people on chairs and me and a couple of others on the floor. The room seemed sort of empty, or unfinished or something, like there wasn't enough furniture in it, or that what there was wasn't big enough. Anyway, I asked somebody what was coming on the telly, what we were going to watch, and they told me it was *The New Adventures of Jesus*—which, in the dream, didn't seem odd to me at all—and I looked over at the screen. Sure enough, the titles were just rolling up and the scene was fading up beneath them. I think it was Jesus with his cross on his shoulder, but I couldn't be sure because there was interference on the telly and the picture went all wobbly. As soon as that happened, there was a knock on the front door.

"Nobody else moved or said anything, just stayed there watching the screen even though it was just static and snow by now, and I got this sense that I had to answer the door. That it was expected of me. It was around then that I started to feel scared, I think, and also then that it all began to feel... I don't know... *pre-destined*, I suppose. It wasn't as if I knew what was going to happen, more that I knew that what *was* going to happen was going to happen, if you know what I mean. And that it was going to be bad. But even though I knew it was going to be bad, I didn't say or do anything to show that I knew. I just played along as if I didn't understand anything. I suppose I was hoping not to stand out, or something. Hoping that if I played along and saw the game through then there wouldn't be any special punishment for me, that I'd just be one of the crowd.

"Anyway, I stood up and left the room and went out into a dark hallway. I sort of recognize it now, when I think about it —I think it was the dream country's version of the hallway in the house we lived in when I was *really* small—but in the dream I didn't. It didn't seem odd to me or anything. Just scary.

"The knocking was still going on. Hadn't ever stopped, just carried on, slow and steady, like it knew it was going to be answered. Not *patient*, exactly. More... expectant. The front door was at the far end of this hallway, and I made my way toward it, still frightened but still acting as if everything was alright even though there was no one else in the hallway to watch me. The knocking stopped at the moment I reached the door—as if whatever was on the other side of it knew exactly where I was—and I opened it.

"It was only a man. To look at, I mean. Very big, though; tall and broad. His hair was thick and black. It was balding on top but he had a beard as if to compensate, short but thick and it rose up on each cheek to within an inch of his lower eyelids. His arms were bare and muscular, and they were covered in hair, too. Now, okay, I was a little girl—maybe *all* adult males look big, broad, and hairy to us—but I don't know. This was different. *He* was different.

"He was walking up the five grey stone steps that rose to the front door—I didn't stop to wonder how he'd knocked on the door if he'd been at the bottom of the steps, I didn't want to make any guesses, didn't want to know—and his eyes were fixed on me as he came up. I couldn't meet his gaze and

I looked out behind him as I stood back to let him pass. The landscape out there was... I don't know... *simultaneous*. I don't know how else to describe it. It was a long English front garden ending in a hedge and a wooden gate and the sun had just set. And at the same time, it was brown and barren, spoiled land with patches of thick mist coalescing and diffusing, hovering over it. It was both of those things together. It didn't fade from one and into the other. It was more like seeing the result of two negatives printed onto the same photo paper. I was very glad to close the door on it.

"But of course, I'd let the worst part in.

"He looked down at me for a second or two as he stood in the hallway by the closed door and then he turned his head in the direction of the room where the others were before looking back at me and nodding. That nod meant lots of things. It meant 'Yes, we're going to that room'. It meant 'Yes, it had to be you who opened the door'. It meant 'Yes, I know you're just playing along'. It meant 'Yes, I am what you think I am'.

"I walked ahead of him in the dark, leading the way back to the television room. I went into the room but realized he hadn't followed me in, so I stopped a few feet inside, not sure what to do or say. I think the telly was still on, I'm not sure. They all turned to face me, and somebody said, 'Who is it, Lisette?' and I didn't say anything and somebody else said 'Who is it, Lisette?' and I still didn't say anything and then they were all saying, 'Who is it, Lisette?', 'Who is it, Lisette?', 'Who is it, Lisette?' And then, from outside the room, he laughed, and they all stopped talking and he walked into the room to stand behind me.

"His voice was like coal. 'Yes,' he said. 'She's brought someone in with her, hasn't she?' And then it all began to go dark. Not slowly. Not quickly. Not normally. The darkness slid down from the ceiling like something almost solid, blacking out the wallpaper and the light inch by inch. People say, 'Darkness fell', don't they? But they don't really mean it. But that's just what was happening. Darkness was falling on us, oozing down the walls like something solid and hungry, something conscious and malicious. It felt... terminal.

"It's hard to tell people your nightmares because the details aren't enough to convey what it felt like. It's the *feeling* that counts, and you can never really tell them the feeling, can you? And this felt so awful, like everything was over. Not like the end of the world, but like the world had never really been there in the first place.

"The darkness didn't stop falling and, as it got about halfway down the room, as all the grownups' heads disappeared inside it, I began to scream. And scream. And scream."

Lisette stopped.

"God," said David's voice. "What happened then?"

"Then I woke up still screaming and my mother came in and held me and told me it was alright."

Lisette exhaled and, for the first time since she began her story, turned her head slightly to look at the man beside her. His face was still turned to the ceiling. He nodded his head slowly.

"Mmm," he said. "A good one. Definitely a good one." His voice had a strange musing quality to it. He reached over Lisette and, from the unit on her side of the bed, helped himself to a cigarette from the packet of Benson & Hedges that was lying there.

"Good job your mum was there, eh?" he said. He put the cigarette in his mouth but remained raised on one elbow, looking down at her. His question had been couched rhetorically but before Lisette could make even a token answer he spoke again. "Where's your mum now?"

Lisette gave him a puzzled look. "She's in Toronto," she said. "Visiting my... don't you want a light for that?"

"No." The cigarette disappeared whole into David's mouth, which began chewing on it.

Lisette giggled, but she could hear the nervous edge to it and stopped herself. "What are you—" she began to say, but David's voice interrupted her.

"*Yes. She's brought someone in with her,*" he said. "Scary. Very scary. Lisette, would you like to see who I've brought in with *me*?"

"David. Don't mess," Lisette said. Telling the story had, as always, both thrilled and frightened her and she felt a little too receptive to enjoy playing any spooky games.

"I'm not messing, Lisette," he said. "Look. Look at me."

Alright, now he was pissing her off. She looked up, annoyed and unafraid. "David!" she snapped. "I'm not fucking kidding!"

"Nor am I," he said. And then he took his shades off.

Lisette began to scream. And scream. And scream.

3.

YAKETY-YAK (DON'T TALK BACK)

On an early morning bus containing seven or eight early-shift weekend laborers making their way to factories and offices and one or two Friday night adulterers making their way to tears and excuses, the thing with the black suit and blood on its collar found a seat halfway down the length of the lower deck. In its hand was a bus ticket, in its jacket pocket one or two grisly souvenirs, and in its head the ceaseless sound of a young man's anguish.

The cuckoo spirit in David's body had amused itself during the course of its adventure with Lisette by switching its host's perceptions on and off at random intervals, so that for David the experience had been like taking part in a movie which had been edited by an impatient drunk and then censored by some hypothetical antithesis of the moral majority.

The whole episode, in David's perceived time, had lasted just over a minute and, apart from an establishing view of the outside of Charles's house, had consisted entirely of jump-cuts between acts of sex and violence: a few seconds of Lisette's beautiful head sliding up and down his erection; her face in the contortion of her climax; random sentences from her telling of what sounded like a creepy story; frightened eyes; a lot of blood. Finally, from the viewpoint of the bedroom door, like a last long-shot needing only closing music and end credits to place it in the sole context he could recognize for it, David had been granted a lingering glimpse of what had once been a girl he had known for four years.

She lay on the bed on her back. On her back, but face-down; her head had been twisted around to an absurdly unnatural degree and her face was pressed into the pillow. A large red stain on the pillow seemed to issue directly from her mouth.

She had been opened from sternum to *mons veneris*. It was not a neat job, though it was clear that a tidy mind had been involved afterwards; several of the internal organs, removed from their home of twenty-three years, were displayed as an orderly though bloody group on a white sheet spread on the floor at the foot of the bed. Taking their place inside Lisette and staring back at David in dumb reproach, its once pristine fur soaked in its mistress's blood, was a large cuddly Garfield cat, the head and shoulders of which alone were visible over the edges of the torn and tortured flesh.

The thing had taken David out of the house before it woke him again and it was only on a wooden bench near the bus stop at the corner of Dovedale road and Rose Lane that David was allowed time to fully realize the enormity of what had happened.

Even as separate predators, grief, fear, and horror can render the wisest philosopher incoherent. Attacking as a pack, they can silence angels and still the mouths of gods. David Holloway was neither angelic nor divine, and such wisdom as he owned was a small and fragile thing which had fled before the fury of this assault, leaving David to stare unaided into the abyss. To describe him as dumbstruck would be accurate but far from adequate. *Gutted*—a word in vogue among David and his friends for the last year or so and used humorously and fecklessly for the most part—began to bounce itself around his mind. The remnants of his sanity seized upon it as a point of focus, as sanity will when catastrophe capers. How the mind gets busy when the world dissolves. How the eye is drawn—in the face of bankruptcy, infidelity, death—to the insignificant detail; to the poor spelling of the bank's typist, to the mole on the faithless cheek, to the scratch on the coffin's handle.

Gutted, David began to repeat to himself. *Gutted. I'm gutted.* And then the other's voice emerged from David's mouth to correct him.

"No, no, David," it said, like a chiding but compassionate teacher who feels your pain but insists on maintaining standards of accuracy. "Let's get it right. *She's* gutted. *You're...* well, I don't really know. Flabbergasted, perhaps?" The voice altered itself before continuing, "Ooh, your gast has never been so flabbered."

The Frankie Howerd imitation was pretty spot-on, but David was neither impressed nor amused. Somewhere inside his head, behind his silent lips, his own voice replied.

You fucking bastard. How could you do that? Why?

"How could *I*? I didn't do anything, David. The sooner you disabuse yourself of that notion, the better. I mean, nobody's going to find *my* fingerprints on the lovely Lisette, are they?"

But—

"No buts, dear boy. It's about time you started facing up to your responsibilities. When the Constabulary come, David, they'll be coming for *you*."

But—

"But *what*? You'll explain? Oh, well, that's alright then. That'll make everything just hunky dory, won't it? I can see it now. *It wasn't me, officer, it was this large glutinous mass of malice that has of recent date taken over my poor innocent body.* 'Oh, I see, Sir. Well, in that case, we'll say no more about it. You're free to go. Only—if you don't mind?—before you pop off and enjoy the rest of your day, would you just rest your testicles on my notepad here while I take a brief moment to express my disgust with the thick end of me truncheon?' Yes indeed, that'll go down a storm, David. A *storm*."

The bus had arrived during the silence the that followed this exchange and David, beyond questions, merely wept silently behind the blank facade of his borrowed face as the creature went through a pantomime of politeness and normality, paying its fare, taking its ticket, nodding at one or two of its fellow passengers, and finding its seat.

The bus drove a circuitous route from the fringes of Mossley Hill to the students and dole-ites section of Wavertree where David's flat was—they could have walked home quicker—and for more than ten minutes of the journey the creature left David alone with his shock, apart from an occasional fondle of the ear and two fingers which were in the pocket of their jacket.

They were still several stops away from home when something caught whatever passed for the creature's eye. Several of the windows on the bus, including the one by which they sat, boasted a transfer stuck on the glass. The transfer, in bright red print, bore a message about vandalism and its consequences:

WILFUL DAMAGE TO SEATS, ETC.
THE EXECUTIVE WILL PRESS
FOR HEAVIEST PENALTIES
AGAINST OFFENDERS

The creature began to giggle, though David at first couldn't tell why. Reaching their hand into a trouser pocket, the creature produced David's front door key and set about amending the Corporation's message by removing certain letters with a scraping action. David's hand worked diligently and neatly and, after a couple of minute's effort, had succeeded in revealing—as if it had always been the hidden subtext of the first—an infinitely more ominous warning:

WILFUL DAMAGE TO SEATS, ETC.
THE EXECUTIVE WILL PRESS
H I S P E N I S
AGAINST OFFENDERS

The creature sat back, beaming with pride at its work. A low chuckle began to escape from its borrowed mouth as it dwelt on the images conjured up by the revised message. David too, against his will and against the claims of despair, found it rather funny and began to add a second silent laugh to the one already issuing from his mouth. The more he thought about it, the funnier it became. Inside his head he spoke, between giggles, to his tenant.

Hey, maybe there's a special room, he said. *Somewhere at the dark end of the depot. Where they take transgressors. Probably got a little plaque outside: Office of her Majesty's Penis Presser.*

The creature burst out into a huge belly laugh, gasping for air and grasping at the seat. Suddenly it realized that the sound of its mirth had drawn attention from the front of the bus, that the driver was staring back along its length via the rear-view mirror in his compartment.

"Hey!" the driver shouted. "You in the suit! Keep it down!"

Keep it down? David said internally. *Tell that to the Executive. He's the one waving his fucking nudger about.* The creature let out a fresh guffaw and the driver, feeling his authority challenged by this, adopted a harsher tone.

"I told you to shut it, mate!" he shouted.

"He's been writing on the window," said a helpful female voice from the back of the bus a couple of rows behind the troublemaker. The driver instantly pulled the bus to a halt.

"Right, you. Off!" he said, opening the front door automatically from his seat and gesturing dramatically with his left arm.

The creature, by now nearly helpless with laughter, stood up and walked obediently toward the indicated exit.

"Go on. Gerrout of it," the driver said as his passenger disembarked. "Think yourself lucky I don't report you."

David's body turned around on the pavement and his face grinned back through the open door at the driver.

"Yeah? Who to?" he said. "The executive? What will he do? Stick his dick in my ear?"

The very accurate Richard Pryor was lost on the driver, but the self-congratulatory laughter was not. "Piss off, you little yob," he said from the safety of his seat.

"Tell you what, mate," said the creature. "I'll leave it with you. Tell him to give it a good press."

The driver felt something hit his face and fall, to land in his lap.

He was still staring, stunned and sickened, at the severed human ear that lay on his knees as the vandal disappeared running down a side street, his hysterical laughter ringing in the air.

4.
AT THE HOP

Seen from the outside, the social club was a large one-storey rectangle of gray concrete. It was set, as if by chance, in an uncared-for field with only its own car park and gravel driveway for company and was several hundred yards away from the last of the tower blocks of the large working-class estate which it had been built to serve.

The club's only external concession to the decorative impulse was the presence of an illuminated sign over each of the two doors which were let into the one of its longer walls that faced west. One of these signs, in a triumph of minimalism, said simply *Bar*, while the other, in happy ignorance of the incongruity of its implicit promise and its actual potential, said *Gaiety Lounge*.

Beyond this second door you would find a small lobby where, should you not be a member of the district social club, you would be asked to pay a nominal sum of money in order to be admitted through a further door into the palace of pleasure itself.

The Gaiety Lounge was of simple design. At one end of its rectangular shape was a stage, at the other a bar, and in the middle were long rows of narrow tables with seats running up and down their length. By half past nine on this particular Saturday night nearly all of those seats were occupied and the temporary owners of those seats who were not at that moment sitting down were either busy in the collecting of liquid or busy in the disposing of it.

The air was full of music and chatter as the jukebox competed with various exchanges of the week's gossip. Like most clubs of its type—and unlike the more sophisticated nightclubs in the heart of the city which drew an almost exclusively young crowd—the clientele of this place ranged in years from teenagers to pensioners and this lack of segregation continued even down to the seating arrangements at the tables. Girlfriends rubbed shoulders with grandmothers and elderly widowers discussed football with boys only just getting used to the taste of beer.

Ahead of all of them was an evening of reassuring familiarity. There'd be the Bingo, there'd be the live entertainment, there'd be a little dancing, and there'd be drunkenness sufficient to convince them that they were all having a good time.

It was generally a friendly place and, unlike some superficially similar clubs, strangers were ignored more for reasons of tact than for reasons of hostility. Furthermore, once two or three people had recognized the weirdo at the bar as Jimmy Holloway's lad, David and his parasite were doubly safe from any unprovoked harassment. Jimmy'd been a good drinking companion and a tough bugger to beat on the snooker table, and his move to the greener fields of Wales following his widowing at the hands of a cruel and leisurely cancer was regretted but not resented by the normally aggressive parochialism of the people among whom he had spent his callow years.

One of the regulars, a contemporary of Jimmy's who had recognized his son when the latter first came in, found himself standing next to him at the bar later in the evening. The Bingo was being cleared away and the turn was about to come on.

"Alright, lad," the man said in greeting, along with a nod and a smile. "How's your dad?"

For a moment, the young man appeared to stiffen and hesitate, and the older man wondered if for some reason he was afraid to speak.

It was not, of course, the act of speaking that David was afraid of, but of what his mouth might say. For the moment, though, his fears proved groundless. "Fine, fine," he heard his voice say. "Haven't seen him for a while, actually. But, you know, we talk on the phone and everything." The imitation was faultless, even down to the nodding and bobbing of the head as the kind of vague signal of friendliness that was entirely appropriate to the situation. "I'll... er... I'll send him your best, eh?"

"Yeah, yeah," said the older man. "Send him me best. Definitely. Definitely. Yeah. And... er... how about yourself, like? Doing alright and everything?"

It was becoming difficult. The divisive specter of Further Education hovered above their conversation and the older man was plainly as relieved as David when his voice replied with a universally acknowledged polite method of excusing oneself. "Oh, I'm fine too, thanks. Yeah. Look, I'm just going to have a quick burst before the band comes on, alright? I'll see you later, yeah?"

"Yeah, alright, lad," the man said. "Take care now." He turned his attention back to trying to catch the barmaid's eye.

By the time the band did come on, David had been fully assimilated into everybody's perception of the evening. Bit of a wanker in the fucking suit and everything, but no skin off anyone's arse. Consequently, no eyes followed him more than casually as he wandered, apparently aimlessly, around and around the internal perimeter of the lounge, sipping at his pint and occasionally standing still and studying the evening's act.

The act in question was a small combo of organ, electric bass, and drums. The vocals were shared out pretty evenly between the bassist and the keyboard player. All three musicians were in their late thirties and all three were inevitably dressed like teenagers, though the energy of teenagers was sadly lacking from their performance. Competent professionalism compensated as much as it ever does and the audience's predisposition to enjoy themselves helped a great deal.

The material the band was offering was the predictable

mix. Some current chart successes, several old rock and roll songs and, scattered throughout the set, both types of sentimental ballad—the irresistibly beautiful and the nauseatingly contrived. Both types were being performed on this occasion with a depressingly fair-minded equality of enthusiasm.

After he and his colleagues had been performing for about twenty-five minutes or so, the bassist graciously surrendered his microphone to a septuagenarian who had arisen unbidden from his place amidst the tables and, advancing to the foot of the stage and turning to face what had been his fellows and were now his audience, had announced that he was going to sing *The Yellow Rose of Texas*. Sing it he undeniably did, though his particular arrangement of it, idiosyncratic to say the least, ensured that the musicians worked harder in their accompaniment of him than they had worked all night. It was no surprise to them, seasoned veterans of the Social Club circuit as they were, that it also received the warmest applause of the set so far.

Harry—for such, judging by the cries of encouragement during his performance, was his name—returned to his proud table-mates while wolf-whistles still pierced the air and glasses still thudded against tabletops in rhythmic approbation. The keyboard player, years of experience having granted him an ability to judge accurately the mood of an audience, shouted through his microphone over the cheers.

"Brilliant! Brilliant!" he said. "Fantastic! Nice one, Harry. Pride of Cantril Farm!" The drummer shot him a look like he'd just played the opening chords of *The Rising of the Green* at an Orange Lodge party.

"Netherly, you fucking tosser!" shouted someone from the audience, and a couple of hard cases rose to their feet from a table at the rear like maybe the evening was going to turn out a little better than they'd hoped.

Wisely, the keyboard player instantly locked eyes with a

blue haired matriarch near the front. "Ah, 'ey, love," he said, still into the microphone. "You'll have to forgive me. I don't half get confused. I'm in agony 'ere." He gestured to his piano stool and twitched his bottom in wounded fashion. "It's the hemorrhoids, you know what I mean?"

The old woman chuckled sympathetically. "Are they giving you gyp, love?" she shouted up at the stage.

"Ah, I'm not messing, darlin'," he said. "Honest. Me arse is like a plate of frigging spaghetti."

The old woman laughed uproariously, and the rest of the crowd followed her lead. Crisis averted, the keyboard player made to get the evening back on track. "Anybody else out there got a song they wanna do?" he shouted. "Or are youse all gonna let Harry walk away with it?"

While all around the club would-be performers wasted precious time in false modesty, a figure in black ran forward, jumped up onto the stage, and had a quick whispered conversation with the bass player. The bass player then turned to cue the other musicians while the new member of the line-up adjusted the mic-stand for height and spoke to the audience.

Said audience was somewhat nonplussed. This kind of thing was normally considered entirely the province of regulars, and the general mood was that it was rather unseemly that a stranger should usurp it. Further, it suggested a kind of seriousness of intent that was entirely out of keeping with the spirit of the thing, and the intruder's introductory remarks did little to lessen the incongruity.

"Right!" he shouted into the mic in an authoritative voice which wouldn't have been out of place for a headline act in a major concert hall. "We're going to start off..."

What are you doing?! I can't fucking sing! What is this!?

"...with what they call a rave from the grave. Let's..."

Oh Christ. Don't. Please don't.

"...see some dancing out there! Let's hear some hands clapping! Let's have..."

I'm shitting meself!

"...a good time! HIT IT!"

This last was of course to the band—who were very nearly as bemused as the punters by this breathtaking pushiness. The guy was clearly a knobhead, they thought, and almost certainly an insane knobhead. That said, he was at least a *confident* insane knobhead, So, what the fuck, they hit it.

BAM!

Dum-dum-dum-dum

BAM-BAM!

With the first explosive staccato chord the figure in black leapt into the air and began a vigorous, flailing dance, a kind of choreographic collage of steps from the Mashed Potato, the Twist, the Pony, the Hand-Jive, and any other hideously outdated dance routine you could care to mention. And all enmeshed within something of his own creation which, even as he was seizing the mic for his vocal debut, he was already christening the Happy Spastic.

"Here she come now, say Mony Mony!"

BAM!

Dum-dum-dum-dum

BAM-BAM!

From the first barked syllable it was clear that he was brilliant. The audience knew it, sensed it the way an audience can, and responded instantly and unselfconsciously, pulled *en masse* into the magic. Throughout the entire Lounge spontaneous clapping broke out, astonishingly in time, miraculously on the off-beat. Several brave couples were on the dance floor in front of the stage before the end of the song's first line. Women whistled, young men howled, mothers taught daughters the Twist, people shook their heads and bodies in wild celebration. It was great. The band members found each other's eyes, exchanged delighted grins, and began to play—for the first time in years—like they actually gave a shit.

He growled. He howled. He twisted and turned. He did the knee drop, the hip flip, the pelvic thrust. He strutted. He strolled. He fell to the floor. And all the time mouthing the nonsense syllables in the perfect manic frenzy, dripping with psychosis and sincerity. He was wilder than Little Richard, more beautifully insane than Jerry Lee. He was *there*. He was *it*. He was the uncrowned King of Garbage. He *was* Tommy James & the Shondells.

And then it was over. With an imperious yanking gesture of his right arm, he stopped the band cleanly on a downbeat, allowing no post-orgasmic trills or rolls to come between him and his audience's gratitude. And even as this gratitude expressed itself in whistles and roars, even as men of forty-five raised clenched fists in victory salutes, even as sixteen-year-old girls pressed against the front of the stage with promises in their eyes, he was gone. One sharp bow and then off the stage in a rush, flinging himself into the closet-with-a-mirror that passed for a dressing room.

David stared in the mirror and saw his fingers run through his sweat-soaked hair, flicking it back and up into a kind of James Dean goes punk. The huge grin came perilously close to vitiating the cool that the black shades conveyed, but it was undeniably charming. From behind him, resonating through the club, he could hear the chanted demands for more. He saw his lips move in the mirror.

"What do you think, David?" he heard his voice say.

Yeah. Yeah! That was great!

"Right. Let's go back out, then. Give the people what they want." The creature paused and David saw his reflection cast an appraising eye up and down his body. "Tell you what," his voice said. "Why don't I twist around a bit inside here? Just to aid the charisma, know what I mean? Slimmer hips, maybe? Broader shoulders? Bigger cock-bulge? What do you think?"

David thought.

I think you've got a fucking big mouth for something made out of pink spaghetti and snot. Let's go.

The creature laughed with delight and affection and ran back on stage. The audience greeted him with louder whistles, louder cheers, and renewed applause. The band was smiling.

"Whatever you want, mate," said the drummer. "You call it, we'll play it."

Requests were being shouted from the floor as the star of the evening took hold of the microphone again, but all of them were ignored. David spoke to the creature.

How about "I've got you under my skin"?

"Nice one, David," the creature replied. "But I've got a better idea."

The audience—who had of course heard only the second part of this exchange—were only allowed a moment or two to be confused by it, because suddenly, deafeningly, in a hoarse scream like that of a laryngitic Hitler, the figure at the microphone proclaimed:

"I AM THE GOD OF HELLFIRE AND I BRING YOU... FIRE!!!"

This was unexpected.

The crowd quietened. The bass player looked at the drummer and shrugged. The drummer looked at his cowbell and sniffed. The keyboard player, unlike his partners, did in fact have a hazy recollection of The Crazy World of Arthur Brown and of their one hit single—the opening line of which the guy at the mic had just howled—but he didn't have a clue as to how to play it and he was frankly unconvinced that it was altogether an inspired choice of encore anyway.

There was a pregnant silence, aborted by a repeated scream from the front of the stage.

"I AM THE GOD OF HELLFIRE AND I BRING YOU—"

And this time, directly on cue...

"—FIRE!"

...in a massive, searing, blinding explosion of color, heat, and horror, the Gaiety Lounge burst into flames.

Some survivors—for there were some survivors—stated later to the Police that the madman had been seen wandering around the edges of the Lounge at an earlier point in the evening, and more than one of them ventured the suggestion that what he must have been doing, for some obscure insane reason, was laying trails of kerosene or something similar all about the place, intending all along to wreak the havoc he wrought. This was one school of thought.

The survivors counted two among their number, however, who espoused a quite different theory. They were both older women, both Roman Catholics, and they both swore that the flames had issued spontaneously and diabolically from the boy's mouth, nose, eyes, and fingertips and had spread almost instantaneously into circles of Hellfire that engulfed the whole of the club's interior and all of its helpless inhabitants.

Whether the ultimate source was human malice or demonic magic, however, the one thing that was certain was that the flames had seized the Lounge in a rapid, virulent, and all but unshakable grasp.

Not a single one of the exits from the place was reachable without first passing through the fire and only those people driven enough by instinct to waste no time in dismay or speculation were able to run through doors or jump through windows without finding on arriving outside that they had brought the fire with them, still forcing its attentions in a more intimate but no less agonizing embrace.

The musicians alone were able to reach the open air completely unscathed as there was a fire door at the rear of the stage area which gave directly onto the car park.

The drummer, whose brother and sister-in-law were in the audience, held his ground for a few seconds longer than his fellows, his panic temporarily held at bay by a murderous rage directed at the person responsible for the carnage.

One look at the singer's face, however, one heart-stopping glance at the unholy glee that lit his features, one moment's listening to the unbalanced laughter, rich in perverse joy, that emanated from his mouth, changed the drummer's attitude. Putting revenge on hold, he threw himself after his colleagues.

On the main floor of the Lounge people screamed, ran, stumbled, and burned. People cried for help, choked on smoke, wept with terror, and burned. People tripped over tables, they tripped over chairs, they tripped over the dead and the dying, and they burned. Hairs raced for scalps like terrified fuses, sweat turned to steam, skin bubbled and burst.

Everywhere was fire and chaos. Hungry flame ate at the oxygen for which panicked lungs were gasping. People ran blind, the eyes clouded both by the tears they were producing in useless defense against the smoke and by the smoke itself. Shattering screams of terminal terror competed for airspace with howls of blistered agony and with hideous racking choking coughs.

The crowd melted into disparate and desperate smaller sections. Some of these were miniature crowds themselves that ran in groups, surrendering individual reaction to the mass mind—which is no mind at all but instinct at its most pathetic and pernicious—and paid the price by discovering, as weaker members fell beneath the feet of stronger, that pressed and panicked flesh can suffocate you just as efficiently as can smoke. Others ran alone, self-determined but still vulnerable.

One woman, sensibly throwing a chair rather than herself through a window, foolishly balanced herself on the back of another chair to haul herself through. This second chair slipped beneath her shifting weight. The woman lost her balance and impaled herself on a large and unremoved shard of glass, hanging there helpless and dying as the flames blistered her legs.

One man, unwisely running against the flow of a crowd rather than with it, was knocked to the floor. Before he could rise to his feet, his hip bones were shattered by a falling table. In the midst of his agonized and probably pointless struggle to free himself, another mass of people ran over him and his left eye was put out by a teenager's stiletto heel. The fire took two minutes to kill him.

Fifty-seven people died within the inferno and five more joined them over the course of the next two days, having lingered for differing amounts of time in the ICU at Sefton General. A further forty suffered severe burns involving varying degrees of disfigurement, and three score more had to have some kind of medical attention.

The evening's main attraction didn't hang around to see the full results of his final number. Instead, like a star diving for the limo even as the band plays the coda, he exited early in the conflagration through the same fire door that his collaborators had used.

The musicians had already rushed to the front of the building to raise the alarm and offer assistance, so he was quite unimpeded as he walked through the car park and into the fields beyond, tie loosened and jacket hooked casually over one shoulder, humming a little tune to himself and staring at the moon.

5.
EBB TIDE

It was during the sodomizing of the dead boy in the attic bedroom of an otherwise empty house that the creature told David it was going to leave.

It explained, as gently as possible, that it felt it had now tasted enough of the world and its pleasures. It had known laughter and debate, had induced rapture, veneration, terror, and death, had had sex with both kinds of people (*Men and women?* David had naively asked. "Living and dead," the creature had explained), and consequently had decided to move on in order to sample other experiences; chiefly that of being deceased. It intended, in short, to vacate David's body via the orgasmic route and to take up residence in that of the dead teenager whom they were currently buggering vigorously.

But what about me? David asked, in a plaintive tone that was a curious mix of fright and possessiveness.

"Don't worry, David," the creature said. "I've made arrangements. You'll be well looked after."

What do you mean?

The creature's reply had that strange tone that parents use when explaining the rapid approach of something they know the child won't like but is, in their opinion, for its own good, like a spanking or a Boarding School. "Well," it said. "I took the liberty of phoning the Police shortly after we broke in. They should be here any moment."

But there's nothing left inside me! David shouted, like a spurned lover or rejected child seizing at some pathetic practical objection when the true one—don't leave me!—is too shaming to voice.

"Oh, that!" said the creature. "Don't worry about that. I'll make sure there's enough substance left to perform the basic motor functions. No one will ever know, I promise.

It'll be like I was never here. I'll even give you some eyes back."

David's panic was now approaching that of the condemned man who, within feet of the scaffold, begins to scream that he has left his room untidy, that he needs a drink, that he needs to make his bed, needs to piss, needs to put a book away, needs...

But how—

"David," the creature interrupted. "Surely it's clear to you by now that I can do *anything*?"

A world of possibilities seemed to be being snatched from David before he had had a chance to even consider them.

But I wanted to... I wanted... I—

"David, I can do anything, but I can't do *everything*. Better to go out on a high, I think. Ah, speaking of which—you're coming. And I'm going."

David's despairing scream was lost in a flurry of chemical and organic activity.

When Inspector Anthony Murrow, the senior policeman on the case, arrived at the scene of the crime, the suspect was sitting quietly in the company of two uniformed officers.

Murrow had had fifteen years on the beat before his ten behind a desk and his instincts for criminal types was still pretty sharp. He could tell at a glance that the lad wasn't going to give them any trouble, despite the grotesque little trail he appeared to have blazed for himself over the last couple of days.

Murrow walked across the attic room to where the body of Leslie Castle, for such was the dead boy's name, lay awaiting the arrival of the coroner and the police photographer. He nodded at Hayes, the more experienced of the two constables, to join him and bring him up to speed.

Hayes told what little he knew of the facts and then

ventured an opinion. "He's obviously off his head, Sir," he said. "He reckons as how it wasn't really him that did it."

"That so?" said Murrow, looking back at David for a moment.

"It was this... this thing inside him," said Hayes. "So he says, anyway. A monster. Made of *worms*. And he reckons he can prove it." Hayes paused significantly.

Murrow let a second or two pass. "Are you expecting me to *guess*, constable?" he said.

"No, Sir. Sorry, Sir," Hayes said. "He says the thing's *gone* now, you see. Gone into the corpse instead. And Holloway says that if we keep watching, we'll see the worms come out of the body when... well, when this thing gets *bored*. Sir."

Murrow raised a slow eyebrow and then walked across the room to sit down opposite the suspect. In a not unkind voice, he asked a question. "This... this *thing*, David?" he said. "What does it *do*?"

The young man—Christ, *boy* really. What could he be? Twenty-two, twenty-three?—stared blankly at him for a few moments, but finally he spoke.

"Sometimes it sings," he said.

"Sometimes it sings," Murrow repeated, and slowly looked across the room to the body. "Is it singing now?" he asked, in a voice skillfully devoid of disbelief, of contempt, of anything beyond honest enquiry.

David turned his head, following the inspector's gaze. Again, there was silence for a time as they both looked at the corpse, at its perfect stillness, and then David looked back at his interrogator and smiled.

He smiled in a manner that Murrow, for he was a man much given to words of resonance and much taken with the strange ambiguities of slaughter, would later describe to his wife as melancholic and wistful.

"Yes," said David. "It's singing now."

Later, Leslie Castle would be buried beneath the ground, his people being old fashioned enough to shy away from cremation.

Later still, just as David had predicted, the worms would emerge from Leslie's body.

As to whether this second event succeeded the first by a matter of minutes or a matter of months, as to whether the worms poured forth prompted by the unnatural boredom of a monster or by the natural process of corruption, as to whether they emerged singly and simpleminded or bonded to each other and to a hideous guiding intelligence, as to all this...

Life and death have their secrets, the world has only guesses.

HERE COMES A CANDLE

PETER ATKINS

"Here comes a candle to light you to bed," said Dominic Moreton. "And here is your pillow—so lay down your head."

He paused, and looked across the room at his wife. "What do you think?"

Lydia had been looking out of their window, down the hill and over the Promenade. The evening dusk had brought a fog with it which was rolling up the Mersey and diffusing the lights on the Liverpool side into a pleasantly impressionist shimmering. But that didn't mean she hadn't been listening. "Oh, it's good, darling," she said quickly. "I like it. Pillow, bedtime. Good. And the diction seems, you know, authentic..."

She left the sentence open, hoping to imply that she hadn't exhausted all she had to say on the subject while at the same time avoiding the possibility of what she did have to say not being quite what Dominic wanted to hear.

"Yeah," he said. "And a hell of a lot healthier than that chopper, right?"

Lydia smiled and nodded, clearly a person who had been just about to say the very same thing, clearly a wife delighted by yet another example of marital telepathy. "Can I hear some of the others?" she asked him, trying to sound eager but not pushy.

"Oh, I think I'm done for tonight," he said. "*Jack and Jill* can wait until tomorrow. Surprisingly tricky, that one, you know. Because I don't want to make any of them *longer* than the originals—wouldn't really be fair, would it? But to cram into a mere four lines the concept of non-sexist cooperation *not* resulting in violent injury to both parties *and* to make it rhyme" He shook his head and grinned ruefully. "Not as easy as you might think."

"Yes," said Lydia. "Yes, I see that. The original does it though, doesn't it?"

Dominic was silent for a moment. "Does what?" he said. He didn't shout or anything—he never shouted, that was one of the things she'd liked about him—but Lydia wished she hadn't brought it up.

"Well…" she said, and waved her hand dismissively, as if whatever thought she may have thought she had wasn't worth pursuing. "Oh, nothing really."

"It can hardly be *nothing*, can it?" said Dominic. "I mean, by definition, it can't be *nothing*. It was something you said, and therefore not actually *nothing*."

"I wasn't being literal, Dom," she said. "I just meant it was of no importance, that's all."

"But it might be," he said. "*The original does it though,* that's what you said. And all I'm asking you is what it is, precisely, that the original does. Not an unreasonable question, surely?"

"I just meant that the original says what it has to say in four lines," Lydia said, her voice a little smaller than she wished it was.

There was a two second silence while Dom just stared at her, his face completely blank. He exhaled through his nose before he spoke, as if calming himself down, as if about to explain something to a particularly stupid ten-year-old and trying his best to do it not with anger but with patience.

"Look," he said. "Violence is *always* easier. Easier to do. Easier to write about. Always easier. And that is exactly why people like us—people lucky enough to be 'clever', lucky enough to be 'educated'—have to do things the hard way. You don't change the world overnight, you know. And you don't do it without a struggle."

"You're right, of course," she said, but he wasn't done and spoke as if she'd disagreed with him.

"And okay—okay maybe I'm *not* in the front line of that struggle. But maybe, *maybe* what I do is—oh, I don't know—sort of important, perhaps? Sneaking behind enemy lines and planting seeds? Helping to ensure their children grow up wearing a different uniform?"

"It *is* important, Dom," Lydia said. "You know that I know that." She was ready to offer more reassurance, but saw that his own speech had calmed him down enough to let his face crease into the little self-mocking smile she'd always liked.

"Ah," he said. "The comforting vision of academic writer as guerilla fighter. Somebody should write a paper on that." He shook his head, amused by the thought, and told her he was going to bed.

Dominic Moreton was thirty-five years old and in the process of crossing over from being merely a respected academic to becoming an example of that increasingly rare creature, the public intellectual. He'd done a fair bit of radio for the local beeb, and Granada had wheeled him out in front of the late-night cameras more than once. He was the well-known author—or, as he modestly chose to term himself, 'translator'—of *The Path through the Forest: Fairy Tales for Modern Children*, a book which had managed the difficult leap from University press to mass market paperback.

Which was all great. But tenure wasn't actually in the bag yet and he knew that his gig at John Moore University—he got really pissed off when people with long memories still referred to it as The Poly; it hadn't been a polytechnic for years—was predicated on his position as a public figure. Which was why he was working on a follow-up volume to his collection of revisionist folk tales, this time taking nursery rhymes and adapting them in what he hoped was an equally enlightened manner.

Perhaps the critics would be kinder this time, though he wasn't holding his breath. He was the first to admit that *The Path through the Forest* was a curious book. Its concern was clearly the path, not the forest, its subject clearly the light, not the dark. In it, the reader found a Hansel and Gretel who received only supper and comfort at the Gingerbread House, a suitor of Rapunzel whose eyes were *not* put out by the brambles. In his versions of the old tales, no loyal retainers or faithful animals were slaughtered or disfigured in the service of their prince, princess, or tailor.

The lessons he wanted people to take from his book were hardly controversial: Co-operation is better than individual struggle; women possess strengths that men do not, as well as vice versa; appearances are nothing on which to base character assessment; peaceful co-existence is rather a good thing. Not much to argue with there. He'd been prepared, nonetheless, for a reactionary backlash and he'd certainly got it. Of course, they'd been smart enough not to attack the message, but the messenger. Personal abuse, most of it. He wished he didn't remember some of their choicest phrases verbatim, but of course he did:

"…anaemic prose and a bloodless imagination."

"…manages to elevate the crude folk-tale to the cultural excellence of Saturday morning television."

"Dr. Moreton stands in relation to the fairy tale in

approximately the same way as the proverbial Arab-with-two-bricks stands to the castrated camel…"

Fuck them. He wore their wounds like medals. Medals, moreover, from a campaign which he'd won. Vocal supporters in civic groups and media had ensured *The Path through the Forest* a home in most public libraries and schools and his trade publisher was making promising noises about the advance that might be coming its successor's way once they'd seen a couple of sample chapters.

He stared in the bathroom mirror as his reflection brushed its teeth. *How many miles to Babylon?* he thought, out of nowhere.

It was Scott Fitzgerald, he remembered, who'd first suggested that 'babylon' was an elision of 'babyland'. "How many miles to Babyland?" he said aloud. "Three score and ten." Yes. That was good. Perhaps he'd put it in the book. A tribute from one writer to another.

He turned off the light and headed for the bedroom, wondering what could be keeping his wife.

Lydia tried another page of the book the woman on that morning show had recommended.

No. Still not interesting.

She tried for a yawn to find out if she was tired.

No. Still wide awake.

She looked across the room, though the open door to Dominic's study on the other side of the hall. His desk light was still on and she could see a small neat pile of print-outs next to his computer.

She turned out the lights in the main room—just because she wasn't tired didn't mean she had to keep Dom awake by leaving lights on everywhere—and made her way to his study. She picked up the tidy stack of pages and, by the small single light, began to read.

Humpty Dumpty sat on a wall.
Humpty Dumpty had a great fall.
But Mummy and Daddy were watching, so then
They put Humpty Dumpty together again!

The first nine or ten sheets of paper each contained little gems of this type and Lydia read them with a vaguely contented approval. It was as she got to the later pages—the pages that she assumed Dom had been working on most recently—that she began to feel something different.

Hush, little baby. Go to sleep.
In the dark, I'll come and creep
And steal your eyes, so you won't weep.
Hush, little baby. Try to sleep.

That couldn't be right, could it?

That surely couldn't fit into Dominic's theme, surely couldn't be something her husband had written? She found it hard to believe that it was even an original, an old rhyme which Dom had yet to correct. It was so… one-sided. So downright nasty. But it wasn't the only one. All of the remaining verses were similar.

Baby pretty, baby blue.
What has mummy brought for you?
Another baby with your face;
A darker twin to take your place.
A darker twin to take your breath
And rock-a-bye you into death.

Lydia didn't like this at all. These things were *horrible*. She didn't want to read any more of them. She replaced the pile next to the printer, a little less neatly than before. She felt strange and unsettled, felt like she should have a drink or something. It wasn't just the rhymes, of course, disturbing as they were. No, it was the sickening and frightening possibility that her husband had written them. Could Dom be *ill*, she wondered?

She felt suddenly and strangely aware of the darkness

behind her and wished she'd put the overhead light on when she came into the room or had left the lights on in the hall. She had a crazy thought that Dominic might have come back downstairs, might have come back very quietly, and walked silently up behind her, waiting patiently in the dark for her to turn and find him, to turn and find a Dominic she didn't know, a Dominic with a slack smile, excited eyes, and something sharp in his hand…

Stop it, she told herself. She was being ridiculous. She took a deep breath and allowed herself to relax.

The floor creaked behind her.

She whirled around, heart racing and explanation already flying from her lips.

"Hello, darling," she said. "Couldn't you sleep? I was just—"

But it wasn't Dominic.

Sunlight streamed into the unshuttered room. Inch by slow inch it made its way across the bedroom floor, creeping up the counterpane, illuminating first fingertips, then hands, arms, chest, chin, nose until finally it shone directly onto the closed eyelids of the sleeping Dominic Moreton, insinuating itself even into his dreams so that the night-time sea in which his unconscious swam was suddenly bathed in light and the krakens and the serpents, the squids and the sea-beasts who had ignored him in the dark roared in unholy delight and rose, dripping and monstrous, above him, tentacles threshing, cavernous mouths open and hungry.

Dominic's eyes jerked open and he sat up in bed still, for a terrifying second or two, awaiting the closing of one of those huge mouths on his flesh.

When none did, his breath calmed and allowed him the luxury of annoyed confusion. It was the sun that had awoken him, he realized, and realized further that this meant it was much later in the morning than it should be. Where was Lydia? Where was his cup of tea?

He looked about him and his confusion deepened. Lydia's side of the bed was in marked contrast to his own rumpled half. The sheets were still tucked in at the top, and her pillow was undented. It looked like she hadn't been to bed at all. And she certainly hadn't woken him at his usual time. What the hell was going on?

"Lydia?" he called, getting out of bed without waiting for a reply.

"Lydia!" he called again, a little louder, pulling himself into his blue toweling robe.

"Lydia!" he shouted, making his way downstairs, even though he realized by then that his wife must have gone out or... or that his wife must have gone out.

He knew his voice would have wakened her if she'd simply fallen asleep in the chair he'd left her in the night before but still the living room was the first place he looked.

Empty.

Well, empty of wives anyway. Dominic turned and looked across the hall. He could see his desk through the open study door. Something was a little off. He knew that he'd left his manuscript in a tidier condition than that and he crossed to the room to check on it.

Flicking rapidly through the loose sheets of paper he saw that, though Lydia must have been doing some peeking last night, there was nothing untoward here. The revised rhymes were still in the order he'd left them in, even though there were five or six blank sheets added to the pile after them. He could only assume Lydia had added the blank pages last night for some unknown reason of her own. What on earth was she thinking? And where the hell *was* she?

"Lydia!" he shouted again, knowing it was pointless, as he walked through to their open plan kitchen and dining area.

Empty.

And no tea brewed nor breakfast begun.

The only downstairs room that he hadn't yet checked was the small television lounge. His wife had lobbied for them to place their TV set in the living room—"Like everybody else in the current century," she'd said, thinking she was funny—but he'd insisted on its exile to a room of its own. People who had televisions in their living room were people who couldn't read and didn't talk. He strode into it briskly, punching the door open so firmly that it swung back and slammed shut behind him.

Empty.

Dominic stared angrily at the TV set, eager to accuse anything of complicity in this mystery. He heard a dripping sound, regular and rhythmic, coming from somewhere behind him. Fucking kitchen tap on the blink again, he thought, and then realized that the sound of the drips were like something hitting not stainless steel, but plush carpet. What the hell was there to drip in *this* room? Had Lydia knocked over a vase, he wondered, and just left it to drain? Dominic turned around to see what the matter was.

Twelve inches above the door, mounted neatly but bloodily on a fine wooden shield which was itself attached firmly to the wall, was the severed head of his wife. Blood gathered in and dripped from her half-open mouth, each drop joining with unerring accuracy the small rust colored circle on the carpet beneath.

"Lydia!" Dominic screamed.

"*Once upon a time...*" the nightmare trophy croaked. A hollow, pain- wracked, curiously distant voice, like a bad connection to a party line in Hell.

"Lydia!" Dominic screamed.

"*Over the hills and far away...*"

"Lydia!"

"*Deep in the forest, there lived...*"

The door slammed open suddenly, crashing back onto the

wall hard enough to make Dominic wince at the thought of the trophy falling from the wall and Lydia's head rolling toward him.

Revealed in the doorway was a small person—dwarf was not a kind word—with a gnarled and dirty face. He had a beard that was matted and tangled and his ears were remarkably pointed. His eyes were not friendly and both his hands gripped tightly on the long wooden handle of an axe almost as tall as he.

Dominic had no time to react. The dwarf moved like lightning, swinging the axe powerfully as he charged, and taking both of Dominic's legs off at the knees in a single vicious stroke. As Dominic toppled to the carpet, too stunned to scream, the dwarf capered around him, chanting into the empty room in a sweet and high-pitched voice:

I chop the tree that has no root.
I chop the tree that bears no fruit.
I chop the hammer that hates the nail.
I chop the teller who hates the tale.

Having finished his rhyme, the dwarf stopped dancing and, putting his hand to his mouth, shouted something out in a voice that was disturbingly reminiscent of the Old Swan bullies of Dominic's youth.

"Come 'ed!" he yelled. "Come and gerrim!"

And in they all came.

Dominic, in surprisingly little pain—due, no doubt, to the profound physical trauma of his amputations—stared up from the floor to the doorway as they all flooded in to his room; the Goose-thing, the bleached Princess, the talking cat, the killer of giants, the killer of dragons, Princes who hopped and croaked, women who glittered and flew, grandmothers with snouts and matted fur.

From somewhere at the rear of the crowd, a voice called out in a tone of authority: "Mind yer backs! King's business. Mind yer backs."

The crowd parted. Dominic looked up to see two finely dressed soldiers—all scarlet and straps straight out of storybooks—advancing towards him. With a brisk military efficiency, they each seized one of his arms and began to drag him behind them, his stumps leaving parallel trails of blood for the crowd in his living room to follow which, at a respectable distance and a somber pace, they did.

Back through the doorway, out into the hallway, past the study, and through the kitchen the King's men took him, professionally unmoved by his cries of pain and refusal. The door into the back garden was open and that was where he was taken, to be laid down finally in the shadow of his high brick wall on his back, stumps to the wall, head to the house.

The crowd flowed into the garden from the kitchen door, fanning out behind the recumbent and mutilated Dominic into a long semicircle, facing the high garden wall. Finally, when everyone had taken their position, a stillness and a silence fell upon the place, broken only by Dominic's wrigglings and whimperings.

Then he heard it and was silent too.

There were panting and scrambling noises coming from the other side of the wall. Loud panting noises. Well-spaced scrambling noises. Something was climbing up the other side of his garden wall. Something big.

A pale hand, surprisingly little, appeared over the top row of bricks and gripped, followed by a second hand—equally tiny but more than eight feet away from the first—and then suddenly, with an energetic flip of a grace astonishing in one so large, it was there.

Sitting on the wall, towering over the yard, puny and useless little legs kicking and flapping obscenely beneath it, staring balefully down at Dominic from its hideously widely-spaced eyes, murmuring invective from the tiny incongruous mouth almost lost in the smoothly curving vastness of its head-cum-torso, its shadow prefiguring its claim on Dominic's body, was the Egg Thing.

To be fair to Dominic it must be admitted that, despite the terror which opened his bowels and despite the shame which accompanied it, it was only the pain of his severed legs, finally breaking through the numbness of shock, which prevented him from enjoying that unspoken last wish of all condemned men—one last bloody good laugh.

In point of fact though, as Humpty Dumpty launched himself from the wall and straight toward the fragile human on the ground, the only laughter came from somewhere on the fringes of the crowd.

The guilty party—well known as one who lacked a proper sense of dignity on these occasions—was nudged and hissed at by his companions, a feline violinist and a very athletic cow. Despite their embarrassed attempts to silence him, though, he laughed and continued to laugh. As the impact fractured several of Dominic's bones, as the sharp edges of shattered shell ripped his flesh open, as he drowned slowly and helplessly in the off-white, viscous, and sharp-smelling contents of his executioner, the little dog laughed to see such fun.

Dominic was discovered late in the afternoon by Julie, the Fazakerley teenager who came in twice a week to do for them. The full heat of the afternoon sun had fused victim and killer together into a kind of academic omelette which, eventually, was scraped off the floor, served up in the more lurid newspapers, and digested by schoolchildren as an item of wonder for several months thereafter. They didn't believe it, of course, but it made for a great story.

BETWEEN THE COLD MOON AND THE EARTH

PETER ATKINS

They only brushed his cheek for a second or two, but her lips were fucking *freezing*.

"Christ, Carol," he said. "Do you want my coat?"

She laughed. "What for?" she asked.

"Because it's one in the morning," he said. "And you're cold."

"It's summer," she pointed out, which was undeniably true but wasn't really the issue. "Are you going to walk me home, then?"

Michael had left the others about forty minutes earlier. Kirk had apparently copped off with the girl from Woolworth's that they'd met inside the pub so Michael and Terry had tactfully peeled away before the bus stop and started walking the long way home around Sefton Park. He could've split a taxi fare with Terry but, given that they were still in the middle of their ongoing argument about the relative merits of T.Rex and Pink Floyd and that it was still a good six months before they'd find Roxy Music to agree on, they'd parted by unspoken consent and Michael had opted to cut across the park alone.

Carol had been standing on the path beside the huge

park's large boating lake. He'd shit himself for a moment when he first saw the shadowed figure there, assuming the worst—a midnight skinhead parked on watch ready to whistle his mates out of hiding to give this handy glamrock faggot a good kicking—but Carol had been doing nothing more threatening than staring out at the center of the lake and the motionless full moon reflected there.

"Alright, Michael," she'd said, before he'd quite recognized her in the moonlight, and had kissed his cheek lightly in further greeting before he'd spoken her name. Now, he fell into step beside her and they began to walk the long slow curve around the lake.

"God, Carol. Where've you been?" he asked. "Nobody's seen you for months."

It was true. Her mum had re-married just before last Christmas and they'd moved. Not far away, still in the same city, but far enough for sixteen-year-olds to lose touch.

"I went to America," Carol said.

Michael turned his head to see if she was kidding. "You went to *America*?" he said. "What d'you mean, you went to America? When? Who with?"

Her eyes narrowed for a moment as if she were re-checking her facts or her memory. "I think it was America," she said.

"You *think* it was America?"

"It might have been an imaginary America," she said, her voice a little impatient. "Do you want to hear the fucking story or not?"

Oh. Michael didn't smile nor attempt to kiss her, but he felt like doing both. Telling stories—real, imagined, or some happy collision of the two—had been one of the bonds between them, one of the things he'd loved about her. Not the only thing of course. It's not like he hadn't shared Kirk and Terry's enthusiastic affection for her astonishingly perfect breasts and for the teasingly challenging way she had about her that managed to suggest two things simultaneously: That, were circumstances to somehow become magically right, she might .. you know .. actually *do it* with you; and that you were probably and permanently incapable of ever conjuring such circumstance. But her stories, and her delight in telling them, were what he'd loved most and what, he now realized, he'd most missed. So yes, he said, he wanted to hear the story.

There was some quick confusion about whether she'd got there by plane or by ship—Carol had never been a big fan of preamble—but apparently what mattered was that, after a few days, she found herself in a roadside diner with a bunch of people she hardly knew.

They were on a road-trip and had stopped for lunch in this back-of-beyond and unpretentious Diner—a place which, while perfectly clean and respectable, looked like it hadn't been painted or refurbished since about 1952. They were in a booth, eating pie and drinking coffee. Her companions were about her age—but could, you know, *drive* and everything. Turned out boys in America could be just as fucking rude as in Liverpool. One of them—Tommy, she thought his name was—was giving shit to the waitress. Hoisting his empty coffee mug, he was leaning out of the booth and looking pointedly down the length of the room.

"Yo! Still need a refill here!" he shouted to the counter.

Carol stood up and, announcing she was going to the ladies' room, slid her way out of the booth. Halfway down the room, she crossed paths with the waitress, who was hurrying toward their booth with a coffee-pot. The woman's name-tag said *Cindi*, a spelling Carol had never seen before and hoped could possibly be short for Cinderella because that'd be, you know, great. Carol spoke softly to her, nodding back towards Tommy, who was impatiently shaking his empty coffee mug in the air.

"Don't mind him, love," Carol said. "He's a bit of a prick, but I'll make sure he leaves a nice tip."

Cindi, who looked to be at least thirty and harried-looking, gave her a quick smile of gratitude. "Little girls' room's out back, sweetheart," she said.

Carol exited the main building of the diner and saw that a separate structure, little more than a shack really, housed the bathrooms. She started across the graveled parking-lot, surrounded by scrub-grass that was discolored and overgrown, looking down the all-but-deserted country road—the type of road, she'd been informed by her new friends, which was known as a two-lane blacktop. The diner and its shithouse annex were the only buildings for as far as her eye could see, apart from a hulking grain silo a hundred yards or so down the road. As Carol looked in that desolate direction, a cloud drifted over the sun, dimming the summer daylight and shifting the atmosphere into a kind of pre-storm dreariness. Carol shivered and wondered, not without a certain pleasure in the mystery, just where the hell she was.

Done peeing and alone in the bathroom, Carol washed her hands and splashed her face at the pretty crappy single sink that was all the place had to offer. The sound of the ancient cistern laboriously and noisily re-filling after her flush played in the background. Carol turned off the tap and looked for a moment at her reflection in the pitted and stained mirror above the sink. As the cistern finally creaked and whistled to a halt, the mirror suddenly cracked noisily across its width as if it was just too tired to keep trying.

"Fuckin' 'ell!" said Carol, because it had made her jump and because she didn't like the newly mis-matched halves of her reflected face. She turned around, ready to walk out of the bathroom, and discovered she was no longer alone.

A little girl—what, six, seven years old?—was standing, silent and perfectly still, outside one of the stall doors, looking up at her. Oddly, the little girl was holding the palm of one hand over her right eye.

"Oh shit," said Carol, remembering that she'd just said

fucking hell in front of a kid. "I didn't know you were .." She paused, smiled, started over. "Hello, pet. D'you live around here?"

The little girl just kept looking at her.

"What's your name?" Carol asked her, still smiling but still getting no response. Registering the hand-over-the-eye thing, she tried a new tack. "Oh," she said. "Are we playing a game and nobody told me the rules? Alright then, here we go."

Raising her hand, Carol covered her own right eye with her palm. The little girl remained still and silent. Carol lowered her hand from her face. "Peek-a-boo," she said.

Finally, the little girl smiled shyly and lowered her own hand. She had no right eye at all, just a smooth indented bank of flesh.

Carol was really good. She hardly jumped at all and her gasp was as short-lived as could reasonably be expected.

The little girl's voice was very matter-of-fact. "Momma lost my eyepatch," she said.

"Oh. That's a shame," said Carol, trying to keep her own voice as equally everyday.

"She's gonna get me another one. When she goes to town."

"Oh, well, that's good. Will she get a nice color? Do you have a favorite color?"

The little girl shrugged. "What are you, retarded?" she said. "It's an eye-patch. Who cares what color it is?"

Carol didn't know whether to laugh or slap her.

"You can go now, if you like," said the little girl. "I have to make water."

"Oh. Alright. Sure. Well, look after yourself," Carol said and, raising her hand in a slightly awkward wave of farewell, headed for the exit door. The little girl called after her.

"You take care in those woods now, Carol", she said.

"I hadn't told her my name," said Carol.

"Well, that was weird," Michael said.

Carol smiled, pleased. "*That* wasn't weird," she said. "It *got* weird. Later. After I got lost in the woods."

"You got lost in the woods?"

Carol nodded.

"Why'd they let you go wandering off on your own?"

"Who?"

"Your new American friends. The people you were in the café with."

"Ha. Café. *Diner*, stupid. We were in America."

"Whatever. How could they let you get lost?"

"Oh, yeah." She thought for a second, looking out to their side at the boating lake and its ghost moon. "Well, p'raps they weren't there to begin with. Doesn't matter. Listen."

Turned out Carol *did* get lost in the woods. Quite deep in the woods, actually. Heart of the forest, Hansel and Gretel shit, where the sunlight, through the thickening trees, was dappled and spotty and where the reassuring blue sky of what was left of the afternoon could be glimpsed only occasionally through the increasingly oppressive canopy of high leafy branches.

Carol was tramping her way among the trees and the undergrowth on the mossy and leaf strewn ground when she heard the sound for the first time. Faint and plaintive and too distant to be truly identifiable, it was nevertheless suggestive of something, something that Carol couldn't quite put her finger on yet. Only when it came again, a few moments later, did she place it. It was the sound of a lonely ship's horn in a midnight ocean, melancholy and eerie. Not quite as eerie, though, as the fact that once the horn had sounded this second time, all the other sounds stopped, all the other sounds that Carol hadn't even been consciously aware of until they disappeared; birdsong, the footsteps of unseen animals moving through the woods, the sigh of the breeze as it whistled through the branches.

The only sounds now were those she made herself; the rustle and sway of the living branches she was pushing her way through and the crackle and snap of the dead ones she was breaking beneath her. Carol began to wonder if moving on in the same direction she'd been going was that great of an idea. She turned around and started heading back and, within a few yards, stepping out from between two particularly close trees, she found herself in a small grove-like clearing that she didn't remember passing through earlier.

There was a downed and decaying tree-trunk lying in the leafy undergrowth that momentarily and ridiculously put Carol in mind of a park bench. But she really wasn't in the mood to sit and relax and it wasn't like there was, you know, a boating lake to look at the moon in or anything. So she kept moving, across the clearing, past the downed trunk, and stopped only when the voice spoke from behind her.

"What's your rush, sweetheart?"

Carol turned back. Sitting perched on the bench-like trunk was a sailor. He was dressed in a square-neck deck-shirt and bell-bottomed pants and Carol might have taken a moment to wonder if sailors still dressed like that these days if she hadn't been too busy being surprised just to see him at all. He was sitting in profile to her, one leg on the ground, the other arched up on the trunk and he didn't turn to face her fully, perhaps because he was concentrating on rolling a cigarette.

"Ready-mades are easier," the sailor said. "But I like the ritual—opening the paper, laying in the tobacco, rolling it up. Know what I mean?"

"I don't smoke," said Carol, which wasn't strictly true, but who the fuck was he to deserve the truth.

"You chew?" he asked.

"Chew what?"

"Tobacco"

"Eugh. No."

The sailor chanted something rhythmic in response, like he was singing her a song but knew his limitations when it came to carrying a tune:

"Down in Nagasaki,
Where the fellas chew tobaccy
And the women wicky-wacky-woo."

Carol stared at him. Confused. Not necessarily nervous. Not yet. She gestured out at the woods. "Where'd you come from?" she said.

"Dahlonega, Georgia. Little town North-east of Atlanta. Foot of the Appalachians."

That wasn't what she'd meant and she started to tell him so, but he interrupted.

"Ever been to Nagasaki, honeybun?"

"No."

"How about Shanghai?"

The Sailor was still sitting in profile to her. Talking to her, but staring straight ahead into the woods and beyond. He didn't wait for a reply. "Docked there once," he said. "Didn't get shore-leave. Fellas who did told me I missed something, boy. Said there were whores there could practically tie themselves in knots. Real limber. Mmm. A man likes that. Likes 'em limber."

Carol was very careful not to say anything at all. Not to move. Not to breathe.

"Clean, too," said the sailor. "That's important to me. Well, who knows? Maybe I'll get back there one of these days. Course, once they get a good look at me, I might have to pay extra." He turned finally to face her. "Whaddaya think?"

Half of his face was bone-pale and bloated, as if it had drowned years ago and been underwater ever since. His hair hung dank like seaweed and something pearl-like glinted in the moist dripping blackness of what used to be an eye-socket.

"Jesus Christ!" Carol said, frozen in shock, watching helplessly as the sailor put his cigarette in his half-ruined mouth, lit it, and inhaled.

"Calling on the Lord for salvation," he said. "Good for you. Might help." Smoke oozed out from the pulpy white flesh that barely clung to the bone beneath his dead face. "Might not."

He rose to his feet and grinned at her. "Useta chase pigs through the Georgia pines, sweet thing," he said, flinging his cigarette aside. "Let's see if you're faster than them little squealers."

And then he came for her.

"I was a lot faster, though," said Carol. "But it still took me ten minutes to lose him."

"Fuck, Carol," said Michael. "That wasn't funny."

"I didn't say it was funny. I said it was weird. Remember?"

Michael turned to look at her and she tilted her face to look up at his, dark eyes glinting, adorably proud of herself. They'd walked nearly a full circuit of the lake now, neither of them even thinking to branch off in the direction of the park's northern gate and the way home.

"Well, it was weird alright," Michael said. "Creepy ghost sailor. Pretty good."

"Yeah," she said. "Turns out there was a ship went down there in the second world war. All hands lost."

"Went down in the woods. That was a good trick."

"It wasn't the *woods*. Didn't I tell you that? It was the beach. That's where it all happened."

"Was it Redondo?"

"The fuck's *Redondo*?" she said, genuinely puzzled.

"It's a beach. In America. I've heard of it. It's on that Patti Smith album."

"Oh, yeah. No. This wasn't in America. It was in Cornwall." She thought about it for a moment. "Yeah. Had to be Cornwall because of the rock pool."

"You didn't say anything about a rock pool."

"I haven't *told* you yet," she said, exasperated. "God, you're rubbish."

Mihael laughed, even though something else had just hit him. He was walking on a moonlit night alone with a beautiful girl and it apparently wasn't occurring to him to try anything. He hadn't even put his arm around her, for Christ's sake. Terry and Kirk would give him such shit for this when he told them. He wondered for the first time if that was something Carol knew, if that was what had always been behind her stories, why she found them, why she told them, like some instinctive Scheherazade keeping would-be lovers at bay with narrative strategies. He felt something forming in him, a kind of sadness that he couldn't name and didn't understand.

"Is everything alright, Carol?" he asked, though he couldn't say why.

"Well, it is *now*," she said, deaf to the half-born subtext in his question. "I got away. I escaped. But that spoils the story, dickhead. You've got to hear what *happened* first."

The park was silver-gray in the light from the moon. He wondered what time it was. "The rock pool," he said.

"Exactly," she said, pleased that he was paying attention.

She hadn't seen it at first. Had kept moving along the deserted beach until the sandy shore gave way to rocky cave-strewn outcrops from the cliffs above the coastline. It was only when she clambered over an algae and seaweed coated rock wall that she found it. Orphaned from the sea and held within a natural basin formation, the pool was placid and still and ringed by several large boulders about its rim. It was about twenty feet across and looked to be fairly deep.

On one of the boulders, laid out as if waiting for their

owner, were some items of clothing. A dress, a pair of stockings, some underwear. Carol looked from them out to the cool inviting water of the pool. A head broke surface as she looked, and a woman started swimming toward the rock where her clothes were. Catching sight of Carol, she stopped and trod water, looking at her suspiciously. "What are you doing?" she said. "Are you spying?" She was older than Carol, about her mum's age maybe, a good-looking thirty-five.

"No, I'm not," Carol said. "Why would I be spying?"

"You might be one of them," the woman said.

"One of who?"

The woman narrowed her eyes and looked at Carol appraisingly. "You know who," she said.

"No, I don't," Carol said. "And I'm not one of anybody. I was with some friends. We went to France. Just got back. The boat's down there on the beach."

"They've all got stories," the woman said. "That's how they get you."

"Who?! Stop talking shit, willya? I .." Carol bit her tongue.

For the first time, the woman smiled. "Are you moderating your language for me?" she said. "That's adorable."

Carol felt strangely flustered. Was this woman *flirting* with her?

"I understand," the woman said, still smiling, still staring straight into Carol's eyes. "I'm an older lady and you want to be polite. But, you know, I'm not really *that* much older." She stepped out of the pool and stood there right in front of Carol, glistening wet and naked. "See what I mean?" she said.

Carol felt funny. She swallowed. The woman kept her eyes fixed on Carol as she stepped very close to her. "I'm going to tell you a secret," she said, and leaned forward to whisper the secret in Carol's ear. "I'm real limber for my age."

Carol jumped back as the woman's voice began a familiar rhythmic chant.

"*Down in Nagasaki,*
Where the fellas chew tobaccy,
And the women wicky-wacky-woo."

Carol tried to run but the woman had already grabbed her by the throat. "What's your rush, sweetheart?" she said, and her voice was different now, guttural and amused. "Party's just getting started."

Carol was struggling in the choking grip. She tried to swing a fist at the woman's head but her punch was effortlessly blocked by the woman's other arm.

"Your eyes are so pretty," the woman said. "I'm going to have them for earrings."

Her mouth opened inhumanly wide. Her tongue flicked out with reptile speed. It was long and black and forked.

"But like I said," said Carol, "I escaped."

"How?" said Michael, expecting another previously unmentioned element to be brought into play, like a knife or a gun or a really sharp stick or a last-minute rescue from her Francophile friends from the recently-invented boat. But Carol had a different ending in mind.

"I walked into the Moon," she said.

Michael looked up to the night sky.

"No," said Carol. "Not that Moon. This one."

She was pointing out towards the center of the utterly calm lake and the perfect Moon reflected there. Looking at it with her, neither of them walking now, Michael felt the cold of the night as if for the first time. He waited in silence, afraid to speak, afraid to give voice to his questions, afraid that they would be answered.

She told another story then, the last, he knew, that his sweet lost friend would ever tell him, the tale of how the other Moon had many ways into and out of this world: Through placid lakes on summer evenings; through city streets on rain-slicked nights; from out the ocean depths for the eyes of lonely night-watch sailors.

And when she was done, when Michael could no longer pretend not to know in whose company he truly was, she turned to him and smiled a heartbreaking smile of farewell.

She looked beautiful in monochrome, in the subtle tones of the Moon that had claimed her for its own. Not drained of color, but richly re-imagined, painted in shades of silver, gray, and black, and delicate lunar blue. She looked almost liquid, as if, were Michael to reach out a hand and even try to touch her, she might ripple into strange expansions of herself.

"Thanks, Michael," she said. "I can make it home from here."

Michael didn't say anything. Didn't know what he could possibly find to say that the tears in his young eyes weren't already saying. The beautiful dead girl pointed a silver finger beyond him, in the direction of his life. "Go on," she said kindly. "Don't look back."

And he didn't look back, not even when he heard the impossible footsteps on the water, not even when he heard the shadow moon sigh in welcome, and the quiet lapping of the lake water as if something had slipped effortlessly beneath it.

He'd later hear the alternative versions of course—the stories of how, one moonlit night, Carol had walked out of the third-floor window of her step-father's house and the vile rumors as to why—but he would prefer, for all his days, to believe the story that the lost girl herself had chosen to tell him.

He continued home through the park, not even breaking step as his fingers sought and found the numb spot on his cheek, the frozen place where her cold lips had blessed him, waiting for her frostbite kiss to bloom in tomorrow's mirror.

THE MYSTERY

PETER ATKINS

"For upwards of two hours, the sky was brilliant with lights"
—The Liverpool Post, Sept 8th 1895

There's actually no mystery at all.

Not if you went the Bluey, anyway.

It used to be the grounds of a house, a big one. No Speke Hall or anything, but still technically a Stately Home. It had been called The Grange and was pulled down in May of 1895.

Four months later, minus an ornamental lake which had been filled in, the grounds were opened as a park for the children of Liverpool by the city council. It was officially named Wavertree Playground but was almost immediately dubbed 'The Mystery' by local people, because the person who bought the land and donated it to the city had asked for anonymity.

The Bluecoat School, a boys' Grammar, backed onto The Mystery and if you were a pupil there, even seventy-five years later, It was made pretty damn clear to you that it was one of our old Governors who'd forked up for the park. Philip Holt – one of our four school houses was named for him – was a maritime magnate in the days of the great ships

71

and the Cast Iron Shore. The money needed to clear the land and create the park was probably no more than loose change to the man whose Blue Funnel Line practically owned the tea trade between Britain and China.

So. No mystery there.

I'll tell you what *was* a mystery, though. The fucking state of the Gents' bogs.

The Liverpool of the mid 'sixties was a city suffering a dizzying drop into recession. No more ships, no more industry, no more Beatles – *Tara, mum. Off to London to shake the world. Don't wait up* – but even so, the public toilets at the northwest corner of the Mystery were astonishingly disgusting. 'Derelict' didn't even come close. They'd been neither bricked up nor pulled down. It was more like they'd been simply forgotten, as if a file had been lost somewhere in the town hall and nobody with any responsibility knew they even existed. Utterly unlooked after in a third world sort of way and alarming to enter, let alone use. No roof, no cubicle doors, no paper, what was left of the plaster over the ancient red bricks completely covered with graffiti of an obsessive and sociopathic nature, and last mopped out sometime before Hitler trotted into Poland.

But, you know, if you had to go you had to go, and I'd had many a piss there back in the day. If you didn't actually touch anything, you had a fighting chance of walking out without having contracted a disease.

But to see that soiled shed-like structure still there on an autumn afternoon thirty years later was more than a little surprising.

I had some business to attend to and shouldn't really have allowed myself to be distracted, but I felt a need to check it out. The boys appeared just as I approached the stinking moss-scarred walkway entrance.

There were two of them, both about thirteen, though one at least a head taller than his friend. Although they weren't actually blocking the path – standing just off to the side, ankle-deep in the overgrown grass – they nevertheless gave the impression of being self-appointed sentries, as if they were there to perhaps collect a toll or something.

"Where are you going, then?" The first one said. His hair was russet and looked home-cut and his face was patchily rosy with the promise of acne.

"The bog," I said.

They looked at each other, and then back at me.

"*This* bog?" said the first.

"Fuckin' 'ell," said the second. He was the shorter one, black Irish pale, unibrowed and sullen.

"You don't wanna go in *there*," said the first.

"Why would you go in *there*?" said his mate.

I shrugged, but I wasn't sure they noticed. They were staring at me with the kind of incipient aggression you'd expect, but weren't actually meeting my eyes. Instead, they were both looking at me at about mid-chest height, as if looking at someone smaller and younger.

"Why wouldn't I?" I said.

"He might get ya," said the black-haired one.

"Who?"

"The feller," said the redhead.

"What feller?" I asked him.

He looked surprised. "Yerav'n 'eard of 'im?" he said.

"No."

"Fuckin' 'ell," said the shorter one.

"He's there all the time," his friend said. "Nights, mostly."

"Yeah," Blackie nodded in support. "Nights."

"Yeah?" I said to the taller one, the redhead, who seemed to be the boss. "What does he do?"

"Waits there for lads," he said.

"What for?"

"You know."

I didn't. He shook his head off my blank look, in pity for my ignorance. "He bums them," he said.

"Shags them up the bum," said his companion helpfully.

"Why?"

"Fuckin' 'ell," said the first one, and looked at his friend with a *we've got a right idiot here* expression. "Because he's an 'omo, that's why."

"A Hom," said the second.

The first looked thoughtful. Came to a decision. "We better go in with ya," he said.

"For safety, like," said the second, with only a trace of his eagerness betraying itself. "He might be in there now."

"Oh, I think I'll be alright," I said. "If he's in there, I'll tell him I'm not in the mood."

My tone was confusing to them. It wasn't going the way it was meant to, the way it perhaps usually did.

"Yeah, burrit's worse than we said," the first one told me, as if worried some opportunity was slipping away. He looked to his friend. "Tell him about the, you know, the thing."

"Yeah, he's gorra nutcracker," Blackie said. "You know warramean?" He mimed a plier-like action in order to help me visualise what he was talking about. "After he's bummed ya, he crushes yer bollocks."

I remembered that. It was a story I'd first heard when I was much younger than them. An urban legend, though the phrase hadn't been coined at the time, conjured into being in the summer of 1965 and believed by nearly every nine year old boy who heard it.

They were still looking at my chest, as if staring down a smaller contemporary.

"How old am I?" I asked them.

"You wha'?" the redhead said.

"How old do you think I am?"

They shared a look, and the taller one shrugged. "Dunno," he said. "About eight?"

"Might be ten," the other one said, not to me but to his friend, and the redhead shot him an angry look as if he didn't want to be bothered with details or sidetracked by debate.

I snapped my fingers loudly, close to my face, and drew their eyes upwards.

They looked confused. Their eyes weren't quite focussing on mine, and I still wasn't sure they could really see me. There was something else hovering behind their confusion; an anxiety, perhaps, as if they feared they might be in trouble, as if something would know they were being distracted from their duty and wouldn't be very pleased with them. As far as they were concerned, this was a day like every other and *needed* to be a day like every other, and any disruption in the pattern was alarming to them, in however imprecise a way.

I didn't doubt that this was how they'd spent a fair portion of their time, back when it was linear. Having a little chat and preparing some eight year old victim for a good battering. They'd probably done it before, and more than once. Done it regularly, perhaps, until their belief in the very predator they used as bait had become their undoing.

"Take a look at this," I said and took something out of my pocket to show them.

A few minutes later, back on the main footpath, I took a look back over my shoulder. It was very dark now and neither the toilets nor the boys were anywhere in sight. The moon had risen in the cloudless sky and I took a glance at my watch. It was an old fashioned watch and its dial was un-illuminated, but I was fairly certain it said it was still four in the afternoon.

I'd kept up a brisk pace while checking the time and, when I looked up again, the house was directly ahead of me, though I hadn't noticed it earlier. Its size alone suggested it was probably magnificent in the daylight, but its lawns were unlit and its windows shuttered and it appeared simply as a great black shape, a mass of deeper darkness against the midnight blue of the sky.

Just outside its black iron gates, half-open as if in tentative invitation, a little girl was standing on the gravel of the driveway.

She was dressed in a simple knee-length smock dress and didn't look up at me as I walked towards her. She was concentrating on her game, her mouth opening and closing in recitation of something. It was a skipping song, as best I remembered it, but she was using it as accompaniment for the rapid bouncing of a small rubber ball between the gravel and her outstretched palm.

"Dip dip dip,
My blue ship.
Sailing on the water
Like a cup and saucer.
O, U, T spells—"

Oh, that's right. Not a skipping song at all. A rhyme of selection or exclusion, a variant of eeny meeny miney mo. The little girl, long and ringleted hair pulled back from her forehead by a wide black ribbon, seemed to remember that at the same moment I did and, just as she mouthed the word *out*, her hand snapped shut around the ball, her eyes flicked up to meet mine, and she thrust her other hand out to point its index finger dramatically at me. Her eyes were jet black and her now silent mouth was pulled in a tight unsmiling line.

"I'm out?" I asked her.

She didn't say anything, and nor did her fixed expression waver. I let the silence build for a few moments as we stared at each other, though I blinked deliberately several times to let her know that if it was a contest it was one she was welcome to win.

"Your concentration's slipping," I said eventually. "Where did the ball go?"

Her little brow furrowed briefly and she looked down at her empty hand. She pulled an annoyed face and then looked back at me.

"Are you going into the house?" she asked.

"In a manner of speaking," I said.

She gave a small tut of derision. "Is that supposed to be clever?" she said.

"No," I said. "Not really."

"Good," she said. "Because it's *not* clever. It's just stupid. Are you going into the house or not?"

"The house isn't really here," I told her.

"Then where are you standing?" she said. "And who are you talking to?"

Without waiting for an answer, she began to lean her head sideways and down. Keeping her unblinking eyes fixed on mine, she continued the movement, slowly and steadily, with no apparent difficulty or discomfort, until her pale little cheek rested flat against her right shoulder and her head was at an impossible right-angle to her neck. At the same time, in some strange counterpoint, her hair rose up into the air, stately and unhurried, until the ringlets were upright and taut, quivering against the darkness like mesmerised snakes dancing to an unheard piper.

I grinned at her. She was good at this.

We exchanged a few more words before I walked through the gates without her, following the wide and unbending path to the house itself. The imposingly large front door was as unlit as the rest of the exterior and was firmly closed. But I knew that others had come to this house before me, and that the door, despite its size and its weight and its numerous locks, had opened as easily for them as it would for me.

The rest of the vast reception room was pretty impressive, but the portrait over the fireplace was magnificent.

The picture itself was at least eight feet tall, allowing for some grass below and some sky above its life-size and black-suited central figure, who stared out into the room with the confident Victorian swagger of those born to wealth and empire. A foxhound cowered low at its master's feet and, in the far background, which appeared to be the grounds of the house, a group of disturbingly young children were playing Nymphs and Shepherds.

The room, like the long hall along which I'd walked to come to it, was illuminated by many candles, though I'd yet to see anyone who might have lit them. Through a half-open door at the far end of the room, though, I could see a shadow flicking back and forth, back and forth, as if somebody was about their business in a repeated pattern of movements.

As I came into the ante-room, the young woman who was pacing up and down looked up briefly from the clipboard she was holding. She appeared to be barely twenty, dressed in what I guessed to be the kind of nurse's uniform women might have worn when they were dressing wounds received in the Crimea, and the stern prettiness of her face and the darkness of her eyes said she could have been an older sister of the little girl I'd met outside the gates.

There was a single bed in the room and, though it was unoccupied, its sheets were rumpled, as if the woman's patient had just recently gone for a little walk. There were wires and cables and drip-feeds lying on the sheets and the other ends of some of them were connected to a black and white television monitor that attempted to hide its anachronism by being cased within a brass and mahogany housing of a Victorian splendour and an H. G. Wells inventiveness.

The young woman, having registered my presence with

neither surprise nor welcome, was back to her job of glancing at the monitor and then marking something on her clipboard.

The image on the monitor – grainy and distorted, washed-out like a barely-surviving kinescope of some long ago transmission – was a fixed-angle image of moonlight-bathed waves, deep-water waves, no shore in sight, as if a single camera were perched atop an impossible tower standing alone in some vast and distant ocean.

I looked at the image for a moment or two while she continued to pace and to make checkmarks on her clipboard.

"So what does that do?" I asked eventually, nodding at the monitor.

She stopped pacing and turned to look at me again. Her expression, while not unfriendly, was conflicted, as if she were both grateful for the break in routine and mildly unsettled by it.

"It used to show his dreams," she said, and turned her head briefly to look again at the endless and unbreaking waves. "But it's empty now."

She looked back at me and tilted her head a little, like she was deciding if I was safe enough to share a confidence with. "It's frightening, isn't it?" she said.

"Frightening?" I said. "I don't know. Perhaps it just means he's at peace."

"No, no," she said, her voice rising in a kind of nervous excitement. "You've misunderstood. That isn't what I meant." And then she caught herself and her voice went flat as if she feared lending emotion to what she said next. "I mean we might be having his dreams *for* him."

She looked at me half-expectantly, her eyes wide, like she was hoping I might tell her that she was wrong, but before I could answer a bell began to ring from a room somewhere deeper in the house.

"Teatime," she said. "You'd best hurry."

The children sat at trestle tables and ate without enthusiasm and there were far too many of them.

Their clothes were a snapshot history lesson; tracksuits and trainers, pullovers and short pants, britches and work-shirts, smocks and knickerbockers. The ones who'd been here longest were an unsettling monochrome against the colours of the more recent arrivals, and it wasn't only their outfits that were fading to grey.

Despite the dutiful shovelling of gruel into their mouths, I knew that they weren't hungry – there was only one inhabitant of this house who was hungry – and I wondered briefly why they even needed to pretend to eat, but figured that habit and routine were part of what helped him chain them here. Not a one of them spoke. Not a one of them smiled. I decided against joining them and headed back down the corridor to which the nurse had pointed me.

I saw something unspeakable in one of the rooms I passed and felt no need to look in any of the others.

The reception room was still empty when I got there. Patience is encouraged in these situations but, you know, fuck it. I decided to break something. There was an exquisite smoked glass figurine resting on top of the piano. I didn't even pick it up, just swept it away with the back of my hand and listened to it shatter against the parquet floor.

I hadn't intended to look, but a rapid skittering caught my eye and I bent down, barely in time to see a tiny something, wretched and limbless, slithering wetly beneath the sofa. I was still crouched down when there was a noise from somewhere behind me, unusually loud for what it most sounded like; the sticky gossamer ripping of a blunder through an unseen spider's web.

I stood up quickly, turning around to look. There was still nobody in the room but, though the large picture over the fireplace was intact and undamaged, its central figure was missing.

"You're a little older than my usual guests," the master of the house said from immediately behind me.

I span back around, very successfully startled. There was nothing overtly threatening about his posture, but he was standing uncomfortably close to me and I wasn't at all fond of his smile.

"A little older," he repeated. "But I'm sure we can find you a room."

"I won't be staying," I said. My voice was steady enough, but I was pissed off at how much he'd thrown me and pissed off more at how much he'd enjoyed it.

"You're very much mistaken," he said. "My house is easy to enter but not so easy to leave."

I understood his confidence. He had a hundred years of experience to justify his thinking that I was one of his usual guests. He could see me, so I had to be dead. Just as most ghosts are invisible to people, most people are invisible to ghosts. But, just as there are a few anomalous ghosts who *can* be seen by people, so are there a few anomalous people who can be seen by ghosts. And he'd just met one.

"Do you know what this is?" I said, and brought the tesseract out of my pocket. They've been standard issue at the department for the last couple of years. Fuck knows where they get them made, but I have a feeling it isn't Hong Kong.

I let it rest in my palm and he looked at it. He tried to keep his expression neutral but I could tell his curiosity was piqued. It always is.

"What does it do?" he said.

"Well, it doesn't really *do* anything," I said. "It just is."

"And what do you want me to do about it?"

"Nothing," I said. "Just look at it for a while."

I gave it a little tap and it slid impossibly through itself.

The room shivered in response, but I don't think he noticed. His eyes were fixed on the little cube and its effortless dance through dimensions.

"There's something wrong with it," he said, but the tone of his voice was fascinated rather than dismissive. "I can't see it properly."

"It's difficult," I agreed. "Because part of it shouldn't be here. Doesn't mean it's not real. Just means it doesn't belong in the space it's in."

The metaphor hit home, as it always did. I don't know why the tesseract works so well on them – I mean, it's utterly harmless, more wakeup call than weapon – but it's definitely made the job easier. He looked up at me. His face was already a little less defined than it had been, but I could still read the fear in it. He was smart, though. Went straight for the important questions and fuck the nuts and bolts.

"Will I be judged?" he said.

"Nobody's judged."

"Will I be hurt?"

"Nobody's hurt."

"Will I be—" He stopped himself then, as an unwilled understanding came to him, and he repeated what he'd just said. Same words. Different stress. "Will I *be*?"

I looked at him.

"Nobody'll be." I said.

It was too late for him to fight, but the animal rage for identity made him try, his imagined flesh struggling against its dissolution and his softening arms reaching out for me uselessly.

"You know who hangs around?" I said. "People with too little will of their own, and people with too much. Let it go. We're just lights in the sky, and their shadows."

"I'll miss it!" he shouted, his disappearing mouth twisting into a final snarl of appetite and terror.

"You won't miss a thing," I said, and watched him vanish.

I'd been in there longer than I thought and, as I walked back through the park towards the Hunter's Lane gate, true night was falling. But it was far from dark. There'd been so many souls in the house, young and old, predator and prey, that the cascade of their dissolution was spectacular and sustained.

For upwards of two hours, the sky was brilliant with lights.

Like an anniversary. Like a half remembered dream. Like a mystery.

CLIVE BARKER

...was born in Liverpool in 1952. He attended Quarry Bank Grammar School where he was a pupil a few years ahead of Doug Bradley and a few behind John Lennon. He wrote his first novel, The Candle in the Cloud *(1971) before attending Liverpool University and cast it aside whilst he studied English and Philosophy there. Although he never returned to this novel he did return to his frustrating time at university in the vengeful fable 'Dread (1984)'. Clive made his directorial debut in 1973 with an adaptation of 'Salomé' that was shot in the cellar of a florists shop on Smithdown Road. With several friends, including Doug Bradley and Peter Atkins, who he was introduced to in Allerton library, they formed the Theatre of the Imagination which would eventually evolve into the Dog Company. Although he was originally reluctant to leave Liverpool the company moved to London and he to the*

horror-tinged area of Crouch End where he would write a number of plays and, almost as a diversion, would produce the Books of Blood *(1984) one of the seminal short story collections of its generation. After writing* The Damnation Game *(1985) and* Weaveworld *(1987) and directing the phenomenally successful* Hellraiser *(1987) he moved again to Beverly Hills, California and from there has continued to script, produce and direct movies, write further bestselling novels for adults and children and produce a world of paintings which have been exhibited widely.*

THE FORBIDDEN

CLIVE BARKER

Like a flawless tragedy, the elegance of which structure is lost upon those suffering in it, the perfect geometry of the Spector Street Estate was only visible from the air. Walking in its drear canyons, passing through its grimy corridors from one grey concrete rectangle to the next, there was little to seduce the eye or stimulate the imagination. What few saplings had been planted in the quadrangles had long since been mutilated or uprooted; the grass, though tall, resolutely refused a healthy green.

No doubt the estate and its two companion developments had once been an architect's dream. No doubt the city-planners had wept with pleasure at a design which housed three and thirty-six persons per hectare, and still boasted space for a children's playground. Doubtless fortunes and reputations had been built upon Spector Street, and at its opening fine words had been spoken of its being a yardstick by which all future developments would be measured. But the planners—tears wept, words spoken—had left the estate to its own devices; the architects occupied restored Georgian houses at the other end of the city, and probably never set foot here.

They would not have been shamed by the deterioration of the estate even if they had. Their brain–child (they would doubtless argue) was as brilliant as ever: its geometries as precise, its ratios as calculated; it was people who had spoiled Spector Street. Nor would they have been wrong in such an accusation. Helen had seldom seen an inner city environment so comprehensively vandalized. Lamps had been shattered and back–yard fences overthrown; cars whose wheels and engines had been removed and chassis then burned, blocked garage facilities. In one courtyard three or four ground–floor maisonettes had been entirely gutted by fire, their windows and doors boarded up with planks and corrugated iron.

More startling still was the graffiti. That was what she had come here to see, encouraged by Archie's talk of the place, and she was not disappointed. It was difficult to believe, staring at the multiple layers of designs, names, obscenities, and dogmas that were scrawled and sprayed on every available brick, that Spector Street was barely three and a half years old. The walls, so recently virgin, were now so profoundly defaced that the Council Cleaning Department could never hope to return them to their former condition. A layer of whitewash to cancel this visual cacophony would only offer the scribes a fresh and yet more tempting surface on which to make their mark.

Helen was in seventh heaven. Every corner she turned offered some fresh material for her thesis: *'Graffiti: the semiotics of urban despair'. It* was a subject which married her two favourite disciplines—sociology and aesthetics—and as she wandered around the estate she began to wonder if there wasn't a book, in addition to her thesis, in the subject. She walked from courtyard to courtyard, copying down a large number of the more interesting scrawlings, and noting their location. Then she went back to the car to collect her camera and tripod and returned to the most fertile of the areas, to make a thorough visual record of the walls.

It was a chilly business. She was not an expert photographer, and the late October sky was in full flight, shifting the light on the bricks from one moment to the next. As she adjusted and re–adjusted the exposure to compensate for the light changes, her fingers steadily became clumsier, her temper correspondingly thinner. But she struggled on, the idle curiosity of passers–by notwithstanding. There were so many designs to document. She reminded herself that her present discomfort would be amply repaid when she showed the slides to Trevor, whose doubt of the project's validity had been perfectly apparent from the beginning.

"The writing on the wall?" he'd said, half smiling in that irritating fashion of his, "It's been done a hundred times."

This was true, of course; and yet not. There certainly were learned works on graffiti, chock full of sociological jargon: *cultural disenfranchisement; urban alienation*. But she flattered herself that *she* might find something amongst this litter of scrawlings that previous analysts had not: some unifying convention perhaps, that she could use as the lynch– pin of her thesis. Only a vigorous cataloguing and cross–referencing of the phrases and images before her would reveal such a correspondence; hence the importance of this photographic study. So many hands had worked here; so many minds left their mark, however casually: if she could find some pattern, some predominant motive, or *motif*, the thesis would be guaranteed some serious attention, and so, in turn, would she.

"What are you doing?" a voice from behind her asked.

She turned from her calculations to see a young woman with a pushchair on the pavement behind her. She looked weary, Helen thought, and pinched by the cold. The child in the pushchair was mewling, his grimy fingers clutching an orange lollipop and the wrapping from a chocolate bar. The bulk of the chocolate, and the remains of previous jujubes, was displayed down the front of his coat.

Helen offered a thin smile to the woman; she looked in need of it. "I'm photographing the walls," she said in answer to the initial enquiry, though surely this was perfectly apparent.

The woman—she could barely be twenty—Helen judged, said: "You mean the filth?"

"The writing and the pictures," Helen said. Then: "Yes. The filth."

"You from the Council?"

"No, the University."

"It's bloody disgusting," the woman said. "The way they do that. It's not just kids, either."

"No?"

"Grown men. Grown men, too. They don't give a damn. Do it in broad daylight. You see "...embroad daylight." She glanced down at the child, who was sharpening his lollipop on the ground. "Kerry!" she snapped, but the boy took no notice. "Are they going to wipe it off?" she asked Helen.

"I don't know," Helen said, and reiterated: "I'm from the University."

"Oh," the woman replied, as if this was new information, "so you're nothing to do with the Council?"

"No."

"Some of it's obscene, isn't it?; really dirty. Makes me embarrassed to see some of the things they draw."

Helen nodded, casting an eye at the boy in the pushchair. Kerry had decided to put his sweet in his ear for safe-keeping.

"Don't do that!" his mother told him, and leaned over to slap the child's hand. The blow, which was negligible, began the child bawling. Helen took the opportunity to return to her camera. But the woman still desired to talk. "It's not just on the outside, neither," she commented.

"I beg your pardon?" Helen said.

"They break into the flats when they go empty. The

Council tried to board them up, but it does no good. They break in anyway. Use them as toilets, and write more filth on the walls. They light fires too. Then nobody can move back in."

The description piqued Helen's curiosity. Would the graffiti on the *inside* walls be substantially different from the public displays? It was certainly worth an investigation.

"Are there any places you know of around here like that?"

"Empty flats, you mean?"

"With graffiti."

"Just by us, there's one or two," the woman volunteered. "I'm in Butts' Court."

"Maybe you could show me?" Helen asked. The woman shrugged.

"By the way, my name's Helen Buchanan."

"Anne–Marie," the mother replied.

"I'd be very grateful if you could point me to one of those empty flats."

Anne–Marie was baffled by Helen's enthusiasm, and made no attempt to disguise it, but she shrugged again and said: "There's nothing much to see. Only more of the same stuff."

Helen gathered up her equipment and they walked side by side through the intersecting corridors between one square and the next. Though the estate was low–rise, each court only five storeys high, the effect of each quadrangle was horribly claustrophobic. The walkways and staircases were a thief 's dream, rife with blind corners and ill–lit tunnels. The rubbish–dumping facilities—chutes from the upper floors down which bags of refuse could be pitched—had long since been sealed up, thanks to their efficiency as fire–traps. Now plastic bags of refuse were piled high in the corridors, many torn open by roaming dogs, their contents strewn across the ground. The smell, even in the cold weather, was unpleasant. In high summer it must have been overpowering.

"I'm over the other side," Anne–Marie said, pointing across the quadrangle. "The one with the yellow door." She then pointed along the opposite side of the court. "Five or six maisonettes from the far end," she said. "There's two of them been emptied out. Few weeks now. One of the family's moved into Ruskin Court; the other did a bunk in the middle of the night."

With that, she turned her back on Helen and wheeled Kerry, who had taken to trailing spittle from the side of his pushchair, around the side of the square.

"Thank you," Helen called after her. Anne–Marie glanced over her shoulder briefly, but did not reply. Appetite whetted, Helen made her way along the row of ground floor maisonettes, many of which, though inhabited, showed little sign of being so. Their curtains were closely drawn; there were no milk–bottles on the doorsteps, nor children's toys left where they had been played with. Nothing, in fact, of *life* here. There was more graffiti however, sprayed, shockingly, on the doors of occupied houses. She granted the scrawlings only a casual perusal, in part because she feared one of the doors opening as she examined a choice obscenity sprayed upon it, but more because she was eager to see what revelations the empty flats ahead might offer.

The malign scent of urine, both fresh and stale, welcomed her at the threshold of number 14, and beneath that the smell of burnt paint and plastic. She hesitated for fully ten seconds, wondering if stepping into the maisonette was a wise move. The territory of the estate behind her was indisputably foreign, sealed off in its own misery, but the rooms in front of her were more intimidating still: a dark maze which her eyes could barely penetrate. But when her courage faltered she thought of Trevor, and how badly she wanted to silence his condescension. So thinking, she advanced into the place, deliberately kicking a piece of charred timber aside as she did so, in the hope that she would alert any tenant into showing himself.

There was no sound of occupancy however. Gaining confidence, she began to explore the front room of the maisonette which had been—to judge by the remains of a disemboweled sofa in one corner and the sodden carpet underfoot—a living-room. The pale-green walls were, as Anne-Marie had promised, extensively defaced, both by minor scribblers—content to work in pen, or even more crudely in sofa charcoal—and by those with aspirations to public works, who had sprayed the walls in half a dozen colours.

Some of the comments were of interest, though many she had already seen on the walls outside. Familiar names and couplings repeated themselves. Though she had never set eyes on these individuals she knew how badly Fabian J. (A.OK!) wanted to deflower Michelle; and that Michelle, in her turn, had the hots for somebody called Mr Sheen. Here, as elsewhere, a man called White Rat boasted of his endowment, and the return of the Syllabub Brothers was promised in red paint. One or two of the pictures accompanying, or at least adjacent to, these phrases were of particular interest. An almost emblematic simplicity informed them. Beside the word *Christos* was a stick man with his hair radiating from his head like spines, and other heads impaled on each spine. Close by was an image of intercourse so brutally reduced that at first Helen took it to illustrate a knife plunging into a sightless eye. But fascinating as the images were, the room was too gloomy for her film and she had neglected to bring a flash. If she wanted a reliable record of these discoveries she would have to come again, and for now be content with a simple exploration of the premises.

The maisonette wasn't that large, but the windows had been boarded up throughout, and as she moved further from the front door the dubious light petered out altogether. The smell of urine, which had been strong at the door, intensified too, until by the time she reached the back of the living–room and stepped along a short corridor into another room beyond, it was cloying as incense. This room, being furthest from the front door, was also the darkest, and she had to wait a few moments in the cluttered glom to allow her eyes to become useful. This, she guessed, had been the 'oom. What little furniture the residents had left behind them had been smashed to smithereens. Only the mattress had been left relatively untouched, dumped in the corner of the room amongst a wretched litter of blankets, newspapers, and pieces of crockery.

Outside, the sun found its way between the clouds, and two or three shafts of sunlight slipped between the boards nailed across the bedroom window and pierced the room like annunciations, scoring the opposite wall with bright lines. Here, the graffitists had been busy once more: the usual clamour of love–letters and threats. She scanned the wall quickly, and as she did so her eye was led by the beams of light across the room to the wall which contained the door she had stepped through.

Here, the artists had also been at work, but had produced an image the like of which she had not seen anywhere else. Using the door, which was centrally placed in the wall, as a mouth, the artists had sprayed a single, vast head on to the stripped plaster. The painting was more adroit than most she had seen, rife with detail that lent the image an unsettling veracity. The cheekbones jutting through skin the colour of buttermilk; the teeth—sharpened to irregular points—all converging on the door. The sitter's eyes were, owing to the room's low ceiling, set mere inches above the upper lip, but this physical adjustment only lent force to the image, giving the impression that he had thrown his head back. Knotted strands of his hair snaked from his scalp across the ceiling.

Was it a portrait? There was something naggingly *specific* in the details of the brows and the lines around the wide mouth; in the careful picturing of those vicious teeth. A nightmare certainly: a facsimile, perhaps, of something from a heroin fugue. Whatever its origins, it was potent. Even the illusion of door–as–mouth worked. The short passageway between living–room and bedroom offered a passable throat, with a tattered lamp in lieu of tonsils. Beyond the gullet, the day burned white in the nightmare's belly. The whole effect brought to mind a ghost train painting. The same heroic deformity, the same unashamed intention to scare. And it worked; she stood in the bedroom almost stupified by the picture, its red–rimmed eyes fixing her mercilessly. Tomorrow, she determined; she would come here again, this time with high–speed film and a flash to illuminate the masterwork.

As she prepared to leave the sun went in, and the bands of light faded. She glanced over her shoulder at the boarded windows, and saw for the first time that one four–word slogan had been sprayed on the wall beneath them.

'*Sweets to the sweet*' it read. She was familiar with the quote, but not with its source. Was it a profession of love? If so, it was an odd location for such an avowal. Despite the mattress in the corner, and the relative privacy of this room, she could not imagine the intended reader of such words ever stepping in here to receive her bouquet. No adolescent lovers, however heated, would lie down here to play at mothers and fathers; not under the gaze of the terror on the wall. She crossed to examine the writing. The paint looked to be the same shade of pink as had been used to colour the gums of the screaming man; perhaps the same hand?

Behind her, a noise. She turned so quickly she almost tripped over the blanket-strewn mattress.

"Who–?"

At the other end of the gullet, in the living–room, was a

scab–kneed boy of six or seven. He stared at Helen, eyes glittering in the half–light, as if waiting for a cue.

"Yes?" she said.

"Anne–Marie says do you want a cup of tea?" he declared without pause or intonation.

Her conversation with the woman seemed hours past. She was grateful for the invitation however. The damp in the maisonette had chilled her.

"Yes…" she said to the boy. "Yes please."

The child didn't move, but simply stared on at her.

"Are you going to lead the way?" she asked him.

"If you want," he replied, unable to raise a trace of enthusiasm. "I'd like that."

"You taking photographs?" he asked.

"Yes. Yes, I am. But not in here."

"Why not?"

"It's too dark," she told him.

"Don't it work in the dark?" he wanted to know.

"No."

The boy nodded at this, as if the information somehow fitted well into his scheme of things, and about turned without another word, clearly expecting Helen to follow.

If she had been taciturn in the street, Anne–Marie was anything but in the privacy of her own kitchen. Gone was the guarded curiosity, to be replaced by a stream of lively chatter and a constant scurrying between half a dozen minor domestic tasks, like a juggler keeping several plates spinning simultaneously. Helen watched this balancing act with some admiration, her own domestic skills were negligible. At last; the meandering conversation turned back to the subject that had brought Helen here.

"Them photographs," Anne–Marie said, "why'd you want to take them?"

"I'm writing about graffiti. The photos will illustrate my thesis."

"It's not very pretty."

"No, you're right, it isn't. But I find it interesting."

Anne–Marie shook her head. "I hate the whole estate," she said. "It's not safe here. People getting robbed on their own doorsteps. Kids setting fire to the rubbish day in, day out. Last summer we had the fire brigade here two, three times a day, 'til they sealed them chutes off. Now people just dump the bags in the passageways, and that attracts rats."

"Do you live here alone?"

"Yes," she said, "since Davey walked out."

"That your husband?"

"He was Kerry's father, but we weren't never married. We lived together two years, you know. We had some good times. Then he just upped and went off one day when I was at me Mam's with Kerry." She peered into her tea–cup. "I'm better off without him," she said. "But you get scared sometimes. Want some more tea?"

"I don't think I've got time."

"Just a cup," Anne–Marie said, already up and unplugging the electric kettle to take it across for a refill. As she was about to turn on the tap she saw something on the draining board, and drove her thumb down, grinding it out. "Got you, you bugger," she said, then turned to Helen: "We got these bloody ants."

"Ants?"

"Whole estate's infected. From Egypt, they are: pharoah ants, they're called. Little brown sods. They breed in the central heating ducts, you see; that way they get into all the flats. Place is plagued with them."

This unlikely exoticism (ants from Egypt?) struck Helen as comical, but she said nothing. Anne–Marie was staring out of the kitchen window and into the back–yard.

"You should tell them—" she said, though Helen wasn't

certain whom she was being instructed to tell, "tell them that ordinary people can't even walk the streets any longer—"

"Is it really so bad?" Helen said, frankly tiring of this catalogue of misfortunes.

Anne–Marie turned from the sink and looked at her hard.

"We've had murders here," she said.

"Really?"

"We had one in the summer. An old man he was, from Ruskin. That's just next door. I didn't *know* him, but he was a friend *of* the sister of the woman next door. I forget his name."

"And he was murdered?"

"Cut to ribbons in his own front room. They didn't find him for almost a week."

"What about his neighbours? didn't they notice his absence?"

Anne–Marie shrugged, as if the most important pieces of information—the murder and the man's isolation—had been exchanged, and any further enquiries into the problem were irrelevant. But Helen pressed the point.

"Seems strange to me," she said.

Anne–Marie plugged in the filled kettle. "Well, it happened," she replied, unmoved.

"I'm not saying it didn't, I just—"

"His eyes had been taken out," she said, before Helen could voice any further doubts.

Helen winced. "No," she said, under her breath.

"That's the truth," Anne–Marie said. "And that wasn't all'd been done to him." She paused, for effect, then went on: "You wonder what kind of person's capable of doing things like that, don't you? You wonder." Helen nodded. She was thinking precisely the same thing.

"Did they ever find the man responsible?"

Anne–Marie snorted her disparagement. "Police don't give a damn what happens here. They keep off the estate as much as possible. When they do patrol all they do is pick up kids for getting drunk and that. They're afraid, you see. That's why they keep clear."

"Of this killer?"

"Maybe," Anne–Marie replied. "Then: He had a hook."

"A hook?"

"The man what done it. He had a hook, like Jack the Ripper."

Helen was no expert on murder, but she felt certain that the Ripper hadn't boasted a hook. It seemed churlish to question the truth of Anne–Marie's story however; though she silently wondered how much of this—the eyes taken out, the body rotting in the flat, the hook—was elaboration. The most scrupulous of reporters was surely tempted to embellish a story once in a while.

Anne–Marie had poured herself another cup of tea, and was about to do the same for her guest.

"No thank you," Helen said, "I really should go."

"You married?" Anne–Marie asked, out of the blue.

"Yes. To a lecturer from the University."

"What's his name?"

"Trevor."

Anne–Marie put two heaped spoonfuls of sugar into her cup of tea. "Will you be coming back?" she asked.

"Yes, I hope to. Later in the week. I want to take some photographs of the pictures in the maisonette across the court."

"Well, call in."

"I shall. And thank you for your help."

"That's all right," Anne–Marie replied. "You've got to tell somebody, haven't you?"

"The man apparently had a hook instead of a hand."

Trevor looked up from his plate of tagliatelle con prosciutto.

"Beg your pardon?"

Helen had been at pains to keep her recounting of this story as un-coloured by her own response as she could. She was interested to know what Trevor would make of it, and she knew that if she once signalled her own stance he would instinctively take an opposing view out of plain bloody–mindedness.

"He had a hook," she repeated, without inflexion.

Trevor put down his fork, and plucked at his nose, sniffing. "I didn't read anything about this," he said.

"You don't look at the local press," Helen returned. "Neither of us do. Maybe it never made any of the nationals."

"Geriatric Murdered By Hook–Handed Maniac?" Trevor said, savouring the hyperbole. "I would have thought it very newsworthy. When was all of this supposed to have happened?"

"Sometime last summer. Maybe we were in Ireland."

"Maybe," said Trevor, taking up his fork again. Bending to his food, the polished lens of his spectacles reflected only the plate of pasta and chopped ham in front of him, not his eyes.

"Why do you say *maybe?*" Helen prodded.

"It doesn't sound quite right," he said. "In fact it sounds bloody preposterous."

"You don't believe it?" Helen said.

Trevor looked up from his food, tongue rescuing a speck of *tagliatelle* from the corner of his mouth. His face had relaxed into that non–committal expression of his—the same face he wore, no doubt, when listening to his students. "Do *you* believe it?" he asked Helen. It was a favourite time–gaining device of his, another seminar trick, to question the questioner.

"I'm not certain," Helen replied, too concerned to find some solid ground in this sea of doubts to waste energy scoring points.

"All right, forget the tale—" Trevor said, deserting his

food for another glass of red wine. "What about the teller? Did you trust her?"

Helen pictured Anne–Marie's earnest expression as she told the story of the old man's murder. "Yes," she said. "Yes; I think I would have known if she'd been lying to me."

"So why's it so important, anyhow? I mean, whether she's lying or not, what the fuck does it matter?"

It was a reasonable question, if irritatingly put. Why *did* it matter? Was it that she wanted to have her worst feelings about Spector Street proved false? That such an estate be filthy, be hopeless, be a dump where the undesirable and the disadvantaged were tucked out of public view— all that was a liberal commonplace, and she accepted it as an unpalatable social reality. But the story of the old man's murder and mutilation was something other. An image of violent death that, once with her, refused to part from her company.

She realized, to her chagrin, that this confusion was plain on her face, and that Trevor, watching her across the table, was not a little entertained by it.

"If it bothers you so much," he said, "why don't you go back there and ask around, instead of playing believe–in–it–or–not over dinner?"

She couldn't help but rise to his remark. "I thought you liked guessing games," she said.

He threw her a sullen look.

"Wrong again."

The suggestion that she investigate was not a bad one, though doubtless he had ulterior motives for offering it. She viewed Trevor less charitably day by day. What she had once thought in him a fierce commitment to debate she now recognized as mere power–play. He argued, not for the thrill of dialectic, but because he was pathologically competitive. She had seen him, time and again, take up attitudes she knew he did not espouse, simply to spill blood. Nor, more's the pity, was he alone in this sport. Academe was one of the last strongholds of the professional time–waster. On occasion their circle seemed entirely dominated by educated fools, lost in a wasteland of stale rhetoric and hollow commitment.

From one wasteland to another. She returned to Spector Street the following day, armed with a flashgun in addition to her tripod and high– sensitive film. The wind was up today, and it was Arctic, more furious still for being trapped in the maze of passageways and courts. She made her way to number 14, and spent the next hour in its befouled confines, meticulously photographing both the bedroom and living– room walls. She had half expected the impact of the head in the bedroom to be dulled by re–acquaintance; it was not. Though she struggled to capture its scale and detail as best she could, she knew the photographs would be at best a dim echo of its perpetual howl.

Much of its power lay in its context, of course. That such an image might be stumbled upon in surroundings so drab, so conspicuously lacking in mystery, was akin to finding an icon on a rubbish–heap: a gleaming symbol of transcendence from a world of toil and decay into some darker but more tremendous realm. She was painfully aware that the intensity of her response probably defied her articulation. Her vocabulary was analytic, replete with buzz–words and academic terminology, but woefully impoverished when it came to evocation. The photographs, pale as they would be, would, she hoped, at least hint at the potency of this picture, even if they couldn't conjure the way it froze the bowels.

When she emerged from the maisonette the wind was as uncharitable as ever, but the boy waiting outside—the same child as had attended upon her yesterday—was dressed as if for spring weather. He grimaced in his effort to keep the shudders at bay.

"Hello," Helen said.

"I waited," the child announced.

"Waited?"

"Anne–Marie said you'd come back."

"I wasn't planning to come until later in the week," Helen said. "You might have waited a long time."

The boy's grimace relaxed a notch. "It's all right," he said, "I've got nothing to do."

"What about school?"

"Don't like it," the boy replied, as if unobliged to be educated if it wasn't to his taste.

"I see," said Helen, and began to walk down the side of the quadrangle. The boy followed. On the patch of grass at the centre of the quadrangle several chairs and two or three dead saplings had been piled.

"What's this?" she said, half to herself.

"Bonfire Night," the boy informed her. "Next week."

"Of course."

"You going to see Anne–Marie?" he asked.

"Yes."

"She's not in."

"Oh. Are you sure?"

"Yeah."

"Well, perhaps *you* can help me..." She stopped and turned to face the child; smooth sacs of fatigue hung beneath his eyes. "I heard about an old man who was murdered near here," she said to him. "In the summer. Do you know anything about that?"

"No."

"Nothing at all? You don't remember anybody getting killed?"

"No," the boy said again, with impressive finality. "I don't remember."

"Well; thank you anyway."

This time, when she retraced her steps back to the car, the boy didn't follow. But as she turned the corner out of the quadrangle she glanced back to see him standing on the spot where she'd left him, staring after her as if she were a madwoman.

By the time she had reached the car and packed the photographic equipment into the boot there were specks of rain in the wind, and she was sorely tempted to forget she'd ever heard Anne–Marie's story and make her way home, where the coffee would be warm even if the welcome wasn't. But she needed an answer to the question Trevor had put the previous night. Do *you* believe it?, he'd asked when she'd told him the story. She hadn't known how to answer then, and she still didn't. Perhaps (why did she sense this?) the terminology of verifiable truth was redundant here; perhaps the final answer to his question was not an answer at all, only another question. If so; so. She had to find out.

Ruskin Court was as forlorn as its fellows, if not more so. It didn't even boast a bonfire. On the third floor balcony a woman was taking washing in before the rain broke; on the grass in the centre of the quadrangle two dogs were absent–mindedly rutting, the fuckee staring up at the blank sky. As she walked along the empty pavement she set her face determinedly; a purposeful look, Bernadette had once said, deterred attack. When she caught sight of the two women talking at the far end of the court she crossed over to them hurriedly, grateful for their presence.

"Excuse me?"

The women, both in middle–age, ceased their animated exchange and looked her over.

"I wonder if you can help me?"

She could feel their appraisal, and their distrust; they went undisguised. One of the pair, her face florid, said plainly: "What do you want?"

Helen suddenly felt bereft of the least power to charm. What was she to, say to these two that wouldn't make her motives appear ghoulish? "I was told" she began, and then stumbled, aware that she would get no assistance from either woman. "…I was told there'd been a murder near here. Is that right?"

The florid woman raised eyebrows so plucked they were barely visible. "Murder?" she said.

"Are you from the press?" the other woman enquired. The years had soured her features beyond sweetening. Her small mouth was deeply lined; her hair, which had been dyed brunette, showed a half–inch of grey at the roots.

"No, I'm not from the press," Helen said, "I'm a friend of Anne–Marie's, in Butts' Court." This claim of *friend* stretched the truth, but it seemed to mellow the women somewhat.

"Visiting are you?" the florid woman asked.

"In a manner of speaking—"

"You missed the warm spell—"

"Anne–Marie was telling me about somebody who'd been murdered here, during the summer. I was curious about it."

"Is that right?"

"—do you know anything about it?"

"Lots of things go on around here," said. the second woman. "You don't know the half of it."

"So it's true," Helen said.

"They had to close the toilets," the first woman put in.

"That's right. They did," the other said.

"The toilets?" Helen said. What had this to do with the old man's death?

"It was terrible," the first said. "Was it your Frank, Josie, who told you about it?"

"No, not Frank," Josie replied. "Frank was still at sea. It was Mrs Tyzack."

The witness established, Josie relinquished the story to her companion, and turned her gaze back upon Helen. The suspicion had not yet died from her eyes.

"This was only the month before last," Josie said." Just about the end of August. It was August, wasn't it?" She looked to the other woman for verification. "You've got the head for dates, Maureen."

Maureen looked uncomfortable." I forget," she said, clearly unwilling to offer testimony.

"I'd like to know," Helen said. Josie, despite her companion's reluctance, was eager to oblige.

"There's some lavatories," she said, "outside the shops—you know, public lavatories. I'm not quite sure how it all happened exactly, but there used to be a boy…well, he wasn't a boy really, I mean he was a man of twenty or more, but he was…" she fished for the words, "…mentally subnormal, I suppose you'd say. His mother used to have to take him around like he was a four year old. Anyhow, she let him go into the lavatories while she went to that little supermarket, what's it called?" she turned to Maureen for a prompt, but the other woman just looked back, her disapproval plain. Josie was ungovernable, however. "Broad daylight, this was," she said to Helen. "Middle of the day. Anyhow, the boy went to the toilet, and the mother was in the shop. And after a while, you know how you do, she's busy shopping, she forgets about him, and then she thinks he's been gone a long time…"

At this juncture Maureen couldn't prevent herself from butting in: the accuracy of the story apparently took precedence over her wariness.

"—she got into an argument," she corrected Josie, "with the manager. About some bad bacon she'd had from him. That was why she was such a time…"

"I see," said Helen.

"—anyway," said Josie, picking up the tale, "she finished her shopping and when she came out he still wasn't there—"

"So she asked someone from the supermarket—" Maureen began, but Josie wasn't about to have her narrative snatched back at this vital juncture.

"She asked one of the men from the supermarket—" she

repeated over Maureen's interjection, "to go down into the lavatory and find him."

"It was terrible," said Maureen, clearly picturing the atrocity in her mind's eye.

"He was lying on the floor, in a pool of blood."

"Murdered?"

Josie shook her head. "He'd have been better off dead. He'd been attacked with a razor—" she let this piece of information sink in before delivering the *coup de grace*,"—and they'd cut off his private parts. Just cut them off and flushed them down a toilet. No reason on earth to do it."

"Oh my God."

"Better off dead," Josie repeated. "I mean, they can't mend something like that, can they?"

The appalling tale was rendered worse still by the *sangfroid* of the teller, and by the casual repetition of 'Better off dead'.

"The boy," Helen said, "Was he able to describe his attackers?"

"No," said Josie, "he's practically an imbecile. He can't string more

than two words together."

"And nobody saw anyone go into the lavatory? Or leaving it?"

"People come and go all the time—" Maureen said. This, though it sounded like an adequate explanation, had not been Helen's experience. There was not a great bustle in the quadrangle and passageways; far from it. Perhaps the shopping mall was busier, she reasoned, and might offer adequate cover for such a crime.

"So, they haven't found the culprit," she said.

"No," Josie replied, her eyes losing their fervor. The crime and its immediate consequences were the nub of this story; she had little or no interest in either the culprit or his capture.

"We're not safe in our own beds," Maureen observed. "You ask anyone."

"Anne–Marie said the same," Helen replied. "That's how she came to tell me about the old man. Said he was murdered during the summer, here in Ruskin Court."

"I do remember something," Josie said. "There *was* some talk I heard. An old man, and his dog. He was battered to death, and the dog ended up... I don't know. It certainly wasn't here. It must have been one of the other estates."

"Are you sure?"

The woman looked offended by this slur on her memory. "Oh yes," she said, "I mean if it had been here, we'd have known the story, wouldn't we?"

Helen thanked the pair for their help and decided to take a stroll around the quadrangle anyway, just to see how many more maisonettes were out of operation here. As in Butts' Court, many of the curtains were drawn and all the doors locked. But then if Spector Street *was* under siege from a maniac capable of the murder and mutilation such as she'd heard described, she was not surprised that the residents took to their homes and stayed there. There was nothing much to see around the court. All the unoccupied maisonettes and flats had been recently sealed, to judge by a litter of nails left on a doorstep by the council workmen. One sight *did* catch her attention however. Scrawled on the paving stones she was walking over—and all but erased by rain and the passage of feet—the same phrase she'd seen in the bedroom of number 14: *Sweets to the sweet*. The words were so benign; why did she seem to sense menace in them? Was it in their excess, perhaps, in the sheer overabundance of sugar upon sugar, honey upon honey?

She walked on, though the rain persisted, and her walkabout gradually led her away from the quadrangles and into a concrete no–man's–land through which she had not previously passed. This was—or had been—the site of the estate's amenities. Here was the children's playground, its metal–framed rides overturned, its sandpit fouled by dogs, its paddling pool empty. And here too were the shops. Several had been boarded up; those that hadn't were dingy and unattractive, their windows protected by heavy wire–mesh.

She walked along the row, and rounded a comer, and there in front of her was a squat brick building. The public lavatory, she guessed, though the signs designating it as such had gone. The iron gates were closed and padlocked. Standing in front of the charmless building, the wind gusting around her legs, she couldn't help but think of what had happened here. Of the man–child, bleeding on the floor, helpless to cry out. It made her queasy even to contemplate it. She turned her thoughts instead to the felon. What would he look like, she wondered, a man capable of such depravities? She tried to make an image of him, but no detail she could conjure carried sufficient force. But then monsters were seldom very terrible once hauled into the plain light of day. As long as this man was known only by his deeds he held untold power over the imagination; but the human truth beneath the terrors would, she knew, be bitterly disappointing. No monster he; just a whey–faced apology for a man more needful of pity than awe.

The next gust of wind brought the rain on more heavily. It was time, she decided, to be done with adventures for the day. Turning her back on the public lavatories she hurried back through the quadrangles to the refuge of the car, the icy rain needling her face to numbness.

The dinner guests looked gratifyingly appalled at the story, and Trevor, to judge by the expression on his face, was furious. It was done now, however; there was no taking it back. Nor could she deny her satisfaction she took in having silenced the inter–departmental babble about the table. It was Bernadette, Trevor's assistant in the History Department, who broke the agonizing hush.

"When was this?"

"During the summer," Helen told her.

"I don't recall reading about it," said Archie, much the better for two hours of drinking; it mellowed a tongue which was otherwise fulsome in its self–corruscation.

"Perhaps the police are suppressing it," Daniel commented.

"Conspiracy?" said Trevor, plainly cynical.

"It's happening all the time," Daniel shot back.

"Why should they suppress something like this?" Helen said. "It doesn't make sense."

"Since when has police procedure made sense?" Daniel replied. Bernadette cut in before Helen could answer. "We don't even bother to read about these things any longer," she said.

"Speak for yourself," somebody piped up, but she ignored them and went on:

"We're punch–drunk with violence. We don't see it any longer, even when It's in front of our noses."

"On the screen every night," Archie put in, "Death and disaster in full colour."

"There's nothing very modern about that," Trevor said. "An Elizabethan would have seen death all the time. Public executions were a very popular form of entertainment."

The table broke up into a cacophony of opinions. After two hours of polite gossip the dinner–party had suddenly caught fire. Listening to the debate rage Helen was sorry she hadn't had time to have the photographs processed and printed; the graffiti would have added further fuel to this exhilarating row. It was Purcell, as usual, who was the last to weigh in with his point of view; and—again, as usual—it was devastating.

"Of course, Helen, my sweet—" he began, that affected weariness in his voice edged with the anticipation of controversy "—your witnesses could all be lying, couldn't they?"

The talking around the table dwindled, and all heads turned in Purcell's direction. Perversely, he ignored the attention he'd garnered, and turned to whisper in the ear of the boy he'd brought—a new passion who would, on past form, be discarded in a matter of weeks for another pretty urchin.

"Lying?" Helen said. She could feel herself bristling at the observation already, and Purcell had only spoken a dozen words.

"Why not?" the other replied, lifting his glass of wine to his lips. "Perhaps they're all weaving some elaborate fiction or other. The story of the spastic's mutilation in the public toilet. The murder of the old man. Even that hook. All quite familiar elements. You must be aware that there's something *traditional* about these atrocity stories. One used to exchange them all the time; there was a certain *frission* in them. Something competitive maybe, in attempting to find a new detail to add to the collective fiction; a fresh twist that would render the tale that little bit more appalling when you passed it on."

"It may be familiar to you—" said Helen defensively. Purcell was always *so poised*; it irritated her. Even if there were validity in his argument—which she doubted—she was damned if she'd concede it. "—*I've* never heard this kind of story before."

"Have you not?" said Purcell, as though she were admitting to illiteracy. "What about the lovers and the escaped lunatic, have you heard that one?"

"I've heard that..." Daniel said.

"The lover is disembowelled—usually by a hook–handed man—and the body left on the top of the car, while the fiancé cowers inside. It's a cautionary tale, warning of the evils of rampant heterosexuality." The joke won a round of laughter from everyone but Helen. "These stories are very common."

"So you're saying that they're telling me lies—" she protested.

"Not lies, exactly—"

"You said *lies*."

"I was being provocative," Purcell returned, his placatory tone more enraging than ever. "I don't mean to imply there's any serious mischief in it. But you *must* concede that so far you haven't met a single *witness*. All these events have happened at some unspecified date to some unspecified person. They are reported at several removes. They occurred at best to the brothers of friends of distant relations. Please consider the possibility that perhaps these events do not exist in the real world at all, but are merely titillation for bored housewives—"

Helen didn't make an argument in return, for the simple reason that she lacked one. Purcell's point about the conspicuous absence of witnesses was perfectly sound; she herself had wondered about it. It was strange, too, the way the women in Ruskin Court had speedily consigned the old man's murder to another estate, as though these atrocities always occurred just out of sight—round the next comer, down the next passageway—but never *here*.

"So why?" said Bernadette.

"Why what?" Archie puzzled.

"The stories. Why tell these horrible stories if they're not true?"

"Yes," said Helen, throwing the controversy back into Purcell's ample lap. "*Why?*"

Purcell preened himself, aware that his entry into the debate had changed the basic assumption at a stroke. "I don't know," he said, happy to be done with the game now that he'd shown his arm. "You really mustn't take me too seriously, Helen. *I* try not to." The boy at Purcell's side tittered.

"Maybe It's simply *taboo* material," Archie said.

"Suppressed—" Daniel prompted.

"Not the way you mean it," Archie retorted. "The whole world isn't politics, Daniel."

"Such naivete."

"What's so *taboo* about death?" Trevor said. "Bernadette already pointed out: It's in front of us all the time. Television; newspapers."

"Maybe that's not close enough," Bernadette suggested.

"Does anyone mind if I smoke?" Purcell broke in. "Only dessert seems to have been indefinitely postponed—"

Helen ignored the remark, and asked Bernadette what she meant by "not close enough"?

Bernadette shrugged. "I don't know precisely," she confessed, "maybe just that death has to be *near*; we have to *know* it's just round the corner. The television's not intimate enough—"

Helen frowned. The observation made some sense to her, but in the clutter of the moment she couldn't root out its significance.

"Do you think they're stories too?" she asked.

"Andrew has a point—" Bernadette replied.

"Most kind," said Purcell. "Has somebody got a match? The boy's pawned my lighter."

"—about the absence of witnesses."

"All that proves is that I haven't met anybody who's actually seen anything," Helen countered, "not that witnesses don't exist."

"All right," said Purcell. "Find me one. If you can prove to me that your atrocity–monger actually lives and breathes, I'll stand everyone dinner at *Appollinaires*. How's that? Am I generous to a fault, or do I just know when I can't lose?" He laughed, knocking on the table with his knuckles by way of applause.

"Sounds good to me," said Trevor. "What do you say, Helen?"

She didn't go back to Spector Street until the following Monday, but all weekend she was therein thought: standing outside the locked toilet, with the wind bringing rain; or in the bedroom, the portrait looming. Thoughts of the estate claimed all her concern. When, late on Saturday afternoon, Trevor found some petty reason for an argument, she let the insults pass, watching him perform the familiar ritual of self–martyrdom without being touched by it in the least. Her indifference only enraged him further. He stormed out in high dudgeon, to visit whichever of his women was in favour this month. She was glad to see the back of him. When he failed to return that night she didn't even think of weeping about it. He was foolish and vacuous. She despaired of ever seeing a haunted look in his dull eyes; and what worth was a man who could not be haunted?

He did not return Sunday night either, and it crossed her mind the following morning, as she parked the car in the heart of the estate, that nobody even knew she had come, and that she might lose herself for days here and nobody be any the wiser. Like the old man Anne–Marie had told her about: lying forgotten in his favourite armchair with his eyes hooked out, while the flies feasted and the butter went rancid on the table.

It was almost Bonfire Night, and over the weekend the small heap of combustibles in Butts' Court had grown to a substantial size. The construction looked unsound, but that didn't prevent a number of boys and young adolescents clambering over it and into it. Much of its bulk was made up of furniture, filched, no doubt, from boarded up properties. She doubted if it could burn for any time: if it did, it would go chokingly. Four times, on her way across to Anne–Marie's house, she was waylaid by children begging for money to buy fireworks.

"Penny for the guy," they'd say, though none had a guy to display. She had emptied her pockets of change by the time she reached the front door.

Anne–Marie was in today, though there was no welcoming smile. She simply stared at her visitor as if mesmerised.

"I hope you don't mind me calling..."

Anne–Marie made no reply.

"...I just wanted a word."

"I'm busy," the woman finally announced. There was no invitation inside, no offer of tea.

"Oh. Well... it won't take more than a moment."

The back door was open and the draught blew through the house. Papers were flying about in the back yard. Helen could see them lifting into the air like vast white moths.

"What do you want?" Anne–Marie asked.

"Just to ask you about the old man."

The woman frowned minutely. She looked as if she was sickening, Helen thought: her face had the colour and texture of stale dough, her hair was lank and greasy.

"What old man?"

"Last time I was here, you told me about an old man who'd been murdered, do you remember?"

"No."

"You said he lived in the next court."

"I don't remember," Anne–Marie said.

"But you *distinctly* told me—"

Something fell to the floor in the kitchen, and smashed. Anne–Marie flinched, but did not move from the doorstep, her arm barring Helen's way into the house. The hallway was littered with the child's toys, gnawed and battered.

"Are you all right?"

Anne–Marie nodded. "I've got work to do," she said.

"And you don't remember telling me about the old man?"

"You must have misunderstood," Anne–Marie replied, and then, her voice hushed: "You shouldn't have come. Everybody *knows*."

"Knows what?"

The girl had begun to tremble. "You don't understand, do you? You think people aren't watching?"

"What does it matter? All I asked was—"

"I don't know *anything*," Anne–Marie reiterated. "Whatever I said to you, I lied about it."

"Well, thank you anyway," Helen said, too perplexed by the confusion of signals from Anne–Marie to press the point any further. Almost as soon as she had turned from the door she heard the lock snap closed behind her.

That conversation was only one of several disappointments that morning brought. She went back to the row of shops, and visited the supermarket that josie had spoken of There she inquired about the lavatories, and their recent history. The supermarket had only changed hands in the last month, and the new owner, a taciturn Pakistani, insisted that he knew nothing of when or why the lavatories had been closed. She was aware, as she made her enquiries, of being scrutinized by the other customers in the shop; she felt like a pariah. That feeling deepened when, after leaving the supermarket, she saw Josie emerging from the launderette, and called after her only to have the woman pick up her pace and duck away into the maze of corridors. Helen followed, but rapidly lost both her quarry and her way.

Frustrated to the verge of tears, she stood amongst the

overturned rubbish bags, and felt a surge of contempt for her foolishness. She didn't belong here, did she? How many times had she criticized others for their presumption in claiming to understand societies they had merely viewed from afar? And here was she, committing the same crime, coming here with her camera and her questions, using the lives (and deaths) of these people as fodder for party conversation. She didn't blame Anne–Marie for turning her back; had she deserved better?

Tired and chilled, she decided it was time to concede Purcell's point. It was all fiction she had been told. They had played with her—sensing her desire to be fed some horrors—and she, the perfect fool, had fallen for every ridiculous word. It *was* time to pack up her credulity and go home.

One call demanded to be made before she returned to the car however: she wanted to look a final time at the painted head. Not as an anthropologist amongst an alien tribe, but as a confessed ghost train rider: for the thrill of it. Arriving at number 14, however, she faced the last and most crushing disappointment. The maisonette had been sealed up by conscientious council workmen. The door was locked; the front window boarded over.

She was determined not to be, so easily defeated however. She made her way around the back of Butts' Court and located the yard of number 14 by simple mathematics. The gate was wedged closed from the inside, but she pushed hard upon it, and, with effort on both parts, it opened. A heap of rubbish—rotted carpets, a box of rain–sodden magazines, denuded Christmas tree—had blocked it.

She crossed the yard to the boarded up windows, and peered through the slats of wood. It wasn't bright outside, but it was darker still within; it was difficult to catch more than the vaguest hint of the painting on the bedroom wall. She pressed her face close to the wood, eager for a final glimpse.

A shadow moved across the room, momentarily blocking

her view. She stepped back from the window, startled, not certain of what she'd seen. Perhaps merely her own shadow, cast through the window? But then *she* hadn't moved; it had.

She approached the window again, more cautiously. The air vibrated; she could hear a muted whine from somewhere, though she couldn't be certain whether it came from inside or out. Again, she put her face to the rough boards, and suddenly, something leapt at the window. This time she let out a cry. There was a scrabbling sound from within, as nails raked the wood.

A dog!; and a big one to have jumped so high.

"Stupid," she told herself aloud. A sudden sweat bathed her.

The scrabbling had stopped almost as soon as it had started, but she couldn't bring herself to go back to the window. Clearly the workmen who had sealed up the maisonette had failed to check it properly, and incarcerated the animal by mistake. It was ravenous, to judge by the slavering she'd heard; she was grateful she hadn't attempted to break in. The dog—hungry, maybe half–mad in the stinking darkness—could have taken out her throat.

She stared at the boarded–up window. The slits between the boards were barely a half-inch wide, but she sensed that the animal was up on its hind legs on the other side, watching her through the gap. She could hear its panting now that her own breath was regularizing; she could hear its claws raking the sill.

"Bloody thing..." she said. "Damn well stay in there."

She backed off towards the gate. Hosts of wood–lice and spiders, disturbed from their nests by moving the carpets behind the gate, were scurrying underfoot, looking for a fresh darkness to call home.

She closed the gate behind her, and was making her way around the front of the block when she heard the sirens; two ugly spirals of sound that made the hair on the back of her neck tingle. They were approaching. She picked up her speed, and came round into Butts' Court in time to see several policemen crossing the grass behind the bonfire and an ambulance mounting the pavement and driving around to the other side of the quadrangle. People had emerged from their flats and were standing on their balconies, staring down. Others were walking around the court, nakedly curious, to join a gathering congregation. Helen's stomach seemed to drop to her bowels when she realized *where* the hub of interest lay: at Anne–Marie's doorstep. The police were clearing a path through the throng for the ambulance men. A second police–car had followed the route of the ambulance onto the pavement; two plain–clothes officers were getting out.

She walked to the periphery of the crowd. What little talk there was amongst the on–lookers was conducted in low voices; one or two of the older women were crying. Though she peered over the heads of the spectators she could see nothing. Turning to a bearded man, whose child was perched on his shoulders, she asked what was going on. He didn't know. Somebody dead, he'd heard, but he wasn't certain.

"Anne–Marie?" she asked.

A woman in front of her turned and said: "You know her?" almost awed, as if speaking of a loved one.

"A little," Helen replied hesitantly. "Can you tell me what's happened?"

The woman involuntarily put her hand to her mouth, as if to stop the words before they came. But here they were nevertheless: "The child—" she said.

"Kerry?"

"Somebody got into the house around the back. Slit his throat." Helen felt the sweat come again. In her mind's eye the newspapers rose and fell in Anne–Marie's yard.

"No," she said.

"Just like that."

She looked at the tragedian who was trying to sell her this obscenity, and said, "No," again. It defied belief; yet her denials could not silence the horrid comprehension she felt.

She turned her back on the woman and paddled her way out of the crowd. There would be nothing to see, she knew, and even if there had been she had no desire to look. These people—still emerging from their homes as the story spread—were exhibiting an appetite she was disgusted by. She was not of them; would never be of them. She wanted to slap every eager face into sense; wanted to say: "It's pain and grief you're going to spy on. Why? Why?" But she had no courage left. Revulsion had drained her of all but the energy to wander away, leaving the crowd to its sport.

Trevor had come home. He did not attempt an explanation of his absence, but waited for her to cross–question him. When she failed to do so he sank into an easy *bonhomie* that was worse than his expectant silence. She was dimly aware that her disinterest was probably more unsettling for him than the histrionics he had been anticipating. She couldn't have cared less.

She tuned the radio to the local station, and listened for news. It came surely enough, confirming what the woman in the crowd had told her. Kerry Latimer was dead. Person or persons unknown had gained access to the house via the back yard and murdered the child while he played on the kitchen floor. A police spokesman mouthed the usual platitudes, describing Kerry's death as an 'unspeakable crime', and the miscreant as 'a dangerous and deeply disturbed individual'. For once, the rhetoric seemed justified, and the man's voice shook discernibly when he spoke of the scene that had confronted the officers in the kitchen of Anne– Marie's house.

"Why the radio?" Trevor casually inquired, when Helen had listened for news through three consecutive bulletins. She saw no point in withholding her experience at Spector Street from him; he would find out sooner or later. Coolly, she gave him a bald outline of what had happened at Butts' Court.

"This Anne–Marie is the woman you first met when you went to the estate; am I right?"

She nodded, hoping he wouldn't ask her too many questions. Tears were close, and she had no intention of breaking down in front of him.

"So you were right," he said.

"Right?"

"About the place having a maniac."

"No," she said. "No."

"But the kid—"

She got up and stood at the window, looking down two storeys into the darkened street below. Why did she feel the need to reject the conspiracy theory so urgently?; why was she now praying that Purcell had been right, and that all she'd been told had been lies? She went back and back to the way Anne–Marie had been when she'd visited her that morning: pale, jittery; *expectant*. She had been like a woman anticipating some arrival, hadn't she?, eager to shoo unwanted visitors away so that she could turn back to the business of waiting. But waiting for what, or *whom*? Was it possible that Anne–Marie actually knew the murderer? Had perhaps invited him into the house?

"I hope they find the bastard," she said, still watching the street.

"They will," Trevor replied. "A baby–murderer, for Christ's sake. They'll make it a high priority."

A man appeared at the corner of the street, turned, and whistled. A large Alsatian came to heel, and the two set off down towards the Cathedral.

"The dog," Helen murmured.

"What?"

She had forgotten the dog in all that had followed. Now

the shock she'd felt as it had leapt at the window shook her again.

"What dog?" Trevor pressed.

"I went back to the flat today—where I took the pictures of the graffiti. There was a dog in there. Locked in."

"So?"

"It'll starve. Nobody knows It's there."

"How do you know it wasn't locked in to kennel it?"

"It was making such a noise—" she said.

"Dogs bark," Trevor replied. "That's all they're good for."

"No..." she said very quietly, remembering the noises through the boarded window. "It didn't bark."

"Forget the dog," Trevor said. "And the child. There's nothing you can do about it. You were just passing through."

His words only echoed her own thoughts of earlier in the day, but somehow—for reasons that she could find no words to convey— that conviction had decayed in the last hours. She was not just passing through. Nobody ever just *passed through*; experience always left its mark. Sometimes it merely scratched; on occasion it took off limbs. She did not know the extent of her present wounding, but she knew it more profound than she yet understood, and it made her afraid.

"We're out of booze," she said, emptying the last dribble of whisky into her tumbler.

Trevor seemed pleased to have a reason to be accommodating. "I'll go out, shall I?" he said. "Get a bottle or two?"

"Sure," she replied. "If you like."

He was gone only half an hour; she would have liked him to have been longer. She didn't want to talk, only to sit and think through the unease in her belly. Though Trevor had dismissed her concern for the dog—and perhaps justifiably so—she couldn't help but go back to the locked maisonette in her mind's eye: to picture again the raging face on the bedroom wall, and hear the animal's muffled growl as it pawed the boards over the window. Whatever Trevor had said, she didn't believe the place was being used as a makeshift kennel. No, the dog was *imprisoned* in there, no doubt of it, running round and round, driven, in its desperation, to eat its own faeces, growing more insane with every hour that passed. She became afraid that somebody—kids maybe, looking for more tinder for their bonfire—would break into the place, ignorant of what it contained. It wasn't that she feared for the intruders' safety, but that the dog, once liberated, would come for her. It would know where she was (so her drunken head construed) and come sniffing her out.

Trevor returned with the whisky, and they drank together until the early hours, when her stomach revolted. She took refuge in the toilet— Trevor outside asking her if she needed anything, her telling him weakly to leave her alone. When, an hour later, she emerged, he had gone to bed. She did not join him, but lay down on the sofa and dozed through until dawn.

The murder was news. The next morning it made all the tabloids as a front page splash, and found prominent positions in the heavyweights too. There were photographs of the stricken mother being led from the house, and others, blurred but potent, taken over the back yard wall and through the open kitchen door. Was that blood on the floor, or shadow?

Helen did not bother to read the articles—her aching head rebelled at the thought—but Trevor, who had brought the newspapers in, was eager to talk. She couldn't work out if this was further peacemaking on his part, or a genuine interest in the issue.

"The woman's in custody," he said, poring over the *Daily Telegraph*. It was a paper he was politically averse to, but its coverage of violent crime was notoriously detailed.

The observation demanded Helen's attention, unwilling or not. "Custody?" she said. "Anne–Marie?"

"Yes."

"Let me see."

He relinquished the paper, and she glanced over the page. "Third column," Trevor prompted.

She found the place, and there it was in black and white. Anne–Marie had been taken into custody for questioning to justify the time–lapse between the estimated hour of the child's death, and the time that it had been reported. Helen read the relevant sentences over again, to be certain that she'd understood properly. Yes, she had. The police pathologist estimated Kerry to have died between six and six–thirty that morning; the murder had not been reported until twelve.

She read the report over a third and fourth time, but repetition did not change the horrid facts. The child had been murdered before dawn. When she had gone to the house that morning Kerry had already been dead four hours. The body had been in the kitchen, a few yards down the hallway from where she had stood, and Anne–Marie had said *nothing*. That air of expectancy she had had about her—what had it signified? That she awaited some cue to lift the receiver and call the police?

"My Christ..." Helen said, and let the paper drop.

"What?"

"I have to go to the police."

"Why?"

"To tell them I went to the house," she replied. Trevor looked mystified. "The baby was dead, Trevor. When I saw Anne–Marie yesterday morning, Kerry was already dead."

She rang the number given in the paper for any persons offering information, and half an hour later a police car came to pick her up. There was much that startled her in the two hours of interrogation that followed, not least the fact that nobody had reported her presence on the estate to the police, though she had surely been noticed.

"They don't want to know—" the detective told her,"— you'd think a place like that would be swarming with witnesses. If it is, they're not coming forward. A crime like this..."

"Is it the first?" she said.

He looked at her across a chaotic desk. "First?"

"I was told some stories about the estate. Murders. This summer."

The detective shook his head. "Not to my knowledge. there's been a spate of muggings; one woman was put in hospital for a week or so. But no; no murders."

She liked the detective. His eyes flattered her with their lingering, and his face with their frankness. Past caring whether she sounded foolish or not, she said: "Why do they tell lies like that. About people having their eyes cut out. Terrible things."

The detective scratched his long nose. "We get it too," he said. "People come in here, they confess to all kinds of crap. Talk all night, some of them, about things they've done, or *think* they've done. Give you it all in the minutest detail. And when you make a few calls, It's all invented. Out of their minds."

"Maybe if they didn't tell you the stories... they'd actually go out and do it."

The detective nodded. "Yes," he said. "God help us. You might be right at that."

And the stories *she'd* been told, were they confessions of uncommitted crimes?, accounts of the worst imaginable, imagined to keep fiction from becoming fact? The thought chased its own tail: these terrible stories still needed a *first cause*, a well-spring from which they leapt. As she walked home through the busy streets she wondered how many of her fellow citizens knew such stories. Were these inventions common currency, as Purcell had claimed? Was there a place, however small, reserved in every heart for the monstrous?

"Purcell rang," Trevor told her when she got home. "To invite us out to dinner."

The invitation wasn't welcome, and she made a face.

"Appollinaires, remember?" he reminded her. "He said he'd take us all to dinner, if you proved him wrong."

The thought of getting a dinner out of the death of Anne–Marie's infant was grotesque, and she said so.

"He'll be offended if you turn him down."

"I don't give a damn. I don't want dinner with Purcell."

"Please," he said softly. "He can get difficult; and I want to keep him smiling just at the moment."

She glanced across at him. The look he'd put on made him resemble a drenched spaniel. Manipulative bastard, she thought; but said: "All right, I'll go. But don't expect any dancing on the tables."

"We'll leave that to Archie," he said. "I told Purcell we were free tomorrow night. Is that all right with you?"

"Whenever."

"He's booking a table for eight o'clock."

The evening papers had relegated The Tragedy of Baby Kerry to a few column inches on an inside page. In lieu of much fresh news they simply described the house–to–house enquiries that were now going on at Spector Street. Some of the later editions mentioned that Anne– Marie had been released from custody after an extended period of questioning, and was now residing with friends. They also mentioned, in passing, that the funeral was to be the following day.

Helen had not entertained any thoughts of going back to Spector Street for the funeral when she went to bed that night, but sleep seemed to change her mind, and she woke with the decision made for her.

Death had brought the estate to life. Walking through to Ruskin Court from the street she had never seen such numbers out and about. Many were already lining the kerb to watch the funeral cortege pass, and looked to have 'claimed their niche' early, despite the wind and the ever-present threat of rain. Some were wearing items of black clothing—a coat, a scarf—but the overall impression, despite the lowered voices and the studied frowns, was one of celebration. Children running around, untouched by reverence; occasional laughter escap- ing from between gossiping adults—Helen could feel an air of anticipation which made her spirits, despite the occasion, almost buoyant.

Nor was it simply the presence of so many people that reassured her; she was, she conceded to herself, happy to be back here in Spector Street. The quadrangles, with their stunted saplings and their grey grass, were more real to her than the carpeted corridors she was used to walking; the anonymous faces on the balconies and streets meant more than her colleagues at the University. In a word, she felt *home*.

Finally, the cars appeared, moving at a snail's pace through the narrow streets. As the hearse came into view—its tiny white casket decked with flowers—a number of women in the crowd gave quiet voice to their grief. One on-looker fainted; a knot of anxious people gathered around her. Even the children were stilled now.

Helen watched, dry-eyed. Tears did not come very easily to her, especially in company. As the second car, containing Anne-Marie and two other women, drew level with her, Helen saw that the bereaved mother was also eschewing any public display of grief. She seemed, indeed, to be almost elevated by the proceedings, sitting upright in the back of the car, her pallid features the source of much admiration. It was a sour thought, but Helen felt as though she was seeing Anne- Marie's finest hour; the one day in an otherwise anonymous life in which she was the centre of attention. Slowly, the cortege passed by and disappeared from view.

The crowd around Helen was already dispersing. She detached herself from the few mourners who still lingered at the kerb and wandered through from the street into Butts' Court. It was her intention to go back to the locked maisonette, to see if the dog was still there. If it was, she would put her mind at rest by finding one of the estate caretakers and informing him of the fact.

The quadrangle was, unlike the other courts, practically empty. Perhaps the residents, being neighbours of Anne–Marie's, had gone on to the Crematorium for the service. Whatever the reason, the place was eerily deserted. Only children remained, playing around the pyramid bonfire, their voices echoing across the empty expanse of the square.

She reached the maisonette and was surprised to find the door open again, as it had been the first time she'd come here. The sight of the interior made her light–headed. How often in the past several days had she imagined standing here, gazing into that darkness. There was no sound from inside. The dog had surely run off; either that, or died. There could be no harm, could there?, in stepping into the place one final time, just to look at the face on the wall, and its attendant slogan.

Sweets to the sweet. She had never looked up the origins of that phrase. No matter, she thought. Whatever it had stood for once, it was transformed here, as everything was; herself included. She stood in the front room for a few moments, to allow herself time to savour the confrontation ahead. Far away behind her the children were screeching like mad birds.

She stepped over a clutter of furniture and towards the short corridor that joined living–room to bedroom, still delaying the moment. Her heart was quick in her: a smile played on her lips.

And there! At last! The portrait loomed, compelling as ever. She stepped back in the murky room to admire it more fully and her heel caught on the mattress that still lay in the corner. She glanced down. The squalid bedding had been turned over, to present its untorn face. Some blankets and a rag–wrapped pillow had been tossed over it. Something glistened amongst the folds of the uppermost blanket. She bent down to look more closely and found there a handful of sweets— chocolates and caramels—wrapped in bright paper. And littered amongst them, neither so attractive nor so sweet, a dozen razor–blades. There was blood on several. She stood up again and backed away from the mattress, and as she did so a buzzing sound reached her ears from the next room. She turned, and the light in the bedroom diminished as a figure stepped into the gullet between her and the outside world. Silhouetted against the light, she could scarcely see the man in the doorway, but she smelt him. He smelt like candy–floss; and the buzzing was with him or in him.

"I just came to look—" she said,"—at the picture."

The buzzing went on: the sound of a sleepy afternoon, far from here. The man in the doorway did not move.

"Well..." she said, "I've seen what I wanted to see." She hoped against hope that her words would prompt him to stand aside and let her past, but he didn't move, and she couldn't find the courage to challenge him by stepping towards the door.

"I have to go," she said, knowing that despite her best efforts fear seeped between every syllable. "I'm expected..."

That was not entirely untrue. Tonight they were all invited to Appollinaires for dinner. But that wasn't until eight, which was four hours away. She would not be missed for a long while yet.

"If you'll excuse me," she said.

The buzzing had quietened a little, and in the hush the man in the doorway spoke. His unaccented voice was almost as sweet as his scent.

"No need to leave yet," he breathed.

"I'm due... due..."

Though she couldn't see his eyes, she felt them on her, and they made her feel drowsy, like that summer that sang in her head. "I came for you," he said.

She repeated the four words in her head. *I came for you.* If they were meant as a threat, they certainly weren't spoken as one.

"I don't... know you," she said.

"No," the man murmured. "But you doubted me."

"Doubted?"

"You weren't content with the stories, with what they wrote on the walls. So I was obliged to come."

The drowsiness slowed her mind to a crawl, but she grasped the essentials of what the man was saying. That he was legend, and she, in disbelieving him, had obliged him to show his hand. She looked, now, down at those hands. One of them was missing. In its place, a hook.

"There will be some blame," he told her. "They will say your doubts shed innocent blood. But I say—what's blood for, if not for shedding? And in time the scrutiny will pass. The police will leave, the cameras will be pointed at some fresh horror, and they will be left alone, to tell stories of the Candyman again."

"Candyman?" she said. Her tongue could barely shape that blameless word.

"I came for you," he murmured so softly that seduction might have been in the air. And so saying, he moved through the passageway and into the light.

She knew him, without doubt. She had known him all along, in that place kept for terrors. It was the man on the wall. His portrait painter had not been a fantasist: the picture that howled over her was matched in each extraordinary particular by the man she now set eyes upon. He was bright to the point of gaudiness: his flesh a waxy yellow, his thin lips pale blue, his wild eyes glittering as if their irises were set with rubies. His jacket was a patchwork his trousers the same. He looked, she thought, almost ridiculous, with his bloodstained motley, and the hint of rouge on his jaundiced cheeks. But people were facile. They needed these shows and shams to keep their interest. Miracles; murders; demons driven out and stones rolled from tombs. The cheap glamour did not taint the sense beneath. It was only, in the natural history of the mind, the bright feathers that drew the species to mate with its secret self.

And she was almost enchanted. By his voice, by his colours, by the buzz from his body. She fought to resist the rapture, though. There was *a monster* here, beneath this fetching display; its nest of razors was at her feet, still drenched in blood. Would it hesitate to slit her own throat if it once laid hands on her?

As the Candyman reached for her she dropped down and snatched the blanket up, flinging it at him. A rain of razors and sweetmeats fell around his shoulders. The blanket followed, blinding him. But before she could snatch the moment to slip past him, the pillow which had lain on the blanket rolled in front of her.

It was not a pillow at all. Whatever the forlorn white casket she had seen in the hearse had contained, it was not the body of Baby Kerry. That was *here*, at her feet, its blood–drained face turned up to her. He was naked. His body showed everywhere signs of the fiend's attentions.

In the two heartbeats she took to register this last horror, the Candyman threw off the blanket. In his struggle to escape from its folds, his jacket had come unbuttoned, and she saw—though her senses protested—that the contents of his torso had rotted away, and the hollow was now occupied by a nest of bees. They swarmed in the vault of his chest, and encrusted in a seething mass the remnants of flesh that hung there. He smiled at her plain repugnance.

"Sweets to the sweet," he murmured, and stretched his

hooked hand towards her face. She could no longer see light from the outside world, nor hear the children playing in Butts' Court. There was no escape into a saner world than this. The Candyman filled her sight; her drained limbs had no strength to hold him at bay.

"Don't kill me," she breathed.

"Do you believe in me?" he said.

She nodded minutely. "How can I not?" she said.

"Then why do you want to live?"

She didn't understand, and was afraid her ignorance would prove fatal, so she said nothing.

"If you would learn," the fiend said, "just *a little* from me... you would not beg to live." His voice had dropped to a whisper. "I am rumour," he sang in her ear. "It's a blessed condition, believe me. To live in people's dreams; to be whispered at street–corners; but not have to *be*. Do you understand?"

Her weary body understood. Her nerves, tired of jangling, understood. The sweetness he offered was life without living: was to be dead, but remembered everywhere; immortal in gossip and graffiti.

"Be my victim," he said.

"No..." she murmured.

"I won't force it upon you," he replied, the perfect gentleman. "I won't oblige you to die. But think; *think*. If I kill you here—if I unhook you..." he traced the path of the promised wound with his hook. It ran from groin to neck. "Think how they would mark this place with their talk... point it out as they passed by and say: "*She* died there; the woman with the green eyes". Your death would be a parable to frighten children with. Lovers would use it as an excuse to cling closer together..."

She had been right: this *was* a seduction.

"Was fame ever so easy?" he asked.

She shook her head. "I'd prefer to be forgotten," she

replied, "than be remembered like that."

He made a tiny shrug. "What do the good know?" he said. "Except what the bad teach them by their excesses?" He raised his hooked hand. "I said I would not oblige you to die and I'm true to my word. Allow me, though, a kiss at least..."

He moved toward her. She murmured some nonsensical threat, which he ignored. The buzzing in his body had risen in volume. The thought of touching his body, of the proximity of the insects, was horrid. She forced her lead–heavy arms up to keep him at bay.

His lurid face eclipsed the portrait on the wall. She couldn't bring herself to touch him, and instead stepped back. The sound of the bees rose; some, in their excitement, had crawled up his throat and were flying from his mouth. They climbed about his lips; in his hair.

She begged him over and over to leave her alone, but he would not be placated. At last she had nowhere left to retreat to; the wall was at her back. Steeling herself against the stings, she put her hands on his crawling chest and pushed. As she did so his hand shot out and around the back of her neck, the hook nicking the flushed skin of her throat. She felt blood come; felt certain he–would open her jugular in one terrible slash. But he had given his word: and he was true to it.

Aroused by this sudden activity, the bees were everywhere. She felt them moving on her, searching for morsels of wax in her ears, and sugar at her lips. She made no attempt to swat them away. The hook was at her neck. If she so much as moved it would wound her. She was trapped, as in her childhood nightmares, with every chance of escape stymied. When sleep had brought her to such hopelessness— the demons on every side, waiting to tear her limb from limb —one trick remained. To let go; to give up all ambition to life, and leave her body to the dark. Now, as the Candyman's face pressed to hers, and the sound of bees blotted out even her own breath, she played that hidden hand. And, as surely as in dreams, the room and the fiend were painted out and gone.

She woke from brightness into dark. There were several panicked moments when she couldn't think of where she was, then several more when she remembered. But there was no pain about her body. She put her hand to her neck; it was, barring the nick of the hook, untouched. She was lying on the mattress she realized. Had she been assaulted as she lay in a faint? Gingerly, she investigated her body. She was not bleeding; her clothes were not disturbed. The Candyman had, it seemed, simply claimed his kiss.

She sat up. There was precious little light through the boarded window—and none from the front door. Perhaps it was closed, she reasoned. But no; even now she heard somebody whispering on the threshold. A woman's voice.

She didn't move. They were crazy, these people. They had known all along what her presence in Butts' Court had summoned, and they had *protected* him—this honeyed psychopath; given him a bed and an offering of bonbons, hidden him away from prying eyes, and kept their silence when he brought blood to their doorsteps. Even Anne-Marie, dry-eyed in the hallway of her house, knowing that her child was dead a few yards away.

The child! That was the evidence she needed. Somehow they had conspired to get the body from the casket (what had they substituted; a dead dog?) and brought it here—to the Candyman's tabernacle—as a toy, or a lover. She would take Baby Kerry with her—to the police— and tell the whole story. Whatever they believed of it—and that would probably be very little—the fact of the child's body was incontestable. That way at least some of the crazies would suffer for their conspiracy. Suffer for *her* suffering.

The whispering at the door had stopped. Now somebody

was moving towards the bedroom. They didn't bring a light with them. Helen made herself small, hoping she might escape detection.

A figure appeared in the doorway. The gloom was too impenetrable for her to make out more than a slim figure, who bent down and picked up a bundle on the floor. A fall of blonde hair identified the newcomer as Anne–Marie: the bundle she was picking up was undoubtedly Kerry's corpse. Without looking in Helen's direction, the mother about–turned and made her way out of the bedroom.

Helen listened as the footsteps receded across the living–room. Swiftly, she got to her feet, and crossed to the passageway. From there she could vaguely see Anne–Marie's outline in the doorway of the maisonette. No lights burned in the quadrangle beyond. The woman disappeared and Helen followed as speedily as she could, eyes fixed on the door ahead. She stumbled once, and once again, but reached the door in time to see Anne–Marie's vague form in the night ahead.

She stepped out of the maisonette and into the open air. It was chilly; there were no stars. All the lights on the balconies and corridors were out, nor did–any burn in the flats; not even the glow of a television. Butts' Court was deserted.

She hesitated before going in pursuit of the girl. Why didn't she slip away now?, cowardice coaxed her, and find her way back to the car. But if she did that the conspirators would have time to conceal the child's body. When she got back here with the police there would be sealed lips and shrugs, and she would be told she had imagined the corpse and the Candyman. All the terrors she had tasted would recede into rumour again. Into words on a wall. And every day she lived from now on she would loathe herself for not going in pursuit of sanity.

She followed. Anne–Marie was not making her way around the quadrangle, but moving towards the centre of the lawn in the middle of the court. To the bonfire! Yes; to the bonfire! It loomed in front of Helen now, blacker than the night–sky. She could just make out Anne–Marie's figure, moving to the edge of the piled timbers and furniture, and ducking to climb into its heart. *This* was how they planned to remove the evidence. To bury the child was not certain enough; but to cremate it, and pound the bones—who would ever know?

She stood a dozen yards from the pyramid and watched as Anne– Marie climbed out again and moved away, folding her figure into the darkness.

Quickly, Helen moved through the long grass and located the narrow space in amongst the piled timbers into which Anne–Marie had put the body. She thought she could see the pale form; it had been laid in a hollow. She couldn't reach it however. Thanking God that she was as

slim as the mother, she squeezed through the narrow aperture. Her dress snagged on a nail as she did so. She turned round to disengage it, fingers trembling. When she turned back she had lost sight of the corpse.

She fumbled blindly ahead of her, her hands finding wood and rags and what felt like the back of an old armchair, but not the cold skin of the child. She had hardened herself against contact with the body: she had endured worse in the last hours than picking up a dead baby. Determined not to be defeated, she advanced a little further, her shins scraped and her fingers spiked with splinters. Flashes of light were appearing at the corners of her aching eyes; her blood whined in her ears. But there!; *there!*; the body was no more than a yard and a half ahead of her. She ducked down to reach beneath a beam of wood, but her fingers missed the forlorn bundle by millimetres. She stretched further, the whine in her head increasing, but still she could not reach the child. All she could do was bend double and squeeze into the hidey–hole the children had left in the centre of the bonfire.

It was difficult to get through. The space was so small she could barely crawl on hands and knees; but she made it. The child lay face down. She fought back the remnants of squeamishness and went to pick it up. As she did so, something landed on her arm. The shock startled her. She almost cried out, but swallowed the urge, and brushed the irritation away. It buzzed as it rose from her skin. The whine she had heard in her ears was not her blood, but the hive.

"I knew you'd come," the voice behind her said, and a wide hand covered her face. She fell backwards and the Candyman embraced her.

"We have to go," he said in her ear, as flickering light spilled between the stacked timbers. "Be on our way, you and I."

She fought to be free of him, to cry out for them not to light the bonfire, but he held her lovingly close. The light grew: warmth came with it; and. through the kindling and the first flames she could see figures approaching the pyre out of the darkness of Butts' Court. They had been there all along: waiting, the lights turned out in their homes, and broken all along the corridors. Their final conspiracy.

The bonfire caught with a will, but by some trick of its construction the flames did not invade her hiding–place quickly; nor did the smoke creep through the furniture to choke her. She was able to watch how the children's faces gleamed; how the parents called them from going too close, and how they disobeyed; how the old women, their blood thin, warmed their hands and smiled into the flames. Presently the roar and the crackle became deafening, and the Candyman let her scream herself hoarse in the certain knowledge that nobody could hear her, and even if they had would not have moved to claim her from the fire.

The bees vacated the fiend's belly as the air became hotter, and mazed the air with their panicked flight. Some, attempting escape, caught fire, and fell like tiny meteors to the ground. The body of Baby Kerry, which lay close to the creeping flames, began to cook. Its downy hair smoked, its back blistered.

Soon the heat crept down Helen's throat, and scorched her pleas away. She sank back, exhausted, into the Candyman's arms, resigned to his triumph. In moments they would be on their way, as he had promised, and there was no help for it.

Perhaps they would remember her, as he had said they might, finding her cracked skull in tomorrow's ashes. Perhaps she might become, in time, a story with which to frighten children. She had lied, saying she preferred death to such questionable fame; she did not. As to her seducer, he laughed as the conflagration sniffed them out. There was no permanence for him in this night's death. His deeds were on a hundred walls and a ten thousand lips, and should he be doubted again his congregation could summon him with sweetness. He had reason to laugh. So, as the flames crept upon them, did she, as through the fire she caught sight of a familiar face moving between the on-lookers. It was Trevor. He had forsaken his meal at Appollinaires and come looking for her.

She watched him questioning this fire-watcher and that, but they shook their heads, all the while staring at the pyre with smiles buried in their eyes. Poor dupe, she thought, following his antics. She willed him to look past the flames in the hope that he might see her burning. Not so that he could save her from death—she was long past hope of that—but because she pitied him in his bewilderment and wanted to give him, though he would not have thanked her for it, something to be haunted by. That, and a story to tell.

DREAD

CLIVE BARKER

There is no delight the equal of dread. If it were possible to sit, invisible, between two people on any train, in any waiting room or office, the conversation overheard would time and again circle on that subject. Certainly the debate might appear to be about something entirely different; the state of the nation, idle chat about death on the roads, the rising price of dental care; but strip away the metaphor, the innuendo, and there, nestling at the heart of the discourse, is dread. While the nature of God, and the possibility of eternal life go undiscussed, we happily chew over the minutiae of misery. The syndrome recognizes no boundaries; in bath-house and seminar-room alike, the same ritual is repeated. With the inevitability of a tongue returning to probe a painful tooth, we come back and back and back again to our fears, sitting to talk them over with the eagerness of a hungry man before a full and steaming plate.

While he was still at university, and afraid to speak, Stephen Grace was taught to speak of why he was afraid. In fact not simply to talk about it, but to analyse and dissect his every nerve-ending, looking for tiny terrors.

In this investigation, he had a teacher: Quaid.

It was an age of gurus; it was their season. In universities up and down England young men and women were looking east and west for people to follow like lambs; Steve Grace was just one of many. It was his bad luck that Quaid was the Messiah he found.

They'd met in the Student Common Room.

"The name's Quaid," said the man at Steve's elbow at the bar.

"Oh."

"You're—?"

"Steve Grace."

"Yes. You're in the Ethics class, right?"

"Right."

"I don't see you in any of the other Philosophy seminars or lectures."

"It's my extra subject for the year. I'm on the English Literature course. I just couldn't bear the idea of a year in the Old Norse classes."

"So you plumped for Ethics."

"Yes."

Quaid ordered a double brandy. He didn't look that well off, and a double brandy would have just about crippled Steve's finances for the next week. Quaid downed it quickly, and ordered another.

"What are you having?"

Steve was nursing half a pint of luke-warm lager, determined to make it last an hour.

"Nothing for me."

"Yes you will."

"I'm fine."

"Another brandy and a pint of lager for my friend."

Steve didn't resist Quaid's generosity. A pint and a half of lager in his unfed system would help no end in dulling the tedium of his oncoming seminars on 'Charles Dickens as a Social Analyst'. He yawned just to think of it.

"Somebody ought to write a thesis on drinking as a social activity."

Quaid studied his brandy a moment, then downed it.

"Or as oblivion," he said.

Steve looked at the man. Perhaps five years older than Steve's twenty. The mixture of clothes he wore was confusing. Tattered running shoes, cords, a grey-white shirt that had seen better days: and over it a very expensive black leather jacket that hung badly on his tall, thin frame. The face was long and unremarkable; the eyes milky-blue, and so pale that the colour seemed to seep into the whites, leaving just the pinpricks of his irises visible behind his heavy glasses. Lips full, like a Jagger, but pale, dry and unsensual. Hair, a dirty blond.

Quaid, Steve decided, could have passed for a Dutch dope-pusher.

He wore no badges. They were the common currency of a student's obsessions, and Quaid looked naked without something to imply how he took his pleasures. Was he a gay, feminist, save-the-whale campaigner; or a fascist vegetarian? What was he into, for God's sake?

"You should have been doing Old Norse," said Quaid.

"Why?"

"They don't even bother to mark the papers on that course," said Quaid.

Steve hadn't heard about this. Quaid droned on.

"They just throw them all up into the air. Face up, an A. Face down, a B."

Oh, it was a joke. Quaid was being witty. Steve attempted a laugh, but Quaid's face remained unmoved by his own attempt at humour.

"You should be in Old Norse," he said again. "Who needs Bishop Berkeley anyhow. Or Plato. Or—"

"Or?"

"It's all shit."

"Yes."

"I've watched you, in the Philosophy Class—"

Steve began to wonder about Quaid.

"—You never take notes do you?"

"No."

"I thought you were either sublimely confident, or you simply couldn't care less."

"Neither. I'm just completely lost."

Quaid grunted, and pulled out a pack of cheap cigarettes. Again, that was not the done thing. You either smoked Gauloises, Camel or nothing at all.

"It's not true philosophy they teach you here," said Quaid, with unmistakable contempt.

"Oh?"

"We get spoonfed a bit of Plato, or a bit of Bentham—no real analysis. It's got all the right markings of course. It looks like the beast: it even smells a bit like the beast to the uninitiated."

"What beast?"

"Philosophy. *True* Philosophy. It's a beast, Stephen. don't you think?"

"I hadn't—"

"It's wild. It bites."

He grinned, suddenly vulpine.

"Yes. It bites," he replied.

Oh, that pleased him. Again, for luck: "Bites."

Stephen nodded. The metaphor was beyond him.

"I think we should feel mauled by our subject." Quaid was warming to the whole subject of mutilation by education. "We should be frightened to juggle the ideas we should talk about."

"Why?"

"Because if we were philosophers worth we wouldn't be exchanging academic pleasantries. We wouldn't be talking semantics; using linguistic trickery to cover the real concerns."

"What would we be doing?"

Steve was beginning to feel like Quaid's straight-man. Except that Quaid wasn't in a joking mood. His face was set: his pinprick irises had closed down to tiny dots.

"We should be walking close to the beast, Steve, don't you think? Reaching out to stroke it, pet it, milk it—"

"What... er... what is the beast?"

Quaid was clearly a little exasperated by the pragmatism of the enquiry.

"It's the subject of any worthwhile philosophy, Stephen. It's the things we fear, because we don't understand them. It's the dark behind the door."

Steve thought of a door. Thought of the dark. He began to see what Quaid was driving at in his labyrinthine fashion. Philosophy was a way to talk about fear.

"We should discuss what's intimate to our psyches," said Quaid. "If we don't... we risk..."

Quaid's loquaciousness deserted him suddenly.

"What?"

Quaid was staring at his empty brandy glass, seeming to will it to be full again.

"Want another?" said Steve, praying that the answer would be no. "What do we risk?" Quaid repeated the question. "Well, I think if we don't go out and find the beast—"

Steve could see the punchline coming.

"—sooner or later the beast will come and find us."

There is no delight the equal of dread. As long as It's someone else's.

Casually, in the following week or two, Steve made some enquiries about the curious Mr Quaid.

Nobody knew his first name.

Nobody was certain of his age; but one of the secretaries thought he was over thirty, which came as a surprise.

His parents, Cheryl had heard him say, were dead. Killed, she thought.

That appeared to be the sum of human knowledge where Quaid was concerned.

"I owe you a drink," said Steve, touching Quaid on the shoulder. He looked as though he'd been bitten.

"Brandy?"

"Thank you."

Steve ordered the drinks.

"Did I startle you?"

"I was thinking."

"No philosopher should be without one."

"One what?"

"Brain."

They fell to talking. Steve didn't know why he'd approached Quaid again. The man was ten years his senior and in a different intellectual league. He probably intimidated Steve, if he was to be honest about it. Quaid's relentless talk of beasts confused him. Yet he wanted more of the same: more metaphors: more of that humourless voice telling him how useless the tutors were, how weak the students.

In Quaid's world there were no certainties. He had no secular gurus and certainly no religion. He seemed incapable of viewing any system, whether it was political or philosophical, without cynicism.

Though he seldom laughed out loud, Steve knew there

was a bitter humour in his vision of the world. People were lambs and sheep, all looking for shepherds. Of course these shepherds were fictions, in Quaid's opinion. All that existed, in the darkness outside the sheep-fold were the fears that fixed on the innocent mutton: waiting, patient as stone, for their moment.

Everything was to be doubted, but the fact that dread existed.

Quaid's intellectual arrogance was exhilarating. Steve soon came to love the iconoclastic ease with which he demolished belief after belief. Sometimes it was painful when Quaid formulated a water-tight argument against one of Steve's dogma. But after a few weeks, even the sound of the demolition seemed to excite. Quaid was clearing the undergrowth, felling the trees, razing the stubble. Steve felt free.

Nation, family, Church, law. All ash. All useless. All cheats, and chains and suffocation.

There was only dread.

"I fear, you fear, we fear," Quaid was fond of saying. "He, she or it fears. there's no conscious thing on the face of the world that doesn't know dread more intimately than its own heartbeat."

One of Quaid's favourite baiting-victims was another Philosophy and Eng. Lit. student, Cheryl Fromm. She would rise to his more outrageous remarks like fish to rain, and while the two of them took knives to each other's arguments Steve would sit back and watch the spectacle. Cheryl was, in Quaid's phrase, a pathological optimist.

"And you're full of shit," she'd say when the debate had warmed up a little. "So who cares if you're afraid of your own shadow? I'm not. I feel fine."

She certainly looked it. Cheryl Fromm was wet dream material, but too bright for anyone to try making a move on her.

"We all taste dread once in a while," Quaid would reply to her, and his milky eyes would study her face intently, watching for her reaction, trying, Steve knew, to find a flaw in her conviction.

"I don't."

"No fears? No nightmares?"

"No way. I've got a good family; I don't have any skeletons in my closet. I don't even eat meat, so I don't feel bad when I drive past a slaughterhouse. I don't have any shit to put on show. Does that mean I'm not real?"

"It means," Quaid's eyes were snake-slits, "it means your confidence has something big to cover."

"Back to nightmares."

"Big nightmares."

"Be specific: define your terms."

"I can't tell you what you fear."

"Tell me what you fear then."

Quaid hesitated. "Finally," he said, "It's beyond analysis."

"Beyond analysis, my ass!"

That brought an involuntary smile to Steve's lips. Cheryl's ass was indeed beyond analysis. The only response was to kneel down and worship.

Quaid was back on his soap-box.

"What I fear is personal to me. It makes no sense in a larger context. The signs of my dread, the images my brain uses, if you like, to *illustrate* my fear, those signs are mild stuff by comparison with the real horror that's at the root of my personality."

"I've got images," said Steve. Pictures from childhood that make me think of—" He stopped, regretting this confessional already.

"What?" said Cheryl. "You mean things to do with bad experiences? Falling off your bike, or something like that?"

"Perhaps," Steve said. "I find myself, sometimes, thinking of those pictures. Not deliberately, just when my

146

concentration's idling. It's almost as though my mind went to them automatically."

Quaid gave a little grunt of satisfaction. "Precisely," he said.

"Freud writes on that," said Cheryl.

"What?"

"Freud," Cheryl repeated, this time making a performance of it, as though she were speaking to a child. "Sigmund Freud: you may have heard of him."

Quaid's lip curled with unrestrained contempt. "Mother fixations don't answer the problem. The real terrors in me, in all of us, are pre-personality. Dread's there before we have any notion of ourselves as individuals. The thumbnail, curled up on itself in the womb, feels fear."

"You remember do you?" said Cheryl.

"Maybe," Quaid replied, deadly serious.

"The womb?"

Quaid gave a sort of half-smile. Steve thought the smile said: "I have knowledge you don't."

It was a weird, unpleasant smile; one Steve wanted to wash off his eyes.

"You're a liar," said Cheryl, getting up from her seat, and looking down her nose at Quaid.

"Perhaps I am," he said, suddenly the perfect gentleman.

After that the debates stopped. No more talking about nightmares, no more debating the things that go bump in the night. Steve saw Quaid irregularly for the next month, and when he did Quaid was invariably in the company of Cheryl Fromm. Quaid was polite with her, even deferential. He no longer wore his leather jacket, because she hated the smell of dead animal matter. This sudden change in their relationship confounded Stephen; but he put it down to his primitive understanding of sexual matters. He wasn't a virgin, but women were still a mystery to him: contradictory and puzzling.

He was also jealous, though he wouldn't entirely admit that to himself. He resented the fact that the wet dream genius was taking up so much of Quaid's time.

There was another feeling; a curious sense he had that Quaid was courting Cheryl for his own strange reasons. Sex was not Quaid's motive, he felt sure. Nor was it respect for Cheryl's intelligence that made him so attentive. No, he was cornering her somehow; that was Steve's instinct. Cheryl Fromm was being rounded up for the kill.

Then, after a month, Quaid let a remark about Cheryl drop in conversation.

"She's a vegetarian," he said.

"Cheryl?"

"Of course, Cheryl."

"I know. She mentioned it before."

"Yes, but it isn't a fad with her. She's passionate about it. Can't even bear to look in a butcher's window. She won't touch meat, smell meat—"

"Oh." Steve was stumped. Where was this leading?

"Dread, Steve."

"Of meat?"

"The signs are different from person to person. She fears meat. She says she's so healthy, so balanced. Shit! I'll find it—"

"Find what?"

"The fear, Steve."

"You're not going to… ?" Steve didn't know how to voice his anxiety without sounding accusatory.

"Harm her?" said Quaid. "No, I'm not going to harm her in any way. Any damage done to her will be strictly self-inflicted.

Quaid was staring at him almost hypnotically.

"It's about time we learnt to trust one another," Quaid went on. He leaned closer. "Between the two of us—"

"Listen, I don't think I want to hear."

"We have to touch the beast, Stephen."

"Damn the beast! I don't want to hear!"

Steve got up, as much to break the oppression of Quaid's stare as to finish the conversation.

"We're friends, Stephen."

"Yes…"

"Then respect that."

"What?"

"Silence. Not a word."

Steve nodded. That wasn't a difficult promise to keep. There was nobody he could tell his anxieties to without being laughed at.

Quaid looked satisfied. He hurried away, leaving Steve feeling as though he had unwillingly joined some secret society, for what purpose he couldn't begin to tell. Quaid had made a pact with him and it was unnerving.

For the next week he cut all his lectures and most of his seminars. Notes went uncopied, books unread, essays unwritten. On the two occasions he actually went into the university building he crept around like a cautious mouse, praying he wouldn't collide with Quaid.

He needn't have feared. The one occasion he did see Quaid's stooping shoulders across the quadrangle he was involved in a smiling exchange with Cheryl Fromm. She laughed, musically, her pleasure echoing off the wall of the History Department. The jealousy had left Steve altogether. He wouldn't have been paid to be so near to Quaid, so intimate with him.

The time he spent alone, away from the bustle of lectures and overfull corridors, gave Steve's mind time to idle. His thoughts returned, like tongue to tooth, like fingernail to scab, to his fears.

And so to his childhood.

At the age of six, Steve had been struck by a car. The injuries were not particularly bad, but concussion left him partially deaf. It was a profoundly distressing experience for him; not understanding why he was suddenly cut off from the world. It was an inexplicable torment, and the child assumed it was eternal.

One moment his life had been real, full of shouts and laughter. The next he was cut off from it, and the external world became an aquarium, full of gaping fish with grotesque smiles. Worse still, there were times when he suffered what the doctors called tinnitus, a roaring or ringing sound in the ears. His head would fill with the most outlandish noises, whoops and whistlings, that played like sound-effects to the flailings of the outside world. At those times his stomach would churn, and a band of iron would be wrapped around his forehead, crushing his thoughts into fragments, dissociating head from hand, intention from practice. He would be swept away in a tide of panic, completely unable to make sense of the world while his head sang and rattled.

But at night came the worst terrors. He would wake, sometimes, in what had been (before the accident) the reassuring womb of his bedroom, to find the ringing had begun in his sleep.

His eyes would jerk open. His body would be wet with sweat. His mind would be filled with the most raucous din, which he was locked in with, beyond hope of reprieve. Nothing could silence his head, and nothing, it seemed, could bring the world, the speaking, laughing, crying world back to him.

He was alone.

That was the beginning, middle and end of the dread. He was absolutely alone with his cacophony. Locked in this house, in this room, in this body, in this head, a prisoner of deaf, blind flesh.

It was almost unbearable. In the night the boy would sometimes cry out, not knowing he was making any sound, and the fish who had been his parents would turn on the light and come to try and help him, bending over his bed making faces, their soundless mouths forming ugly shapes in their attempts to help. Their touches would calm him at last; with time his mother learned the trick of soothing away the panic that swept over him.

A week before his seventh birthday his hearing returned, not perfectly, but well enough for it to seem like a miracle. The world snapped back into focus; and life began afresh.

It took several months for the boy to trust his senses again. He would still wake in the night, half-anticipating the head-noises.

But though his ears would ring at the slightest volume of sound, preventing Steve from going to rock concerts with the rest of the students, he now scarcely ever noticed his slight deafness.

He remembered, of course. Very well. He could bring back the taste of his panic; the feel of the iron band around his head. And there was a residue of fear there; of the dark, of being alone.

But then, wasn't everyone afraid to be alone? To be utterly alone.

Steve had another fear now, far more difficult to pin down.

Quaid.

In a drunken revelation session he had told Quaid about his childhood, about the deafness, about the night terrors.

Quaid knew about his weakness: the clear route into the heart of Steve's dread. He had a weapon, a stick to beat Steve with, should it ever come to that. Maybe that was why he chose not to speak to Cheryl (warn her, was that what he wanted to do?) and certainly that was why he avoided Quaid.

The man had a look, in certain moods, of malice. Nothing

more or less. He looked like a man with malice deep, deep in him.

Maybe those four months of watching people with the sound turned down had sensitized Steve to the tiny glances, sneers and smiles that flit across people's faces. He knew Quaid's life was a labyrinth; a map of its complexities was etched on his face in a thousand tiny expressions.

The next phase of Steve's initiation into Quaid's secret world didn't come for almost three and a half months. The university broke for the summer recess, and the students went their ways. Steve took his usual vacation job at his father's printing works; it was long hours, and physically exhausting, but an undeniable relief for him. Academe had overstuffed his mind, he felt force-fed with words and ideas. The print work sweated all of that out of him rapidly, sorting out the jumble in his mind.

It was a good time: he scarcely thought of Quaid at all.

He returned to campus in the late September. The students were still thin on the ground. Most of the courses didn't start for another week; and there was a melancholy air about the place without its usual melee of complaining, flirting, arguing kids.

Steve was in the library, cornering a few important books before others on his course had their hands on them. Books were pure gold at the beginning of term, with reading lists to be checked off, and the university book shop forever claiming the necessary titles were on order. They would invariably arrive, those vital books, two days after the seminar in which the author was to be discussed. This final year Steve was determined to be ahead of the rush for the few copies of seminal works the library possessed.

The familiar voice spoke.

"Early to work."

Steve looked up to meet Quaid's pin-prick eyes.

"I'm impressed, Steve."

"What with?"

"Your enthusiasm for the job."

"Oh."

Quaid smiled. "What are you looking for?"

"Something on Bentham."

"I've got 'Principles of Morals and Legislation'. Will that do?"

It was a trap. No: that was absurd. He was offering a book; how could that simple gesture be construed as a trap?

"Come to think of it," the smile broadened, "I think it's the library copy I've got. I'll give it to you."

"Thanks."

"Good holiday?"

"Yes. Thank you. You?"

"Very rewarding."

The smile had decayed into a thin line beneath his—

"You've grown a moustache."

It was an unhealthy example of the species. Thin, patchy, and dirty-blond, it wandered back and forth under Quaid's nose as if looking for a way off his face. Quaid looked faintly embarrassed.

"Was it for Cheryl?"

He was definitely embarrassed now.

"Well…"

"Sounds like you had a good vacation."

The embarrassment was surmounted by something else.

"I've got some wonderful photographs," Quaid said.

"What of?"

"Holiday snaps."

Steve couldn't believe his ears. Had C. Fromm tamed the Quaid? Holiday snaps?

"You won't believe some of them."

There was something of the Arab selling dirty postcards

about Quaid's manner. What the hell were these photographs? Split beaver shots of Cheryl, caught reading Kant?

"I don't think of you as being a photographer."

"It's become a passion of mine."

He grinned as he said 'passion'. There was a barely-suppressed excitement in his manner. He was positively gleaming with pleasure.

"You've got to come and see them."

"I—"

"Tonight. And pick up the Bentham at the same time."

"Thanks."

"I've got a house for myself these days. Round the corner from the Maternity Hospital, in Pilgrim Street. Number sixty-four. Some time after nine?"

"Right. Thanks. Pilgrim Street." Quaid nodded.

"I didn't know there were any habitable houses in Pilgrim Street."

"Number sixty-four."

Pilgrim Street was on its knees. Most of the houses were already rubble. A few were in the process of being knocked down. Their inside walls were unnaturally exposed; pink and pale green wallpapers, fireplaces on upper storeys hanging over chasms of smoking brick. Stairs

leading from nowhere to nowhere, and back again.

Number sixty-four stood on its own. The houses in the terrace to either side had been demolished and bull-dozed away, leaving a desert of impacted brick-dust which a few hardy, and foolhardy, weeds had tried to populate.

A three-legged white dog was patrolling its territory along the side of sixty-four, leaving little piss-marks at regular intervals as signs of its ownership.

Quaid's house, though scarcely palatial, was more welcoming than the surrounding wasteland.

They drank some bad red wine together, which Steve had brought with him, and they smoked some grass. Quaid was far more mellow than Steve had ever seen him before, quite happy to talk trivia instead of dread; laughing occasionally; even telling a dirty joke. The interior of the house was bare to the point of being spartan. No pictures on the walls; no decoration of any kind. Quaid's books, and there were literally hundreds of them, were piled on the floor in no particular sequence that Steve could make out. The kitchen and bathroom were primitive. The whole atmosphere was almost monastic.

After a couple of easy hours, Steve's curiosity got the better of him.

"Where's the holiday snaps, then?" he said, aware that he was slurring his words a little, and no longer giving a shit.

"Oh yes. My experiment."

"Experiment?"

"Tell you the truth, Steve, I'm not so sure I should show them to you."

"Why not?"

"I'm into serious stuff, Steve."

"And I'm not ready for serious stuff, is that what you're saying?"

Steve could feel Quaid's technique working on him, even though it was transparently obvious what he was doing.

"I didn't say you weren't read—"

"What the hell is this stuff?"

"Pictures."

"Of?"

"You remember Cheryl."

Pictures of Cheryl. Ha.

"How could I forget?"

"She won't be coming back this term."

"Oh."

"She had a revelation."

Quaid's stare was basilisk-like.

"What do you mean?"

"She was always so calm, wasn't she?" Quaid was talking about her as though she were dead. "Calm, cool and collected."

"Yes, I suppose she was."

"Poor bitch. All she wanted was a good fuck."

Steve smirked like a kid at Quaid's dirty talk. It was a little shocking; like seeing teacher with his dick hanging out of his trousers.

"She spent some of the vacation here."

"Here?"

"In this house."

"You like her then?"

"She's an ignorant cow. She's pretentious, she's weak, she's stupid. But she wouldn't *give*, she wouldn't give a fucking thing."

"You mean she wouldn't screw?"

"Oh no, she'd strip off her knickers soon as look at you. It was her fears she wouldn't give—"

Same old song.

"But I persuaded her, in the fullness of time."

Quaid pulled out a box from behind a pile of philosophy books. In it was a sheaf of black and white photographs, blown up to twice postcard size. He passed the first one of the series over to Steve.

"I locked her away you see, Steve." Quaid was as unemotional as a newsreader. "To see if I could needle her into showing her dread a little bit."

"What do you mean, locked her away?"

"Upstairs."

Steve felt strange. He could hear his ears singing, very quietly. Bad wine always made his head ring.

"I locked her away upstairs," Quaid said again, "as an experiment. That's why I took this house. No neighbours to hear." No neighbours to hear what?

Steve looked at the grainy image in his hand.

"Concealed camera," said Quaid, "she never knew I was photo- graphing her."

Photograph One was of a small, featureless room. A little plain furniture.

"That's the room. Top of the house. Warm. A bit stuffy even. No noise."

No noise.

Quaid proffered Photograph Two.

Same room. Now most of the furniture had been removed. A sleeping bag was laid along one wall. A table. A chair. A bare light bulb.

"That's how I laid it out for her."

"It looks like a cell."

Quaid grunted.

Photograph Three. The same room. On the table a jug of water. In the corner of the room, a bucket, roughly covered with a towel.

"What's the bucket for?"

"She had to piss."

"Yes."

"All amenities provided," said Quaid. "I didn't intend to reduce her to an animal."

Even in his drunken state, Steve took Quaid's inference. He didn't *intend* to reduce her to an animal. However...

Photograph Four. On the table, on an unpatterned plate, a slab of meat. A bone sticks out from it.

"Beef," said Quaid.

"But she's a vegetarian."

"So she is. It's slightly salted, well-cooked, good beef."

Photograph Five. The same. Cheryl is in the room. The

door is closed. She is kicking the door, her foot and fist and face a blur of fury.

"I put her in the room about five in the morning. She was sleeping: I carried her over the threshold myself. Very romantic. She didn't know what the hell was going on."

"You locked her in there?"

"Of course. An experiment."

"She knew nothing about it?"

"We'd talked about dread, you know me. She knew what I wanted to discover. Knew I wanted guinea-pigs. She soon caught on. Once she realized what I was up to she calmed down."

Photograph Six. Cheryl sits in the corner of the room, thinking.

"I think she believed she could out-wait me."

Photograph Seven. Cheryl looks at the leg of beef, glancing at it on the table.

"Nice photo, don't you think? Look at the expression of disgust on her face. She hated even the smell of cooked meat. She wasn't hungry then, of course."

Eight: she sleeps.

Nine: she pisses. Steve felt uncomfortable, watching the girl squatting on the bucket, knickers round her ankles. Tear-stains on her face.

Ten: she drinks water from the jug.

Eleven: she sleeps again, back to the room, curled up like a foetus.

"How long has she been in the room?"

"This was only fourteen hours in. She lost orientation as to time very quickly. No light change, you see. Her body clock was fucked up pretty soon."

"How long was she in here?"

"'Till the point was proved."

Twelve: Awake, she cruises the meat on the table, caught surreptitiously glancing down at it.

"This was taken the following morning. I was asleep: the camera just took pictures every quarter hour. Look at her eyes..."

Steve peered more closely at the photograph. There was a certain desperation on Cheryl's face: a haggard, wild look. The way she stared at the beef she could have been trying to hypnotize it.

"She looks sick."

"She's tired, that's all. She slept a lot, as it happened, but it seemed just to make her more exhausted than ever. She doesn't know now if it's day or night. And she's hungry of course. It's been a day and a half. She's more than a little peckish."

Thirteen: she sleeps again, curled into an even tighter ball, as though she wanted to swallow herself.

Fourteen: she drinks more water.

"I replaced the jug when she was asleep. She slept deeply: I could have done a jig in there and it wouldn't have woken her. Lost to the world."

He grinned. Mad, thought Steve, the man's mad.

"God, it stank in there. You know how women smell sometimes; It's not sweat, It's something else. Heavy odour: meaty. Bloody. She came on towards the end of her time. Hadn't planned it that way."

Fifteen: she touches the meat.

"This is where the cracks begin to show," said Quaid, with quiet triumph in his voice. "This is where the dread begins."

Steve studied the photograph closely. The grain of the print blurred the detail, but the cool mama was in pain, that was for sure. Her face was knotted up, half in desire, half in repulsion, as she touched the food.

Sixteen: she was at the door again, throwing herself at it, every part of her body flailing. Her mouth a black blur of angst, screaming at the blank door.

"She always ended up haranguing me, whenever she'd had a confrontation with the meat."

"How long is this?"

"Coming up for three days. You're looking at a hungry woman."

It wasn't difficult to see that. The next photo she stood still in the middle of the room, averting her eyes from the temptation of the food, her entire body tensed with the dilemma.

"You're starving her."

"She can go ten days without-eating quite easily. Fasts are common in any civilized country, Steve. Sixty per cent of the British population is clinically obese at any one time. She was too fat anyhow."

Eighteen: she sits, the fat girl, in her corner of the room, weeping.

"About now she began to hallucinate. Just little mental ticks. She thought she felt something in her hair, or on the back of her hand. I'd see her staring into mid-air sometimes watching nothing."

Nineteen: she washes herself. She is stripped to the waist, her breasts are heavy, her face is drained of expression. The meat is a darker tone than in the previous photographs.

"She washed herself regularly. Never let twelve hours go-by without washing from head to toe."

"The meat looks..."

"Ripe?"

"Dark."

"It's quite warm in her little room; and there's a few flies in there with her. They've found the meat: laid their eggs. Yes, It's ripening up quite nicely."

"Is that part of the plan?"

"Sure. If the meat revolted when it was fresh, what about her disgust at rotted meat? That's the crux of her dilemma, isn't it? The longer she waits to eat, the more disgusted she becomes with what she's been given to feed on. She's trapped with her own horror of meat on the one hand, and her dread of dying on the other. Which is going to give first?"

Steve was no less trapped now.

On the one hand this joke had already gone too far, and Quaid's experiment had become an exercise in sadism. On the other hand he wanted to know how far this story ended. There was un undeniable fascination in watching the woman suffer.

The next seven photographs—twenty, twenty-one, two, three, four, five and six pictured the same circular routine. Sleeping, washing, pissing, meat-watching. Sleeping, washing, pissing—

Then twenty-seven.

"See?"

She picks up the meat.

Yes, she picks it up, her face full of horror. The haunch of the beef looks well-ripened now, speckled with flies" eggs. Gross.

"She bites it."

The next photograph, and her face is buried in the meat.

Steve seemed to taste the rotten flesh in the back of his throat. His mind found a stench to imagine, and created a gravy of putrescence to run over his tongue. How could she do it?

Twenty-nine: she is vomiting in the bucket in the corner of the room.

Thirty: she is sitting looking at the table. It is empty. The water-jug has been thrown against the wall. The plate has been smashed. The beef lies on the floor in a slime of degeneration.

Thirty-one: she sleeps. Her head is lost in a tangle of arms.

Thirty-two: she is standing up. She is looking at the meat again, defying it. The hunger she feels is plain on her face. So is the disgust.

Thirty-three. She sleeps.

"How long now?" asked Steve.

"Five days. No, six."

Six days.

Thirty-four. She is a blurred figure, apparently flinging herself against a wall. Perhaps beating her head against it, Steve couldn't be sure. He was past asking. Part of him didn't want to know.

Thirty-five: she is again sleeping, this time beneath the table. The sleeping bag has been torn to pieces, shredded cloth and pieces of stuffing littering the room.

Thirty-six: she speaks to the door, through the door, knowing she will get no answer.

Thirty-seven: she eats the rancid meat.

Calmly she sits under the table, like a primitive in her cave, and pulls at the meat with her incisors. Her face is again expressionless; all her energy is bent to the purpose of the moment. To eat. To eat 'til the hunger disappears, 'til the agony in her belly, and the sickness in her head disappear.

Steve stared at the photograph.

"It startled me," said Quaid, "how suddenly she gave in. One moment she seemed to have as much resistance as ever. The monologue at the door was the same mixture of threats and apologies as she'd delivered day in, day out. Then she broke. Just like that. Squatted under the table and ate the beef down to the bone, as though it were a choice cut."

Thirty-eight: she sleeps. The door is open. Light pours in. Thirty- nine: the room is empty.

"Where did she go?"

"She wandered downstairs. She came into the kitchen, drank several glasses of water, and sat in a chair for three or four hours without saying a word."

"Did you speak to her?"

"Eventually. When she started to come out of her fugue state. The experiment was over. I didn't want to hurt her."

"What did she say?"

"Nothing."

"Nothing?"

"Nothing at all. For a. long time I don't believe she was even aware of my presence in the room. Then I cooked some potatoes, which she ate."

"She didn't try and call the police?"

"No."

"No violence?"

"No. She knew what I'd done, and why I'd done it. It wasn't preplanned, but we'd talked about such experiments, in abstract conversations. She hadn't come to any harm, you see. She'd lost a bit of weight perhaps, but that was about all."

"Where is she now?"

"She left the day after. I don't know where she went."

"And what did it all prove?"

"Nothing at all, perhaps. But it made an interesting start to my investigations."

"Start? This was only a start?"

There was plain disgust for Quaid in Steve's voice.

"Stephen—"

"You could have killed her!"

"No."

"She could have lost her mind. Unbalanced her permanently."

"Possibly. But unlikely. She was a strong-willed woman."

"But you broke her."

"Yes. It was a journey she was ready to take. We'd talked of going to face her fear. So here was I, arranging for Cheryl to do just that. Nothing much really."

"You forced her to do it. She wouldn't have gone otherwise."

"True. It was an education for her."

"So now you're a teacher?"

Steve wished he'd been able to keep the sarcasm out of his voice. But it was there. Sarcasm; anger; and a little fear.

"Yes, I'm a teacher," Quaid replied, looking at Steve obliquely, his eyes not focussed. "I'm teaching people dread."

Steve stared at the floor. "Are you satisfied with what you've taught?"

"And learned, Steve. I've learned too. It's a very exciting prospect: a world of fears to investigate. Especially with intelligent subjects. Even in the face of rationalization—"

Steve stood up. "I don't want to hear any more." "Oh? OK."

"I've got classes early tomorrow."

"No."

"What?"

A beat, faltering.

"No. don't go yet."

"Why?" His heart was racing. He feared Quaid, he'd never realized how profoundly.

"I've got some more books to give you."

Steve felt his face flush. Slightly. What had he thought in that moment? That Quaid was going to bring him down with a rugby tackle and start experimenting on his fears?

No. Idiot thoughts.

"I've got a book on Kierkegaard you'll like. Upstairs. I'll be two minutes."

Smiling, Quaid left the room.

Steve squatted on his haunches and began to sheaf through the photographs again. It was the moment when Cheryl first picked up the rotting meat that fascinated him most. Her face wore an expression completely uncharacteristic of the woman he had known. Doubt was written there, and confusion, and deep—

Dread.

It was Quaid's word. A dirty word. An obscene word,

associated from this night on with Quaid's torture of an innocent girl.

For a moment Steve thought of the expression on his own face, as he stared down at the photograph. Was there not some of the same confusion on his face? And perhaps some of the dread too, waiting for release.

He heard a sound behind him, too soft to be Quaid.

Unless he was creeping.

Oh, God, unless he was—

A pad of chloroformed cloth was clamped over Steve's mouth and his nostrils. Involuntarily, he inhaled and the vapours stung his sinuses, made his eyes water.

A blob of blackness appeared at the comer of the world, just out of sight, and it started to grow, this stain, pulsing to the rhythm of his quickening heart.

In the centre of Steve's head he could see Quaid's voice as a veil. It said his name.

"Stephen."

Again.

"—ephen."

"—phen."

"—hen."

"en."

The stain was the world. The world was dark, gone away. Out of sight, out of mind.

Steve fell clumsily amongst the photographs.

When he woke up he was unaware of his consciousness. There was darkness everywhere, on all sides. He lay awake for an hour with his eyes wide before he realized they were open.

Experimentally, he moved first his arms and his legs, then his head. He wasn't bound as he'd expected, except by his ankle. There was definitely a chain or something similar around his left ankle. It chafed his skin when he tried to move too far.

The floor beneath him was very uncomfortable, and when he investigated it more closely with the palm of his hand he realized he was lying on a huge grille or grid of some kind. It was metal, and its regular surface spread in every direction as far as his arms would reach. When he poked his arm down through the holes in this lattice he touched nothing. Just empty air falling away beneath him.

The first infra-red photographs Quaid took of Stephen's confinement pictured his exploration. As Quaid had expected the subject was being quite rational about his situation. No hysterics. No curses. No tears. That was the challenge of this particular subject. He knew precisely what was going on; and he would respond logically to his fears. That would surely make a more difficult mind to break than Cheryl's.

But how much more rewarding the results would be when he did crack. Would his soul not open up then, for Quaid to see and touch? There was so much there, in the man's interior, he wanted to study.

Gradually Steve's eyes became accustomed to the darkness.

He was imprisoned in what appeared to be some kind of shaft. It was, he estimated, about twenty feet wide, and completely round. Was it some kind of air-shaft, for a tunnel, or an underground factory? Steve's mind mapped the area around Pilgrim Street, trying to pinpoint the most likely place for Quaid to have taken him. He could think of nowhere.

Nowhere.

He was lost in a place he couldn't fix or recognize. The shaft had no corners to focus his eyes on; and the walls offered no crack or hole to hide his consciousness in.

Worse, he was lying spreadeagled on a grid that hung

over this shaft. His eyes could make no impression on the darkness beneath him: it seemed that the shaft might be bottomless. And there was only the thin network of the grill, and the fragile chain that shackled his ankle to it, between him and falling.

He pictured himself poised under an empty black sky, and over an infinite darkness. The air was warm and stale. It dried up the tears that had suddenly sprung to his eyes, leaving them gummy. When he began to shout for help, which he did after the tears had passed, the darkness ate his words easily.

Having yelled himself hoarse, he lay back on the lattice. He couldn't help but imagine that beyond his frail bed, the darkness went on forever. It was absurd, of course. Nothing goes on forever, he said aloud.

Nothing goes on forever.

And yet, he'd never know. If he fell in the absolute blackness beneath him, he'd fall and fall and fall and not see the bottom of the shaft coming. Though he tried to think of brighter, more positive, images, his mind conjured his body cascading down this horrible shaft, with the bottom a foot from his hurtling body and his eyes not seeing it, his brain not predicting it.

Until he hit.

Would he see light as his head was dashed open on impact? Would he understand, in the moment that his body became offal, why he'd lived and died?

Then he thought: Quaid wouldn't dare. "Wouldn't dare!" he screeched. "Wouldn't dare!"

The dark was a glutton for words. As soon as he'd yelled into it, it was as though he'd never made a sound.

And then another thought: a real baddie. Suppose Quaid had found this circular hell to put him in because it would *never* be found, *never* be investigated? Maybe he wanted to take his experiment to the limits.

To the limits. Death was at the limits. And wouldn't that

be the ultimate experiment for Quaid? Watching a man die: watching the fear of death, the motherlode of dread, approach. Sartre had written that no man could ever know his own death. But to know the deaths of others, intimately— to watch the acrobatics that the mind would surely perform to avoid the bitter truth—that was a clue to death's nature, wasn't it? That might, in some small way, prepare a man for his own death. To live another's dread vicariously was the safest, cleverest way to touch the beast.

Yes, he thought, Quaid might kill me; out of his own terror.

Steve took a sour satisfaction in that thought. That Quaid, the impartial experimenter, the would-be educator, was obsessed with terrors because his own dread ran deepest.

That was why he had to watch others deal with their fears. He needed a solution, a way out for himself.

Thinking all this through took hours. In the darkness Steve's mind was quick-silver, but uncontrollable. He found it difficult to keep one train of argument for very long. His thoughts were like fish, small, fast fish, wriggling out of his grasp as soon as he took a hold of them.

But underlying every twist of thought was the knowledge that he must out-play Quaid. That was certain. He must be calm; prove himself a useless subject for Quaid's analysis.

The photographs of these hours showed Stephen lying with his eyes closed on the grid, with a slight frown on his face. Occasionally, paradoxically, a smile would flit across his lips. Sometimes it was impossible to know if he was sleeping or waking, thinking or dreaming.

Quaid waited.

Eventually Steve's eyes began to flicker under his lids, the unmistakable sign of dreaming. It was time, while the subject slept, to turn the wheel of the rack—

Steve woke with his hands cuffed together. He could see a bowl of water on a plate beside him; and a second bowl, full of luke-warm unsalted porridge, beside it. He ate and drank thankfully.

As he ate, two things registered. First, that the noise of his eating seemed very loud in his head; and second, that he felt a construction, a tightness, around his temples.

The photographs show Stephen clumsily reaching up to his head. A harness is strapped on to him, and locked in place. It clamps plugs deep into his ears, preventing any sound from getting in.

The photographs show puzzlement. Then anger. Then fear.

Steve was deaf.

All he could hear were the noises in his head. The clicking of his teeth. The slush and swallow of his palate. The sounds boomed between his ears like guns.

Tears sprang to his eyes. He kicked at the grid, not hearing the clatter of his heels on the metal bars. He screamed until his throat felt as if it was bleeding. He heard none of his cries.

Panic began in him.

The photographs showed its birth. His face was flushed. His eyes were wide, his teeth and gums exposed in a grimace. He looked like a frightened monkey.

All the familiar, childhood feelings swept over him. He remembered them like the faces of old enemies; the chittering limbs, the sweat, the nausea. In desperation he picked up the bowl of water and upturned it over his face. The shock of the cold water diverted his mind momentarily from the panic-ladder it was climbing. He lay back down on the grid, his body a board, and told himself to breathe deeply and evenly.

Relax, relax, relax, he said aloud.

In his head, he could hear his tongue clicking. He could hear his mucus too, moving sluggishly in the panic-constricted passages of his nose, blocking and unblocking in his ears. Now he could detect the low, soft hiss that waited under all the other noises. The sound of his mind—

It was like the white noise between stations on the radio, this was the same whine that came to fetch him under anaesthetic, the same noise that would sound in his ears on the borders of sleep.

His limbs still twitched nervously, and he was only half-aware of the way he wrestled with his handcuffs, indifferent to their edges scouring the skin at his wrists.

The photographs recorded all these reactions precisely. His war with hysteria: his pathetic attempts to keep the fears from resurfacing. His tears. His bloody wrists.

Eventually, exhaustion won over panic; as it had so often as a child. How many times had he fallen asleep with the salt-taste of tears in his nose and mouth, unable to fight any longer?

The exertion had heightened the pitch of his head-noises. Now, instead of a lullaby, his brain whistled and whooped him to sleep.

Oblivion was good.

Quaid was disappointed. It was clear from the speed of his response that Stephen Grace was going to break very soon indeed. In fact, he was as good as broken, only a few hours into the experiment. And Quaid had been relying on Stephen. After months of preparing the ground, it seemed that this subject was going to lose his mind without giving up a single clue.

One word, one miserable word was all Quaid needed. A little sign as to the nature of the experience. Or better still, something to suggest a solution, a healing totem, a prayer even. Surely some Saviour comes to the lips, as the personality is swept away in madness? There must be *something*.

Quaid waited like a carrion bird at the site of some atrocity, counting the minutes left to the expiring soul, hoping for a morsel.

Steve woke face down on the grid. The air was much staler now, and the metal bars bit into the flesh of his cheek. He was hot and uncomfortable.

He lay still, letting his eyes become accustomed to his surroundings again. The lines of the grid ran off in perfect perspective to meet the wall of the shaft. The simple network of crisscrossed bars struck him as pretty. Yes, pretty. He traced the lines back and forth, 'til he tired of the game. Bored, he rolled over onto his hack, feeling the grid vibrate under his body. Was it less stable now? It seemed to rock a little as he moved.

Hot and sweaty, Steve unbuttoned his shirt. There was sleep-spittle on his chin but he didn't care to wipe it off. What if he drooled? Who was to see?

He half pulled off his shirt, and using one foot, kicked his shoe off the other.

Shoe: lattice: fall. Sluggishly, his mind made the connection. He sat up. Oh poor shoe. His shoe would fall. It would slip between the bars and be lost. But no. It was finely balanced across two sides of a lattice-hole; he could still save it if he tried.

He reached for his poor, poor shoe, and his movement shifted the grid.

The shoe began to slip.

"Please," he begged it, "don't fall." He didn't want to lose his nice shoe, his pretty shoe. It mustn't fall. It mustn't fall.

As he stretched to snatch it, the shoe tipped, heel down, through the grid and fell into the darkness.

He let out a cry of loss that he couldn't hear.

Oh, if only he could listen to the shoe falling; to count the seconds of its descent. To hear it thud home at the bottom of the shaft. At least then he'd know how far he had to fall to his death.

He couldn't endure it any longer. He rolled over on to his stomach and thrust both arms through the grid, screaming:

"I'll go too! I'll go too!"

He couldn't bear waiting to fall, in the dark, in the whining, silence, he just wanted to follow his shoe down, down, down the dark shaft to extinction, and have the whole game finished once and for all.

"I'll go! I'll go! I'll go!" he shrieked. He pleaded with gravity.

Beneath him, the grid moved.

Something had broken. A pin, a chain, a rope that held the grid in position had snapped. He was no longer horizontal; already he was sliding across the bars as they tipped him off into the dark.

With shock he realized his limbs were no longer chained.

He would fall.

The man wanted him to fall. The bad man—what was his name? Quake? Quail? Quarrel—

Automatically he siezed the grid with both hands as it tipped even further over. Maybe he didn't want to fall after his shoe, after all? Maybe life, a little moment more of life, was worth holding on to—

The dark beyond the edge of the grid was so deep; and who could guess what lurked in it?

In his head the noises of his panic multiplied. The thumping of his bloody heart, the stutter of his mucus, the dry rasp of his palate. His palms, slick with sweat, were losing their grip. Gravity wanted him. It demanded its rights of his body's bulk: demanded that he fall. For a moment, glancing over his shoulder at the mouth that opened under him, he thought he saw monsters stirring below him. Ridiculous, loony things, crudely drawn, dark on dark. Vile graffiti leered up from his childhood and uncurled their claws to snatch at his legs.

"Mama," he said, as his hands failed him, and he was delivered into dread.

"*Mama.*"

That was the word. Quaid heard it plainly, in all its banality.

"Mama!"

By the time Steve hit the bottom of the shaft, he was past judging how far he'd fallen. The moment his hands let go of the grid, and he knew the dark would have him, his mind snapped. The animal self survived to relax his body, saving him all but minor injury on impact. The rest of his life, all but the simplest responses, were shattered, the pieces flung into the recesses of his memory.

When the light came, at last, he looked up at the person in the Mickey Mouse mask at the door, and smiled at him. It was a child's smile, one of thankfulness for his comical rescuer. He let the man take him by the ankles and haul him out of the big round room in which he was lying. His pants were wet, and he knew he'd dirtied himself in his sleep. Still, the Funny Mouse would kiss him better.

His head lolled on his shoulders as he was dragged out of the torture-chamber. On the floor beside his head was a shoe. And seven or eight feet above him was the grid from which he had fallen.

It meant nothing at all.

He let the Mouse sit him down in a bright room. He let the Mouse give him his ears back, though he didn't really want them. It was funny watching the world without sound, it made him laugh.

He drank some water, and ate some sweet cake.

He was tired. He wanted to sleep. He wanted his Mama. But the Mouse didn't seem to understand, so he cried, and kicked the table and threw the plates and cups on the floor. Then he ran into the next room, and threw all the papers he could find in the air. It was nice watching them flutter up and flutter down. Some of them fell face down, some face up. Some were covered with writing. Some were pictures. Horrid pictures. Pictures that made him feel very strange.

They were all pictures of dead people, every one of them. Some of the pictures were of little children, others were of grown-up children. They were lying down, or half-sitting, and there were big cuts in their faces and their bodies, cuts that showed a mess underneath, a mish-mash of shiny bits and oozy bits. And all around the dead people: black paint. Not in neat puddles, but splashed all around, and finger-marked, and hand-printed and very messy.

In three or four of the pictures the thing that made the cuts was still there. He knew the word for it.

Axe.

There was an axe in a lady's face buried almost to the handle. There was an axe in a man's leg, and another lying on the floor of a kitchen beside a dead baby.

This man collected pictures of dead people and axes, which Stevie thought was strange.

That was his last thought before the too-familiar scent of chloroform filled his head and he lost consciousness.

The sordid doorway smelt of old urine and fresh vomit. It was his own vomit; it was all over the front of his shirt. He tried to stand up, but his legs felt wobbly. It was very cold. His throat hurt.

Then he heard footsteps. It sounded like the Mouse was coming back. Maybe he'd take him home.

"Get up, son."

It wasn't the Mouse. It was a policeman.

"What are you doing down there? I said get up."

Bracing himself against the crumbling brick of the doorway Steve got to his feet. The policeman shone his torch at him.

"Jesus Christ," said the policeman, disgust written over his face. "You're in a right fucking state. Where do you live?"

Steve shook his head, staring down at his vomit-soaked shirt like a shamed schoolboy.

"What's your name?"

He couldn't quite remember.

"Name, lad?"

He was trying. If only the policeman wouldn't shout. "Come on, take a hold of yourself."

The words didn't make much sense. Steve could feel tears pricking the backs of his eyes.

"Home."

Now he was blubbering, sniffing snot, feeling utterly forsaken. He wanted to die: he wanted to lie down and die.

The policeman shook him.

"You high on something?" he demanded, pulling Steve into the glare of the streetlights and staring at his tear-stained face. "You'd better move on."

"Mama," said Steve, "I want my Mama."

The words changed the encounter entirely.

Suddenly the policeman found the spectacle more than disgusting; more than pitiful. This little bastard, with his bloodshot eyes and his dinner down his shirt was really getting on his nerves. Too much money, too much dirt in his veins, too little discipline.

"Mama" was the last straw. He punched Steve in the stomach, a neat, sharp, functional blow. Steve doubled up, whimpering.

"Shut up, son."

Another blow finished the job of crippling the child, and then he took a fistful of Steve's hair and pulled the little druggy's face up to meet his.

"You want to be a derelict, is that it?"

"No. No."

Steve didn't know what a derelict was; he just wanted to make the policeman like him.

"Please," he said, tears coming again, "take me home."

The policeman seemed confused. The kid hadn't, started fighting back and calling for civil rights, the way most of them did. That was the way they usually ended up: on the ground, bloody-nosed, calling for a social worker. This one just wept. The policeman began to get a bad feeling about the kid. Like he was mental or something. And he'd beaten the shit out of the little snot. Fuck it. Now he felt responsible. He took hold of Steve by the arm and bundled him across the road to his car.

"Get in."

"Take me—"

"I'll take you home, son. I'll take you home."

At the Night Hostel they searched Steve's clothes for some kind of identification, found none, then scoured his body for fleas, his hair for nits. The policeman left him then, which Steve was relieved about. He hadn't liked the man.

The people at the Hostel talked about him as though he wasn't in the room. Talked about how young he was; discussed his mental-age; his clothes; his appearance. Then they gave him a bar of soap and showed him the showers. He stood under the cold water for ten minutes and dried himself with a stained towel. He didn't shave, though they'd lent him a razor. he'd forgotten how to do it.

Then they gave him some old clothes, which he liked. They weren't such bad people, even if they did talk about him as though he wasn't there. One of them even smiled at him; a burly man with a grizzled beard. Smiled as he would at a dog.

They were odd clothes he was given. Either too big or too small. All colours: yellow socks, dirty white shirt, pin-stripe trousers that had been made for a glutton, a thread-bare sweater, heavy boots. He liked dressing up, putting on two vests and two pairs of socks when they weren't looking. He felt reassured with several thicknesses of cotton and wool wrapped around him.

Then they left him with a ticket for his bed in his hand, to wait for the dormitories to be unlocked. He was not impatient, like some of the men in the corridors with him. They yelled incoherently, many of them, their accusations laced with obscenities, and they spat at each other. It frightened him. All he wanted was to sleep. To lie down and sleep.

At eleven o'clock one of the warders unlocked the gate to the dormitory, and all the lost men tiled through to find themselves an iron bed for the night. The dormitory, which was large and badly-lit, stank of disinfectant and old people.

Avoiding the eyes and the flailing arms of the other derelicts, Steve found himself an ill-made bed, with one thin blanket tossed across it, and lay down to sleep. All around him men were coughing and muttering and weeping. One was saying his prayers as he lay, staring at the ceiling, on his grey pillow. Steve thought that was a good idea. So he said his own child's prayer.

"Gentle Jesus, meek and mild,
Look upon this little child,
Pity my —
What was the word?
Pity my — simplicity,
Suffer me to come to thee."

That made him feel better; and the sleep, a balm, was blue and deep.

Quaid sat in darkness. The terror was on him again, worse than ever.

His body was rigid with fear; so much so that he couldn't even get out of bed and snap on the light. Besides, what if this time, this time of all times, the terror was true? What if the axe-man was at the door in flesh and blood? Grinning like a loon at him, dancing like the devil at the top of the stairs, as Quaid had seen him, in dreams, dancing and grinning, grinning and dancing.

Nothing moved. No creak of the stair, no giggle in the shadows. It wasn't him, after all. Quaid would live 'til morning.

His body had relaxed a little now. He swung his legs out of bed and switched on the light. The room was indeed empty. The house was silent. Through the open door he could see the top of the stairs. There was no axe-man, of course.

Steve woke to shouting. It was still dark. He didn't know how long he'd been asleep, but his limbs no longer ached so badly. Elbows on his pillow, he half-sat up and stared down the dormitory to see what all the commotion was about. Four bed-rows down from his, two men were fighting. The bone of contention was by no means clear. They just grappled with each other like girls (it made Steve laugh to watch them), screeching and pulling each other's hair. By moonlight the blood on their faces and hands was black. One of them, the older of the two, was thrust back across his bed, screaming: "I will not go to the Finchley Road! You will not make me. Don't strike me! I'm not your man! I'm not!"

The other was beyond listening; he was too stupid, or too mad, to understand that the old man was begging to be left alone. Urged on by spectators on every side, the old man's assailant had taken off his shoe and was belabouring his victim with it. Steve could hear the crack, crack of his blows: heel on head. There were cheers accompanying each strike, and lessening cries from the old man.

Suddenly, the applause faltered, as somebody came into the dormitory. Steve couldn't see who it was; the mass of men crowded around the fight were between him and the door.

He did see the victor toss his shoe into the air however, with a final shout of "Fucker!"

The shoe.

Steve couldn't take his eyes off the shoe. It rose in the air, turning as it rose, then plummeted to the bare boards like a shot bird. Steve saw it clearly, more clearly than he'd seen anything in many days.

It landed not far from him.

It landed with a loud thud.

It landed on its side. As his shoe had landed. His shoe. The one he kicked off. On the grid. In the room. In the house. In Pilgrim Street.

Quaid woke with the same dream. Always the stairway. Always him looking down the tunnel of the stairs, while that ridiculous sight, half-joke, half-horror, tip-toed up towards him, a laugh on every step.

He'd never dreamt twice in one night before. He swung his hand out over the edge of the bed and fumbled for the bottle he kept there. In the dark he swigged from it, deeply.

Steve walked past the knot of angry men, not caring about their shouts or the old man's groans and curses. The warders were having a hard time dealing with the disturbance. It was the last time Old Man Crowley would be let in: he always invited violence. This had all the marks of a near-riot; it would take hours to settle them down again.

Nobody questioned Steve as he wandered down the corridor, through the gate, and into the vestibule of the Night Hostel. The swing doors were closed, but the night air, bitter before dawn, smelt refreshing as it seeped in.

The pokey reception office was empty, and through the door Steve could see the fire-extinguisher hanging on the wall. It was red and bright. Beside it was a long black hose, curled up on a red drum like a sleeping snake. Beside that, sitting in two brackets on the wall, was an axe.

A very pretty axe.

Stephen walked into the office. A little distance away he heard running feet, shouts, a whistle. But nobody came to interrupt Steve, as he made friends with the axe.

First he smiled at it.

The curve of the blade of the axe smiled back.

Then he touched it.

The axe seemed to like being touched. It was dusty, and hadn't been used in a long while. Too long. It wanted to be picked up, and stroked, and smiled at. Steve took it out of its brackets very gently, and slid it under his jacket to keep warm. Then he walked back out of the reception office, through the swing-doors and out to find his other shoe.

Quaid woke again.

It took Steve a very short time to orient himself. There was a spring in his step as he began to make his way to Pilgrim Street. He felt like a clown, dressed in so many bright colours, in such floppy trousers, such silly boots. He was a comical fellow, wasn't he? He made himself laugh, he was so comical.

The wind began to get into him, whipping him up into a frenzy as it scooted through his hair and made his eye-balls as cold as two lumps of ice in his sockets.

He began to run, skip, dance, cavort through the streets, white under the lights, dark in between. Now you see me, now you don't. Now you see me, now you—

Quaid hadn't been woken by the dream this time. This time he had heard a noise. Definitely a noise.

The moon had risen high enough to throw its beams through the window, through the door and on to the top of the stairs. There was no need to put on the light. All he needed to see, he could see. The top of the stairs were empty, as ever.

Then the bottom stair creaked, a tiny noise as though a breath had landed on it.

Quaid knew dread then.

Another creak, as it came up the stairs towards him, the ridiculous dream. It had to be a dream. After all, he knew no clowns, no axe-killers. So how could that absurd image, the same image that woke him night after night, be anything but a dream?

Yet, perhaps there were some dreams so preposterous they could only be true.

No clowns, he said to himself, as he stood watching the door, and the stairway, and the spotlight of the moon. Quaid knew only fragile minds, so weak they couldn't give him a clue to the nature, to the origin, or to the cure for the panic that now held him in thrall. All they did was break, crumble into dust, when faced with the slightest sign of the dread at the heart of life.

He knew no clowns, never had, never would.

Then it appeared; the face of a fool. Pale to whiteness in the light of the moon, its young features bruised, unshaven and puffy, its smile open like a child's smile. It had bitten its lip in its excitement. Blood was smeared across its lower jaw, and its gums were almost black with blood. Still it was a clown. Indisputably a clown even to its ill-fitting clothes, so incongruous, so pathetic.

Only the axe didn't quite match the smile.

It caught the moonlight as the maniac made small,

chopping motions with it, his tiny black eyes glinting with anticipation of the fun ahead.

Almost at the top of the stairs, he stopped, his smile not faltering for a moment as he gazed at Quaid's terror.

Quaid's legs gave out, and he stumbled to his knees.

The clown climbed another stair, skipping as he did so, his glittering eyes fixed on Quaid, filled with a sort of benign malice. The axe rocked back and forth in his white hands, in a petite version of the killing stroke.

Quaid knew him.

It was his pupil: his guinea-pig, transformed into the image of his own dread.

Him. Of all men. Him. The deaf boy.

The skipping was bigger now, and the clown was making a deep-throated noise, like the call of some fantastical bird. The axe was describing wider and wider sweeps in the air, each more lethal than the last.

"Stephen," said Quaid.

The name meant nothing to Steve. All he saw was the mouth opening. The mouth closing. Perhaps a sound came out: perhaps not. It was irrelevant to him.

The throat of the clown gave out a screech, and the axe swung up over his head, two-handed. At the same moment the merry little dance became a run, as the axeman leapt the last two stairs and ran into the bedroom, full into the spotlight.

Quaid's body half turned to avoid the killing blow, but not quickly or elegantly enough. The blade slit the air and sliced through the back of Quaid's arm, sheeting off most of his triceps, shattering his humerus and opening the flesh of his lower arm in a gash that just missed his artery.

Quaid's scream could have been heard ten houses away, except that those houses were rubble. There was nobody to hear. Nobody to come and drag the clown off him.

The axe, eager to be about its business, was hacking at

Quaid's thigh now, as though it was chopping a log. Yawning wounds four or five inches deep exposed the shiny steak of the philosopher's muscle, the bone, the marrow. With each stroke the clown would tug at the axe to pull it out, and Quaid's body would jerk like a puppet.

Quaid screamed. Quaid begged. Quaid cajoled.

The clown didn't hear a word.

All he heard was the noise in his head: the whistles, the whoops, the howls, the hums. He had taken refuge where no rational argument, no threat, would ever fetch him out again. Where the thump of his heart was law, and the whine of his blood was music.

How he danced, this deaf-boy, danced like a loon to see his tormentor gaping like a fish, the depravity of his intellect silenced forever. How the blood spurted! How it gushed and fountained!

The little clown laughed to see such fun. There was a night's entertainment to be had here, he thought. The axe was his friend forever, keen and wise. It could cut, and cross-cut, it could slice and amputate, yet still they could keep this man alive, if they were cunning enough, alive for a long, long while.

Steve was happy as a lamb. They had the rest of the night ahead of them, and all the music he could possibly want was sounding in his head.

And Quaid knew, meeting the clown's vacant stare through an air turned bloody, that there was worse in the world than dread. Worse than death itself.

There was pain without hope of healing. There was life that refused to end, long after the mind had begged the body to cease. And worst, there were dreams come true.

COMING TO GRIEF

CLIVE BARKER

Miriam had not taken the shortcut along the rim of the quarry for almost eighteen years. Eighteen years of another life, quite unlike the life she'd lived in this all but forgotten city. She'd left Liverpool to taste the world: to grow; to prosper; to learn to live; and, by God, hadn't she done just that? From the naive and frightened nineteen-year-old she had been when she had last set foot on the quarry path, she had blossomed into a wholly sophisticated woman of the world. Her husband idolized her; her daughter grew more like her with every year; she was universally adored.

Yet now, as she stepped onto the ill-bred gravel path that skirted the chasm of the quarry, she felt as though a wound had opened in her heel and that hard-won poise and self-reliance were draining out of her and running away into the dark; as though she'd never left her native city, never grown wiser with experience. She felt no more prepared to face this hundred-yard stretch of walled walkway than she had been at nineteen. The same doubts, the same imagined horrors that had always haunted her on this spot, clung now to the inside of her brainpan and whispered about the certainty of secrets. They still lay in wait here, idiot fears concocted of street-corner gossip and childish superstition. Even now the old myths came running back to embrace her. Tales of hook- handed men, and secret lovers slaughtered in the act of love; a dozen rumored atrocities that, to her burgeoning and overheated imagination, had always had their source, their epicenter, here: on the Bogey-Walk.

That's what they'd called it; and that was what it would always be to her: the Bogey-Walk. Instead of losing its potency with the passage of the years, it had grown gross. It had prospered as she had prospered; it had found its vocation as she had done. Of course, she had grown into contentment, and perhaps that weakened her. But it, oh, *it* had merely fed on its own frustration and become encrusted with desire to take her for itself. Maybe, as time had passed, it had fed a little to keep its strength up: but it needed, in its immutable heart, only the certainty of its final victory to stay alive. Of this she was suddenly and incontestably certain: that the battles she had fought with her own weakness were not over. They had scarcely begun.

She attempted to advance a few yards along the Walk but faltered and stopped, the so-familiar panic turning her feet to lead weights. The night was not soundless. A jet droned over, a longing roar in the darkness; a mother called her child in from the street. But here, on the Walk itself, signs of life were a world away and could not comfort her. Cursing her own vulnerability, she turned back the way she'd come and traipsed home through the warm drizzle by a more roundabout route.

Grief, she half reasoned, had battened upon her and sapped her will to fight. In two days' time perhaps, when her mother's funeral was over and the sudden loss was more manageable, then she would see the future plainly and that pathway would fall into its proper perspective. She'd recognize the Bogey-Walk as the excrement-ridden, weed-lined gravel path that it was. Meanwhile she'd get wetter than she needed taking the safe road home.

The quarry was not in itself such a terrifying spot; nor, to any but her, was the path along its rim. There'd been no murders there that she knew of, no rapes or muggings committed along that sordid little track. It was a public footpath, no less and no more: a poorly kept, poorly illuminated walkway around the edge of what had once been a productive quarry and was now the communal rubbish-tip. The wall that kept the walkers from falling a hundred feet to their deaths below was built of plain red brick. It was eight feet high, so that nobody could even see the depth on the other side, and was lined with pieces of broken milk bottles set in concrete, to dissuade anyone from scrambling up onto it. The path itself had once been tarmac, but subsidence had opened cracks in it, and the Council, instead of resurfacing, had seen fit simply to dust it with loose gravel. It was seldom, if ever, weeded. Stinging nettles grew to child height in the meager dirt at the bottom of the wall, as did a sickly scented flower whose name she did not know but which, at the height of summer, was a Mecca to wasps. And that—wall, gravel, and weeds—was the sum of the place.

In dreams, however, she'd scaled that wall—her palms magically immune to the pricking glass—and in those vertiginous adventures she'd peer down and down the black, sheer cliff of the quarry into its dark heart. It was impenetrable, the gloom at the bottom, but she knew that there was a lake of green and brackish water somewhere below. It could be seen, that choked pool of filth, from the other side of the quarry; from the safe side. That's how she knew it was there, in her dreams. And she knew, too, walking on the unpiercing glass, tempting gravity and providence alike, that the prodigy of malice that lived on the cliff face would have seen her and would be climbing, even now, hand over clawed hand, up the steep side toward her. But in those dreams she always woke up before the nameless beast caught hold of her dancing feet, and the exhilaration of her escape would heal the fear; at least until the next time she dreamed.

The opposite end of the quarry, far from the sheer wall and the pool, had always been safe. Abandoned diggings and blastings had left a litter of boulders of Piranesian magnitude, in whose crevices she had often played as a child. There was no danger here: just a playground of tunnels. It seemed miles and miles (at least to her child's eye) across the wasteland to the rainwater lake and the tiny line of red brick wall that beetled along the top of the cliff. Though there had been days, she remembered, even in the safety of the sun, when she would catch sight of something the color of the rock itself stretching its back on the warm face of the quarry, clinging to the cliff in a tireless and predatory pose not a dozen yards beneath the wall. Then, as her child's eyes narrowed to try to make sense of its anatomy, it would sense her gaze and freeze itself into a perfect copy of the stone.

Stone. Cold stone. Thinking about absence, about the disguise required by a thing that wished not to be seen, she turned into her mother's road. As she selected the house key, it occurred to her, absurdly, that perhaps Veronica was not dead: simply perfectly camouflaged in the house somewhere, pressed against the wall or at the mantelpiece; unseen but seeing. Perhaps then visible ghosts were simply inept chameleons: the rest had the trick of concealment down pat. It was a foolish, fruitless train of thought, and she chided herself for entertaining it. Tomorrow, or the day after, such thoughts would again seem as alien as the lost world in which she was presently stranded. So thinking, she stepped indoors.

The house did not distress her; it simply reawakened a sense of tedium her busy, clever life had put aside. The task of dividing, discarding, and packing the remnants of her mother's life was slow and repetitive. The rest—the loss, the remorse, the bitterness—were so many thoughts for another day. There was sufficient to do as it was, without mourning. Certainly the empty rooms held memories; but they were all pleasant enough to be happily recalled, yet not so exquisite as to be wished into being again. Her feelings, moving around the deserted house, could only be defined by what she no longer saw or felt: *not* her mother's face; *not* the chiding voice, the preventing hand; just an unknowable nothing that was the space where life used to be.

In Hong Kong, she thought, Boyd would be on duty, and the sun would be blazing hot, the streets thronged with people. Though she hated to go out at midday, when the city was so crowded, today she would have welcomed the discomfort. It was tiresome sitting in the dusty bedroom, carefully sorting and folding the scented linen from the chest of drawers. She wanted life, even if it was insistent and oppressive. She longed for the smell of the streets to be piercing her nostrils, and the heat to be beating on her head. No matter, she thought, soon done.

Soon done. Ah, there was a guilt there: the ticking off of the days until the funeral, the pacing out of her mother's ritual removal from the world. Another seventy-two hours and the whole business would be done with, and she would be flying back to life.

As she went about her daughterly duties, she left every light burning in the house. It was more convenient to do so, she told herself, with all the to-ing and fro-ing the job required. Besides, the late November days were short and dismal, and the work was dispiriting enough without having to labor in a perpetual dusk.

Organizing the disposal of personal items was taking the longest time. Her mother had acquired a sizable wardrobe, all of which had to be sorted through: the pockets emptied, the jewelry removed from the collars. She sealed up the bulk of the clothes in black plastic bags, to be collected by a local charity shop the following day, keeping only a fur wrap and a gown for herself. Then she selected a few of her mother's favorite possessions to give to close friends after the funeral: a leather handbag; some china cups and saucers; a herd of ivory elephants that had belonged... she had forgotten who they had belonged to. Some relative, long gone.

Once the clothes and bric-a-brac had been organized, she turned her attention to the mail, sorting the outstanding bills into one pile and the personal correspondence, whether recent or remote, into another. Each letter, however old or difficult to follow, she read carefully. Most she dispatched to the small fire she had lit in the living-room grate. It was soon a cave of bat-wing ashes; black and veined with burned words. Once only, a letter found tears in her: a note, written in her father's gossamer hand, which awakened agonies of regret for the wasted years of antagonism between them. There were photographs among the leaves, too; most as frozen as Alaska: arid, fruitless territory. Some, however, catching a true moment between the poses, were as fresh as yesterday, and a din of voices spilled from the aged image:

—*Wait! Not yet! I'm not ready!*

—*Daddy! Where's Daddy? We must have Daddy in this one!*

—*He's tickling me!*

Laughter pealed off these images; their fixed joy parodied the truth of deterioration and annihilation whose proof was borne by the empty house.

—*Wait!*

—*Not yet!*

—*Daddy!*

She could hardly bear to look at some of them. She burned first the ones that hurt the most.

—*Wait!*, someone shouted. Herself, perhaps, a child in the arms of the past. *Wait!*

But the pictures cracked in the heart of the fire, then browned and burst with blue flame, and the moment—

—*Wait!*

—the moment went the way of all the moments that had surrounded the instant that the camera had fixed, gone away forever like fathers and mothers and, in time, daughters too.

She retired to bed at three-fifteen A.M., the bulk of her self-assigned chores done for the day. Her mother would have applauded her efficiency, she suspected. How ironic that Miriam, the daughter who had never been daughterly enough, who had always wanted the world instead of being content to stay at home, was now being as meticulous as any parent could have possibly wished. Here she was, cleaning away a whole history; consigning the leavings of a life to the fire, scouring the

house more thoroughly than her mother had ever done.

A little after three-thirty, having mentally arranged the business of the following day, she drained the last of the half tumbler of whiskey she'd been sipping all evening and sank, almost immediately, into sleep.

She dreamed nothing. Her mind was clear. As clear as darkness is clear, as emptiness is clear; not even Boyd's face, or his body (she often dreamed of his chest, of the fine pattern of hair on his stomach) crept into her head to pollute the featureless bliss.

It was raining when she awoke. Her first thought was: *Where am I?*

Her second thought was: *Is today the funeral, or tomorrow?*

Her third thought was: *In two days I'll be back with Boyd. The sun will be shining. I'll forget all of this.*

For today, however, there was more unappetizing work ahead. The funeral was not until tomorrow, which was Wednesday. Today the business was mundane: checking the cremation arrangements with Beckett and Dawes, writing notes of thanks for the many letters of condolence she'd received, a dozen other minor duties. In the afternoon she would visit Mrs. Furness, a friend of her mother's who was now too crippled with arthritis to attend the funeral. She would give the old lady that leather handbag, as a keepsake. In the evening it would be again the same, sorry business of sorting through her mother's belongings and organizing their redistribution. There was so much to give to the needy—or the greedy—whichever asked first. She didn't care who took the stuff, as long as the job was finished soon.

About mid-morning, the telephone rang. It was the first noise she'd heard in the house since waking that she hadn't made herself, and it startled her. She lifted the receiver, and a warm word was spoken in her ear: her name.

"Miriam?"

"Yes. Who is this?"

"Oh, love, you sound absolutely washed out. It's Judy, sweetheart; Judy Cusack."

"Judy?"

The very name was a smile.

"Don't you remember?"

"Of course I remember. How lovely to hear your voice."

"I didn't ring any earlier. I thought you'd have so much on your hands. I'm so sorry, pet, about your mother. It must have been a blow. My dad died the year before last. It really knocked me sideways."

Vaguely Miriam could picture Judy's father, a slender, elegant man who'd smiled once in a while and had said very little.

"He'd been very ill. It was a blessing, really. God, I never thought I'd hear myself say that. Funny, isn't it?"

Judy's voice had scarcely changed at all; she frothed with

pleasure the way she always had, the body Miriam saw in her mind's eye was still rounded, with a lingering puppy fat. Eighteen years ago they had been the best of friends, soul mates; and for a moment, exchanging pleasantries with that breezy voice, it was as though the time between this conversation and their last had shrunk to hours.

"It's so good to hear your voice," said Miriam.

It *was* good. It was the past speaking, but it was a good past, a sunlit past. She had almost forgotten, in the toil of this autopsy she was busy with, how fine some memories could be.

"I heard from the people next door about your coming home," Judy said, "but I was of two minds whether to call. I know it must be a very difficult time for you. So sad and all."

"Not really," Miriam said.

The plain truth sneaked out without her meaning to say it; but there it was now, said. It *wasn't* a sad time. It was a drudge, it was a limbo, but she wasn't holding a flood of sorrows in abeyance. She saw that now, and her heart lightened with the simplicity of the confession. Judy offered no reproof, only an invitation.

"Are you feeling well enough to come over for a drink?"

"I've still got a lot of sorting to do."

"I promise we won't talk about old times," Judy said. "Not one word. I couldn't bear it; it makes me feel antiquated." She laughed.

Miriam laughed with her. "Yes," she said. "I'd love to come..."

"Good. It's a bind, isn't it, when you're an only child, and It's all your responsibility. Sometimes you really think there's no end to it."

"It's crossed my mind," Miriam replied.

"When it's all over, you'll wonder what the fuss was about," Judy said. "I coped with Dad's funeral, though at the time I thought I was going to fall apart."

"You didn't have to handle it alone, did you?" Miriam asked. "What about…" She wanted to name Judy's husband; she recalled her mother writing to her about Judy's late—and if she remembered correctly, scandalous—marriage. But she couldn't remember the groom's name.

"Donald?" Judy prompted her.

"Donald."

"Separated, pet. we've been separated two and a half years."

"Oh, I'm sorry."

"I'm not." The answer came back in a flash. "It's a long story. I'll tell you about it this evening. About seven?"

"Could we make it a little later? I've got so much to do. Is eight all right?"

"Anytime, love, don't rush yourself. I'll expect you when I see you; we'll leave it at that."

"Fine. And thanks for ringing."

"I've been itching to call since I heard you were back. It's not often you get a chance to see old friends, is it?"

A few minutes shy of noon, Miriam faced what she expected to be the most debilitating of her duties. Though she wouldn't confess it to herself, she felt a tremor of disgust as she parked outside the funeral home. There was a dull, stale taste at the back of her throat, and her eyes seemed spoiled with grit. She frankly had no wish to see her mother again, not now that they couldn't talk, and yet when the urbane Mr. Beckett had said to her on the phone, "You will want to view the deceased?" she had replied, "Of course," as though the request had been on the tip of her tongue all along.

And what was there to fear? Veronica Blessed was dead; she'd died peacefully in her sleep. But Miriam found that a phrase, a random phrase that she remembered from school, had crept into the back of her head that morning and she couldn't rid herself of it:

"Everyone dies because they run out of breath."

That thought was there now, as she looked at Mr. Beckett, and the paper lilies and the scuffed corner of his desk. To run out of breath, to choke on a tongue, to suffocate under a blanket. She had known all those fears when she was young, and now they came back to her in Mr. Beckett's office and held her hand. One of them leaned over and whispered maliciously in her ear: Suppose one day you simply forget to breathe? Black face, tongue bitten off.

Was that what made her throat so dry? The thought that Mama, Veronica, Mrs. Blessed, widow of Harold Blessed, now deceased, would be lying on silk with her face as black as the Earl of Hell's riding boots? Vile notion: vile, ridiculous notion.

But they kept coming, these unwelcome ideas, one quick upon the heels of another. Most she could trace back to childhood; absurd, irrelevant images floating up from her past like squid to the sun.

The Levitation Game, a favorite school pastime, came to mind: six girls ranged around a seventh, trying to lift her up with one finger apiece. And the accompanying ceremony:

"She looks *pale*," says the girl at the head.

"She *is* pale."

"She *is* pale."

"She *is* pale."

"She *is* pale."

"She *is* pale," the attendants answer by rote, counterclockwise.

"She looks *ill*," the high priestess announces.

"She *is* ill."

"She *is* ill."

"She *is* ill."

"She *is* ill."

"She *is* ill," the others reply.

"She looks *dead*—"

She is—

There'd been a murder, too, when she was only six, two streets down from where they'd lived. The body had been wedged behind the front door—she'd heard Mrs. Furness tell all to her mother—and it was so softened by putrefaction that when the police forced the door open it had concertinaed into a bundle that proved impossible to unglue. Sitting now beside the scentless lilies, Miriam could smell the day she'd stood, hand in her mother's hand, listening to the women talk of murder. Crime, come to think of it, had been a favorite subject of Mrs. Furness. Had it been through her good offices that Miriam had first learned that her nightmares of the Bogey-Walk had their counterpart in the adult world?

Miriam smiled, thinking of the women casually debating slaughter as they stood in the sun. Mr. Beckett seemed not to notice her smile; or, more likely, was well prepared for any manifestation of grief, however bizarre. Perhaps mourners came in here and threw off all their clothes in their anguish or wet their pants. She looked at him more closely, this young man who had made a profession of bereavement. He was not unattractive, she thought. He was an inch or two shorter than she, but height didn't matter in bed; and moving coffins around would put some muscle on a body, wouldn't it?

Listen *to yourself*, she thought, pulling herself up short. *What are you contemplating?*

Mr. Beckett plucked at his pale ginger mustache and offered a look of practiced condolence to Miriam. She saw his charm—what meager supply there was—vanish in that one look.

He seemed to be waiting for some cue from her; she wondered what. At last he said:

"Shall we go through to the Chapel of Rest, or shall we discuss the business first?"

Ah, *that* was it. Better to get the farewells over with, she thought. He could wait a while longer for his money. "I'd like to see my mother," she said.

"Of course you would," he replied, nodding as though he'd known all along that she wanted to view the body; as if he were somehow completely conversant with her most intimate workings. She resented his fake familiarity but made no sign of it.

He stood up and ushered her through the glass-paneled door and into a corridor flanked by vases of flowers. They, like the lilies on his desk, were artificial. The scent she could smell was that of floor polish, not blossoms; no bee had hope of succor here, unless there was nectar to be taken from the dead.

Mr. Beckett halted at one of the doors, turned the handle, and ushered Miriam ahead of him. This was it, then: face-to-face at last. *Smile, Mother, Miriam's home.* She entered the room. Two candles burned on a small table against the far wall, and there was a further abundance of artificial flowers, their fake fecundity more distasteful here than ever.

The room was small. Space enough for a coffin, a chair, a table, bearing the candles, and one or two living souls.

"Shall I leave you with your mother?" Mr. Beckett asked.

"No," she said with more urgency and more volume than the tiny room could accommodate. The candles coughed lightly at her indiscretion. More softly she said, "I would prefer you to stay, if you don't mind."

"Of course," Mr. Beckett dutifully replied.

She wondered briefly how many people, at this juncture, chose to keep their vigil unaccompanied. It would be an interesting statistic, she thought, her mind dividing into disinterested observer and frightened participant. How many mourners, faced with the dear dead, asked for company, however anonymous, rather than be left alone with a face they had known a lifetime?

Taking a deep breath, she stepped toward the coffin, and

there, snoozing on a sheet of pale cream cloth in this narrow, high-sided bed, was her mother. What a foolish and neglectful place to fall asleep in, she thought; and in your favorite dress. So unlike you, Mother, to be so impractical. Her face had been tastefully rouged, and her hair recently brushed, although not in a style she had favored. Miriam felt no horror at seeing her like this; just a sharp thrill of recognition and the instinct, barely suppressed, to reach into the coffin and shake her mother awake.

Mother, I'm here. It's Miriam.

Wake up.

At the thought of that, Miriam felt her cheeks flush, and hot tears well up in her eyes. The tiny room was abruptly a single sheet of watery light; the candles two bright eyes. "Mama," she said once.

Mr. Beckett, clearly long inured to such spectacles, said nothing, but Miriam was acutely aware of his presence behind her and wished she'd asked him to leave. She took hold of the side of the coffin to steady herself, while the tears dripped off her cheeks and fell into the folds of her mother's dress.

So this was death's house; this was its shape and nature. Its etiquette was perfect. At its visitation there had been no violence; only a profound and changeless calm that denied the need for further show of affection.

Her mother, she realized, didn't require her any longer; it was as simple as that. Her first and final rejection. *Thank you,* said that cold, discrete body, *but I have no further need of you. Thank you for your concern, but you may go.*

She stared at Veronica's well-dressed corpse through a haze of unhappiness, not hoping to wake her mother now, not hoping even to make sense of the sight. Then she said, "Thank you," very quietly. The words were for her mother; but Mr. Beckett, taking Miriam's arm as she turned to go, took it for himself.

"It's no trouble," he replied. "Really."

Miriam blew her nose and tasted the tears. The duty was done. Time now for business. She drank weak tea with Beckett and finalized the financial arrangements, watching for him to smile once, to break his covenant with sympathy. He didn't. The interview was conducted with indecent reverence, and by the time he ushered her out into the cold afternoon, she had grown to despise him.

She drove home without thinking, her mind not blank with the loss but with the exhaustion of having wept. It was not a conscious decision that made her choose the route back to the house that led alongside the quarry. But as she turned into the street that ran past her old playground, she realized that some part of her wanted—perhaps even *needed*—a confrontation with the Bogey-Walk.

She parked the car at the safe end of the quarry, a short walk from the path itself, and got out. The wire gates she'd scrambled through as a child were locked, but a hole had been torn in the wire, as ever. Doubtless the quarry was still a playground. New wire, new gates; but the same games. She couldn't resist ducking through the gap, though her coat snagged in a hook of wire as she did so. Inside, little seemed to have changed. The same chaos of boulders, steps and plateaus, litter, weeds and puddles, lost and broken toys, bicycle parts. She thrust her fists into her coat pockets and ambled through the rubble of childhood, keeping her eyes fixed on her feet, easily finding again the familiar routes between the stones.

She would never get lost here. In the dark—in death, even, as a ghost—she would be certain of her steps. Finally she located the spot she'd always loved the best and, standing in the lee of a great stone, raised her head to look at the cliff across the quarry. From this distance the Walk was barely visible, but she scanned its length meticulously. The quarry face looked less imposing than she'd remembered; less majestic. The intervening years had shown her more perilous heights, more tremendous depths. And yet she still felt her bowels contracting as though an octopus had been sewn up at the crux of her body, and she knew that the child in her, insusceptible to reason, was searching the cliff for a sign, however negligible, of the Walk's haunter. The twitch of a stone-colored limb, perhaps, as it kept its relentless vigil; the flicker of a terrible eye.

But she could see nothing.

Almost ashamed of her fears, she retraced her steps through the canyon of stones, slipped through the gate like an errant child, and returned to the car.

The Bogey-Walk was *safe*. Of course it was safe. It held no horrors, and never had. The sun was valiantly trying to share her exhilaration now, forcing wan and heatless beams through the rain clouds. The wind was at her side, smelling of the river. Grief was a memory.

She would go to the Walk now, she decided, and give herself time to savor each fearless step she took along it, jubilating in her victory over history. She drove around the side of the quarry and slammed the car door with a smile on her face as she climbed the three steps that led off the pavement onto the footpath itself.

The shadow of the brick wall fell across the Walk, of course; and its length was darker than the street behind her. But nothing could sour her confidence. She walked from one end of the weed-clogged corridor to the other without incident, her whole body high with the sheer ease of it. *How could I ever have feared this?* she asked herself as she turned and began the journey to the waiting car.

This time, as she walked, she allowed herself to think back on the specifics of her childhood nightmares. There had been a place—halfway along the Walk and therefore at the greatest distance from help—that had been the high-water mark of her terror. That particular spot—that forbidden few yards that, to the unseeing eye, were no different from every other yard along the Walk—was the place the thing in the quarry would choose to pounce when her last moments came. That was its killing ground, its sacrificial grove, marked, she had fervently believed, with blood of countless other children.

Even as the taste of that memory returned to her, she approached the point. The signs that had marked the place were still to be seen: an arrangement of five discolored bricks; a crack in the cement that had been minuscule eighteen years ago and had grown larger. The spot was as recognizable as ever; but it had lost its potency. It was just another few of a hundred identical yards, and she bypassed the spot without the contentment on her face faltering for more than an instant. She didn't even glance behind her.

The wall of the Bogey-Walk was old. It had been built a decade before Miriam was born, by men who had known their craft indifferently well. Erosion had eaten at the quarry face beneath the teetering brick, unseen by Council inspectors and safety officials from the Department of the Environment; in places the rain-sodden sandstone had crumbled and fallen away. Here and there, the bricks were unsupported across as much as half their breadth. They hung over the abyss of the quarry while rain and wind and gravity ate at the crumbling mortar that kept them united.

Miriam saw none of this. She would have had to have waited a while before she heard the uneasy grinding of the bricks as they leaned out against the air, waiting, aching, begging to fall. As it was, she went away, elated, certain that she'd sloughed off her terrors forever.

That evening she saw Judy.

Judy had never been beautiful; there had always been an excess in her features: her eyes too big, her mouth too broad. Yet now, in her mid-thirties, she was radiant. It was a sexual bloom, certainly, and one that might wither and die prematurely, but the woman who met Miriam at the front door was in her prime.

They talked through the evening about the years they'd been apart— despite their contract not to discuss the past— exchanging tales of their defeats and their successes. Miriam found Judy's company enchanting; she was immediately comfortable with this bright, happy woman. Even the subject of her separation from Donald didn't inhibit her flow.

"It's not *verboten* to talk about old husbands, pet; It's just a bit boring. I mean, he wasn't a bad sort."

"Are you divorcing him?"

"I suppose so; if I have a moment. These things take months, you know. Besides, I'm a Libra; I can never make up my mind what I want." She paused. "Well," she said with a half-secret smile, "That's not altogether true."

"Was he unfaithful?"

"Unfaithful?" She laughed. "That's a word I haven't heard in a long time."

Miriam blushed a little. Was life really so backward in the colonies, where adultery was not yet compulsory?

"He screwed around," said Judy. "That's the simple truth of it. But then, so did I."

She laughed again, and this time Miriam joined in with the laughter, not quite certain of the joke. "How did you find out?"

"I found out when *he* found out."

"I don't understand."

"It was all so obvious, it sounds like a farce when I tell it;

but he found a letter, you see, from someone I'd been with. Nobody particularly important to me—just a casual friend, really. Anyway, he was *triumphant*; I mean, he *really* crowed about it, said he'd had more affairs than I had. Treated it all like some sort of competition—who could cheat the most often and with whom." She paused; the same mischievous smile appeared again. "As it was, when we put our cards on the table, I was doing rather better than he was. That *really* pissed him off."

"So you separated?"

"There didn't seem to be much point in staying together; we didn't have any kids. And there wasn't any love lost between us. There never really had been. The house was in his name, but he let me have it."

"So you won the competition?"

"I suppose I did. But then, I had a hidden advantage."

"What?"

"The other man in my life was a woman," Judy said, "and poor Donald couldn't handle that at all. He more or less threw in the towel as soon as he found out. Told me he realized he'd never understood me and that we were better apart." She looked up at Miriam and only now saw the effect her statement had had. "Oh," she said, "I'm sorry. I just opened my mouth and put my foot in it."

"No," said Miriam, "It's me. I'd never thought of you..."

"...as a Lesbian? Oh, I think I've always known it, right back to school days. Writing love letters to the games mistress."

"We all did that," Miriam reminded her.

"Some of us meant it more seriously than others." Judy smiled.

"And where's Donald now?"

"Oh, somewhere in the Middle East, last I heard. I'd like him to write to me, just to tell me he's well. But he won't. His pride wouldn't let him. It's a pity. We might have been good friends if we hadn't been husband and wife."

That seemed to be all there was to say on the subject; or all Judy wanted to say.

"Shall I go and make some coffee?" she suggested, and went through to the kitchen, leaving Miriam to toy with the cat and her thoughts. Neither were particularly fleet-footed that night.

"I'd like to go to your mum's funeral," Judy called through from the kitchen. "Would you mind?"

"Of course not."

"I didn't know her well, but I used to see her out shopping. She always looked so *smart*."

"She was," Miriam said. Then: "Why don't you come in the lead car with me?"

"I'm not a relative."

"I'd like you to." The cat turned over in its sleep and presented its winter-furred belly to Miriam's comforting fingers. "Please."

"Then thank you. I will."

They spent the remaining hour and a half drinking coffee, and then whiskey, and then more whiskey, and talking about Hong Kong and their parents, and finally about memory. Or rather, about the irrational nature of memory; how their minds had selected such odd details to fix events while neglecting others more apparently significant: the smell in the air when the words of affection were spoken, not the words themselves; the color of a lover's shoes, but not of their eyes.

At last, way after midnight, they parted.

"Come to the house about eleven," Miriam said. "The cars are leaving at about a quarter past."

"Right. I'll see you tomorrow, then."

"Today," Miriam pointed out.

"That's right, today. Take care driving, love, It's a foul night."

The night *was* breezy; the car radio reported gale-force winds in the Irish Sea. She drove home cautiously through the empty streets, the same gusts that buffeted the car raising leaves from the dead and whirling them up into the glare of the headlamps. In Hong Kong, she thought, there would still be plenty of life in the streets this time of night. Here? Just sleep-darkened houses, closed curtains, locked doors. As she drove, she mentally followed her footsteps through the day and the three encounters that had marked it out. With her mother, with Judy, and with the Bogey-Walk. By the time she'd done her thinking, she was home.

Sleep came fitfully through the blustery night, punctuated by dustbin lids whipped off by vicious licks of wind, the rain, and the scratching of sycamore branches against the windows.

The next day was Wednesday, December 1, and the rain had turned to sleet by dawn.

The funeral was not insufferable. It was at best a functional farewell to someone Miriam had once known and now had lost sight of; at worst, its passionless solemnity and well-oiled ritual smacked of frigidity, ending as a conveyor belt took the coffin through a pair of lilac curtains to the furnace and the chimney beyond. Miriam could not help but imagine the interior of the coffin as it shuddered through the theatrical divide of the curtains; could not help but visualize the way her mother's body shook with each tiny jerk of her box toward the incinerator. The thought, though self-inflicted, was all but unbearable. She had to dig her fingernails into the flesh of her palm simply to prevent herself from standing up and demanding a halt to the proceedings: to have the lid prised off the coffin, to fumble in the shroud, and to pluck that blank body up in her arms one more time; lovingly, adoringly thanking her. That moment was the worst; she held herself in check until the curtains closed, and then it was over.

As partings went, it was perfunctory, but it clung, in its plain way, to a measure of dignity.

The wind was biting as they left the tiny red brick chapel of the crematorium, the mourners already dividing to their cars with murmurs of thanks and faint looks of embarrassment. There were flakes of snow in the wind: too large and too wet to amount to much as they flopped to the ground, but rendering the glum surroundings yet more inhospitable. Miriam's teeth ached in her head; and the ache was spreading up her nose to her eyes.

Judy hooked her arm.

"We must get together again, love, before you leave."

Miriam nodded. Leaving was less than twenty-four hours away, and tonight, as a foretaste of liberty, Boyd would ring. He'd promised to do so, and he was sweetly reliable. She knew she'd be able to smell the heat of the street down the telephone wire.

"Tonight..." Miriam suggested to Judy. "Come round to the house tonight."

"Are you sure? Isn't it a bit of a trial being there?"

"Not really. Not now."

Not now. Veronica had gone, once and for all. The house was not a home any longer.

I've still got a lot of cleaning up to do," Miriam said. "I want to hand it over to the agents with all Mother's belongings dealt with. I don't like the thought of strangers going through her stuff."

Judy murmured her agreement.

"I'll help, then," she said. "If you don't think I'll get in the way."

"A working evening?"

"Fine."

"Seven?"

"Seven."

A sudden, vehement gust of wind caught Miriam's breath, dispersing a few lingering mourners to the warmth of their cars. One of her mother's neighbors—Miriam could never remember the woman's name—lost her hat. It blew off and bowled across the Lawn of Remembrance, her pop-eyed husband clumsily pursuing it across the ash-enriched grass.

At the height of the quarry, the wind was even stronger. It came up from the sea and down the river, funneling its fury into a snow-specked fist; then it scoured the city for victims.

The wall of the Bogey-Walk was ideal material. Weak from the flux of years, it needed little bullying to persuade it to surrender. In the late afternoon, a particularly ambitious gust took three or four glass-crowned bricks off the top of the wall and pitched them into the quarry lake. The structure was weakest there, in the middle of its length, and once the wind had started the demolition, gravity lent its elbow to the work.

A young man, cycling home, was just about to reach the middle of the footpath when he heard a roar of capitulation and saw a section of the wall buckle outward in a cloud of mortar fragments. There was a diminishing percussion of bricks against rock as the ruins danced their way down to the foot of the cliff. A gap, fully six feet across, had opened up in the wall, and the wind, triumphant, roared through it, tugging at the exposed edges of the wall and coaxing them to follow. The young man got off his bicycle and wheeled it to the spot, grinning at the spectacle.

It was a long way down, he thought as he stepped toward the breach and cautiously peered over the edge. The wind was at his heels and at the small of his back, curling around him, begging him to step a little farther. He did. The vertigo he felt excited him, and the idiot urge to fling himself over, though resistible, was strong. Leaning over, he was able to see the bottom of the quarry; but the face of the stone directly beneath the hole in the wall was out of sight. A small overhang obscured the place.

The young man leaned farther out, the icy wind hot for him. *Come on*, it said. *Come on, look closer, look deeper.*

Something, not a yard below the yawning gap in the wall, moved. The young man saw, or thought he saw, a form—whose bulk was hidden by the overhang—move. Then, sensing that it was observed, freeze against the cliff wall.

Get on with it, said the wind. *Give in to your curiosity.*

The young man thought better of it. The thrill of the test was souring. He was cold; the fun was over. Home time. He stepped back from the hole and began to wheel his bicycle away, a whistle coming to his lips that was part in celebration of escape and part to keep whatever he felt at his back at bay.

At seven, Miriam was sorting through the last of her mother's jewelry. There was very little of value in the small perfumed boxes, but there were one or two pretty brooches nesting in beds of greying cotton wool that she had decided to take home with her, for remembrance. Boyd had rung a little after six, as he had promised, his voice watery on a bad line, but full of reassurance and affection. Miriam was still high from his conversation. Now the telephone rang again. It was Judy.

"Lovey, I don't think I ought to come over this evening. I'm feeling pretty bad at the moment. I came on at the funeral, and the pains are always bad when it's cold."

"Oh, dear."

"I'd be lousy company, I'm afraid. Sorry to let you down."

"Don't worry; if you're not well..."

"Pity is, I might not get to see you again before you go back." She sounded genuinely distressed at the thought.

"Listen," Miriam said, "if I get this work finished before it gets too late, I'll wander round your way. I hate telephone farewells."

"Me too."

"I can't promise."

"Well, if I see you, I see you; we'll leave it at that, eh? If I don't, take care, love, and drop me a line to tell me you got home safely."

By the time she stepped out of the house at nine-fifty, the gale had long since blown itself out, only to be followed by a stillness so profound, it was almost more unnerving than the preceding din. Miriam locked the door and took a step back to look at the front of the house. The next time she set foot here (if, indeed, she ever did), the house would be re-occupied and, no doubt, repainted. She would have no right-of-way here; the pains of remembrance she had experienced in the last few days would themselves be memories.

She walked to the car, keys in hand, but decided on the spur of the moment that she would walk to Judy's house. The gale-cleansed air was invigorating, and she would take the opportunity to wander around the old neighborhood one final time.

She would even take the Bogey-Walk, she thought; she'd be at Judy's in five or ten minutes.

There was a long, deceptive curve in the Walk as it followed the rim of the quarry. From one end, it was not, possible to see the other, or even the middle. So Miriam was almost upon the gap in the wall before she saw it. Her confident step faltered. In her lower belly something uncoiled its arms in welcome.

The hole gaped in front of her, vast and inviting. Beyond the edge, where the meager light from the street had no strength to go, the darkness of the quarry was apparently infinite. She could have been standing on the edge of the world; there was neither depth nor distance beyond the lip of the path, just a blackness that hummed with anticipation.

Even as she stared, morsels of cement crumbled into space. She heard them patter away from her; she could even hear their distant splashes.

But now, entranced by her sudden dread, she heard another noise, close by, a noise she had prayed never to hear in the waking world, the grit of nails on the stone face of the quarry, the rush of caustic breath from a creature that had waited oh, so patiently for this moment and was now slowly and purposefully dragging its way up the last few feet of the cliff toward her. And why should it hurry? It knew she was frozen to the spot.

It was coming; there was no help to be had. Its arms were splayed over the stone, and its head, dark with grime and depravity, was almost at the rim of the Walk. Even now, with its victim almost in view, it didn't hasten its steady climb but took its awful time.

The little girl Miriam had been wanted to die now, before it saw her, but the woman she was wanted to see the face of her ageless tormentor. Just to see, for the horrid instant before it took her, what the thing was like. After all, it had been here so long, waiting. It had its reasons for such patient malice, surely; maybe the face would show them.

How could she have thought there could ever be escape from this? In sunlight she'd laughed off her fears, but that had been a sham. The sweat of childhood, the night tears (hot, and running straight from the corners of her eyes into her hair), the unspeakable terrors, were here. They had come out of the dark, and she was, at the last, alone. Alone as only children are alone: sealed in with feelings beyond articulation, in private hells of ignorance whose corridors run, unseen, into adulthood.

Now she was crying, loudly, bawling like a ten-year-old,

her crumpled face red and shining with tears. Her nose ran, her eyes burned.

In front of her, the Bogey-Walk was weakening, and she felt the irrevocable pull of the dark. One of her steps toward the gap in the wall was matched by another hauling of the flat black belly over the quarry's face. Another step, and now she was a foot from the crumbling edge of the Bogey-Walk, and in a matter of moments it would take her by the hair and split her apart.

She stood by the dizzying edge, and the face of her dread swam up from the bottomless night to look at her. *It was her mother's face.* Horribly bloated to twice or three times its true size, her jaundiced eyelids flickering to reveal whites without irises, as though she were hanging in the last moment between life and death.

Her mouth opened; her lips blackened and stretched to thin lines around a toothless hole, which worked the air uselessly, trying to speak Miriam's name. So even now there was to be no moment of recognition; the thing had cheated her, offering that dead, beloved face in place of its own.

Her mother's mouth chewed on, her rasping tongue trying vainly to shape the three syllables. The beast wanted to summon her, and it knew, with its age-old cunning, which face to use to make the call. Miriam looked down through her tears at the flickering eyes; she could half see the deathbed pillow beneath her mother's head, half smell her last, sour breath.

The name was almost said. Miriam closed her eyes, knowing that when the word was spoken, that would be the end. She was without will. The Bogey had her; this brilliant mimicry was the final, triumphant turn of the screw. It would speak with her mother's voice, and she would go to it.

"*Miriam,*" it said.

The voice was lovelier than she'd anticipated.

"Miriam." It called in her ear, its claws now on her shoulder.

"Miriam, for God's sake," it demanded. *"What are you doing?"*

The voice was familiar, but it was not her mother's voice, nor that of the beast. It was Judy's voice, Judy's hands. They dragged her back from the gap and all but threw her against the opposite wall. She felt the security of cold brick at her back, against the cushion of her palms. The tears cleared a little.

"What are you doing?"

Yes, no doubt of it. Judy, plain as day.

"Are you all right, love?"

Behind Judy, the dark was deep, but from it there came only a pattering of stones as the Bogey retreated down the quarry face. Miriam felt Judy's arms around her, tight; more possessive of her life than she had been.

"I didn't mean to give you such a heave," she said, "I just thought you were going to jump."

Miriam shook her head in disbelief. "It hasn't taken me," she said.

"What hasn't, sweetheart?"

She couldn't bring herself to talk in earshot of it. She just wanted to be away from the wall; and the Walk.

"I thought you weren't coming," said Judy, "so I thought —bugger it—I'll go round and see you. It's a good thing I took the shortcut. What in heaven's name possessed you to go peering over the edge like that? It's not safe."

"Can you take me home?"

"Of course, love."

Judy put her arm around her and led her away from the gap in the wall.

Behind them, silence and darkness. The lamp flickered. The mortar crumbled a little more.

They stayed together through the night at the house, and they shared the big bed in Miriam's room innocently, as they had as children. Miriam told the story from beginning to end: the whole history of the Bogey-Walk. Judy took it all in, nodded, smiled, and let it be. At last, in the hour before dawn, the confessions over, they slept.

At that same hour, the ashes of Miriam's mother were cooling, mingled with the ashes of thirteen others who had gone to the incinerator that Wednesday, December 1. In the morning, the remaining bones would be ground up and the dust would be divided into four- teen equal parts, then shoveled scrupulously into fourteen urns bearing the names of the loved ones. Some of the ashes would be scattered; some sealed in the Wall of Remembrance; some would go to the bereaved, as a focus for their grief.

At that same hour, Mr. Beckett dreamed of his father and half woke, sobbing, only to be soothed back to sleep by the girl at his side.

And, at that same hour, the husband of the late Marjorie Elliot took a shortcut along the Bogey-Walk. His feet crunched on the gravel, the only sound in the world at that weary hour before dawn. He had come this way every day of his working life, exhausted from the night shift at the bakery. His fingernails were lined with dough, and under his arm he carried a large white loaf and a bag of six crusty rolls. These he had carried home, fresh each morning, for almost twenty-three years. He still repeated the ritual, though since Marjorie's premature death, most of the bread was uneaten and went to the birds.

Toward the middle of the Bogey-Walk, his steps slowed. There was a fluttering in his belly; a scent in the air had awakened a memory. Was it not his wife's scent? Five yards farther on and the lamp flickered. He looked down at the gap in the wall and from out of the quarry rose his long-mourned Marjorie, her face huge.

It spoke his name once, and without bothering to reply to her call, he stepped off the Walk and was gone.

The loaf he had been carrying was left behind on the gravel.

Loosened from its tissue wrapping, it cooled, slowly forfeiting the warmth of its birth to the night.

RAMSEY CAMPBELL

...was born in Liverpool in 1946 and has never left Merseyside. His local library—no bigger than a corner shop—was Childwall, where he first encountered the work of Lovecraft and M. R. James and many others in the field. He was educated at Christ the King School on Queens Drive and Ryebank Preparatory on Edge Lane before graduating to St Edward's College in Sandfield Park. Among his classmates at St Edward's were the politician Peter Kilfoyle and the historian Paul Preston. Many of the books in his teenage collection were bought from Bascombe's in Smithdown Road and from Leslie Johnson, the science fiction bookseller who lived off the Rocket. In his mid-teens he haunted all the cinemas Liverpool and Merseyside had to offer, and was a member of the Liverpool Science Fiction Society (LiG) at 69A Bold Street. From 1962 to 1966 he worked for the Inland Revenue in

Church Street, and between 1962 to 1964 he attended Childwall Hall College of Further Education, where he posted film reviews weekly on the noticeboard. From 1966 to 1973 he worked in libraries —Wavertree, Picton, the Music Library in Church Alley (where a youthful Simon Rattle was a frequent borrower), finally Edge Hill. Since then he has written full-time. He was the film reviewer for BBC Radio Merseyside from 1969 until 2007. In 2015 Liverpool John Moores University awarded him an Honorary Fellowship for outstanding services to literature. His novel Creatures of the Pool *is set entirely in Liverpool, and draws upon many local legends and traditions, while his trilogy—*The Searching Dead, Born to the Dark *and* The Way of the Worm *— begins in 1950s Liverpool and depicts several decades of the city up to something like the present day.*

COMING TO LIVERPOOL

RAMSEY CAMPBELL

This isn't fiction, but there are ghosts in it. Some of them are me.

We begin in 1942 or thereabouts. My father is living with some of his family at 40 Nook Rise in Wavertree Garden Suburb, a development built immediately before the First World War "to provide a residential suburb for the people of Liverpool amid surroundings which conduce to both health and pleasure". So confident of their purpose were the developers that they made their telegraphic address Antislum, Liverpool. Tree-shaded cruciform Nook Rise is beyond a bowling green and tennis courts off Thingwall Road, where as a youngster I hoped that a Thing might lurk behind the wall. I'm not yet born, however, since my mother hasn't long met my father, and they won't be married for several years. Nevertheless, is this in some sense me?

"...chubby, mischievous, rosy – sleek black hair, blue eyes..." and bearing some resemblance to his mother "but with decent features; and one day [he] will be famous..."

This is from my mother's first novel, *Portrait of Greta Walton*. The speaker is describing her future son. She's Toni Richardson, who represents my mother in this highly auto-

217

biographical novel. It's told mostly from the viewpoint of Greta Walton, her workmate and friend. Greta, "wholly enraptured", further learns that "Toni would be pal as well as mother to him – such a pal as man seldom had. His ideals should be cherished and his offences receive sympathetic guidance. In short, [he] would be so enlightened that at all times he would differentiate the good from the bad." Greta imagines "Toni and he together, several years ahead. It was the same Toni, the same figure – only a few grey hairs to mark the passing of time. Holding the grubby hand of a small boy, she was talking to him and he was hanging upon her every word – looking at her with adoration."

The boy's name is in fact Michael Christopher, a good Catholic pairing. "So that was Michael Christopher," Greta reflects, "influenced from the outset by the mind of a fine woman – and one day, justifying his existence, he, too, would be great." Toni is a writer of fiction for children, but has ambitions to write a great adult novel. "So that's another reason why the novel must succeed," she tells Greta. "No success – no Michael Christopher!" By contrast, the unnamed putative father is barely taken into account; he's at best a vague idealised figure who might be imagined as uninvolved in the birth.

In May 1942 my mother writes to my father that she's posting him a copy of *Portrait of Greta Walton*. "Although I am deeply ashamed of it, of having written it, (and of what I have written) I have spoken too much to you about it that it is natural for you to be curious about it. It would not, therefore, have been fair to you if I had just forwarded it to 'Greta'..." It's the first of her letters to him that survives. In it she addresses him as "my big brother", perhaps because he was thirteen years older.

Why was she ashamed of the novel? While it never quite admits to a lesbian theme, Greta's infatuation with Toni is clearly meant to be viewed as suspect, which we can assume was my mother's view of the actual relationship, or at least that aspect of it. The book was written at the suggestion of "Greta", who approved each chapter as it was completed. It draws on my mother's experience as a saleswoman and ultimately a drapery buyer at Rushworth's department store in Huddersfield, where I assume "Greta" was a workmate. The final section has Greta reflect that "in seeking reflection as a novelist, [Toni] had combined it with an attempt to bring her to her senses by, in making her the novel's central character, deliberately magnifying all that was abnormal in her". Now that this is established, the novel is to have "a very different ending", since Greta has formed a relationship with a man. In time Toni's dream of authorship would turn into desperation.

At least that's clear, but some things are less so. In May 1942 my mother writes the letter I quoted, addressed to Alex and signed Nora. In June, however, she hasn't sent the novel and has failed to write the final section. She thanks my father for advice on writer's block, calling him Mr Campbell and signing herself Sheila (the name she used when advertising, apparently in a writers' journal, for authors who would correspond with her and criticise her work). At this stage theirs is a literary friendship, if with a certain perverse flirtatiousness: she asks for "harshness and contempt – and let it be stinging", and acknowledges her "apparently abnormal desire for harsh treatment". One problem with this history is that I'm drawing almost exclusively on letters written by my mother.

In April 1943 they've moved on to discuss their love lives. There's little sense of a war going on around them, although my mother works for the Ministry of War Transport and my father is apparently in the Home Guard (which prompts her to send him a blessed medal of St Bernadette in May). Both had romances that fell short of their notion of an ideal partner; his ideal was his mother. (Among his few surviving papers are a twenty-eight-page letter to "My dear mother", dated August 1928, describing with a keen eye for detail how he's revisiting France – from Dijon to Fontainebleau to Paris and eventually Le Havre, where the letter was written – in the company of his friend E., who apparently resembled a retired colonel and who kept to his bed while my father took walks at dawn. They appear to have been great cinemagoers, but of *Metropolis* my father wrote "A more gloomy and uneventful film could hardly be imagined.") One of his romances was with a woman twenty years his senior. He's involved in a French circle and in running a youth club. My mother has had several proposals of marriage and turned them all down. One of the men subsequently turned to drink.

That month, although they haven't met, she imagines them together. "You are sitting by the fire, and it is lighting up your eyes, discovering occasional gleams – not, mind you, only occasional ones; but mostly they are into dark, because they cannot turn away from my unwavering, searching look; whilst I am in (being your guest!) your chair, and therefore in the shadow!" Some process appears to have begun – perhaps that their correspondence, while appearing to bring them closer, is keeping them at a dangerously idealised distance. This is in the midst of a letter explaining why she won't return to Rushworth's when her present job ends – because "Greta" works there. The novel is still incomplete, and "Greta" (in whom my mother finds "generosity of spirit" while describing herself as "smug and conceited") has asked to have it if it remains so. My mother thinks this the best solution: she writes that it may "wash me clean".

Next month she sends my father two fairy tales by "Nora Bernadette" (her Christian names). In "The Magic Land of Almost-Sure", Ordinary Everyday Maiden ("neither beautiful nor even pretty") sets out upon an unspecified but worthy task, encouraged by Fairy Hopeful. She's told that many pilgrims are engaged on it, but while she can't see them, their voices overwhelm her until her fairy godmother leads her "beyond the deafening presence of the 'voices'" and then places her hand in an invisible man's hand. He proves to be Prince Charming of the Kingdom of Generous Hearts. While she can't see him, he has managed to look at her once, an indulgence that may have lowered his opinion of her. In the sequel, "The Not-So-Nice-Land-of-Perplexities", they are still journeying together along the Sunlit Pathway of Mutual Trust and Understanding, although they're geographically remote. This time the maiden's vision lets her see "a very handsome, dark haired Prince watching her". She can't decide whether to let him know she has recognised him or to pretend otherwise, or even if she should send him a message in case she was mistaken. At last she decides that "Prince Charming can't help but understand." I believe all this to refer to my mother's belief that my father had been to Huddersfield for a secret look at her. Whether he actually had is unclear.

She's disconcerted by his view that "what Greta felt was, at root, a beautiful thing", although she criticises herself severely for her treatment of the real person. She admits to finding it hard to love, because she always hoped to meet "someone whom I should love whole heartedly, spiritually, mentally, and physically". My father maintains that the only reason for a couple to marry is to have children, which she takes to mean that marriage does not "purify the gratification of their physical instincts" and agrees. He feels it's a pity if they know too much about sex before marriage. This kind of analysis is spread over several long letters. She suggests he should burn her novel but is relieved when he declines. At last she admits that she befriended "Greta" after breaking off an engagement with a young man who had grown too physical for her taste.

In June she sends my father booklets published by the Catholic Truth Society. Perhaps they are simply meant to promote discussion, but in those days they were often used as a means of converting a partner in a mixed relationship before marriage. In August the two of them appear to be about to meet; at least, my mother speaks of identifying him by a badge on his left lapel. There's then a two-month hiatus in my mother's letters. The next thanks my father for three letters and appears to recall their meeting, but that's the only reference.

At the end of October my father sends a copy of Walter de la Mare's poetry anthology *Come Hither* as a birthday present. The inscription reads "By this token, Alexander Ramsay reminds Nora Bernadette of happy things, that never lose their freshness, and reminds her, too, of the duty, which lies so lightly upon her, to see in the happiness she inspires in others a reflection of her own good nature."

In December another meeting is planned. She has sent him a portrait photograph of herself. Just before Christmas she and her mother move from their house at 36 Armitage Road to a flat in 64 Trinity Street, also in Huddersfield. At the beginning of 1944 she and my father discuss a leap year tradition that allows women to propose marriage. Otherwise there's little sign that the couple will be wed within a year, though a teasing coyness has begun to overtake sections of my mother's letters, where she often refers to herself in the third person (or rather as Nora B). She still signs herself "Yours, very sincerely" and discusses at an objective distance the appropriateness of various forms of kiss. She does declare that his letters are "the most interesting and nicest" she has ever had.

Although his visit isn't scheduled until March, in January he lets my mother know that he'll attend a Presbyterian church service while she goes to a Catholic one. She has advised a seventeen-year-old colleague to tell her parents that she's in love with a nineteen-year-old in the Forces, which prompts an extended discussion of how to handle marriage and some thoughts of the perils of war. (She was often asked for advice by younger workmates.) Over the next few weeks her letters anticipate Alexander Ramsay's visit at length and in considerable detail.

On 13 March she writes "Now that our weekend is in the past, I am hoping that you had a pleasant journey home. I am hoping, too, that you can say (without calling forth even the teeniest, weeniest bit of diplomacy) that you enjoyed every minute of the time we spent together. I did, Alex. And that is the absolute truth.

"Thank you, most sincerely, for coming. And forgive me if you don't like the question I am now going to ask. For I must, and so, please, Alex, won't you give me a straightforward honest reply? I have a feeling that you may have come to Huddersfield this weekend, and, as you say, will come again in another six months' time, because you do not want to disappoint Nora B.; because you are well aware she very much wants you to come. Is that a fact, Alex? Or do you really want to come just as much as I want you to?

"...It was lovely to see you again, and to see you looking well and most distinguished. And I mean that most sincerely, Alex.

Always my most special wishes for you.

Yours, very sincerely,

Nora."

His reply appears to have been positive, since next week she says "The happy moments we enjoyed together and which you recollected in your last letter are the ones that most impressed me, too." She adds that a longer ramble in June "will prove whether Alexander Ramsay, really and truly and without it being any kindness on his part, wants to come." It's clear that she feels compelled to worry at words. He responds with, apparently, a frank letter and half his wartime ration of lemons. She agrees that they've viewed their friendship as "a beautiful adventure" and reassures him that "what has to be, will be" (by which, she explains in her next missive, she is "certainly not expressing an angry, dissatisfied surrender to what may be my destiny"). She tells him that she couldn't bear losing his friendship and is glad that they "can discuss this importantly personal matter with reasonable calm". She's convinced that ideals can "become, and remain, reality. It depends entirely on the idealists themselves."

Six months pass. The June meeting has taken place, and others may well have, but no letters have survived. The next is dated in early October and addressed to "My dearest". The last three weeks have been "a 'mutual' heaven". She knows "without a shadow of a doubt, that Alex and Nora will be very, very happy together". She assures him that she likes "small, comfortable houses" and predicts that she will find "that wonderful fairy place '40, NOOK RISE'" is "just very, very snug". She's sure it will provide a room for her mother. It seems he has described having both women come to live with him after the marriage as "a privilege".

My mother soon makes it clear that she has a bed-sitting room in mind, although she has yet to tell her mother of the plan to move her in. She hopes my father won't have to get rid of too much of his own furniture, since she hopes to bring nearly all of her mother's. Her sister Kathleen doesn't need it, since she lives in a well-furnished house "too big to appeal to me". She and her husband Leslie "are always bickering[1]" whereas my parents will set them an example "of contentment, of peace, and of true and mutual love".

By mid-October they're engaged to be married in early January. My mother would like the wedding to be as quiet as practicable (ideally "only our two selves, but I suppose that is impossible"). She's coming to Liverpool in a month to see the house. She agrees that they will make the best of it, since my father has suggested she may want it "doing up", and he's

---

1. True enough, though in my childhood I found it entertaining, and have no reason to doubt their mutual affection.

repainting some of it. They are exchanging letters daily, or as often as the post allows. Hers are anticipatory and romantic.

At the end of October (immediately after the anniversary of her father's death) she's struck down by a bilious attack. She will have to attend the surgery in Huddersfield when she was planning her first visit to Liverpool, and proposes bringing the visit forward a day. Her letters suggesting it grow terser, if no less affectionate, until he phones the day before to put her off. The doctor finds her run down and wants to examine her again next weekend, and so she asks to advance her rescheduled visit a day. She imagines having visited the house after all and saying to his sister Barbara (who presently lives with him) "I can see that my beloved Alex has been working very hard to make it lovely for his Nora."

By mid-November the visit appears to have taken place. Making the best is becoming an issue. She would like new curtains for the front room and a new modern fireplace – failing that, at least the removal of the mantelpiece, to which she has taken a particular dislike. She praises her mother's taste in furniture and begs him to buy a suite the women have chosen, with a large chair to be exclusively her mother's. If they can't afford that and a honeymoon, she would rather spend the honeymoon in their house. She's eager to see the sights of "Liverpool, Wavertree, Cheshire and the docks". She assures him that they "shall never for one moment regret our marriage to each other". Similar reassurances are sought and given at considerable length several times before the marriage. They seem to be able to manage a honeymoon (at Berners Close in Grange-over-Sands in the Lake District) after all. She feels she already knows the place and will love it – my father has often been on holiday there – though she wants it "to be very nearly deserted, except for us".

They are now meeting each weekend. On a Saturday early in November my father says a prayer for them and moves them both to tears. In remembering this my mother adds a prayer that "the three of us will live in true harmony together". He has received some instruction in Catholicism. A new fireplace seems to be imminent, but then finances prove unequal to it. My father suggests foregoing the new suite, to my mother's dismay. There will surely be space in the front room for her mother's furniture (dining chairs, a revolving bookcase, a secretaire and a work table). If this influx crowds out items that are already there, surely my father can dispose of these unless they are of sentimental value. Her salutations to him are becoming increasingly fulsome. At one point she refers to his "terrible withdrawal" while they took a walk around some golf links.

"Greta" sends an affectionate letter and wants to meet my father over Christmas. Perhaps she does. On Boxing Day my mother pleads with him to write to her mother "telling her that you sincerely and whole-heartedly want her to be with us and for good, and that you cannot 'allow' her to stay away from us after the 30th of January" (less than a month after the marriage). My mother is anxious because flying bombs are in the air. At the beginning of January she restates her concerns for her mother. "I want her to stay in bed when, and as long as, she wants, and I want her to get up, on the other hand, when she wants."

My parents are married on 6 January 1945 as planned, although three days beforehand my mother takes to her bed with a severe chill. The wedding doesn't quite end their letters; one more of hers survives. On 4 January 1946 I'm born, rivalling (in terms of this memoir, at least) Tristram Shandy for length of preamble. In early February she's back in Huddersfield, prolonging a reunion with her mother. "I feel so strange at being back here; and I miss you so. For, though it is only 2.0 P. M., the thought will not leave me that I will not be with my beloved from 'as much before six as possible' tonight. Yet, dearest, it will very soon be Thursday, when we shall have our glorious reunion. For, my dearest, I should like to stay until then. Mother was, and is, so very delighted to see me, that I should like to prolong that pleasure…" My parents have had a quarrel over the training of my father's pet dog. My mother apologises for her temper and spends two pages reiterating her affection. "You are much nicer and sweeter than I, even in my most inspired hopings, thought you might be…"

September 1946 finds her in Huddersfield once more, apparently to help sell some family property, and my father's extant letters date from this period. They're addressed daily to "Dearest" and signed "With fondest love, Alex." The first is dated the 10th, immediately after my mother and I leave. "The strong air of your native heath should do those healthy lungs the good that a tonic should… I don't think I have ever seen such searchingly friendly eyes, and you have so looked after him that he is already a credit to your training and care." That's me, and I'm discovering how to crawl. For the duration of this narrative I'm John, though I later left that behind and contented myself with my middle name or more precisely my spelling of it. On the 11th my father writes "It was really thrilling when I returned home on Tuesday night to find you waiting for me! Oh but no, it was nothing quite so satisfactory as that but a very good substitute. You had laid the table in complete readiness for my arrival. That was most graciously thoughtful, dearest."

On the 13th "I was amused beyond my studious wont to read that John has had his first big bath. How he would revel in it, I can easily imagine. Did he holler to be left in amongst the soap suds a minute or two longer than the necessary? Or did he bellow, as only he knows how to, to be let out? You would have had a fleet of toy ducks circling round inside the bath and he would enjoy pushing them below the surface while you seized the opportunity to soap the as yet unwashed parts. I am so pleased, dearest, at this news of his first real bath that I am inclined to excuse him from his next one until a week or two have elapsed. And I must apologise to him for missing such a great occasion in his most important life. Did the soap get in his eyes? Did those eyes look up to you appealingly to ask you to give over or to urge you to put still more and more bubbly lather all over his portly frame? These are the questions I should like to have had answered by actual visual experience. But I have no hesitation in saying you thoroughly enjoyed yourself."

On 17 September he exhorts her to "have that sunny tour of Greenhead Park that I have been promising myself for you. You must show our little John the ducks we used to talk to, or at least their grandchildren and watch the lively sparkle in his eyes. Kiss him under the chin for me." On the 18th "I am thinking that by your next letter, darling, you may be able to give some clear indication of your return, although it is a trifle doubtful," but the following day he writes "As regards your return, darling, wouldn't it be nice if you could find some homely place in Huddersfield to stay on in until the 12/10, when I could then call for you. It would still further save our coal and would in addition afford you a very well-deserved holiday." One reason she needs it may well be their hefty son. It seems that I was fed "body-building Farex", an infant food. "I did tell you, didn't I, of how even I felt the presence of John's frame on my arm long after I left you at the station. It amused me at the time to think how a big fellow like myself could find cause for such complaint. So I am likely to listen to you sympathetically when you tell me in future that you feel fit to drop after bouncing your playmate round for an hour or so." He signs himself "With fondest affection, Alex", beside which appear three symbols, a large X with NORA fitted in its interstices, flanked by two smaller ones each similarly containing JOHN.

"Fast, fast, I must send you the enclosed. I will send the other 10/= when I know how I stand at Crayke. Because last year I had the most peculiar experience of not having a ½ d to my name, and had to depend on the good weather of the first Monday to put me in funds. I am hoping, how I'm hoping, that the work will be constant, and the company companionable, and that the resulting grist to the mill will be worth sneezing with. That I shall miss you, darling, and that I miss you now to see me off on my journey goes without even thinking…" This is from the 26th. Two days later he's writing from Crayke Castle, some miles north of York. "The old place is just as old and friendly and well-run as ever it was. I am surprised to learn that I occupy the last vacancy for this work. A popular resort this for servants of the public willing to lend their backs in lifting the produce of the earth… Even hay-making may be included. And sugar-beet pulling. And a bit of leg-pulling as well, I shouldn't be surprised… But oh what a disappointment awaited me when the train stopped at Huddersfield for five minutes and more. I hung out of the window and stretched up my highest in the hope of seeing yourself and John waiting on the platform for a word of greeting. I had indeed looked forward to that grand moment, darling. A month and more's absence is rather a bit too long. The break would have been particularly lovely…"

Does this refer to a prearranged meeting, or just a dream? Perhaps it gives us a first glimpse of the truth behind the letters. The trouble with romantic idealism is that it may need its opposite in order to seem real. When an ideal is shattered, the shards pierce the heart. There is one more letter, dated the 30th.

"My very dearest,

"If it was raining early on this morning, and it was and had been all night, the likelihood is that we shall have sunshine later on in the day. The lively group of harvesters was taken round in a covered wagon at 7.30 am. on visits to the neighbouring farmers who smiled through their rain-soaked moustaches and refused our help meanwhile. We may be called for at noon and sit about in various attitudes of studious repose, aping the carefree abandon of casual labourers trained in the art of waiting for things to turn up.

"But, darling, there is a more hopeful sign which is a source of pleasure to me as I write. If it is raining today Monday, it may not and must not rain at all anywhere to-morrow Tuesday. For such an important transport of property and persons takes place then. A great trek begins from Huddersfield to Liverpool. Not so cinematographically glamorous perhaps as 'Covered Wagon' or some tale of the Wild West, but intensely, personally important for us all. I'll be with you in thought, trying to carry the responsibility of your undertaking and the weight of John on first one arm, then the other.

"So I hope, darling, that it will be delightfully agreeable weather that you'll have for that critically exciting journey. And that John, who looked so ravishing in his waterproof cape, will enjoy the freedom of not having to wear it. And that your strong arms will find him as light as a feather and that your heart will be as gay as a lightsome song.

"They've called for us, or at least I think so.

"Au revoir darling

"Safe landing for you all & every good luck

"Your devoted

"Alex"

Very shortly afterwards – perhaps as a member of that trek – her mother comes to live with them.

"I, Nora Campbell, am a practicing Roman Catholic, and I married my husband, Alexander Ramsay Campbell, at St. Patrick's Roman Catholic Church, New North Rd., Huddersfield, on the 6th of January, 1945. Canon Grogan performed the ceremony.

"When I agreed to marry my husband, I asked him to make two promises first; one was that the children of any marriage should be brought up in the Roman Catholic faith;

the other was that my widowed mother should make her home with us. My husband assured me that he very readily agreed to both...

"After a week's honeymoon, I came to live in the house where my husband, his two sisters, and his mother (who had been dead about a year), had lived for the past ten years or so. Since his mother's death, his married sister and her husband had lived with him. The other sister was in The Forces.

"I had been to this house only once before, though my husband visited me often in Huddersfield before our marriage... On this first occasion when I saw the house, I said at once that though I did not mind living there at the start of our marriage, I should want to get a more suitable house as soon as possible. My husband assured me it would only be a temporary arrangement. He realised only too well that I was used to something very much superior to it...

"The first Sunday I came back from my honeymoon to this rented home of his, he coolly announced to my great distress that the house we were in was to be our home for good."

It is 1954. My mother has written this account of her marriage in an attempt to obtain a legal separation. She has been trying to get one since 1947. She refers to a novel (clearly *Portrait of Greta Walton*) that she "had been writing since 1937; it was more than three quarters finished, but in 1940-41, due to the war activities, I somehow couldn't go on with it. So I put an advert in THE WRITER, which is a writers' publication, requesting some fellow-writer to collaborate." Where does the truth lie – in the letters or this account, or somewhere in between? In fact my paternal grandmother, Rebecca Johnston (or Johnstone) Campbell, died in March 1943. Perhaps my mother's reference the following month to her as my father's ideal woman touches on correspondence (now lost) about this. Rebecca died aged 94, and was exactly half that age when she gave birth to my father (his sisters, I believe, were younger). She had lived at 40 Nook Rise at least since 1919. No voters' lists exist for the years of either world war, but it seems entirely possible that the Campbells were the first tenants. My father is listed at the address from the beginning of the twenties, but there is never a sign of his father, presumably a fatality of the war.

Ignorance before marriage wasn't such a good idea, since sex seems to have come as a horrid shock. In those days some women allegedly lay there thinking of England, though in my mother's case it was more likely to have been Huddersfield. "He thought he had a right to intimacy every night; and that took place until I went into hospital about a month before the child's birth... When I refused his demands on the occasions when I felt they were more than I could be expected to stand (not every time he sought to be intimate, by any means) he then started unnatural practises. He did this on about six occasions. I felt degraded, disgusted, and humiliated." There may have been a sadistic component to my father's sexuality: "When I told him how I despised him for it, he ran the side of his large hand across my throat, as though with a knife; he then pressed lightly on my throat with his two hands; his heavy body was on top of me so that I could not move-----he said, in a deliberate, cold voice: 'What a nice little throat you've still got.'"

My mother describes the house in some detail. "The rooms, all of them, were in a disgraceful state. All very badly needed doing. The bathroom and one bedroom were painted in a bottle green, making the rooms depressingly dark and dismal; the ceiling of the living room was a dark, dirty yellow. When I pointed this out to him, he informed me that the dark green painting had been done by himself, also the ceiling. He reminded me that I had planned to have green for the bedroom; he had done it in that dark shade he said, also the bathroom and ceiling, so that it wouldn't need doing again for a very long time...

"I tried to make him realise how the house appeared to

me, at the start of my married life; how inconvenient and out-of-date it was. I pointed out its deficiencies, which were very many. All the rooms are exceedingly small, there is no hall-----just a small space between the living room, the stairs, and the front door. The kitchen sink is under the hot water cylinder cupboard in such an uncomfortable position that your back feels broken when you have been there more than a moment or so; the untiled walls are so damp that distemper will not stay on them; the damp is green and slimy. The hot water is heated from the kitchen, a room with a cold stone floor and far too small and altogether too uninviting to live in. The toilet too is absolutely out-of-date and unhygienic; the taps are still clumsy brass..."

Much, perhaps all, of this was true. It seems to have left my mother few places to go except inside her own head, first as a fiction writer and then, alas, too far in. There is much more.

"I have never invited anyone to my home. Just at first, a few of my friends came uninvited from Huddersfield, but when they did, if they had not gone when he arrived home from work, he walked out of the house, and stayed out until they had gone. Then he went on to display his rage at my having them there. So, eventually, they ceased to come. (I still have no proper friends in Liverpool, though a few people have invited me to their homes. I have always had to refuse because I should never have recovered from the shame had they seen the inside of my home.) He has wrecked everything I have done to improve this squalid, miserable home...

"I had the living room distempered last December, along with having the electricity made safe... Almost immediately my husband deliberately made dirty marks on every wall. Not content with that, he left his finger prints here, there, and everywhere. He has left marks where he struck his matches... It has upset me so much that in my frequent nightmares, that are growing more frequent, always my husband is there in that room, showing me what he has done with the walls and telling me that whatever I do he'll spoil it, boasting, sneering, threatening me, as in real life. Night after night I have wakened in terror, and once I found him in the middle of the night standing in the doorway of the bedroom where John and I sleep, watching us, a look of horrifying hate on his face. I was shaking with fear for us but I pretended to be asleep... Often he prowls about downstairs during the night. Often, too, he throws things about in his bedroom. It is a shocking strain waiting for that to happen and listening to it when it comes. Always I fear what he will do next..."

Her mother moved to Southport in 1952 "because she could no longer stand the misery and atmosphere of this home" but has returned "because she feared for my safety, as I did... So, though my sister and her husband have pleaded with my mother to make her home with them, she has consistently refused to leave me... Since my mother came back to me she has stayed in her bedroom from straight after tea, to be out of my husband's way in case he returned home. There is no fire there; so she is obliged to be in bed. All the light she has is a NIGHTLIGHT. (My husband started a row on one occasion by accusing her of turning on the electric light. He had obviously been standing outside the house watching, because the light was only on a few minutes... I had put it on because I was speaking to her. It was twenty minutes to one in the morning and my husband had not come home...

"It was when John was about four months old that THE CHRISTIAN SCIENCE MONITOR started coming to the house. It is a daily paper published in America, and comes to the house from America... During the first few years of their coming, he used to pick them up off the small floor space between the front door and the stairs. He used to stack them on top of the wardrobe, on a bedroom chair, and behind a clock, also in a radiogram... They were seldom opened. Then he took them to piling them in John's room, which was already crammed with books, old, musty books... When I ceased to sleep with him... my husband settled himself in that room; and so for a while I put the papers in that room as fast as they came, with the result that they were stacked there, still unopened. So it was that I left them where they were after coming through the letter box; and he left them there, too, unopened. The sight of them fills me with horror... I said that only the doctor is allowed in this house, but, of course, I am obliged to admit the electricity reader and the gas meter reader, as well as the man who visits mother about her pension; and then, too, before the electricity was changed, the electrician was always doing repairs. And, of course, the decorators saw inside the house. And all of them stare at the papers with horror and amazement. And then they stare at me... So the papers are still in the tiny passage, filling it, reaching towards the ceiling in the boxes I have had to put them in to keep the floor clear, and already a third of the way up the stairs... I suppose they will go on coming indefinitely...

"I sincerely believe he has been trying in a diabolical, though horribly subtle way (sometimes I think his mind is so distorted that he must be mad) to cause me to have a mental collapse; and having failed is now systematically working to drive me out of the house, so that he won't have to support me..."

As for their son, "he is a very, very nervous child. He has a very active mind and a very vivid imagination; so that, as I realise only too well, he requires a peaceful environment, and the most careful, understanding handling. I know that if he does not soon get away from here tremendous, irreparable damage will be done to his health, his mentality, and his future."

Among the documents she kept is an undated cutting

from the letter column of *The Christian Science Monitor*. Under the deadline "Britain's Younger Face" this appears:

"My father, he is a policeman, sometimes gets The Christian Science Monitor at the railway station and he brings it home for me to read. The children's part is very good.

"But I have had a blow. Here is The Christian Science Monitor of January 6 and there is 'Drawing Rhymes' done by Mabel Livingston and it says that there's no more, because it's a set.

"Is there a set I could have to stick in a book and show teacher? If there isn't, don't bother, please, because you have enough to do and it wouldn't be fair to make you more busy.

"Please do what you can and thank you.

"The ice is melting here and there is more coal to keep us warm. I hope you have plenty.

"Thank you again.

MASTER JOHN RAMAY (sic) CAMPBELL

40 Nook Rise, Liverpool 15, England."

An editor's note follows: "We think Master John has written at the end of his letter the best commentary we've seen on the way Britain meets a crisis."

I didn't write the letter. My father wasn't me.

There's a great deal more detail in my mother's single-spaced twenty-one-page typescript. I believe I read almost all of it at the time, although she withheld one page – obviously the one about their sexual behaviour. She ends "I have tried to set this statement down in a restrained, quiet manner, so that, in view of my writing hobby, I should not be accused of being dramatic." If she still regards her writing as a hobby, her attitude to it soon grows more desperate. She comes to invest it with her hopes of earning an income of her own, and writes several novels and a number of short stories. None will be published.

She may have submitted for publication a letter she wrote to the *Liverpool Echo* on 13 June 1955. Parts of the carbon copy are illegible, but the surviving text is eloquent enough. It's addressed from "Queen's Drive, Liverpool".

"Dear Sir,

"How qualified [several words obscured] of Kathleen D. Rogers, S. R. N. (whose letter appeared in the Liverpool Echo dated the 8th of June.) She was disgusted by what she read in the Lancet; I wonder, then, how she would feel if she were the victim of 'the scourge of gossip'. I wonder how anyone else would feel----including the ones whose tongues have been so busy if they were persecuted in this way. And I mean 'persecuted'.

"As Kathleen Rogers says, it is caused by boredom, malice, and jealousy; and, I would add, disappointment, frustration, and very often, as in my case, a deliberate attempt to harm the victim to let off poisonous steam. Also, in the background of their small, undeveloped minds is the ruthless determination to detract attention from themselves.

"It is started off by one person who has a willing listener, who repeats it, and does not forget to enlarge upon it, adding comments of her own. The recipient of this also repeats it, also adding to it-----and so this wickedly destructive snowball goes on its way, all the time growing in size and strength.

"Not the least horrifying thing about it is the injustice and gullibility of those who first listen and then actively join in. But, then, of course, it is far easier to let everyone know you are on the side that has the most weight, and if you show you are contributing you will [several words illegible] (except the victim's, which, of course, don't matter. It takes courage, apparently too much, to either keep an open mind about what you don't understand or to openly defend the victim. I say, thank God, there are just a few left of the former.

"Ah well. It is obviously great fun baiting someone, first subtilly (sic), and then, if your victim does not appear to be cracking as quickly as you hoped, by more and more open, and ruthless, methods, by lies and any other under hand way that comes to mind. Well, baiting seems to appeal to a certain type. It appealed to the Germans, if you remember, in their treatment of the Jews.

"But, of course, I mustn't forget to mention the really subtle type. What they do has the same cause, but they cloak it under a pretence of being anxious about the victim. They approach officials (in extreme confidence) and are sufficiently plausible to be believed. Then, triumphantly, they are really sure that the things will come to the conclusion that they have been working for-----except, just what is the end they are wanting? Supposing it is a tragic one? Will they feel any guilt [words obscured – probably "or will"] they be able to persuade themselves that they acted in the best of good faith, to help in every way in their power? I would only add to that, that one's conscience is not only the hardest thing to quieten, but it also grows, like the gossip, in strength.

"And all this for base, petty motives, maybe because, as in my case, they have an imperfect knowledge, and, therefore, understanding, of the subject. But when it reaches the [words obscured – probably "stage when the"] victim's word is no longer given credence; when the victim is discussed and ridiculed even by strangers, then the situation is exceedingly grave. For that is SLANDER."

The carbon bears no valediction or signature. I rather doubt that the letter saw print. It's dated six days after her last letter to the publisher of the monthly magazine *Stores and Shops*, to whom she had submitted her non-fiction book *Behind the Counter – Sales Careers in Stores and Shops* by Nora B. Walker (her maiden name). On 2 March 1955 she writes to A. W. Plowman, M. A. "I am forwarding my book on Salesmanship as promised... I have tried to closely follow all your directions, so I do hope I have succeeded..."

The next extant letter is dated 19 May, from W. H. Newman, the managing director. "Mr Plowman has passed to me your letter of 12 May. We are sorry to hear that your son is ill and hope that he will soon make a permanent recovery…"

He has made "certain slight amendments to the text" and is showing it to retail experts for an opinion, meanwhile asking if she would prefer an outright fee rather than royalties. On 23 May he offers £40 and adds "I am enclosing a few stamps as we do not want you to pay for our letters."

On 3 June he writes "As promised, I am writing to let you know about the first opinion we have had about your MS from a Store staff expert. This is disappointing because the view is taken that whilst there is a lot of good stuff in it there are matters of retail technique and so on which are out of date…

"We are getting another expert's view and will try and obtain also the specific detailed points on which opinion differs from yours. This may bring us near enough to the answer to enable us to give you data on which to devise amendments…"

On 6 June, this from my mother.

"I would like to confirm my request made to you on the 'phone. I should be greatly obliged if you would return my Ms. On Salesmanship & Staff Training as soon as possible, so that I may revise it and then use it as I think best.

"Thank you for the offer to get the second opinion before returning it, but I feel able to make an unbiased criticism and then revise it, if necessary, myself. I may add to it, as I now find I can, and I may treat it from quite a different angle; but I would like it back as soon as you can possibly manage it, so that I may go ahead and sell it.

"May I say, quite respectfully, that I am not anxious for it to be seen by too many Store Staff Experts before publication. I would not like them to be inspired to write a similar book themselves.

"I would just like to add that I did not think my book was so much a technical one as a psychological one. As I said on the phone, the CAN I HELP YOU was meant, and inferred, to be taken as the spirit of the approach, and of the actual, Salesmanship. It was never meant to be spoken (except on very fitting occasions, which the assistant who has this spirit comes to automatically know.) What I would like to stress is that there is a great need, and sad want, of such a spirit in these days. Too many assistants just don't care two hoots whether they serve you or not. Their attitude is, take it or leave it. Few of them are courteous, and discipline seems to be a thing of the past. All this I have constantly, and closely observed, and, I may say, am still observing. Whether it is my book, or someone else's, that is published in order that a different spirit may prevail, there is, I can assure you, a change for the better very much overdue. In the store where I was employed, a Yorkshire one, (which rose from a small shop and is all the time extending,) you had to be always on your toes.

"With this book in mind, I have made it my business to listen and watch from the 'other side' of the counter, and I repeat that the relationship between customer and assistant has seriously deteriorated.

"All this, plus my experience over seventeen years, is why I wrote my book. I don't think I have failed to convey what I intended, though maybe the book will gain if I enlarge, and clarify, certain points. It is because I shall have to take up more time to bring about these changes that I request you, Mr. Newman, if you do not feel to have sufficient confidence in my book to take the risk of its being successful, to please let me have it back without more delay."

W. H. Newman replies at once.

"Mr Plowman, who is getting your MS vetted by a second authority, is away in Norwich and so I do not expect to be able to get hold of the typescript until the end of the week. I am sorry there will be this delay in returning it.

"It may well be that when we get the second opinion we shall be able to say 'yes', as our own reaction is favourable…"

On the 9th my mother writes to him

"I did not realise until I received back my MS. how much work you had been spending on it. I do thank you most sincerely. I feel that as you have taken such pains with it, it is only fair to give you the first chance of considering it again, after I have made what I hope will be improvements…

"I also now understand that… it has to be read and recommended by Store staff [words obscured on the carbon – probably "experts before"] publication in order to interest the firms to buy. It was stupid of me, but I just could not appreciate this before.

"With the idea of improving my MS., I have in mind to add another chapter, YOUR CUSTOMERS' REMARKS and SOME SHOP PHRASES, the former to be an analysis of such remarks as: 'I'll tell her'; 'You see, it's not for me'; 'Are these all you've got?'; 'I'll think it over'; 'Not exactly what I want'; 'I think I'll leave it'. (This chapter is to get to the root of their true meaning, and also to advise how to deal with them.) The other chapter expresses comments on some much used shop phrases, and also gives advice…

"Would you please tell me whether you would want to reconsider it? I do hope you will not think I am pestering you. That is the very last thing I want to do. I would not presume to ask you except that you have put in so much work on it that it seems only right to do so. I hope, too, that you will not consider me erratic. The fact is that I have a great many worries at the moment, and, too, I did not realise that the whole business would take so long…"

This appears to cross with W. H. Newman's handwritten letter of the same date.

"A hasty note before I dash off to our printers in Dewsbury (to act as a courier because of the railway strike). It was kind of you to ring up and Mr Plowman and I are pleased to know that you appreciate that our efforts on the book were on a positive and practical line. We should certainly like to see it again if you decide to alter parts. One of the specific things which would have to be altered is that referring to the dress worn. The rules vary so much that the book's contention one way or the other would have to be left out – and the matter of choice could remain open. No other detailed comment which I could pass on was made.

"We agree there is scope for this and we could do the publishing as effectively as anyone because of our continuing contact with its market.

"I therefore hope we shall be able to have another go."

If there was any further correspondence, it's lost. The following week my mother writes her letter to the *Liverpool Echo*. The book never saw print, and in August she writes to a Mr *Bourne* (apparently a writer whose work she had undertaken to type) "I have just had my book on Salesmanship returned, after almost twelve months and a great deal of encouraging, most misleading correspondence."

In May 1955 she had sent Rider & Company a proposal for a book on her favourite author, Jane Austen, to "mark my appreciation… and also to express my views (which I believe are different from other people's) on some debatable points" but was told that "it does not seem suitable for inclusion in our list." Most of her early tales were love stories ("Romance for Little Miss Muffet", for instance). There's the occasional animal story ("Rags the Hero"). She submitted *Portrait of Greta Walton* as early as the end of 1947, to the Vansittart Novel Competition, which gained it a barely legible handwritten rejection letter from Kathleen White, the Comp Secy (as she styles herself). "I am returning it with a synopsis of the readers' criticisms which may be interesting to you. Its' (sic) a case of Try, Try, Try again!" The synopsis says "This story is much too immature for the standard of our Competition. As one of the judges exclaimed 'What a portrait!' The plot is thin – a girl shy gauche and ordinary falls in love with another girl of more character and intelligence. After emotional scenes and jealousies Greta finally learns to be more normal in the company of a boy. Within its limits the story is not badly told but the product is no more than promising. The author lacks experience."

A novel, *Accent on Love*, dates from the late fifties. The title (which she changed to *A View from the Peak*) suggests that her roots as a writer lie in romantic fiction. The book as a whole demonstrates her ambitions and, alas, the limits of her literary engagement with reality. Perhaps for that very reason the book says more than it intends.

The heroine, Catherine Cummings, is the founder of "a new kind of grammar school" in Pooltown. It will be known as the Thirteen Plus School and require "an entirely new kind of examination" (which is to say, one taken two years later than the one I'd recently passed). Catherine has set it up with money a benefactor, Susan Mortimer, gave her to devote to some good cause. At the opening day she warns the pupils that "you will need to be totally idealistic." The school motto is *Honour Before Honours*. As she takes the stage, "many of [the children] were reminded of Her Majesty, Elizabeth the Queen Mother."

Later, alone, she "dwelled for a moment on a new world where wars and violence were only history. Where disease was at an end. Where the colour of your skin wasn't even noticed. And where juvenile delinquency had no meaning because it had never existed. Where the strong concentrated on helping the weak. Where everyone went out of their way to assist others less fortunate or in trouble to carry their burdens, and only from the highest motives.

"Did she really expect such a miracle from her school? Could such perfection ever be reality? Well, yes, all things were possible. With God's help..." She cleaves to her beliefs although someone concealed by a pen name ("Realistic") writes newspaper articles about her, apparently all in capitals. "CATHERINE CUMMINGS IS AT WORK ON HER DREAMS AGAIN... CATHERINE CUMMINGS, IT WOULD SEEM, IS TRYING TO SHAPE THE CHARACTER OF HUMANITY. WELL, IF IT NEEDS SAYING, PSYCHIATRISTS HAVE BEEN TRYING TO DO THAT FOR SOME TIME. AND CATHERINE CUMMINGS IS NOT A PSYCHIATRIST..."

One pupil at the school is twelve-year-old Danny Hopewell. He doesn't join in sports "because the doctor won't let me". He and his mother Clair live in a cottage with a tiny hall. "It had seemed, and still was, just what they wanted; and, goodness knows, they had had a long enough search for it... It had to be a place where his mother, a novelist, could work out her inspirations. Where he, too, Danny Hopewell, could also write." One of their private jokes is that "Clair Hopewell was an individualist, the joke being on her because of the price she sometimes had to pay for being one." They are "alike in expression, though she was dark and he was fair."

Danny is asked "to set the pace for his fellow pupils by promising never to slack – not even slightly – in his work." At home he writes stories of the supernatural, encouraged by his mother, who is his first reader. "Writers always had to be prepared for the creative fever that seized them at the oddest times and because of the oddest things." Hearing from a schoolmate, Jill, that the founder was prevented from marrying her one true love, Bert Trotter, "Danny, being a writer, was naturally mapping out the romantic chapters, not forgetting the happy ending, that ought to follow." He tells Jill that "often the best writers take the longest time to get into print", to which she responds that she expects "that's because their work is so out of the ordinary that it's a risk to print and publish it because it mightn't be appreciated by the public." He lends Jill his supernatural tales, and although he wants them to see first publication as a book she submits one, "The

Stream", to a short story competition without telling him. "For the stories were stunning. They were thrilling and mystifying and would still have been clever if they had been the work of Edgar Allan Poe – but because Danny, a twelve year old boy, had written them, they were astounding."

The sight of a man watching the cottage has inspired him to write "The Stream", which concerns a cottage by a stream. Peter Hartley and his younger brother live in it with their mother. A male ghost is frequently seen near the stream as a child or older. It appears as an old man to Peter before disappearing for good. The stream dries up, exposing a document addressed to him by name, willing the cottage to him and revealing that the benefactor is about to be murdered by his own brother. Peter turns it over and finds "The writing on that side of the paper was red as blood. It looked like blood. It was blood. It said that the body of an old man had been recovered from the stream behind the cottage earlier that day, and that the body was so mutilated that it was obvious the man had been murdered. It added, in brackets, that the man's name was <u>Peter Hartley</u>."

Jill's brother Simon, a pupil at the local secondary modern, finds the book and scoffs at it before setting out to do worse. "For though Simon was totally ignorant of political issues, and, though having heard of communism, it, and the way it worked, was a mystery, he was enraged by Danny's individuality and determined to overpower all that was unusual in him." He taunts Danny with gibes such as "How's the authorship business, Mr. Conan Doyle?" and "What does it feel like to be a celebrated novelist? Let's be knowing, <u>author boy</u>!" Next day he's reduced to "making insinuating references to Poe, Dickens, Wells, and M. R. James, who were the only authors of 'queer' stories that he knew" although later he comes up with Graham Greene. He lures Danny into the clutches of Fred Smith's teenage gang, one of whom enquires "This the goof wot writes?" Having roughed him up they vandalise the Thirteen Plus School and eventually set fire to it. Danny wins second prize in the competition and a personal comment from an editor that "he had been much impressed by Danny's work and that he believed Danny would be a leading writer in the future."

Simon runs away but returns to face the music. Danny encounters the mysterious man and, discovering that he's Bert Trotter back from having made his fortune in America, reflects that "Somehow, he and Miss Cummings had to be reunited. Supernatural stories were different, of course, but romantic ones had to have a happy ending!"

At the trial of the arsonists Fred Smith gives an impassioned speech. "You ain't never been that blooming hungry that any blessed living thing would do to eat. You ain't never felt too sick to eat because you'd gone without that long that yer belly wouldn't take it when yer got it. And how would you like not having a corner where you could do what you wanted wivvout being gaped at! You've never been treated as though you was a snail or a bit of muck. I hate that bloody, swanking school!" It confronts Catherine with the limits of her charity, and she resolves to embrace his kind. Bert Trotter intervenes and offers to take Fred under his wing. Later he walks Catherine home and, in a lane that revives a romantic memory of theirs, proposes to her. Simon and Danny make up. Jill undertakes to learn to type perfectly, and Danny agrees she can be his secretary when he's famous. Fred becomes a farmer in America, and his slum family move to a better house, his father having gained "a safe, steady job in the corporation cleansing department." Their first visitors are Bert and Catherine Trotter.

I'm Danny, of course, having been at St Edward's College for a year and written my first book, *Ghostly Tales*. Indeed, the competition editor's comments resemble Tom Boardman Jr's about that book. I was furious about being represented, especially with "chubby pink knees bulging out of neatly pulled up socks. His blazer, too, was on the tight side. His hair was flat and tidy and obviously just dressed." (I don't recall feeling so embarrassed to find a similarly pudgy self in an earlier novel, *The Ghost of Spooky Manor*, dedicated "To my own, very dear, eight year old John, who revels in such mysteries.") My objections must have been taken to heart, because in a rewrite that my mother didn't finish, Danny has become Juliette and appropriately altered. Otherwise it seems to me that the novel was always founded on acts of denial, especially of Liverpool. Although the location is named Pooltown, there's virtually no sense of place, and the little we're shown bears no resemblance to the town where my mother is living. The book seems to reach for fading memories of a lost Huddersfield, of idealism, even of a lost ability to stand back from oneself.

Perhaps she could no longer afford or bear to see herself. She encouraged me to submit my work, I imagine partly in the hope that it would bring us some financial stability, as she continued doggedly submitting her own. Inspiration kept striking, and she would often grab a notebook to scribble ideas down, whether for the work in progress or a future tale. One notebook of uncertain date appears to contain the names under which actual people from Liverpool and Huddersfield would figure as characters in a novel. Mr Atkinson (parenthesised as "Snooper – Liverpool – N. Rise") would be Marmaduke Appleyard. Harold Broadbent, the lost love for whom she yearned, becomes John Broad. Alex = Ian Mackenzie. The Carlines, neighbours in Nook Rise, are listed as "kind but afraid for themselves and Hazel" (their daughter, with whom I used to play). Father Grogan is changed into Canon Smith. Mrs Van Dyke gets a long parenthesis ("Catholic – Mrs Tyson been 'trying' to 'work' on her? But she's nice, I think!") and a transformation into Mrs Hungerford. Mr and Mrs Weston ("were 'nice' but obviously 'worked on') are destined to be Mr and Mrs Wicks. "Lady from Waldgrave Road who said in Dr's about not having son at table" ("Catholic – Snooper") = Mrs Brady. Many folk are characterised as "snoopers", including Gladys and Bob Trenery (distantly related to Gladys Gordon Trenery, I suppose, who wrote for *Weird Tales* as G. G. Pendarves), the next-door neighbours who had looked after her and three-year-old me when she cut her hand in a marital squabble. Alder Hey Psychiatrist ("needed one herself") acquires a name, Dr Payne. It seems likely that she was the doctor who in my medical history from the 1950s suggests my mother might well be the problem with my nerves. I recall my mother opining more than once that using Liverpool or Liverpudlians as material for fiction was liable to invite reprisals, and whatever her intentions for this book, it appears to have progressed in written form no farther than these notes.

September 1954 brings a letter from an associate editor at Museum Press, regretting that they no longer publish juvenile novels and adding "One thing I should mention to you, and that is that you are being very optimistic in hoping to have a book which is written in the next few weeks in print by Christmas – I fear that even the liveliest publishers take far longer than that!"

At least as early as that year she had an agent for her fiction, Kay Routledge, co-director of Charles Lavell Limited. This brought her no success. While in 1954 the agent enthused about her short story "No Washing Machine" (based on an encounter with a salesman who apparently expressed shock at her lack of that household item), by June 1957 Kay Routledge writes of another tale "I regret I cannot offer to negotiate the short story for you. It is not along the lines of the material I handle for the women's magazines, and actually it is based on a false premise: I do not think an astrologer will commit himself so far as to predict a marriage within a short period. We represent a leading astrologer so I am well informed about this… I hope you will enjoy your holiday and that you and your young son are now much better. I will send the manuscript – and the old one, which has failed to appeal to all the editors – to your address when you return home."

By September my mother had reverted to attempting to place her own work. W. & R. Holmes (Books) Ltd of Glasgow respond "We are sorry to be returning herewith your children's thriller <u>The Gillian Kershaw Mystery</u>, but would advise you that our publications are for the most part of an educational nature. We suggest you try one of the publishing firms specialising in children's books."

A letter from her sister Kay in December 1961 includes the paragraph "I had not written to you before, because I hadn't heard from you, even a thankyou note after you returned home. If you still feel that your correspondence is being interfered with write to the Postmaster General. You'll get satisfaction from Head Office."

My mother carries on submitting her work directly nonetheless. She couldn't sell a science fiction – or rather, science fantasy – novel called *The Wish Machine*, or the script for a comic-book serial, *The Character Building School*, or a short school story, "The Mystery at Belgrave School", or much else. Indeed, from 9 February 1963 we have this, to Miss Nora B. Walker:

"Dear Miss Walker,

"Many thanks for sight of your stories, which go back to you under separate cover today. These are light, interesting, but not with sufficient body to be meaningful to Arkham House readers. The Wish Machine seems to me a promising vehicle to enable you to make some observations about life within the framework of fantasy, but it lacks the impact desirable in the field of the fantastic, and there is no very sound reason why these observations should be cast in the fantasy form. A book of this kind would not interest Arkham

House, I am sorry to say. ... I should think THE PRICE OF POPULARITY is a better title than POPULARITY IS EXPENSIVE.

"May you have good sailing in your new book!

"Sincerely,

"August Derleth."

Later that month she tries another agent, Frederick G. Richford:

"...In particular, and firstly, I want to place two short stories – around 1,500 and 1,000 words – which I have written recently and which have not yet been sent to any British editor. They are of the Fantasy?/Imagination type and are the first of many I intend to write. I have now sufficient material for a book of them and am working on them at the moment. It is my belief that they are something a little 'different'; and if you are interested in trying to place them for me, I should like you to keep in mind that the two completed, and the ones to be written in the near future, are collectively intended for book publication. However, I should like them to appear separately first. (I should be interested to hear your opinion on this.) the finished book would come under the heading (as a subtitle) of Stories of Fantasy, Imagination, and the Unusual..."

Alongside her books and short stories she also sent entries every week to a magazine competition called Bullets, where entrants selected phrases from a list provided and added one of their own to make a witty observation. As I recall quite a few of my mother's were slyly knowing, but they never won a prize.

While she and my father very seldom spoke (and even less did he to me), she occasionally wrote him letters. The carbon of one from March 1958 survives.

"A few months ago, I asked you, for John's sake, to buy a house away from this district. You ignored that letter, as well as one I wrote some years back.

"You have said that you have finished with me, even though I did ask you, for John, to co-operate with me in making a fresh start. If ever you change your mind about that, it will be for you to approach me.

"There are some things I would remind you of, however. I married you almost fourteen years ago and came to live in a strange town among strangers. I came to live in a house I disliked but which I believed was only a temporary residence. I left all my friends behind me, and I had (and still have) very many.

"I have already told you, and it is the truth, that John is most unhappy in this neighbourhood[2]. As you are well aware, so am I. We are resented, including yourself, for John's cleverness despite his frequent illnesses...

"But it is for John's sake that I am making a last appeal to you. John has a right to a home that he is not ashamed of, one where he can bring his friends. He needs to study and to entertain..."

She had found such a house and urged its purchase. Presumably there was no response.

In 1964 my first book was published, and I took my mother to Paris for a few days on the advance against royalties. We travelled via London, and my mother wrote to "Greta", now living in South Kensington. The reply is the only one of her letters I've found.

"Dear Nora,

"Thank you so much for the presentation copy of John's victory. It must be a jubilant and satisfying feeling, to see oneself in print. You must be most proud and gratified, by his success, & so young. That's what comes, I suppose, of his mixture of Jewish and Scottish blood, & should I add, Irish?

"Your Husband must be frightfully proud of him too – &

---

2. I don't recall this as a problem.

it's a pity your mother never knew – for she never had much faith in <u>your</u> talents, had she?!

"I can't imagine how you've managed to be married, a housewife, a mother, & to have written all those novels, books, plays etc. which you listed – <u>I</u> can scarcely find time to write a letter! Have they all been published? for it amounts to practically a lifetime's work. How <u>do</u> you look after a home as well?

"I was most touched when I saw John's photograph on the back cover. You've produced a good looking son, Nora. He looks to have beautiful eyes, & a very sweet mouth…

"Well now, after all this preamble, we shall be away, in Bavaria, when you come to London. Just imagine, out of a whole year, the dates co-incide…

"I wonder how life is treating you – I sincerely hope that happiness has come your way, for good health, & <u>un</u>-happiness don't go hand in hand.

"Why do you have to wait until you've sold a novel, before having your innards put in order? Wouldn't you be better for everything, if the trouble were cleared up? If I remember correctly, you seem to have been putting it off for about 18-20 years!

"Couldn't your husband make arrangements for you? Surely he and John could manage whilst you were away – it could be even <u>fun</u>…

"Kindest regards to you all three, and congrats to John. ['Greta'.]"

In 1970 my future wife and I set up home together. In 1971 my father was fatally injured, perhaps while defending the place where he worked (Holt's Fireplaces on Edge Lane) as a night watchman. I visited him in hospital as seldom as possible, a gruelling and well-nigh mute experience relieved by his death. I thought this might come as a relief to my mother as well, but being alone in the house appears to have sent her further inwards. Soon it became a lair from which she would observe anyone who ventured into the cul-de-sac. Watching through the nets is a suburban pastime, but I suspect she told herself tales about strangers. By then she wasn't writing much. The fictions may have festered in her head.

Among her surviving papers is a letter that was never sent, for reasons that will become clear. It may or may not be related to a note written on an envelope, which reads

"<u>Private</u>

"Don't use that key. I know you've got it. If you do, I shall get my own back, I promise you."

The letter is dated 19/2/75.

"Dear Honey,

"Your attention, please!

"Though I should not be writing this letter at all except for the fact that I believe you to be a friend of the past with whom I have lost touch, you have the advantage of me; but let me add at once that I have no intention of posting it. However, as we both know, that is not necessary. Not only are you in the almost omnipotent position of being able to see me, and hear me, inside and outside my home whenever you choose, but you are also able to translate my typescript.

"So it is that I prefer to convey this message in the comfort, such as it is, of my own home. Before that I would stress that I shall not at any time be inserting an advertisement in any paper, nor shall I be post- any letter to you (which would seem to be almost impossible anyway as I am not only not convinced of your identity but, also, I do not know your address) <u>except in answer to yours</u>. (After all, if you are as genuine as you would have me believe – and as I want to believe – there should be no difficulty in that.)

"Now we come to the question of the significance of your strange behaviour – that is, your concentration on me, whilst, however, you remain invisible to me. (Don't you think that is not exactly playing the game, no matter what your motive is?)

And what EXACTLY is your motive? Am I the victim of some scientific experiment, are you guarding me from some kind of danger (if so, what? or whom?) I realise there is a possibility (that is, more, <u>much more</u>, than a possibility – or I should not be writing this at all, as I have already said,) that you actually are the person I have been led to believe you are, in which case you may still be just a little interested in me, as I am in you. If you are that person, you will remember that at the end of both short periods of friendship we parted on <u>un</u>friendly terms; and here I must point out that when we met the second time I did not recognise you – but it was wartime, when much is rightly excused, and at once I liked you. (Although I look back on that interlude with some amazement.)

"I also think of the difference in your appearance and also what was, (or could be,) unaltered, plus some more cryptic observations you made about me. The seemingly peculiar thing is (which tantalises me) that I have always prided myself on my photographic memory for faces, but I have worked it out that faces are imprinted on my mind but if I do not see them again for a long period, if they have altered in the meantime, although I get a clear picture of the face as it has become, I do not always recognise it – until in retrospect I put the two faces side by side when all the differences blend into one.

"After all, however, you may not be my friend of the past. In fact you may be someone with whom I am totally unacquainted. You know the answer to that. But one thing is certain. If you are genuine, you will agree that it is <u>your</u> privilege to get in touch with <u>me</u>; and, most definitely, <u>I</u> shall not get in touch with <u>you</u> except in reply to <u>your</u> letter."

It's unsigned.

There is one more letter. In 1980 I was a guest at the World Fantasy Convention. While I was in America she apparently wrote to me care of my New York agent but used ordinary inland postage. I didn't receive the letter until months after my return, and felt it best not to refer to it. She never did. It reads:

"My very dear John,

"When _are_ you coming home? I am being very brave – but do, please, come soon. Will you be here at the end of this week, or even before? It was great news that you had heard that you had won another outstanding award, and I am very, very proud of you – but, please, tell me when you are coming home.

"Thank you for your lovely card, and by the way, the only reason that I have not written before is that I have a very weak wrist at the moment.

"Very little news, but Jenny brought Tammy to see mee last week. She was full of liffe and fun!

"Well, John, I shall be hoping to see you now very, very soon. Do let me hear from you. A card would be welcome. The one you have sent is very interesting.

"All my love,

"Mum."

In 1981 my wife and I and our daughter moved out of Liverpool, though not at all far – to Wallasey, still very much on Merseyside, although across the river. It must have seemed too far to my mother. Her house grew full of people, most if not all of them menacing or worse. One of her objections to the house had always been that it was rented, and so we bought her a house in Wallasey, less than a mile away from ours. I was unable to grasp that the only place she lived now was inside her own mind. If anything, the move disoriented her further. Next year she died. Some years afterwards I had a phone call from "Greta", who had traced me through Directory Enquiries. She seemed more saddened than surprised to learn her friend was dead.

I've visited the house in Nook Rise several times since – with J. K. Potter, with David Mathew, more recently with Poppy Z. Brite. The owners, a pleasant friendly family, gave

David and me the tour. The house is remarkably neat and compact now, and feels loved. I was disconcerted by how small it seemed at last – even the back garden and its neighbours, the view of all of which from my bedroom window had appeared considerable for as long as I'd lived in the house. I should have expected this shift of perception to have taken place much earlier – certainly in the years I was visiting my mother there. Perhaps I was haunted by my childhood image of the house. Now the place feels very snug.

Are there any ghosts? Poppy said she found our brief visit disturbing, although we didn't even enter the house. As we drove to it the sky above the garden suburb turned as black as the heart of a storm – as some of my memories. Sometimes I dream I'm back in the house I remember. Perhaps it's haunted only by me, or will be. I'd rather hope it's haunted by what could have been.

THE MAN IN THE UNDERPASS

RAMSEY CAMPBELL

I'm Lynn. I'm nearly eleven. I was born in Liverpool, in Tuebrook.

I go to Tuebrook County Primary School. This year I've been taking my little brother Jim to the Infants. Every morning we walk to school. It's only six hundred yards away. I know that because our class had to find out for Mrs Chandler for a project. We cross one street and then walk up Buckingham Road. At the end we go down the underpass under West Derby Road. My little brother calls it underpants. And then just at the other end, there's the school.

The underpass is what my story's all about.

It isn't very high, my best friend June's big sister can touch the roof without jumping. In the roof there are long lights like ice chopped up. That's what Mrs Chandler means when she says something is a nice image. Usually some of the lights are broken, and there are plugs hanging down like buds. When you walk through you can hear the traffic overhead, it feels as if your ears are shaking when buses drive over. When we were little we used to stand in the middle so the buses would make our ears tickle. And we used to shout and make ghosty noises because then it sounded like a cave.

Then the skinheads started to wait for the little kids in the underpass, so they got a lollipop man to cross us over and we weren't supposed to go down. Sometimes we did, because some of the traffic wouldn't stop for the lollipop man and we wanted to watch our programmes on tv. Then the lady in the greengrocer's would tell on us and we got spanked. I think we're too old to be spanked. June would cry when she was spanked, because she's a bit of a little kid sometimes. So we stopped going down until the skinheads went somewhere else. June's big sister says they're all taking LSD now.

When we could go down again it wasn't like the same place. They'd been spraying paint all over the walls. The walls used to be white, but now they were like the advertisements you see at the films, when the colours keep changing and dazzling you. They were green and gold and pink like lipstick and white and grey and blood red. They were words we wouldn't say at home, like tits, and all the things skinheads say. Like "tuebrook skins rule ok," only they'd painted it over twice, so it was as if something was wrong with your eyes.

June and I were reading everything on the way to school when Tonia came down. She lives in the next street from me, with her father. She used to go to St John the Evangelist, but now she goes to Tuebrook County Primary with us. June doesn't like her because she says Tonia thinks she's better than us and knows more. She never comes round to play with me, but I think she's lonely and her mother doesn't live with them, only a lady who stays with them sometimes. I heard that in the sweetshop before the sweetshop lady started nodding to tell them I was there. Anyway, Tonia started acting shocked at the things they'd painted on the walls. "I don't think you should let your little brother see these things. They aren't good for him." Jim's seen our mother and father with no clothes on, but June said "Oh come on, Lynn. We weren't looking anyway, only playing," and she pretended to pee at Tonia, and we ran off.

Tonia was nearly late for assembly. She'd been looking at the man painted on the wall where the underpass dips in the middle. Mrs Chandler smiled at her but didn't say anything. If it had been us she'd have pretended to be cross, but she wouldn't really mind if we laughed, because she likes us laughing. I suppose Tonia must have been looking at the man on the wall because she hadn't seen anything like him before, she was flushed and biting her lip and smiling at the same time. My story's about him too, in a funny way, at least I think it is. He was as tall as the roof, and his spout was sticking up almost as far as his chin. Someone had painted him in white —really they'd just drawn round him, but then someone else had written on the wall, so he was full of colours. He'd got one foot on each side of the drain in the middle of the underpass, that the gutter runs down to. Jim said the man was going to pee, so I had to tell him he wouldn't be going to pee when his spout's like that.

Anyway, that was the day Mrs Chandler told us the theatre group was coming to do a play for us. June said "Are they going to make us laugh?" and Mrs Chandler said "Oh yes, they'll shout at you if you don't laugh."

Then we had to write about our parents. I like writing about people, but June likes writing about football and music best. Tonia suddenly started crying and tore up her paper, so Mrs Chandler had to put her arms round her and talk to her, but we couldn't hear what she was saying. June got jealous and kept asking Mrs Chandler things, so Mrs Chandler put her in charge of the mice's cage all week.

When we got home Tonia stayed behind in the playground. I saw her go into the underpass, but the last time I looked she hadn't come out. My mother was still at Bingo, and Jim was crying so I smacked him, then I had to make him a fried egg so he'd stop. When my father came in he said

"Should have made me one as well. You're a lot better housewife than," and he stopped. But my mother had won and gave him half, so he didn't shout at her.

After tea I went to the wine shop to get them some crisps. Jim sat on the railings at the top of the underpass and was seeing how far he could lean back holding on with his heels, so I had to run out and smack him. I broke my arm when I was little, doing that on the railings. Then I saw Tonia coming out of the underpass. "Haven't you had your tea yet?" I said. She must have been in a mood, because she got all red and said "I've had my dinner, if that's what you mean. We have it exactly the same time every day, if you must know. You don't think I've been down there all this time, do you?" I do try to make friends with her, but it's hard.

The next afternoon we had the play. There were five people in it, three men and two women. It was very good, and everyone laughed. I liked the part best when one of the men has to be the moon, so he has a torch and tries to get into it to be the man in the moon. They borrowed Mrs Chandler's guitar that she brings when we have singing, and they all sang at the end and we pretended to throw money, then they threw sweets for us. I told Mrs Chandler I liked it, and she said it was from *A Midsummer Night's Dream* because it was nearly midsummer. I said I'd like to read it, so she said to ask for it at the library.

Then it was time to go home, and June asked one of the actors to cross her over the road. She told him he'd got a lovely face. Well, he had, but it's just like June to say something like that. She's bold sometimes. She said "Oh, and this is Lynn. She's my best friend, so you can talk to her too." I think she wanted him to come on his own, but he called the others to look at the colours in the underpass. So we all went down there instead. I saw Tonia watching us, and she looked as if she was going to cry, as if we'd found her special hiding-place or something, then she ran after us. They all started shouting and gasping like little kids watching fireworks. "Look at the figure in the middle. It's almost a work of art," one of the women said. "Ebsolutely Eztec," a man said. I don't think he really talked like that, he was just trying to be funny. Tonia pulled at the one with the lovely face and said "What does he mean?"

"He means Aztec, love," he said. "I'm not your love," Tonia said. The man looked upset, because he was only being friendly, but he spelt Aztec for her. "Just the place for a midsummer sacrifice," one of the men said. "I don't think the Aztecs were bothered about seasons. They cut hearts out all the year round," another one said. Then they all walked us home and said we should try to start a youth theatre with Mrs Chandler. But Tonia stayed in the underpass.

The next day I went to the library after school. It's a nice place, except they chase you if you mess even a little bit. The librarian has a red face and shouts at the little kids if they don't understand what he means, and doesn't like showing you where the books are. But the girls are nice, and they'll talk to you and look for books for you. I got *A Midsummer Night's Dream* out. I didn't really understand it, except for the funny parts we saw at school. I'd like Mrs Chandler to help me with it, but I think she'd be too busy. I can read it again when I'm older.

I saw Tonia's father when I was there. He was getting a book about Aztecs for her. He said it was for a project. She must have told him that. It's stupid, because she could have told the truth. The librarian got him a book out of the men's library. "This will probably be a bit advanced for her," he said. Tonia's father started shouting. "Don't talk about what you don't know. She's an extremely intelligent child. I've had more than enough of that sort of comment at home." The librarian was getting redder and redder, and he saw me looking, so I ran out.

Next morning Tonia brought the book to school. "I've got

something to show you," she told June and me. Then she heard Mrs Chandler coming, so she hid the book in her desk. She could have shown her, Mrs Chandler would have been interested. At playtime she brought it out with her. We all had to crowd round her so the teachers wouldn't see. There were pictures of Aztec statues that looked like the floors you see in really old buildings. And there were some drawings, like the ones little kids do, funny but you aren't supposed to laugh. Some of them had no clothes on. "Don't let everyone see," Tonia said. "I don't know what you're worried about. They don't worry us," I said, because the way she was showing us made the pictures seem dirty, though they weren't really. It was like a picture of Jesus we used to giggle at when we were little, because he was only wearing a cloth. I suppose she never used to play doctors and nurses, so she couldn't have seen anything like the man in the underpass.

When we went out to play at dinnertime she brought the book again. She started reading bits out of it, about the Aztecs using pee for dyeing clothes, and eating dogs and burning people and cutting their hearts out and eating them. She said one part meant that when they made a sacrifice their gods would appear. "No it doesn't," June said. "They were just men dressed up." "Well, it does," Tonia said. "The gods came and walked among them." "You're the best reader, Lynn. You say what it says," June said. Actually June was right, but Tonia was biting her lip and I didn't want to be mean, so I said she was right. June wouldn't speak to me when we walked home.

But the next day I had to be specially nice to June, because Mrs Chandler said so, so we were friends again. June was upset all day, that was why Mrs Chandler said to be nice to her. Someone had left the mice's cage unlocked and they'd escaped. June was crying, because she liked to watch them and she loves animals, only she hadn't any since when her kitten tried to get up under the railway bridge where you can hear pigeons, and fell off and got killed. Mrs Chandler said for everyone to be nice to June, so we were. Except Tonia, who avoided us all day and didn't talk to anyone. I thought then she was sad for June.

On Saturday we went to the baths by the library. The baths are like a big toilet with tiled walls and slippery floors. We said we'd teach Tonia to swim, but her father wouldn't let her come in case she got her asthma and drowned. We had to stop some boys pushing Jim and the other little kids in. There must be something wrong with them to do that. I think they ought to go and see a doctor, like Tonia with her asthma. Only June's big sister says it isn't the ordinary doctor Tonia needs to go and see.

Then we went home to watch Doctor Who. It was good, only Jim got all excited watching the giant maggots chasing Doctor Who and nearly had to go to bed. My mother had bought some lovely curtains with her Bingo money, all red and purple, and she was putting them up in the front room so our maisonette would look different from the others. There wasn't any football on tv, so my father went out for a drink and gave us money for lemonade. June had to go home because her auntie was coming, so I took Jim to get the lemonade.

On the way we met Tonia. She didn't speak to us. She was running and she looked as if she'd been sick. I wasn't sure, because it had got all dark as if someone had poured dirty dishwater into the sky. Anyway, I went to the wine shop and when I'd bought the lemonade I looked for Jim but he wasn't there. I didn't hear him go out, because I'd told him to stay in the shop but they'd left the door open to let air in. He'd run down the underpass. Little kids are like moths when they see a light sometimes. So I went to get him and I nearly slipped, because someone had just been throwing red paint all over the place. It was even on the lights, and someone had tried to paint the man on the wall with it. Jim said it was blood and I told him not to be soft. But it did look nasty. I didn't even want my supper.

It rained all Sunday, so nothing happened. Except June brought the *Liverpool Echo* round because one of my poems was in it. I'd sent it in so long ago that I'd forgotten. They only put your first name and your age, as if you didn't want anyone to know it was you. I think it's stupid.

Next day when we were coming home we saw the man who empties the bins on West Derby Road talking to the ladies from the wine shop. There's a concrete bin on top of the underpass, with a band going round it saying litter litter litter. He'd found four mice cut up in the bin. June started crying when we got to our road. She cries a lot sometimes and I have to put my arm round her, like my father when he heard Labour hadn't won the election. She thought they were the mice from our classroom. I said they couldn't be, because nobody could have caught them.

The next night June and I took Jim home, then we went to the library. We left him playing with the little girls from up the street. When we got back he wasn't there. My mother got all worried but we said we'd look for him. We looked under the railway bridge, because he likes to go in the workshop there to listen to the noise, that sounds like the squeak they put on the tv to remind you to switch it off. But he wasn't there, so we looked on the waste ground by the railway line, because he likes playing with the bricks there more than the building blocks he got for Christmas. He was sitting there waiting to see a train. He said a girl had taken the little girls to see a man who showed them nice things.

Some policemen came to school one day to tell us not to go with men like that, because they were ill, so we thought we'd better tell our parents. But just as we were coming home we saw Tonia with the little girls. She looked as if she wanted to run away when she saw us, then June shouted "What've you been doing with those kids?"

"It wasn't anything, only a drawing on the wall," one of the little girls said. "You wouldn't even let Jim look at him the other day," I said. "Well, he wouldn't have wanted to come," Tonia said. "You just let them play next time. Jim was having fun," I said.

The next day a puppy came into the playground and we all played with it. It rolled on its back to make us tickle it, then it peed on the caretaker's bike and he chased it away. Tonia played with it most and when it came back to the playground, she threw sweets out of the window for it until Mrs Chandler said not to. We were painting, and Tonia did a lovely one with lots of colours, instead of the ones she usually does which are all dark. Mrs Chandler said it was very good, and you could tell she was really pleased. But she asked Tonia why the man was standing with his back to us, and Tonia blushed and said she couldn't paint faces very well, though she can when she wants to. I painted a puppy eating a bone and Mrs Chandler liked that too.

When it was time to go home Tonia stayed behind to ask Mrs Chandler about painting faces, as if she didn't know how. We thought she wanted to walk along with Mrs Chandler, but instead she ran out of the school when everyone had gone and went down the underpass with the puppy. We saw her because I had to get some apples from the greengrocers. That's a funny shop, because the boards have got all dirty with potatoes, and sometimes the ladies talk to people and forget we're there. So we were in there a long time and Tonia and the puppy hadn't come up. "Let's see what she's doing," June said. Just as we went down the ramp the puppy ran out with Tonia chasing it. She had a penknife. "I was only pretending. I wouldn't kill it really," she said. "You shouldn't have a knife at all," I said. Then she went off because we wouldn't help her find the puppy.

After tea Jim and the little girls were climbing on a lorry, so I had to tell them the man would shout when he came back. They all ran up the street and started shouting "Pop a cat a petal, pop a cat a petal." Little kids are funny sometimes. I asked them what it meant and one of the little girls said "That's what that girl said we had to say to the man on the wall." I told her not to play with Tonia, because Tonia could do things they shouldn't.

Next day I asked Mrs Chandler what it meant. She had to look it up, then she said it was a volcano in Mexico. At dinnertime I asked Tonia why she'd told the little girls to say it. Tonia went red and said it was her secret. "Then you shouldn't have told them. Anyway, it's only a volcano," June said, because she'd heard Mrs Chandler tell me. "No, it isn't," Tonia said. "It's his name. It's a god's name." "It's a volcano in Mexico," I said. "Lynn should know. She's the best reader, and she had a poem in the paper," June said. "I didn't see it," Tonia said. "Well, I did. It said Lynn," June said. "That could be anyone," Tonia said. "You're making it up." "No she isn't," June said. "She'll have you a fight." So we went behind the school and had a fight, and I won.

Tonia was crying and said she'd tell Mrs Chandler, but she didn't. She was quiet all afternoon, and she waited for us when we were going home. "I don't care if you did have a poem in the paper," she said. "I've seen something you haven't." "What is it?" I said. "If you meet me tonight I'll show you," she said. "Just you. She can't come." "June's my best friend. She's got to come too or I won't," I said. "All right, but you've got to promise not to tell anyone," Tonia said. "Wait till it's nearly dark and meet me at the end of my road."

So I had to say I was going to hear a record at June's, and she had to say she was coming to ours. We met Tonia at nine o'clock. She was very quiet and wouldn't say anything, just started walking and didn't look to see if we were coming. Sometimes I don't like the dark, because the cars look like animals asleep, and everything seems bigger. It makes me feel like a little kid. We could see all the people in the houses watching tv with the lights out, and I wished I was back at home. Anyway, we followed Tonia, and she stopped at the top of the underpass.

"Oh, it's only that stupid thing on the wall," June said. "No, it isn't," Tonia said. "There's a real man down there if you look." "Well, I don't want to see him," June said. "What's so special about him?" I said. "He's a god," Tonia said. "He's not. He's just a man playing with his thing," June said. "He probably wouldn't want you to see him anyway," Tonia said. "I'm going down. You go home." "We'll come with you to make sure you're all right," I said, but really I was excited without knowing why.

We went down the ramp where nobody would see us and Tonia said we had to take our knickers off and say "Pop a cat a petal," only whisper it so people wouldn't hear us. "You're just like a little kid," June said. "I'm not taking my knickers off." "Well, pull your dress up then," Tonia said. "No, you do it first," I said. "I don't need to," Tonia said. "You've got to go first," I said. So she did, and we all started whispering "Pop a cat a petal," and when we were behind her we pulled our dresses down again. Then Tonia was in the underpass and we were still round the corner of the ramp. We dared each other to go first, then I said "Let's go in together."

So June pushed me in and I pulled her in, and we started saying "Pop a cat a petal" again, only we weren't saying it very well because we couldn't stop giggling. But then I got dizzy. All the lights in the underpass were flickering like a fire when it's going out, and the colours were swaying, and all the passage was like it was glittering slowly, and Tonia was standing in the middle swaying as if she was dancing with the light. Then June screamed and I think I did, because I thought I saw a man.

It must have been our eyes because the light was so funny. But we thought we saw a giant standing behind Tonia. He was covered with paint, and he was as tall as the roof. He hadn't any clothes on, so he couldn't have been there really, but it looked as if his spout was swaying like an elephant's trunk reaching up. But it must have been just the light, because he hadn't got a face, only paint, and he looked like those cutout photographs they put in shop windows. Anyway, when we screamed Tonia looked round and saw we were nowhere near her. She looked as if she could have hit us. And when we looked again there wasn't any giant, only the man back on the wall.

"He wanted you," Tonia said. "You should have gone to him." "No thank you," June said. "And if we get into trouble at home I'll batter you." Then we ran home, but they didn't ask me anything, because they'd heard my father had to be on strike again.

Next day Tonia wouldn't speak to us. We heard her telling someone else that she knew something they didn't, so we told them that she only wanted you to take your knickers down. Then she wanted to walk home with us. "He's angry because you ran away," she said. "He wanted a sacrifice." June wouldn't let her, but I said "You can walk on the other side of the road if you want, but we won't talk to you." So she did, and she was crying and I felt a bit mean, but June wouldn't let me go over.

Saturday was horrible, because my parents had a row about the strike, and Jim started crying and they both shouted at him and had another row, and he was sick all down the stairs, so I cleaned it up. Then there wasn't any disinfectant, and my mother said my father never bought anything we needed, and he said I wasn't the maid to do all the dirty jobs. So I went upstairs and had a cry, then I played with Jim in our room, and it was just getting dark when I saw June coming down our road with her mother.

I thought they might have found out where we'd been last night, but it wasn't that. June's mother wanted her to stay with us, because her big sister had been attacked in the underpass and she didn't want June upset. So Jim slept with my parents and they had to be friends again, and June and I talked in bed until we fell asleep. June's big sister had just been walking through the underpass when a man grabbed her from behind. "Did he rape her?" I said. "He must have. Do you think it hurts?" June said. "It can't hurt much or people wouldn't do it," I said.

On Sunday June went home again, because her big sister had gone to hospital. I heard my parents talking about it when I was in the kitchen. "It's most peculiar," my mother said. "The doctor said she hadn't been touched." "I wouldn't have thought people needed to imagine that sort of thing these days at her age," my father said. I don't know what he meant.

On Monday Mrs Chandler said we weren't to go in the underpass again until she said. Tonia said we couldn't get hurt in the daytime, with the police station just up the road. But Mrs Chandler said she'd spank us herself if she heard we'd been down, and you could tell she wasn't joking.

At dinnertime there were policemen in the underpass. We went to the top to listen. The traffic was noisy, so we couldn't hear everything they said, but we heard one shout "Bring me an envelope. There's something caught on the drain." And another one said "Drugs, by the look of it." Then Tonia started coughing and we all had to run away before they caught us. I think she did it on purpose.

When I went home I had to go to the greengrocers. So I pretended I was waiting for someone by the underpass, because I saw a policeman going down. He must have gone to tell the one who was watching, because I heard him say "You won't believe this. They weren't drugs at all. They were hearts." "Hearts?" said the other one. "Yes, of some kind of small animal," he said. "Two of them. I'm wondering how they tie in with those mice in the bin up there. They'd been

269

mutilated, if you remember. But there ought to be two more hearts. They couldn't have gone down the drain because it's been clogged for weeks." "I'll tell you something else," the other one said. "I don't think that's red paint on this light." I didn't want to hear any more, so I turned round to go, and I saw Tonia listening at the other end. Then she saw me and ran away.

So I know who took the mice out of the classroom, and I think I know why she looked as if she'd been sick that night, but I don't want to speak to her to find out. I wish I could tell Mrs Chandler about it, but we promised not to tell about the underpass, and June would be terribly upset if she knew about the mice. Her big sister is home again now, but she won't go out at night, and she keeps shivering. I suppose Tonia might leave it alone now, because it's nearly the holidays. Only I heard her talking the other day in the playground. She might just have been boasting, because she looked all proud of herself, and she looked at the policeman at the top of the underpass as if she wished he'd go away, and she said "Pop a cat a petal did it to me too."

MACKINTOSH WILLY

RAMSEY CAMPBELL

To start with, he wasn't called Mackintosh Willy. I never knew who gave him that name. Was it one of those nicknames that seem to proceed from a group subconscious, names recognised by every member of the group yet apparently originated by none? One has to call one's fears something, if only to gain the illusion of control. Still, sometimes I wonder how much of his monstrousness we created. Wondering helps me not to ponder my responsibility for what happened at the end.

When I was ten I thought his name was written inside the shelter in the park. I saw it only from a distance; I wasn't one of those who made a game of braving the shelter. At ten I wasn't afraid to be timid — that came later, with adolescence.

Yet if you had walked past Newsham Park you might have wondered what there was to fear: why were children advancing, bold but wary, on the red-brick shelter by the twilit pool? Surely there could be no danger in the shallow shed, which might have held a couple of dozen bicycles. By now the fishermen and the model boats would have left the pool alone and still; lamps on the park road would have

271

begun to dangle luminous tails in the water. The only sounds would be the whispering of children, the murmur of trees around the pool, perhaps a savage incomprehensible muttering whose source you would be unable to locate. Only a game, you might reassure yourself.

And of course it was: a game to conquer fear. If you had waited long enough you might have heard shapeless movement in the shelter, and a snarling. You might have glimpsed him as he came scuttling lopsidedly out of the shelter, like an injured spider from its lair. In the gathering darkness, how much of your glimpse would you believe? The unnerving swiftness of the obese limping shape? The head that seemed to belong to another, far smaller, body, and which was almost invisible within a grey Balaclava cap, except for the small eyes which glared through the loose hole?

All of that made us hate him. We were too young for tolerance – and besides, he was intolerant of us. Ever since we could remember he had been there, guarding his territory and his bottle of red biddy. If anyone ventured too close he would start muttering. Sometimes you could hear some of the words: "Damn bastard prying interfering snooper... thieving bastard layabout... think you're clever, eh? ... I'll give you something clever..."

We never saw him until it was growing dark: that was what made him into a monster. Perhaps during the day he joined his cronies elsewhere – on the steps of ruined churches in the centre of Liverpool, or lying on the grass in St John's Gardens, or crowding the benches opposite Edge Hill Public Library, whose stopped clock no doubt helped their draining of time. But if anything of this occurred to us, we dismissed it as irrelevant. He was a creature of the dark.

Shouldn't this have meant that the first time I saw him in daylight was the end? In fact, it was only the beginning.

It was a blazing day at the height of summer, my tenth. It was too hot to think of games to while away my school holidays. All I could do was walk errands for my parents, grumbling a little.

They owned a small newsagent's on West Derby Road. That day they were expecting promised copies of the *Tuebrook Bugle*. Even when he disagreed with them, my father always supported the independent papers – the *Bugle*, the *Liverpool Free Press*: at least they hadn't been swallowed or destroyed by a monopoly. The lateness of the *Bugle* worried him; had the paper given in? He sent me to find out.

I ran across West Derby Road just as the traffic lights at the top of the hill released a flood of cars. Only girls used the pedestrian subway so far as I was concerned; besides, it was flooded again. I strolled past the concrete police station into the park, to take the long way round. It was too hot to go anywhere quickly or even directly.

The park was crowded with games of football, parked prams, sunbathers draped over the greens. Patients sat outside the hospital on Orphan Drive beside the park. Around the lake, fishermen sat by transistor radios and whipped the air with hooks. Beyond the lake, model boats snarled across the shallow circular pool. I stopped to watch their patterns on the water, and caught sight of an object in the shelter.

At first I thought it was an old grey sack that someone had dumped on the bench. Perhaps it held rubbish – sticks that gave parts of it an angular look. Then I saw that the sack was an indeterminate stained garment, which might have been a mackintosh or raincoat of some kind. What I had vaguely assumed to be an ancient shopping bag, resting next to the sack, displayed a ragged patch of flesh and the dull gleam of an eye.

Exposed to daylight, he looked even more dismaying: so huge and still, less stupefied than dormant. The presence of the boatmen with their remote-control boxes reassured me. I ambled past the allotments to Pringle Street, where a terraced house was the editorial office of the *Bugle*.

Our copies were on the way, said Chrissie Maher the editor, and insisted on making me a cup of tea. She seemed a little upset when, having gulped the tea, I hurried out into the rain. Perhaps it was rude of me not to wait until the rain had stopped – but on this parched day I wanted to make the most of it, to bathe my face and my bare arms in the onslaught, gasping almost hysterically.

By the time I had passed the allotments, where cabbages rattled like toy machine-guns, the downpour was too heavy even for me. The park provided little cover; the trees let fall their own belated storms, miniature but drenching. The nearest shelter was by the pool, which had been abandoned to its web of ripples. I ran down the slippery tarmac hill, splashing through puddles, trying to blink away rain, hoping there would be room in the shelter.

There was plenty of room, both because the rain reached easily into the depths of the brick shed and because the shelter was not entirely empty. He lay as I had seen him, face upturned within the sodden Balaclava. Had the boatmen avoided looking closely at him? Raindrops struck his unblinking eyes and trickled over the patch of flesh.

I hadn't seen death before. I stood shivering and fascinated in the rain. I needn't be scared of him now. He'd stuffed himself into the grey coat until it split in several places; through the rents I glimpsed what might have been dark cloth or discoloured hairy flesh. Above him, on the shelter, were graffiti which at last I saw were not his name at all, but the names of three boys: MACK TOSH WILLY. They were partly erased, which no doubt was why one's mind tended to fill the gap.

I had to keep glancing at him. He grew more and more difficult to ignore; his presence was intensifying. His shapelessness, the rents in his coat, made me think of an old bag of washing, decayed and mouldy. His hand lurked in his sleeve; beside it, amid a scattering of Coca-Cola caps, lay fragments of the bottle whose contents had perhaps killed him. Rain roared on the dull green roof of the shelter; his staring eyes glistened and dripped. Suddenly I was frightened. I ran blindly home.

"There's someone dead in the park," I gasped. "The man who chases everyone."

"Look at you!" my mother cried. "Do you want pneumonia? Just you get out of those wet things this instant!"

Eventually I had a chance to repeat my news. By this time the rain had stopped. "Well, don't be telling us," my father said. "Tell the police. They're just across the road."

Did he think I had exaggerated a drunk into a corpse? He looked surprised when I hurried to the police station. But I couldn't miss the chance to venture in there – I believed that elder brothers of some of my schoolmates had been taken into the station and hadn't come out for years.

Beside a window which might have belonged to a ticket office was a bell you rang to make the window's partition slide back and display a policeman. He frowned down at me. What was my name? What had I been doing in the park? Who had I been with? When a second head appeared beside him he said reluctantly "He thinks someone's passed out in the park."

A blue and white Mini called for me at the police station, like a taxi; on the roof a red sign said POLICE. People glanced in at me as though I were on my way to prison. Perhaps I was: suppose Mackintosh Willy had woken up and gone? How long a sentence did you get for lying? False diamonds sparkled on the grass and in the trees. I wished I'd persuaded my father to tell the police.

As the car halted, I saw the grey bulk in the shelter. The driver strode, stiff with dignity, to peer at it. "My God," I heard him say in disgust.

Did he know Mackintosh Willy? Perhaps, but that wasn't the point. "Look at this," he said to his colleague. "Ever see a corpse with pennies on the eyes? Just look at this, then. See what someone thought was a joke."

He looked shocked, sickened. He was blocking my view as he demanded "Did you do this?"

His white-faced anger, and my incomprehension, made me speechless. But his colleague said "It wouldn't be him. He wouldn't come and tell us afterwards, would he?"

As I tried to peer past them he said "Go on home, now. Go on." His gentleness seemed threatening. Suddenly frightened, I ran home through the park.

For a while I avoided the shelter. I had no reason to go near, except on the way home from school. Sometimes I used to see schoolmates tormenting Mackintosh Willy; sometimes, at a distance, I had joined them. Now the shelter yawned emptily, baring its dim bench. The dark pool stirred, disturbing the green beards of the stone margin. My main reason for avoiding the park was that there was nobody with whom to go.

Living on the main road was the trouble. I belonged to none of the side streets, where they played football among parked cars or chased through the back alleys. I was never invited to street parties. I felt like an outsider, particularly when I had to pass the groups of teenagers who sat on the railings above the pedestrian subway, lazily swinging their legs, waiting to pounce. I stayed at home, in the flat above the newsagent's, when I could, and read everything in the shop. But I grew frustrated: I did enough reading at school. All this was why I welcomed Mark. He could save me from my isolation.

Not that we became friends immediately. He was my parents' latest paperboy. For several days we examined each other warily. He was taller than me, which was intimidating, but seemed unsure how to arrange his lankiness. Eventually he said "What're you reading?"

He sounded as though reading was a waste of time. "A book," I retorted.

At last, when I'd let him see that it was Mickey Spillane, he said "Can I read it after you?"

"It isn't mine. It's the shop's."

"All right, so I'll buy it." He did so at once, paying my father. He was certainly wealthier than me. When my resentment of his gesture had cooled somewhat, I realised that he was letting me finish what was now his book. I dawdled over it to make him complain, but he never did. Perhaps he might be worth knowing.

My instinct was accurate: he proved to be generous – not only with money, though his father made plenty of that in home improvements, but also in introducing me to his friends. Quite soon I had my place in the tribe at the top of the pedestrian subway, though secretly I was glad that we never exchanged more than ritual insults with the other gangs. Perhaps the police station looming in the background restrained hostilities.

Mark was generous too with his ideas. Although Ben, a burly lad, was nominal leader of the gang, it was Mark who suggested most of our activities. Had he taken to delivering papers to save himself from boredom – or, as I wondered afterwards, to distract himself from his thoughts? It was Mark who brought his skates so that we could brave the slope of the pedestrian subway, who let us ride his bicycle around the side streets, who found ways into derelict houses, who brought his transistor radio so that we could hear the first Beatles records as the traffic passed unheeding on West Derby Road. But was all this a means of distracting us from the park?

No doubt it was inevitable that Ben resented his supremacy. Perhaps he deduced, in his slow and stolid way, that Mark disliked the park. Certainly he hit upon the ideal method to challenge him.

It was a hot summer evening. By then I was thirteen. Dust and fumes drifted in the wakes of cars; wagons clattered repetitively across the railway bridge. We lolled about the pavement, kicking Coca-Cola caps. Suddenly Ben said "I know something we can do."

We trooped after him, dodging an aggressive gang of taxis, towards the police station. He might have meant us to play some trick there; when he swaggered past, I'm sure everyone was relieved – everyone except Mark, for Ben was leading us onto Orphan Drive.

Heat shivered above the tarmac. Beside us in the park, twilight gathered beneath the trees, which stirred stealthily. The island in the lake creaked with ducks; swollen litter drifted sluggishly, or tried to climb the bank. I could sense Mark's nervousness. He had turned his radio louder; a misshapen Elvis Presley blundered out of the static, then sank back into incoherence as a neighbourhood waveband seeped into his voice. Why was Mark on edge? I could see only the dimming sky, trees on the far side of the lake diluted by haze, the gleam of bottle caps like eyes atop a floating mound of litter, the glittering of broken bottles in the lawns.

We passed the locked ice-cream kiosk. Ben was heading for the circular pool, whose margin was surrounded by a fluorescent orange tape tied between iron poles, a makeshift fence. I felt Mark's hesitation, as though he were a scared dog dragged by a lead. The lead was pride: he couldn't show fear, especially when none of us knew Ben's plan.

A new concrete path had been laid around the pool. "We'll write our names in that," Ben said.

The dark pool swayed, as though trying to douse reflected lights. Black clouds spread over the sky and loomed in the pool; the threat of a storm lurked behind us. The brick shelter was very dim, and looked cavernous. I strode to the orange fence, not wanting to be last, and poked the concrete with my toe. "We can't," I said; for some reason I felt relieved. "It's set."

Someone had been there before us, before the concrete had hardened. Footprints led from the dark shelter towards us. As they advanced, they faded, no doubt because the concrete had been setting. They looked as though the man had suffered from a limp.

When I pointed them out Mark flinched, for we heard the radio swing wide of comprehensibility. "What's up with you?" Ben demanded.

"Nothing."

"It's getting dark," I said, not as an answer but to coax everyone back towards the main road. But my remark inspired Ben; contempt grew in his eyes. "I know what it is," he said, gesturing at Mark. "This is where he used to be scared."

"Who was scared? I wasn't bloody scared."

"Not much you weren't. You didn't look it," Ben scoffed, and told us "Old Willy used to chase him all round the pool. He used to hate him, did old Willy. Mark used to run away from him. I never. I wasn't scared."

"You watch who you're calling scared. If you'd seen what I did to that old bastard – "

Perhaps the movements around us silenced him. Our surroundings were crowded with dark shifting: the sky unfurled darkness, muddy shapes rushed at us in the pool, a shadow huddled restlessly in one corner of the shelter. But Ben wasn't impressed by the drooping boast. "Go on," he sneered. "You're scared now. Bet you wouldn't dare go in his shelter."

"Who wouldn't? You watch it, you!"

"Go on then. Let's see you do it."

We must all have been aware of Mark's fear. His whole body was stiff as a puppet's. I was ready to intervene – to say, lying, that the police were near – when he gave a shrug of despair and stepped forward. Climbing gingerly over the tape as though it were electrified, he advanced onto the concrete.

He strode towards the shelter. He had turned the radio full on; I could hear nothing else, only watch the shifting of dim shapes deep in the reflected sky, watch Mark stepping in the footprints for bravado. They swallowed his feet. He was nearly at the shelter when I saw him glance at the radio.

The song had slipped awry again; another waveband seeped in, a blurred muttering. I thought it must be Mark's infectious nervousness that made me hear it forming into words. "Come on, son. Let's have a look at you." But why shouldn't the words have been real, fragments of a radio play?

Mark was still walking, his gaze held by the radio. He seemed almost hypnotised; otherwise he would surely have flinched back from the huddled shadow which surged forward from the comer by the bench, even though it must have been the shadow of a cloud.

As his foot touched the shelter I called nervously "Come on, Mark. Let's go and skate." I felt as though I'd saved him. But when he came hurrying back, he refused to look at me or at anyone else.

For the next few days he hardly spoke to me. Perhaps he thought of avoiding my parents' shop. Certainly he stayed away from the gang – which turned out to be all to the good, for Ben, robbed of Mark's ideas, could think only of shoplifting. They were soon caught, for they weren't very skilful. After that my father had doubts about Mark, but Mark had always been scrupulously honest in deliveries; after some reflection, my father kept him on. Eventually Mark began to talk to me again, though not about the park.

That was frustrating: I wanted to tell him how the shelter looked now. I still passed it on my way home, though from a different school. Someone had been scrawling on the shelter. That was hardly unusual – graffiti filled the pedestrian subway, and even claimed the ends of streets – but the words were odd, to say the least: like scribbles on the walls of a psychotic's cell, or the gibberish of an invocation. DO THE BASTARD. BOTTLE UP HIS EYES. HOOK THEM OUT. PUSH HIS HEAD IN. Tangled amid them, like chewed bones, gleamed the eroded slashes of MACK TOSH WILLY.

I wasn't as frustrated by the conversational taboo as I might have been, for I'd met my first girlfriend. Kim was her name; she lived in a flat on my block, and because of her parents' trade, seemed always to smell of fish and chips. She obviously looked up to me – for one thing, I'd begun to read for pleasure again, which few of her friends could be bothered attempting. She told me her secrets, which was a new experience for me, strange and rather exciting – as was being seen on West Derby Road with a girl on my arm, any girl. I was happy to ignore the jeers of Ben and cronies.

She loved the park. Often we strolled through, scattering charitable crumbs to ducks. Most of all she loved to watch the model yachts, when the snarling model motorboats left them alone to glide over the pool. I enjoyed watching too, while holding her warm if rather clammy hand. The breeze carried away her culinary scent. But I couldn't help noticing that the shelter now displayed screaming faces with red bursts for eyes. I have never seen drawings of violence on walls elsewhere.

My relationship with Kim was short-lived. Like most such teenage experiences, our parting was not romantic and poignant, if partings ever are, but harsh and hysterical. It happened one evening as we made our way to the fair that visited Newsham Park each summer.

Across the lake we could hear shrieks that mingled panic and delight as cars on metal poles swung girls into the air, and the blurred roaring of an ancient pop song, like the voice of an enormous radio. On the Ferris wheel, coloured lights sailed up, painting airborne faces. The twilight shone like a Christmas tree; the lights swam in the pool. That was why Kim said "Let's sit and look first."

The only bench was in the shelter. Tangles of letters dripped trails of dried paint, like blood; mutilated faces shrieked soundlessly. Still, I thought I could bear the shelter. Sitting with Kim gave me the chance to touch her breasts, such as they were, through the collapsing deceptively large cups of her bra. Tonight she smelled of newspapers, as though she had been wrapped in them for me to take out; she must have been serving at the counter. Nevertheless I kissed her, and ignored the fact that one corner of the shelter was dark as a spider's crevice.

But she had noticed; I felt her shrink away from the corner. Had she noticed more than I had? Or was it her infectious wariness that made the dark beside us look more solid, about to shuffle towards us along the bench? I was uneasy, but the din and the lights of the fairground were reassuring. I determined to make the most of Kim's need for protection, but she pushed my hand away. "Don't," she said irritably, and made to stand up.

At that moment I heard a blurred voice. "Popeye," it muttered as if to itself; it sounded gleeful. "Popeye." Was it part of the fair? It might have been a stallholder's voice, distorted by the uproar, for it said "I've got something for you."

The struggles of Kim's hand in mine excited me. "Let me go," she was wailing. Because I managed not to be afraid, I was more pleased than dismayed by her fear – and I was eager to let my imagination flourish, for it was better than reading a ghost story. I peered into the dark corner to see what horrors I could imagine.

Then Kim wrenched herself free and ran around the pool. Disappointed and angry, I pursued her. "Go away," she cried.

"You're horrible. I never want to speak to you again." For a while I chased her along the dim paths, but once I began to plead I grew furious with myself. She wasn't worth the embarrassment. I let her go, and returned to the fair, to wander desultorily for a while. When I'd stayed long enough to prevent my parents from wondering why I was home early, I walked home.

I meant to sit in the shelter for a while, to see if anything happened, but someone was already there. I couldn't make out much about him, and didn't like to go closer. He must have been wearing spectacles, for his eyes seemed perfectly circular and gleamed like metal, not like eyes at all.

I quickly forgot that glimpse, for I discovered Kim hadn't been exaggerating: she refused to speak to me. I stalked off to buy fish and chips elsewhere, and decided that I hadn't liked her anyway. My one lingering disappointment, I found glumly, was that I had nobody with whom to go to the fairground. Eventually, when the fair and the school holidays were approaching their end, I said to Mark "Shall we go to the fair tonight?"

He hesitated, but didn't seem especially wary. "All right," he said with the indifference we were beginning to affect about everything.

At sunset the horizon looked like a furnace, and that was how the park felt. Couples rambled sluggishly along the paths; panting dogs splashed in the lake. Between the trees the lights of the fairground shimmered and twinkled, cheap multicoloured stars. As we passed the pool, I noticed that the air was quivering above the footprints in the concrete, and looked darkened, perhaps by dust. Impulsively I said "What did you do to old Willy?"

"Shut up." I'd never heard Mark so savage or withdrawn. "I wish I hadn't done it."

I might have retorted to his rudeness, but instead I let myself be captured by the fairground, by the glade of light amid the balding rutted green. Couples and gangs roamed, harangued a shade half-heartedly by stallholders. Young children hid their faces in pink candy floss. A siren thin as a Christmas party hooter set the Dodgems running. Mark and I rode a tilting bucket above the fuzzy clamour of music, the splashes of glaring light, the cramped crowd. Secretly I felt a little sick, but the ride seemed to help Mark regain his confidence. Shortly, as we were playing a pinball machine with senile flippers, he said "Look, there's Lorna and what's her name."

It took me a while to be sure where he was pointing: at a tall bosomy girl, who probably looked several years older than she was, and a girl of about my height and age, her small bright face sketched with makeup. By this time I was following him eagerly.

The tall girl was Lorna; her friend's name was Carol. We strolled for a while, picking our way over power cables, and Carol and I began to like each other; her scent was sweet, if rather overpowering. As the fair began to close, Mark easily won trinkets at a shooting gallery and presented them to the girls, which helped us to persuade them to meet us on Saturday night. By now Mark never looked towards the shelter – I think not from wariness but because it had ceased to worry him, at least for the moment. I glanced across, and could just distinguish someone pacing unevenly round the pool, as if impatient for a delayed meeting.

If Mark had noticed, would it have made any difference? Not in the long run, I try to believe. But however I rationalise, I know that some of the blame was mine.

We were to meet Lorna and Carol on our side of the park in order to take them to the Carlton cinema nearby. We arrived late, having taken our time over sprucing ourselves; we didn't want to seem too eager to meet them. Beside the police station, at the entrance to the park, a triangular island of pavement, large enough to contain a spinney of trees, divided the road. The girls were meant to be waiting at the nearest point of the triangle. But the island was deserted except for the caged darkness beneath the trees.

We waited. Shop windows on West Derby Road glared fluorescent green. Behind us trees whispered, creaking. We kept glancing into the park, but the only figure we could see on the dark paths was alone. Eventually, for something to do, we strolled desultorily around the island.

It was I who saw the message first, large letters scrawled on the corner nearest the park. Was it Lorna's or Carol's handwriting? It rather shocked me, for it looked semiliterate. But she must have had to use a stone as a pencil, which couldn't have helped; indeed, some letters had had to be dug out of the moss that coated stretches of the pavement. MARK SEE YOU AT SHELTER, the message said.

I felt him withdraw a little. "Which shelter?" he muttered.

"I expect they mean the one near the kiosk," I said to reassure him.

We hurried along Orphan Drive. Above the lamps, patches of foliage shone harshly. Before we reached the pool we crossed the bridge, from which in daylight manna rained down to the ducks, and entered the park. The fair had gone into hibernation; the paths and the mazes of tree trunks were silent and very dark. Occasional dim movements made me think that we were passing the girls, but the figure that was wandering a nearby path looked far too bulky.

The shelter was at the edge of the main green, near the football pitch. Beyond the green, tower blocks loomed in glaring auras. Each of the four sides of the shelter was an alcove housing a bench. As we peered into each, jeers or curses challenged us.

"I know where they'll be," Mark said. "In the one by the bowling-green. That's near where they live."

But we were closer to the shelter by the pool. Nevertheless I followed him onto the park road. As we turned towards the bowling-green I glanced towards the pool, but the streetlamps dazzled me. I followed him along a narrow path between hedges to the green, and almost tripped over his ankles as he stopped short. The shelter was empty, alone with its view of the decaying Georgian houses on the far side of the bowling-green.

To my surprise and annoyance, he still didn't head for the pool. Instead we made for the disused bandstand hidden in a ring of bushes. Its only tune now was the clink of broken bricks. I was sure the girls wouldn't have called it a shelter, and of course it was deserted. Obese dim bushes hemmed us in. "Come on," I said, "or we'll miss them. They must be by the pool."

"They won't be there," he said – stupidly, I thought.

Did I realise how nervous he suddenly was? Perhaps, but it only annoyed me. After all, how else could I meet Carol again? I didn't know her address. "Oh, all right," I scoffed, "if you want us to miss them."

I saw him stiffen. Perhaps my contempt hurt him more than Ben's had; for one thing, he was older. Before I knew what he intended he was striding towards the pool, so rapidly that I would have had to run to keep up with him – which, given the hostility that had flared between us, I refused to do. I strolled after him rather disdainfully. That was how I came to glimpse movement in one of the islands of dimness between the lamps of the park road. I glanced towards it and saw, several hundred yards away, the girls.

After a pause they responded to my waving – somewhat timidly, I thought. "There they are," I called to Mark. He must have been at the pool by now, but I had difficulty in glimpsing him beyond the glare of the lamps. I was beckoning the girls to hurry when I heard his radio blur into speech.

At first I was reminded of a sailor's parrot. "Aye aye," it was croaking. The distorted voice sounded cracked, uneven, almost too old to speak. "You know what I mean, son?" it grated triumphantly. "Aye aye." I was growing uneasy, for my mind had begun to interpret the words as "Eye eye" – when suddenly, dreadfully, I realised Mark hadn't brought his radio.

There might be someone in the shelter with a radio. But I was terrified, I wasn't sure why. I ran towards the pool calling "Come on, Mark, they're here!" The lamps dazzled me; everything swayed with my running – which was why I couldn't be sure what I saw.

I know I saw Mark at the shelter. He stood just within, confronting darkness. Before I could discern whether anyone else was there, Mark staggered out blindly, hands covering his face, and collapsed into the pool.

Did he drag something with him? Certainly by the time I reached the margin of the light he appeared to be tangled in something, and to be struggling feebly. He was drifting, or being dragged, towards the centre of the pool by a half-submerged heap of litter. At the end of the heap nearest Mark's face was a pale ragged patch in which gleamed two round objects – bottle caps? I could see all this because I was standing helpless, screaming at the girls "Quick, for Christ's sake! He's drowning!" He was drowning, and I couldn't swim.

"Don't be stupid," I heard Lorna say. That enraged me so much that I turned from the pool. "What do you mean?" I cried. "What do you mean, you stupid bitch?"

"Oh, be like that," she said haughtily, and refused to say more. But Carol took pity on my hysteria and explained "It's only three feet deep. He'll never drown in there."

I wasn't sure that she knew what she was talking about, but that was no excuse for me not to try to rescue him. When I turned to the pool I gasped miserably, for he had vanished – sunk. I could only wade into the muddy water, which engulfed my legs and closed around my waist like ice, ponderously hindering me.

The floor of the pool was fattened with slimy litter. I slithered, terrified of losing my balance. Intuition urged me to head for the centre of the pool. And it was there I found him, as my sluggish kick collided with his ribs.

When I tried to raise him, I discovered that he was pinned down. I had to grope blindly over him in the chill water, feeling how still he was. Something like a swollen cloth bag, very large, lay over his face. I couldn't bear to touch it again, for its contents felt soft and fat. Instead I seized Mark's ankles and managed at last to drag him free. Then I struggled towards the edge of the pool, heaving him by his shoulders, lifting his head above water. His weight was dismaying. Eventually the girls waded out to help me.

But we were too late. When we dumped him on the concrete, his face stayed agape with horror; water lay stagnant in his mouth. I could see nothing wrong with his eyes. Carol grew hysterical, and it was Lorna who ran to the hospital, perhaps in order to get away from the sight of him. I only made Carol worse by demanding why they hadn't waited for us at the shelter; I wanted to feel they were to blame. But she denied they had written the message, and grew more hysterical when I asked why they hadn't waited at the island. The question, or the memory, seemed to frighten her.

I never saw her again. The few newspapers that bothered to report Mark's death gave the verdict "by misadventure." The police took a dislike to me after I insisted that there might be somebody else in the pool, for the draining revealed nobody. At least, I thought, whatever was there had gone away. Perhaps I could take some credit for that at least.

But perhaps I was too eager for reassurance. The last time I ventured near the shelter was years ago, one winter night on the way home from school. I had caught sight of a gleam in the depths of the shelter. As I went close, nervously watching both the shelter and the pool, I saw two discs glaring at me from the darkness beside the bench. They were Coca-Cola caps, not eyes at all, and it must have been the wind that set the pool slopping and sent the caps scuttling towards me. What frightened me most as I fled through the dark was that I wouldn't be able to see where I was running if, as I desperately wanted to, I put up my hands to protect my eyes.

CONCUSSION

RAMSEY CAMPBELL

For some weeks Kirk Morris had been gnawed by the knowledge that he must die. He had tried to feign indifference; then, when he realised that at his death Liverpool, if not the rest of the world, would cease to exist, he had determined to return for one last confrontation of his memories.

That day a few private vehicles were coasting in the streets; he signalled one and heaved his case onto the seat beside him. The new transport must have hit a snag again, calling forth these vehicles in imitation of the bygone taxis. He sped across London. The high concrete and metal buildings were mobiles of sunlight that ached in his eyes. Since weather control had cleared the city skies the bleached bone streets had become yet more unreal to Kirk; his journeys through them had the obsessive quality of a flight down the corridors of some surrealist film. Nowhere could he find the overpowering solidity of the black grime-encrusted buildings, surrounding one reassuringly for miles, for which he had moved so long ago to London in an attempt to be convinced by his surroundings of their reality. Instead, he existed, robbed of referent and drained of emotion, on a lower floor of a stark rectangular housing block in the suburbs, occasionally meeting families in the lift or young couples at the meal dispenser round the corner, and it was partly the conviction that he would die unnoticed that had persuaded him to undertake this journey into nostalgia. Of course, he thought, shaking himself awake, this was nonsense; when he died they would cease to be, as much illusion as the GLCPT that had pensioned him off when the buses ceased to run. But if Liverpool was illusion, why did he need to spend time and energy on the illusion of returning?

The vehicle drew up beside the gap in the buildings like slabs of sand that denoted Victoria Coach Station. Kirk handed a note over the driver's shoulder; the man hesitated, looking unsure whether to be grateful for or insulted by the size of the tip—after all, he'd picked up Kirk out of sympathy, not to profit. Kirk couldn't believe in his indecision; it had been decades since Kirk had trusted anyone. He dragged his case onto the pavement. The passers-by looked shifty, as if smug with a knowledge they thought withheld from him. He'd buttonhole one and worm the truth out of him—then suddenly he giggled: nonexistent money to a nonexistent driver!

He had to drop the case three times before he reached what had been the coach station: a sheltered square of concrete approached by two lanes between the buildings flecked as tweed that rose towards another square, one of blue sky stained with spilled milk, invisible from beneath the shelter. Queues stamped, swayed and complained on the four platforms closing in the square, and Kirk joined that for Manchester and Liverpool. Preceding him was a young man, glancing frequently at the entrances, waiting for someone or perhaps merely keeping their place. He unbuttoned his 1960-style sports jacket—nostalgia was all the rage these days among the younger set—and cast it over his shoulder, flicking Kirk's face like a challenge. Kirk recoiled grumbling and touched his cheek, feeling wrinkles that could never now be smoothed. He sat down on the concrete bench against the building; the stone was cold as a tomb through his trousers. Across the square a bus snored awake. It caught at Kirk's throat with nostalgia, and after all the presence of the bus could only be related to the nostalgia of Kirk's generation who were sick in other than surface transport and prepared to pay extra for comfort and the sight of a bus still on the ground. It was comfort Kirk sought— but the comfort of remembering the day he met Anne.

The young man with the sports-coat turned from the exhaust and coughed; Kirk adjusted his glasses, held together for a year with tape, to focus on each detail of the vehicle, to realise memory. Through the grey fumes a girl, mysteriously glimpsed, was shoving her luggage aboard the rack, and when Kirk woke Anne was struggling with her case above him. He'd fallen asleep before the coach moved out; this girl must have arrived at Victoria after he'd dozed off, to materialise above him now as from a dream. He blinked through the windows: a country lane at speed, somewhere near Stratford; a mauve mist of flowers skimmed by. "Did I wake you?" she said. "I'm ever so sorry."

"Not at all," Kirk said, and grimaced inwardly at his swift response; why must he always cap their remarks so finally, never talk to them? He stood up, tottering as the driver wrenched the wheel at a curve. "Let me help," and he jammed the case into place. "Thanks, you're awfully good," Anne said and smiled into his eyes; he sat down beneath the smile. At last she seated herself and picked up a book.

If only this were real! It had never returned to Kirk so vividly since he had ridden the bus down to London, abandoning Liverpool after all was over. He could feel her body warm on his, her tongue—as he'd felt it while he waited for her during their lost week, when time had seemed annihilated; for a moment Anne might have appeared on the concrete platform and run to greet him. As if to mock him, the young man in the queue leaned out and scanned the grey square for his girl; Kirk closed his eyes and reached back to Anne for consolation. What had come next? The hot coach upholstery—hushed conversation round him, laughter— pages turning—

Anne's reading speed astonished him. The pages passed almost as swiftly as the flowers. The book fascinated him too; bound in bright plastic, the corners of its pages rounded off— but his eyes strayed to her bare neck, her sleek piled blonde hair, and framed in the space between the headrests her fresh flowered cotton frock, the creases in its short sleeves flattening and sharpening as she flipped rapidly onwards. If he could make her speak to him again— She put up her hand to adjust her glasses; the bus squealed to a stop at a roundabout; the book was torn from her hand. Of course it hadn't been so satisfyingly timed; he'd shifted in his seat as with insomnia, searching for words that eluded him like a dream; but memory had edited, tightening up the cues. He almost fell into the aisle and had the book before she could stoop.

"Oh, aren't you good," praised Anne. He held the book a second after she had taken it; their fingers touched. He'd read about that somewhere. "Lousy driver," he said, glaring up the coach. Cars chased their tails around the roundabout. "I could do better myself. I mean really—I'm sure I could manage a bus." God, you cretin, he snarled at himself, why should she be interested? But apparently she was. "Can you drive, then?" she asked as if enthralled. "I often drive. But I don't have a car."

"Nor do we. I'd love to have one." The driver saw a gap and rammed in the bus; Kirk almost fell. "Don't kill yourself for me," she implored. "Why don't you join me?"

Across the aisle a middle-aged couple nodded to each

other like disapproving puppets, but Kirk was too contented to care. "Are you from London, then?" she asked.

"Me? No, I'm from Liverpool. I can tell you're London, of course."

"Actually I'm Southend. Why, you mean the accent? I put that on a lot because it makes me think of flower-sellers and all that sort of thing. You know—all the past. I love the past. Sometimes when I'm going to sleep I think I'll wake up—oh, before I was born, when everything was lovely—well, not everything, there were the wars, but I don't know, the past seems awfully romantic. Sometimes when I woke up and found I was still me I used to cry. When I was younger. But Liverpool has lots of the past still preserved, doesn't it? That's why I'm staying there."

Kirk had been basking in her monologue. Somehow she was the first girl with whom he'd felt at ease since his trauma with Shirley. Liverpool has lots of the past still preserved? He thought of the ossified spire that rose above the roof of Owen Owen's in imitation of the GPO Tower in London, of the boutiques on Bold Street emulating Chelsea, of the garish Meal in a Moment hamburger cafes on Lime Street, vanguards from London of a life lived at such speed as to outdistance emotion. "There are pockets of the past round Liverpool, you're right," he told her, remembering lonely walks in Bidston, West Kirby, Frankby. "I've visited most of them. You know, in search of atmosphere."

"Have you honestly? How marvellous," she cried. "You'll have to be my cicerone."

This time they both saw Punch and Judy draw together. "This'll never do," she declared, "us sitting together and not even introduced. I'm Anne and I'm so pleased to make your acquaintance."

"I'm Kirk," he searched, "and I'm a student. What are you?"

"Kirk, what a lovely name," said Anne, "like an actor. For

the cinematograph. Isn't that a wonderful word, cinematograph? Much nicer than—" something that eluded Kirk; but he'd always been shy of asking for words to be repeated, preferring to agree or grunt intelligently. "Oh, what am I? A romantic little girl, wouldn't you say? And in term time I'm a student too. My question. In what are you a student?"

"French is my main subject." Memory dashed like water in his face: Adrienne's letter in his pocket, still to be answered. And on the cold stone bench Kirk's fingers clutched the letter, rubbing against the other later letter he wanted still more to forget, tufted both with the fluff of decades. Somewhere in there was her photo too: head and shoulders a little askew, a touch of soft-focus by virtue of inexpert lensmanship, lending her long blonde hair a delicate glow and her eyes a hint of moisture above her smile. And never a photograph of Anne; he tried not to think about that. Adrienne, with whom he'd corresponded for years, promising finally to visit her in Paris if he could collect the money, Adrienne to whom he'd written with a kind of desperate passion after the Shirley incident, calling her "cherie" and "ma petite chou" and all the other words he'd learned outside the French class and believed in because he'd never been to France. Adrienne, and then he thought of Anne's Auntie Ethel: the second time he'd killed. He shrugged them off. Anne—what's your subject? He couldn't think of them all the time; he'd go mad. "Anne?"

"But we've been introduced. We know each other. You mean to say you can't guess my subject? History! You knew all along, really." She touched his arm; her skin was warm on his. "Here, look at my history book."

She found the plastic cover in her flowered lap. Ahead a car shot from a turning; the coach driver stood on the brake; Kirk was thrown forward as he turned to Anne and his head thudded on the seat in front. Something cracked.

"Oh, your poor head!" cried Anne. "Are you all right, darling?"

Was that what happened? Did she really call him "darling" so soon? Yes, he was sure she did. Perhaps there was more dialogue, but again memory was speeding up the action. Certainly he never saw her book. He sat back stunned, examining his divided spectacles.

"My wounded Kirk," mourned Anne, then became more serious: "Can't you see very well? Look, let me put them in my bag. This lens has smashed. It didn't go in your eye? Have you any others?"

"No, unfortunately," said Kirk, eyes closed, waiting for the rhythm to weaken. "I can't see a yard without them, either."

"That's terrible. Can't you even see me? I'll be so sad if you can't."

"I can see that far, don't worry," he told her, and at once realised what he'd done. He cursed himself; Shirley had tied his tongue for ever. No doubt Anne didn't think he cared about her now. Perhaps she'd find another cicerone. She might even have been joking, unaware of how his mind had brightened. He strained to speak: too late.

"I think you look handsome without them, anyway," she continued. "But with them you look more studious, so either way is fine. I'll take them to the optician's tomorrow for you. You probably wouldn't be able to find the door. Just think, going into a museum by mistake. They'd probably buy them: unique Victorian eyeglasses, slightly damaged. Glasses can be awfully stupid sometimes, don't you think? I mean when you're kissing sometimes: clink-clink. The boy I was going out with in Southend said I looked like an owl. We broke it off the other day. He seemed awfully hurt. Still, 'twas but infatuation. How do I get your glasses back to you?"

"You could bring them round." That's not what she means, he moaned at himself. "No, now I think about it, I'd better know how much they're going to cost. Why don't we meet somewhere tomorrow?"

The young man in the coach queue—who might have been strategically placed on stage to represent Kirk's younger self—patrolled the platform for his girlfriend, brushing from his sports-coat dust sneezed away by the exhaust, and Kirk glanced down at his sagging grey suit as he hurried towards the Pier Head. The Liver Clock above him tolled eleven. He'd taken everything he could out of the pockets to give the suit some shape—including Adrienne's letter, now a fortnight old, that he must answer as soon as he had time—but the trousers still bulged shapelessly at the knee, his wallet still outlined a rectangle of grey on his jacket; for too long he'd had nobody for whom to dress. He plunged beneath the shadow of the long Pier Head bus station hall, pale as the bore of a blown bone; about him milled a vague crowd, prams, motorcyclists scented with petrol manoeuvring their machines to the ferry, a hive of shade and colour. A smell of hot pastry lured him to the baker's stall. At the adjacent bookstall a figure in white moved away and blurred completely; next second it had run to him and focused. Anne smiled apologetically. "I shouldn't tease you when you can't see," she apologised. "I won't do it again, I promise. I found an optician's near Bidston, such a lovely one, all antique. You must see it sometime. He said your glasses won't be ready for a week, so you won't be able to see me really at all. It's terribly sad."

She was wearing a white sweater, white sharply pleated skirt, white patterned socks. Or was that the next day? It was all so long ago. He clutched the stone bench: let her be wearing these, he liked them best. "Don't worry, I can see you," he replied, and his toes squirmed. "You look great," he said.

"You're nice. Where shall we go?"

He hadn't thought. "Having fun"—where did you go for that? What could you do in Liverpool on a summer morning?

The art gallery, the parks, to which he'd gravitate in London, seemed a little cheerless; the cinemas weren't open—besides, he couldn't see. "Let's walk down and I'll think," he said, and led the way down the ramp to the river, where figures fuzzed against the dazzling water. Anne took his arm: "You don't mind, do you?"

"On the contrary," he responded, immediately bitter at his stock response, his inaction. "There's always New Brighton fairground," he said, and swore at himself: you provincial idiot, that's not the place to take a London girl!—not London, Southend, whose fairground must long ago have earned her contempt. But Anne clutched his arm: "That'd be fabulous, I love fairgrounds, so nostalgic."

He couldn't see the coloured lights above the fairground; he imagined them set in a velvet sky. Blocks of paint whirled and lifted screaming. A few couples sat on warm benches; others sought the shade of the amusement arcade, drawn by the purr of fruit machines and the infrequent rush of coins. Kirk took Anne's hand and settled her in a Ghost Train car. They plunged into darkness; the car jerked back from death-grins—Kirk saw only luminous clothed eggs. Anne huddled closer and he put his arm around her, inhaling the scents of talc and laundered wool. Her hair lay light and warm against his cheek.

"But ghosts aren't really like that," she insisted as they came to rest in sunlight. "I think they'd be just like people, and you wouldn't know what they really were until afterwards. Those things in there are straight out of a Gothic novel. Mind you, I don't mind Gothic novels. Being carried away by a horseman in a black cloak over the mountains under the moon to a castle—No, I'm only joking, I'd rather be with you. My turn now." And she pulled him towards a circular platform. The car whirled about, was lifted spinning and suddenly was hurled almost from its axis. The fairground tilted, fell away. Kirk closed his eyes. The sky was swimming;

he couldn't move for fear of being thrown clear, though Anne weighed on his arm and sand rubbed between his fingers.

"Wasn't that marvellous?" Anne panted. "Where shall we go next? Oh, poor Kirk, don't you feel well?"

"Not very. Maybe because I haven't got my glasses."

"Oh dear, and I was going to buy you an ice cream. Sorry, darling, shouldn't have said that. Come on, I'll get you a drink. It'll do you the world of good."

Reaching the main street, they found themselves opposite the Court Cinema, dwarfed by a poster for taxis; two children ran by with propellers. "What a strange little place," said Anne. "*Vertigo*, what's that? Oh, I'm sorry, that wasn't exactly in good taste."

"No it's all right," mumbled Kirk. "*Vertigo*—it's the Alfred Hitchcock film about James Stewart becoming obsessed with Kim Novak, I should say the girl he thinks she is, and in trying to mould her into his dream of her, he causes her death."

"That's awfully sad. I wish we could see it. Come on, I'm going to give you your medicine."

The Scotch settled Kirk's stomach, but not his thoughts; perhaps he should suggest a visit tonight to *Vertigo*, even though it would be invisible to him. He felt ill at ease in the empty parlour, holding hands with Anne, watched by the barman as he polished glasses and flicked flies; he'd rather be showing Anne off to the crowds. Again the move was hers. "Do you think we could go to Ellesmere Port?" she said. "I'd so like to see the docks before they're all demolished."

On the bus to Ellesmere Port she caught his eye. "You like my pleats, don't you? I think you'd like to touch them. But that'd be wicked." So that was what she'd been wearing. She'd said that on the bus that day. He was sure she had.

Their visit to Ellesmere Port had faded; it jerked from image to image like an old film. The stern of a ship behind high stern grey buildings, the grey seeping into the sky; Anne waving to someone at the ship's rail. "Now, I'm only teasing," she told Kirk as he tensed. "Let's go back to my auntie's. You do know how to get to Bidston from here?" Unfortunately, Kirk couldn't correlate the bus routes this side of the Mersey; he suggested they walk for a while. Along the road they reached a gate into a field. "Look, marvellous, a bridle-path," cried Anne. Kirk thought it more likely the path of tractor-treads, but let himself be led. Then the grey sky darkened and pattered on the grass; they piled beneath the shelter of a tree. Kirk's arm was round Anne's shoulders; she was silent, regaining her breath. He felt the bark rough against his back; he stared across the field, trying to forget that the next move was his, but the dull green was curtained by indolent raindrops against a faster distant mist, and he sensed rather than saw that the indistinct horizon was blocked off by the squat curves of an oil refinery. As if of its own accord, his hand edged round and stroked Anne's soft warm cheek. The rain slowed. "We'd better go before it starts again," Anne said. "I like it here," Kirk protested weakly; he'd tried and failed, he knew. "I know, darling," and she smiled up at him, "but it'd be nicer at home."

"Auntie Ethel, come and meet Kirk." They stood in a hall bright as an aquarium; Kirk was aware of surfaces of glass and plastic, the open treads of a staircase, what seemed to his limited vision like indirect lighting. A door opened at the end of the hall; a figure in slacks moved towards them, graceful yet shy as a tropical fish, halted and said in a voice a little cracked by age "He's gorgeous. You'd better watch out or I'll have him for myself. Hello, Kirk, can you see me from there? Then I'd better warn you that you may get a shock." The face swam forward; the projectionist focused, and Kirk saw that beneath the grey hair and eyes, one side of Auntie Ethel's lined yet lively face was covered by a purple birthmark. "Now why on earth should I get a shock?" he asked, shaking hands. "Unless you mean because you're nicer-looking than your niece." Anne kicked his ankle, but not hard. "There you are, men are fickle," said Auntie Ethel. "Sorry if I embarrassed you, Kirk. I go like that sometimes. Ever since someone—well, I won't bore you. It's odd, you remind me of him. I know your face, I'm sure. It's all right, Anne, I'm not trying a line." She seemed to recollect herself. "Now you children go and get dry and I'll make you something to eat. You're not going to help, Annie, you're too wet. It's been a long time since I've got dinner for more than one."

"It is sad, Kirk," Anne said, taking his coat and leading him into the sitting-room. "Auntie Ethel's husband was killed in a car crash before they'd had children, and I know she so wanted children. She was ever so worried about my coming down by bus, in case—you know. Well, we'll be her children all this week, won't we?"

Kirk, trying to settle himself on an odd curved couch made of cane, agreed, but his thoughts were elsewhere: how long before he had to kiss Anne? The aquarium seemed timeless, unreal; he couldn't ponder properly. "I'll help her set the table, anyway," Anne said, and leaned down to kiss his cheek. He remembered *Brighton Rock*, more strongly than when he'd been with Shirley; Pinkie kissing a girl and missing her mouth—he couldn't see that Graham Greene had been at his shoulder, whispering doubts. He thrust his fingers through Anne's hair and pulled her down to him, kissed her mouth, which was scented and moist. Then he let go, waiting. "Gosh, you're strong," Anne said, "but let's eat first, darling."

"This is a marvellous house," Anne told Auntie Ethel. Though the latter had protested, Anne had insisted on sitting with her to keep her company, leaving Kirk facing them as at an interview. "All these lovely things," and she looked to Kirk for confirmation; but he was still adjusting to the plates and tablecloth, both made of paper. The latest trend, he supposed, and realised that Anne was deliberately suppressing her love of the antique.

"I've only been here once before, you know," she told Kirk, who was struggling to saw his lettuce with a plastic knife. "I haven't even been to Bidston Village."

"No, so you haven't. You'll have to escort her there, Kirk."

"I certainly will." His knife slipped and tomato-seeds glittered on the paper cloth like coloured tears. "Don't be so tidy," Auntie Ethel rebuked as he tried to scoop them up, "you'll show up the rest of us. Plenty more cloths where that came from."

"I stayed with Auntie Ethel just for a day last year. They drove me down from Manchester because they couldn't put me up there. Manchester's too modern, anyway. I was asleep in the back all the way here. I wished I hadn't been, I like night driving—" She stopped. "I was in Manchester for a wedding."

"They say one wedding leads to another," said Auntie Ethel, smiling.

The sitting-room again; Anne lifted the lid of a red record-player. "I'd like to dance with you."

"I can't," said Kirk. "Never mind, darling," and she put her arms round his neck. Her perfume was as subtle as her outline in the evening. There was a brief struggle; he tried to pull her aboard his knee, she was lifting him. "Wait a minute," she said, and pulled away. She collected cushions from the furniture and arranged them expertly on the floor. "Lie down," she told him, and as he did so "Darling, take my glasses off." He wished she wouldn't direct so much; it was like a rehearsal. Then she knelt above him, stroked his hair, brushed her lips down from his forehead to his mouth. He drew her down to him. He was filled with a timeless peace; so much for Shirley and for Graham Greene! When he felt her tongue he was suddenly dismayed; but tenderness passed through the slow luxurious movement of her mouth and gradually formed into his caresses, tenderness that drifted through them and became the dusk that merged their bodies, their warmth like a cocoon, until the coach roared round the concrete courtyard and out into the world.

Kirk blinked weakly; the dust lay on his lips like tasteless salt. Why must the future drain his last days of Anne? The Liverpool queue had lengthened, but the young man with the sports-coat still turned at each new footstep. Sadly Kirk closed his eyes, but Anne had gone. Some link was needed. Kirk touched his pockets, his trousers full of change; he jangled the money—

Next day the sun was a golden coin; the last few patches of rain were dwindling, like continents eroded by time. Kirk waited outside Woolworth's on Church Street; for some reason Anne had suggested they meet there. Blobs of flesh rushed headlong past, hot cloth waited at the crossing. For a moment he wanted to cut this scene; it was too full of a lost future. But then he gave the cue; to skip it would be to lose part of Anne. Coins. As the doors of Woolworth's were unbolted to give vent to the chatter of counted change like the musings of a vast computer, Anne was at his side. "I'm ever so sorry I'm late, darling. You can slap me if you like," and when he aimed, "No, not here, darling." She pulled him into the store and across to the jewellery counter; a lesser mathematician was still counting, a coin rang for each digit. "Please buy me a ring," she pleaded, "just a little one."

"Which one do you like?" He was playing for time, but she'd already chosen. God, which hand? He had never before had occasion to look. He couldn't close his eyes; he closed his mind. The odds were even: left hand. But which finger? The overalled assistant's eyes were on them; no doubt in her mind she was already describing the scene to her colleagues. "Want some help, luv?" she called. Kirk slid the ring down the only finger it fitted, Anne's third. "I don't think so," he replied, and led Anne towards the door with an obscure sense of victory. "Is this a holiday engagement?" he could not help asking.

"That's up to you, Kirk, isn't it?" For a moment her eyes were as lifeless as her glasses. She caught sight of the photo booth near the basement staircase. "I've never seen one of those before," she said, but her voice was sinking. "Let's, Kirk."

"There we are, together for ever." She examined each blurred shot of her ring held towards the camera. "Let's have half each. Then we'll each have part of each other." And she tore off two for Kirk like an inexperienced film editor cutting shots that made nonsense of the climax.

He took her to Bidston Hill. The grass was damp as reeds. They admired the proud white windmill on the Hill, to Kirk a rough white texture of stone; they progressed through the marshy grass to the cockpit further down the slope, where Anne said "The past must have been cruel sometimes." Kirk knew why but couldn't act; he wasn't sure of her. They passed the futuristic house at the bottom of the Hill, as full of bright rectangles as a Mondrian painting. "If only," Anne said, "I could go back into the past." She wasn't speaking to him, he knew; her hand was limp in his. He showed her Bidston Village: stone walls, old grey houses, a little shop, a lamp-post before the church porch, the occasional car roaring by unheeding. "It'll be swallowed up by a council estate any day now," he told her. "Poor village," she said, but it wasn't there for her. "Anne darling," he said; the first time. She rushed into his eyes. "If we go up to Caldy Village we can have tea on the lawn. If you'd like to."

"Oh, darling," she told the countryside, "you made the effort for me." He led her through the woods to Caldy Hill; clusters of leaves hung aloft like clouds. From the rocks, carved with initials that perhaps had survived their authors, she took in the sunset; Kirk visualised Hilbre Island far below in the Dee, holding its place in the waters, if it were not Hilbre that forged forward through a static medium. At last they returned to the bench to join a presumed series of lovers before sunsets. If only he could tell her why he'd brought her here—to exorcise Shirley; Shirley, the student from his course who'd come with him one evening to Caldy, the only haunt of his that freed him to enter the glittering water, the distant trees on the edge of the universe. He'd cast his gaze into the feathers of colour laid along the horizon for minutes before he'd slid one arm round Shirley's shoulders and leaned across to kiss her. For a moment she had stared at him; then she'd burst out laughing. No, he couldn't tell Anne; she might resent this substitution; besides, he didn't feel ready to trust such a secret to her. He covered her face; her eyes closed.

Among the trees the shadows shaped the passing of a breeze. "Sometimes I wonder where you go when you dream," said Anne. "Do I go into the past, do you think? Just now I feel I'm in a dream. A lovely dream."

"Yes, I know."

Anne watched her feet flicker through the bars of shadow like a film about to stop. "I wish you knew what to say to girls," she said.

A colossal green leper stood on the horizon; the Liver Clock, flaking off each second from the future. Kirk paced the bare wood of the Woodside landing-stage and peered at the bilious lights floating with the current. He did know what to say to girls, it was simply that he couldn't often verbalise; he sought peace, not to strain for words. What about his letters to Adrienne? Writing in French was different; to declare love in a language other than your own was like placing it in quotes—you weren't emotionally committed. Adrienne. No, Anne; he loved Anne; was he still flinching from Shirley's laughter? But his hand was groping in his pocket for Adrienne's letter; if he must exorcise her too before he could reach Anne, then he would. Hurriedly he stuffed back the other letter with the note attached and placed the envelope on the stone bench, perhaps hoping that it would blow away. "My dearest Kirk—I was so glad to hear that you intend to come to Paris. I hope you will be able to—the money (decades of pockets had erased that word: "gather", if he recalled correctly). If you could find a job here—" No, that was enough; he settled himself on the stone bench, finding new areas of cold, fighting cramp. Time might have frozen on this concrete square like a film; no direct sunlight told the time of day. Victoria Station— No, that took him back before Anne— or afterwards. The light behind his memories went out. Anne had gone. He could remember his love for Anne, like a film he'd once seen. "I love you, Anne," he whispered to the dust. And jerked out of sequence, their last scene lit up in his memory.

A pub on the approach to the Pier Head; lights like inverted hanging wineglasses; maritime prints of outward-bound ships; from one table a rush of laughter; Anne sitting chin on hand, sipping a vodka. "What will you do eventually, Kirk?" That could mean anything; he chose one meaning. "I hope I'll make London sometime in the future," he said, Paris forgotten; after all, he mightn't be equipped to earn a living there, and he'd never even met Adrienne. "I hope you do," Anne said. "And please come and see me in Southend. You remember how to reach me? But until you do, you will write to me, won't you?"

"Of course I will. Do you mind them typed? I type faster than I can write."

"Oh, don't. I want them in your writing."

"All right." The bell for closing time pealed between them. Kirk helped her don the jacket of the suit she'd worn for him; he didn't look down at his own. They left without speaking, struggling through the maze of tables from which a girl collected glasses of soapsuds. The night was chill; a drunk yelled after them and gesticulated, almost overbalancing. As they waited at the traffic-lights on the last stretch to the Pier Head, Anne gripped Kirk's arm. They stepped on the disused railway track between the cobbles and Anne turned: "Kirk, I love you. Please—" He knew what she was forbidden to say; he was on the edge of acting out so many movies that he'd seen. The lights blazed down into his face. "Je t'adore," he said. It was the best he could do; he didn't know whether it was enough, he felt the light fading. But at once she looked up at the clock; he couldn't be sure if she'd even heard.

They had crossed the river; it rushed by unobstructed. As they climbed the Woodside ramp, past a newspaper flattened on the grey wall like a poster, Anne said: "I can't pay for a taxi and I suppose you can't either, Kirk?"

"I can't," he told her; he didn't like to add that she had cleaned him out. "Oh, Kirk, five minutes to my last bus," she mourned. They kissed feverishly in the bus shelter, then on the platform, beneath averted eyes; then the engine snarled. Anne moved up the aisle; Kirk's hand clung limply to the pole. Suddenly she cried his name and running back, pressed something into his hand: "My darling, your glasses, I almost forgot!" The bell rang. The bus pulled out. Anne waved as she was drawn away, blurred, was gone. A light was carried off into the night. He couldn't see. He struggled with the case, opened it, fumbled on his glasses; but the bus had turned a corner, the street was dark, cold, empty.

His glasses brought the pavement closer, sharp as the sights of a delirium—but why go on? If only that was how it had ended!—on one last luminous image he gave himself of a tiny Anne borne waving away around the corner. The pain of parting was more bearable than the dull ache of disillusionment, which itself was preferable to the all-embracing horror of disorientation. But his memories were headlong in their flight from happiness; already they'd rushed through the Liverpool coach station at Edge Lane, bypassing a tableau of a man with a hose and the grey trails of buses like snail-tracks, and had dumped him on the coach to Southend, his first visit to Anne. Penniless, he'd sold his typewriter; the girls in the downstairs flat on Smithdown

Road had complained of its nocturnal tapping—not that he cared, but Anne had said she wanted him to write. And allowing for the remainder of the month he'd still realised enough to pay his fare to Southend. He'd written to Anne two days ago to herald his arrival, but she hadn't replied yet. The letter from Adrienne lay in his flat unanswered. But he knew how to reach Anne, and next week he'd be back to class and Shirley.

The doubts commenced on the edge of Southend; as in a film, he glanced up and gazed out across the first laps of sand. Had it been a holiday romance? Had she called him "darling" in the casual London way? Had she declared her love to intensify their parting, to create a scene for her album? He wished he'd waited for a reply to his letter. If she were eager to show him the door, if there were someone else sitting in the front room waiting for him to leave, it would annihilate him. Trivial, trivial, his future self scoffed on the bench; but doubt now was all he could trust. He willed it to dissipate like morning mist over Southend: the amazingly protracted pier, thrusting entertainment seawards to hold steady on the water, faceted yet featureless as time; the sea unfolding sibilantly on the sand; the flowers bordering the streets; the street-names elevated on poles like varieties of flowers. Flowers for love or for a wedding. A wedding night on Mount Pleasant, street of Liverpool's hotels and "of all the Mr and Mrs Smiths of the world," as he'd told Anne. Having wavered and chosen a hotel, they found the desk-clerk suspicious; but Anne in her white skirt looked too innocent to be guilty. The desk-clerk smiled, perhaps at some remembered escapade, and unlocked the double room. As soon as the door had closed Kirk stroked Anne's hair, found the fastening of her dress, opened it and led her to the bed. Gently he pushed her back and lifted her legs onto the coverlet. As he began to draw her dress down from her shoulders he realised she was trembling. He glanced at her face. She was shaking with laughter.

A girl laughed in the dry square; Kirk awoke. He kept his eyes closed; he was afraid to open them on tears. "Don't be long for heaven's sake, the bus must be due," said the young man in the coach queue. High heels clicked away. How could he have dreamed that of Anne? Of course they'd never been to a hotel; he'd never seen a girl naked; but if it had been Anne, she'd never have done that to him. She couldn't do that to me, he told himself, passing an old man wheeling his wife along Southend promenade. And he turned up the side street leading to Arlen Street, where Anne lived.

Down the blazing street came two figures, arms about each other. Even with his glasses and in the piercing sunlight, he could not make out their faces. Kirk's fist clenched in his pocket. They came closer; a young bearded man strolling with a girl Kirk had never seen before. His fist opened, already feeling Anne's fingers between his, and he ran to the end of the street, to Arlen Street, and was confronted by a desert of waste ground.

That image was clearest of all: the humps of spewed earth, the ruts and folds of bulldozer treads like the gums of a toothless mouth, a dog urinating brightly in the sunlight against the noticeboard that claimed the wasteland; the abandonment, the disorientation. Kirk moaned. He must have been mistaken. He stumbled back towards the promenade and overtook the couple; he put his hand on the girl's warm shoulder to make them turn and to feel a human body. "I'm wrong for Arlen Street, aren't I?" he pleaded. "Can you put me right?"

"Allen Street you want, mate," suggested the girl's escort.

"No, A-r-l-e-n," Kirk spelled desperately, hearing Anne say "Like Michael Arlen, you know."

"Wrong town, I'd say," the girl broke in. "You're not from round here, are you?"

"Are you from round here?" Kirk caught at the possibility.

"I'm half a mile up the front, mate, and Anne's in the next street." Kirk's stomach twisted; then he saw that the other was referring to the girl on his arm. Kirk moved away, almost fleeing; sand stung his cheeks. As he reached the promenade they called behind him "There's a map up the prom if you don't believe us."

Of course no Arlen Street was noted on the map. Chaos churned in Kirk like the breeze-blown sand. He shuffled towards a group of shops; beside one a staircase led beneath a dead electric sign to a basement coffee-bar. He took one step towards it; Anne might be there—then a pang shot up from his stomach, blocking his way. He no longer wanted to meet her. He wanted to go home. He made for the bus-station, past inverted chairs defending cafe tables, signs on stalls: "Novelty Hats", "Torture Thro' the Ages"; the illuminations hung lifeless in sunlight, and "The Longest PIER in the World" had been drained of all but a pink tinge. The next bus was for London; but anything to escape Southend.

The sight of Victoria Station as it had once been, movie posters vast against the sky, actresses of cardboard, drivers sipping coffee from paper cups beside a photo booth (of course, thought future Kirk, he should have known then), was superimposed over the sounds of the concrete square, like a film whose dubbing emphasises its unreality; on the stone bench Kirk felt the world receding, revealing itself as his hallucination. If he opened his eyes he might find figures mouthing like fish, their dialogue continuing unsynchronised —while in his memory, more vivid, more intense and more convincing, he found he had three hours to wait for the Liverpool coach. He lost himself in the night. Presently, the lights of a cinema blazed; the film was *Vertigo*. No, it was too cruel. But he refused to tire himself for three hours in pursuit of a memory when he could be grappling with it. The film had started; the camera moved alluringly through the shadows of a night-club, and suddenly, bright in a blonde aura, there was Kim Novak. Kirk watched wide-eyed; then he shook and buried his face in his hands. Inexorably the film continued. A giant kiss filled the screen: flaps of skin engulfing each other like the jaws of cannibal snails, thought Kirk, still shaking. Beneath the kiss the audience rustled and coughed; neither was real. Abruptly Kirk stood up. Above him in the circle a couple took the cue; as they stood, silhouetted on the fan of light that was Kim Novak, they kissed luminously. Kirk spun about, rammed into a vacated seat and stumbled blindly out.

At Victoria Station a man staggered into the bar, stuttering that life was a bad joke played on humanity, and Kirk directed him out with such force that even this man's fervour failed. Kirk found a stained table, its plastic top decorated with linked brown rings like a Chinese puzzle, arranged his plate of sandwiches and glass of Coca-Cola and threw his coat on the next chair. Before his slumped coat stood a half-empty glass, stained with drink like dismal clouds. A waitress somnolently sponged the tables, shovelling the debris onto a single plate as if to feed a dog; she saw the half-drained glass and left it for Kirk's girlfriend, whose place he must be keeping with his coat. Oh God, he said, realising. He wondered what he'd do until the coach arrived; sit and stare at the bare bar, people the seat beside him and weep if necessary; another drunk, they'd think.

The coach seemed stalled for ever; the air-conditioning insinuated a faint nauseating whine into Kirk's ears. Muted conversations hemmed him in as at a sickbed. Just before he leapt up and screamed, the coach pulled out. He couldn't sleep; Anne was there. He stared out with burning eyes at cardboard houses exhibited beneath sodium lighting, then at last the first unlit road where the headlights wiped darkness from vignettes of lonely mansions, caught scurrying small forms and brushed over mysteriously empty cars in laybys, and suddenly he remembered: he could question Anne's Auntie Ethel and discover Anne's address!—if Anne hadn't warned her in advance. He gripped the stone bench to absorb its chill and be weighed down by what reality was left, but already he was flying helpless through the Pier Head on the Sunday afternoon, past old women screaming at old women screaming the Gospel, youths jeering as they aimed from the roof of the police station, unwashed wailing children dragged along by unwashed parents, over the worn boards littered with cigarette packets and knotholes surrounded by arrested ripples, onto the bus to Bidston, where the "No Spitting" sign had received the obvious amendment, and out into the sun; for a moment the leaf-shadows that strayed about the pavement were the dapplings of light on the Dee beneath Caldy Hill. He strode towards the house, but his steps faltered. The memorable cry of the gate's hinges was silent, the empty socket of the bellpush was somehow filled by a new screw. The door opened.

A girl of Kirk's age smiled and turned her head shyly; she was not Anne. "Could I speak to Mrs Ethel...?" More than that he didn't know. "I'm an Ethel but I'm not married yet. Who told you I was?" She wavered so near the edge of shrillness that she must be compensating; she looked directly at him, and he saw why. One side of her face was covered by a purple birthmark.

He caught at the burning wood of the doorframe and managed not to fall; he clutched the concrete bench and fell, knowing what was to come. His mouth opened and forced deeper into chaos, like a kiss. "You don't have relations—in Southend?"

"Why yes, my sister's there."

"Married with a daughter?" The doorframe flaked beneath his fingers like a block of salt; the grit of the concrete bench coated his hands—he was merging into it, a memorial to chaos.

"Good Lord no, not yet. She's younger than I am, she's staying with our friends down there. Though I do hope she will be married one day. Me too if it comes to that. Did you meet her on holiday? I think she's got her eye on our friends' son. She didn't tell you about me, did she? You must come in and have a cup of tea."

"I have to go. It's the wrong address," Kirk faltered and almost ran from the garden. On the pavement he looked back. She was staring at him sadly. He closed his eyes and stepped into the road. She must think he'd fled the birthmark, but there was nothing he could say. A car swept by on each side of him, and he remembered: thus she would lose her husband. He beat at the wake of the car and staggered gasping to the pavement. What could he say? She'd think he was insane. At last, from the shadow of the trees, he glanced back. The door was closed.

The bus back to Woodside felt more solid now than when he'd caught it, perhaps draining its solidity from the concrete bench, in which, like everything, he'd once again ceased to believe. As he was carried from Bidston to his flat he began to suspect how all was staged for him. That night he prowled, even though term began next day, until the night rain lashed him back; he started at laughing girls on motorcycles borne by a V-shaped spray, he stared into the black hypnotic mirrors of the flagstones, seeking Anne, who was nowhere. He couldn't understand; he was no scientist or mystic; the knowledge that Anne had never been filled him with a doubt of everything he'd taken for granted. At last he sank into bed and was whirled into sleep, dreaming of Anne so vividly that her smile, her voice, her scent, her warmth were more real than the jagged alarm, the slits of light in his room and the hall, and the two letters on the hall table.

One he knew: his only letter to Anne. A blotched grid ("No Such Address", "Gone Away") had encroached on his careful writing, and beside it someone had scribbled: "Arlen

Street not built yet!!" No, it wasn't possible; if he hadn't been with Anne for a week, where had he been? Had he strode round Liverpool arm in arm with air, talking to himself? Then he chilled; without his glasses he couldn't have known if the crowds had edged away from him and branded him insane. But no, this betrayed Anne. He'd held her, felt her tongue, her body; no ghost could be so solid. Or if her body had been illusion— He didn't want to think; he rushed upstairs, the letters crushed in his hand, and wrested open the wardrobe door. The brown back of the wardrobe was still solid. He found the shirt into whose pocket he'd thrust the photographs Anne had given him. The pocket was empty. As he fought the nylon folds a hint of Anne's perfume seemed to touch the air. He lifted the shirt and inhaled; no perfume, only a trace of his own sweat. He slumped on the bed. Before him lay the ruthless grid. His hand crept towards it. No, don't! he cried on the concrete bench. But already he'd torn the letter to shreds, and on the bench his hand went limp in his pocket, its fingers slackly touching the other letter, Adrienne's.

On the bed he opened the letter; the writing on the envelope was not Adrienne's, but the postmark he knew. Inside was a folded note in French and another envelope, addressed to him by Adrienne. He didn't feel equal to the French; he wrenched open the second envelope. "My dearest Kirk—you have not yet written, and I have been thinking; I would not want you to come to Paris without knowing all about me. I should have said before, I cannot get about so well, that is what I want to say. You have seen my photograph and I hope you like it, but maybe you did not guess that I have to use a wheelchair—" Trembling, Kirk laid the letter on the tangled sheet and unfolded the note. It was from Adrienne's father: she had been rushing to post this letter to Kirk; the road had been busy, and when the wheelchair had overturned, the car had been unable to brake— On the bench he stuffed the letter back into his pocket, certain once more that all was illusion. Everything was too pat. Adrienne's death was the ending of a movie, Auntie Ethel was the stock sympathiser with romance, Anne was his true love—it was all too scripted for words, he thought, not realising that only life dares stage such coincidences.

When he left the flat as if stepping from one dream to another, he was overwhelmed by unreality: twigs intricately depicted on the sky; a milk-van rounding the corner on cue; a train drawing its whistle along the skyline—you couldn't tell him all that wasn't staged to impress him. By his own mind, of course: a brilliant hallucination. No wonder he felt sick on the bus to college; his body was fighting to correlate the illusion of movement with the conviction of stasis, as in a Cinerama film. The college corridors were prolonged into the impossible perspectives of a surrealist painting. In the classroom, between the black speckled plane of the blackboard and the canted dim reflection of the chatting groups, he was amazed by the talent that had contrived the improvised conversations: six separate improvisations, all for him. Then Shirley entered through the doorway, left. He beckoned her over, anxious to know what lines she'd been given. As she approached he lost control; he burst out laughing. "How very intriguing," she said, turning away; she shouldn't have said that, he'd have liked his moment of triumph. When the lecture began—

No, that was enough. There was no need to recall how absurd he'd found the idea of being taught by an hallucination, how he'd fled Liverpool and the ghost of Anne in every street, taken refuge in London where at least he'd never seen her—for he could only fall through his memories of her into a void; if she had not been real, how could he trust any evidence presented by his senses? Yet he was troubled to recall that he'd had the illusion of starving in London until he'd taken a job on the buses, a choice whose source he couldn't determine. Sometimes he felt that he'd dreamed

Anne, and sometimes, on the rim of the void, that she'd dreamed him. If so, she'd abandoned him to decades swept bare as by a night-wind, walks through streets where light existed only to carve shadows, glimpses of couples, always young, meeting outside cinemas he would never enter. By now the void was visible through her; soon she would tatter and fade like mist, and the void would close in. He was dying.

"I'm ever so sorry I was so late," Anne said. "You know I don't like travelling in London. I just had to wait for one of those lovely taxis."

Kirk's eyelids trembled. The young man with the sportscoat was no longer alone; Anne was with him, swinging one leg and clapping her hands as the Liverpool coach entered the square. She wore her cotton frock, each flower as Kirk remembered it; it was like emerging from darkness into sunlight. For a moment he thought he'd gone mad. "I'll be leaving before you know," Anne told the young man, "it's ever so sad." And instantly the continuity clarified. The young man's hand covered a flower. For a second Kirk was ready to fight him for Anne, but he knew he was powerless. They had yet to meet.

The coach dozed to a halt and the queue shuffled forward. Kirk stood up and almost fell; his stone legs had disintegrated. He dragged his case through the concrete dust. Anne's escort lifted her luggage onto the rack as she seated herself behind the driver. An old couple sat in the seat behind Anne; Kirk knew he must sit there. He groaned; his toes scrabbled like imprisoned insects. The old couple conferred over the view across the aisle and moved to the seat opposite. Kirk plunged into the place they had vacated. He struggled with his case, and a hand took the handle from him. "Allow me," said the young man. Anne smiled and waited until the case was safe. Crushed, Kirk sank into his place.

The driver slammed his gate. From the front seat came an

outburst of confused and hurried leave-taking, silenced by a kiss. Kirk closed his eyes. When he opened them at the first jerk of the bus, he met Anne's gaze. It was passing over him as she craned to wave to the young man. She hadn't recognised Kirk; she couldn't. The bus rushed through the pale planed streets and Anne regarded herself in a pocket mirror. Had her ghost cast a reflection? He would never know. It was unimportant; here she was before him in the flesh; he had only to lean forward and speak, the one thing he couldn't do. Though he knew her love she had never met him; she was a stranger. And he no longer trusted strangers.

Half an hour later, in a landscape of lopped trees grey as the pedestals of monuments, he leaned forward. One of Anne's fingers followed the curved corner of her book, lifting to turn; the golden sunlit down on her forearm was warm as her arm in his. His hand lost its grip between the headrests; his lips collapsed together as he fell back, aching. His breath proved the window. Something should happen to bring them together, but he knew nothing would; she wouldn't drop the book, this time it was up to him to plunge into the past, to reinstate reality. "Excuse me—" he cried, thrust forward by the brake. Anne's face appeared in the gap; her eyes were wide; she smiled encouragement. Perhaps she saw him as a cache of memories, of the past she loved. His mouth worked. "Do you—do you know where we are?" he stammered. "I think we're in Stratford," she said, and returned to her book as he muttered thanks. Oh God, he thought, she was close enough to touch and yet he'd lost her for ever.

Metal glinted in the sky; a steel curve formed on the horizon and passed above them with a sigh. The streets of the new Stratford were lifeless: slabs of concrete left to whiten in the sun; the silver panels of the meal dispensers flashed cold as scalpels as they passed. A love song ebbed from a portable tv; an athlete padded alongside the coach for a few seconds before falling back. For Kirk he, at least, had not been robbed by time of familiarity. It was time that had thrust between them, wearing out his body, setting Anne before him like a fragile perfect doll. Yet for a week they had wandered outside time. If only he could release them once more—

Then he thought he knew. Firm as it had felt, it had not been Anne's body he had held to him; it had been their spirits, essences—he couldn't find the right expression—that had met, somewhere outside time. Their bodies were the clocks that marked the end of their love. Destroy their bodies and they would be reunited. But could he take the final step? He answered himself: what other step could he take? He stood up tottering behind Anne; each limit of him was trembling as if ready to release him. Ahead green grassy banks streamed towards him and were gone, like time; beyond the grey stumps started into sight. "Anne," he whispered. She glanced up from her book, puzzled. He clutched the headrest; if only he could touch her, just her hair! "Anne, I know you don't know me—" Her mouth opened. He stammered out "We met fifty years ago. You went back into the past somehow and we met on a coach, maybe it was here —your case was falling off the rack and I helped you—I love you, Anne." It's no use, he thought. Her eyes widened; her pink parted lips moved—and Kirk stumbled forward, drove his elbow into the driver's face and wrenched the wheel hard over.

When they'd asked the last question Anne lay back and tried to sleep. She hated the hospital ward, the glass panels around each bed as if to enclose a vacuum, the curtains that drew together at the touch of a button, the beds that could turn traitor and convert into stretchers within a minute; she hoped she would dream of the past. The doctor had disliked her being questioned, but she'd insisted on the facts. They told her of the man who'd caused the crash by attacking the driver, killing himself and concussing the driver and several passengers, including Anne. They said he had spoken to her, but she didn't remember; one never remembers the events before concussion. They showed her a photograph of the old man, but she'd never seen him; so they left her to rest. And yet— Somehow, as she drifted, she felt she'd met him; somehow she referred this to the week she'd lost under concussion. Poor old man, she thought, he must have been miserable to do what he did; mad with his memories, perhaps, now all destroyed. She hoped his last thoughts had been of something beautiful. And quietly, as she hovered on the edge of dream, she began to weep.

THROUGH THE WALLS

RAMSEY CAMPBELL

Hugh Pears was gathering mint in the back yard when he heard the crash. It sounded like someone hurled onto a sheet of tin. God, not the children! As he ran through the kitchen, Chris glanced at him, puzzled; she hadn't recognised the sound. "You aren't going out now," she protested. "The children will be home any minute." But he hadn't reached the front door when they ran in. "There's a man hurt outside," Linda shouted.

"They nearly ran us over," Andrew shouted louder.

Pears let go of his fear with a gasp of relief, and hurried out. A red Mini had slewed into the wall of the house next door. The driver was lifting a figure from the passenger seat. Its head was a raw red bulb; blood had rusted its hair.

When Pears opened his eyes he'd regained control. The driver was supporting his passenger, whose forehead was bleeding copiously. Pears wondered why he should have seen anything else. He wasn't fond of the sight of blood, but nor was he given to building nightmares out of it. "Bring him in here," he called. "My wife's a nurse."

As Pears helped them up the path, he saw the young man in the ground-floor flat next door gazing expressionlessly at

320

them. Only his gaze moved, as if he were peering from behind a pale gaunt mask. If you can't help, Pears raged, then have the decency to take yourself elsewhere. The gaze followed them blankly, indifferent as the fog that massed at the edge of the streetlight like dim spectators.

Chris sat the man in one of the white wood dining-chairs. "What happened?" she asked, tilting his head back.

"We skidded on a patch of oil," the driver said. "It looked big enough for a lorry—I wouldn't have thought they were supposed to come down a residential street, not a narrow one like this."

"Too many people don't care about that," Chris said.

The passenger was holding his trouser leg away from his shin, down which blood was running incontinently into his shoe. "This'll teach me to wear my seat belt," he said, shaking.

She cleaned the wound and gave him a compress to hold against it. "I don't think it's serious, but we'd better be sure," she said, turning down the cooker. "I'll drive you to the hospital."

Andrew was sponging blood from the back of the chair. That jarred Pears out of the reverie through which he'd watched Chris caring for the man. The thoughts had streamed through his mind like smoke; he felt vaguely that he would prefer not to remember them. He shook his head. All this nonsense came of boredom, inertia, probably of feeling incapable of helping Chris. Get on with something. He strode into the back yard.

He'd finished gathering the mint when he heard Linda's cry of disgust. A spider, he thought, or a cranefly or a slug. As he hurried through the kitchen and the dining area he saw, beyond the open front door down the hall, the young man from the flat standing on the pavement, gazing in. If he's what you're saying yuk to, Pears told Linda, I can't say I blame you. But she was staring at the hall wall.

Just inside the front door, the wallpaper had acquired a splotch of blood. Trickles were making their way towards the skirting-board. "Damn," Pears said. "He must have done it as they went out. Get me a cloth, Linda, quick."

He closed the front door. As Pears hid the blood from him, the young man gaped in appalled disbelief. You're absolutely right, Pears told him, we're going to scrape it off and use it for soup.

He dabbed at the blood. Mrs Tarrant can get the worst of it off, she'll be here tomorrow. That's what she's paid for. He scrubbed as hard as he dared. The stain remained, but fainter. Eventually he sat and waited for his dinner, minutely lining up the cutlery, listening to Linda and Andrew playing pole-vaulting in the yard. His mind felt full of rapid formless smoke.

Over dinner Chris asked "What exactly happened?"

"He shouldn't have driven down our road so fast," Andrew said.

"If someone hadn't been so stupid they ran out in front of him, there wouldn't have been an accident," Linda said.

"I didn't see him. He came straight round the corner." He glared at her, the threat of angry tears in his eyes. "I bet you'd have been glad if I'd been run over."

"That's right. No, I wouldn't," Linda amended, trying to head off his mood. She put an arm round him, but he threw her off.

"You're quite right, Andrew," Chris said. "He shouldn't have been driving so fast. But for your own sake you must be more careful how you go."

Pears listened blankly. He heard the words, but it was as though he heard them through a wall; they seemed separate from him. He stared at the table, at the white wood and its reflected hints of the violet and lilac walls. The words affected him in the same way: they were there, that was all.

He gazed at his food as he ate. Wherever he looked, there

seemed to be movement at the edge of his eye. Dark spots moved on the walls, as though the kitchen were a sweating cave, or as if the walls were the throat of a chimney, fluttering with soot. When he looked, the movements snapped into corners of the room or behind the furniture. His eyes must be tired. Perhaps he could blame the tree in the next yard, its shadow on the curtain swaying sluggishly, blurred by the gathering November fog. Perhaps he was overworked, though he hadn't thought himself to be more so than anyone else at the bank.

Andrew had been mollified, or nearly. "Sisters," he said witheringly. When he'd eaten his fruit he said "May I leave the table? I'm going to dust Fritz."

Linda had been waiting for a chance at the last word in the argument. She was too much of a young lady now to stick out her tongue. "Aren't you too old for that thing yet?" she demanded. "When are you going to throw away that horrible doll?"

"Linda, you're only two years older," Chris said. "Hardly the voice of maturity."

"Well, I didn't want that doll when I was eight."

An aunt had brought her Fritz from Germany, but Linda had mislaid the doll behind her bed almost at once, complaining "Alice's father brought her back a lovely German dress." "Give me the doll if you don't want him," Andrew had said. Pears supposed that now it was up to him to intervene. Anything to drag his mind free of the slow heavy dance of the nodding shadow on the curtains, to shake off the darkly teeming walls. "There's nothing horrible about Andrew's doll, Linda," he said.

"There is too. You come and look."

She pulled him into the hall. "Go outside and see," she said. "I used to like to look up at our bedroom when I came home. Now he makes it look nasty. I'll switch on the light so you can see."

She ran upstairs, pleats flirting from her bare thighs. A Majorca tan was fading from her legs. He must talk to Chris about making her wear longer skirts. She was far too enticing. One of these days— What? He snatched his gaze away from Linda as she reached the top of the stairs, and rushed himself out.

As Pears emerged, the young man next door was letting in three others. One displayed a fat hand-rolled multicoloured cigarette for approval. Stupid fools. No wonder the fellow in the flat looked so inert. And him an industrial chemist, if Pears wasn't misinterpreting his salary cheque: should know better.

When Linda switched on the light, the fog sprang forward, towering blankly on the opposite pavement. It settled clammily on Pears, who shivered and looked up. Fritz the doll was standing on the sill in the centre of the bay window, grinning out. Pears could just see his red knees over the sill, beneath his lederhosen. His raised tankard was halfway to his mouth; his painted wooden face was edged with light. He looked hideous.

Fog crept insinuatingly down Pears's spine, fog was a dwindling blank-faced box around him. The lawn stirred feebly, as if drowned. He tried to shake himself, but shuddered. Good God, he was standing in his own front garden, looking at his own house: what could be so terrible in that? But he could hardly keep his eyes on the doll.

It looked like an overgrown bloated schoolboy mottled with red paint as if its skin were bursting. Beneath the blue glass eyes, the grin had become secretive, knowingly obscene. Its free hand hovered near its flies. It was all the effect of the fog; fog had tinted its face shinily grey, slimy, diseased. It looked swollen with waste that might gush forth at any moment.

Linda read his expression. "See?" she called.

"I must say," Pears said warily, "he looks rather a nasty little man today."

He didn't realise that Andrew was in the bedroom until the boy appeared behind Linda, weeping. He pushed her out of the way and threw up the sash, then he hurled the doll into the road. Pears heard it break. "Did you see that?" someone said in the flat. "Far out."

Cretins, Pears snarled. Tears were streaming between Andrew's fingers, Linda was trying to comfort him and fighting to pull his hands away from his face, Chris was hurrying upstairs, irritably shouting "What's going on?" Pears opened the front gate; wet flakes of rust chafed beneath his fingers. He stooped to pick up the doll. Then he recoiled.

The fog had dimmed the streetlights. The shadow of the doll was blurred, the wet road was uneven. He wasn't really seeing a thick dark lumpy fluid, seeping slowly from the doll's cracked head.

The fog was muttering; the sound grew into an open-mouthed snarl. A car swung into the road. Pears reached for the doll, then pulled back his hand and ran towards the house. Behind him he heard the car grind the doll into splinters.

Andrew had heard it too; Chris was trying to calm him down. "Will you stay out of this," she shouted. Pears gladly took the order for himself. He went into the living-room. Beyond the garden the privet leaves looked thick, coated with fog; he knew how they felt. He drew the curtains and sat in the bay window.

When Chris came down, she stared at him. He frowned enquiringly. If she didn't say what she was thinking, they couldn't talk about it. His mind seemed clearer now; he relaxed, smiling. She sat opposite him, shaking her head. The subdued children trudged into the next room, the playroom; Linda whispered. "It's not my job to run this family singlehanded," Chris said.

"I never said it was."

"But you act it. If you don't intend to help at least don't make things more difficult."

She sounded weary. "Have you a migraine?" Pears said.

"It's taken you long enough to notice."

"I'm not feeling too well myself. I expect that hasn't helped my behaviour."

"Your behaviour isn't that unusual."

This was hardly the time to discuss it: if she felt as odd as he did, they would only end up screaming. He moved his chair out of the bay and switched on the television, but found he couldn't watch for long. The image whirred silently, as his eye refused to aid the illusion of continuous movement. Blackfaced minstrels danced and sang, hurtling forward to fill the bulging screen, grimacing with painted lips. Pears reached for the switch. "I'm listening to that," Chris said.

He sank back and gazed at the fire. On the edge of his vision colours boiled beneath glass, as if an aquarium had gone mad. The fire swayed gently, flickering high and vanishing. When he emerged from his reverie, the programme had been ousted by another. A sandy brown desert, a bright amber sky: the colours didn't clamour for attention. Calm now, he looked. Men in khaki shorts were gently spading out a pit. Archaeologists? Two of them were coaxing something from the soil. He leaned closer.

It came up with its arms held stiff at its sides, its skin pulled back from a yellowing fixed smile. The pit was surrounded by fleshless bodies, rigidly contorted or lying supine with their lips wrenched back as if by hooks, grinning. "So far the mass graves have yielded at least five hundred dead," an announcer was pronouncing. The camera tilted up to show that it had been keeping back a vista of ranked corpses as far as the horizon. In the next room the children were putting toys away. "I don't think we should risk the children seeing this," he said, turning to Chris.

As he spoke something moved to the edge of the screen and emerged into the room. A shadow, of course. When Pears glared at the corner where it had halted, there was nothing. How could television cast a shadow? It must have come from the street. The screen piled up with swarms of brown emaciated manikins. Their dried-out sockets were turned to the sun, their jaws protruded through their skins. He surged out of his chair and switched off the television.

All he achieved was to send the announcer into hiding. "There are almost certainly further graves to be discovered," the man continued, muffled now, as if he'd put his hand over his mouth. Not until Pears heard someone shout "Jesus, that's sick. Turn it off," did he realise that the voice was persisting in the flat through the wall.

He slumped back, and began to cough. Had the fog managed to insinuate itself into the room? There was a faint unpleasant smell. In the corner a faint shadow remained—an after-image, of course. The smell reminded him of old meat, but wasn't quite like that. Had a mouse died beneath the floor? He'd look tomorrow—he didn't feel at all like searching now. "I think we'd all benefit from an early night," he said. "It's past their bedtimes, anyway."

"Do what you want," Chris said.

Andrew was morosely obedient, and Linda made only a token protest; yet Pears found himself becoming irritable. Suppose Chris noted the smell, what might she find? Nothing, for God's sake. Get to bed.

Reading his mood, the children allowed themselves to be herded quickly to the bathroom. Pears stood outside as they splashed; Linda was trying to wheedle Andrew into her game. We aren't such a bad family, Pears thought. I can hold Chris, we don't need to talk.

Abruptly Linda was out of the bathroom. She ran naked to him, towelled pink, her bald pubes and tentatively swelling breasts framed in her tan, and put her arms around him. "Carry me to bed," she pleaded.

Her hair was warm beneath his chin. She moved against him, soft to his touch, instinctive and guileless as a young animal. As she gazed up at him, sleepy and innocently sensuous, she looked exactly as Chris sometimes did. For a moment of illusion she was Chris, renewed. "Not tonight, love," he said. "Your mother and I aren't feeling very well."

He smacked her bottom gently. She wriggled with delight, gazing at him, until he pushed her away. "Go on, now," he said, close to panic. "We want to get to bed."

He hurried into the bathroom. "Finish your teeth quickly, Andrew, and I'll tuck you in." He leaned against the wall, his nails squeaking on the tiles. As soon as Andrew had closed the door, Pears was seized by a violent and prolonged orgasm.

He lay in bed, making a lair of the darkness. Even there he wasn't safe. When he closed his eyes, grinning faces floated up, plump and sticky. Suppose Chris wanted him to make love to her? That was often the way they expunged their arguments. He could hear her scrubbing the blood from the wall.

Her climbing footsteps seemed to take forever, as if she were sadistically prolonging her approach. She knows, he thought. I've broadcast to her what I've done. He pressed himself as near to his edge of the bed as he could, pretending to sleep.

He held himself still as she slipped into bed. Too still. He moved slightly, muttering. "Hugh?" she said. He glared into the darkness, grinding his teeth silently. "Hugh, listen," she said.

He turned over violently. "What is it?"

He hadn't meant to shout. "Nothing," she said, turning away.

"No, what is it?"

"It doesn't matter."

He could feel her turning restlessly for hours. He held himself rigid, willing her to sleep. She turned against him, rubbery; the bed felt like a tropical tent. When at last she was quiet, he couldn't be sure she wasn't pretending. He didn't dare leave the bed in case he disturbed her. Fog hung in the gap between the curtains, glowing feebly, thick and blank as his mind. His eyes itched hotly. He gazed at nothing.

At breakfast his eyes felt bloated and raw. Around dawn the chattering of birds had suddenly toppled with him into sleep. He stared at his plate. His knife sliced a poached egg; yellow liquid leaked from its pupil. The sounds of Chris and the children nagged at him, annoying as radio voices bumbling against an exhausted battery. He didn't know how he would be able to face work.

"I don't want to go to school today," Andrew said. "I don't feel well."

"Neither do I," Linda said.

"What's the matter with you?" Chris demanded.

They looked at each other, baffled. "Come on, both of you," she said. "No nonsense. Once you come home tonight, you've the whole weekend."

Pears forced himself to look at them directly. They were rummaging for an argument. "Listen, don't fret," he told them. "It won't be so bad, once you're there. I don't always want to go out in the mornings, you know. I don't this morning. But we have to go."

"And what about me?" Chris demanded angrily. "Do you think it's a picnic for me to go shopping, the way they look at you round here? It's an effort of will, I assure you."

He stared at her. "Only last week you said you liked these shops."

She was flushed with anger that she'd let her feelings show. "Well, that's how I feel now," she said defiantly.

"Well," he said, glancing at his watch. "Time's getting on. If I go now, I can walk up with you two. Are you coming?" he asked Chris, rather discouragingly: her revelation had annoyed him, for he didn't know how to handle it.

"I've the washing-up to do. I'll manage, don't worry." When he hesitated she said "I've told you not to worry about me."

Fog was blocking the way just outside the gate, a dull featureless thug. Behind the thickening grey screen, the privet leaves looked fat and plastic. Pears could see nothing he would be able to bear to touch. He gazed back down the hall, past the dining-table to Chris at the sink, and almost retreated. Instead he urged the children out. Glancing back at their bright orange curtains, which looked shabby now with fog, he caught sight of the young man in the flat, gazing apathetically through the uncurtained window.

The hinges of the gate shrieked jaggedly; Pears felt as if the sound were being dragged through his ears. The children waited restlessly. "Go on then," he said, impatient with everything, and strode out, thinking: I should make them want to go, not bully them.

The fog settled on him like wet cobwebs, drawing him deeper into itself. It closed him in with silence. He could hear no sound from the main road two hundred yards away. His muffled footsteps clopped; he could hardly hear the children's. Andrew and Linda were diluted, dissolving smudgily into the fog.

Odd blurs bobbed past: the mirror of a parked car, the overhanging tips of a tree. They faded, and the street seemed to fade with them. He was alone with fog. It closed on his face like a cold soft mask, trickling thickly into his lungs. A single paving-stone repeated itself underfoot, again and again, in a frame of fog. He couldn't see the children now. He began coughing uncomfortably. Nor could he hear them.

He gagged himself with one hand, and strained his ears. All his senses were muffled; his mouth and nose felt stuffed with wet smoke. The flat inexorable wall of fog stood close to him, boxing him in. He opened his mouth to shout, but it filled with a foggy cough. The children had gone. As he fought to speak, a dreadful suspicion choked him. He and the children hadn't been alone in the fog. There had been a hulking shape that paced them just behind the blinding wall, waiting until they became separated. He could feel its stealthy presence now, somewhere near. Its hands had grabbed the children's mouths. It had dragged the children into an alley and stuffed gags into their mouths. Now it was turning to Linda—

He heard the children's muffled screams.

For a moment he was fog, fluid, helpless. Then he smashed his way blindly forward, towards the cries. The grey slammed against his eyes, then fell back, acquiring an orange tinge. The children were waiting beneath the sodium lights of the main road, giggling nervously. Traffic moved by like a glacier, bleary lights gazing tearfully ahead. He'd never expected to be so glad to see a traffic jam.

The children must have been playing hide and seek in the fog, they must have scared each other. Pears felt angry, and anxious to be sure that that was what had happened. To interrogate them, or to lose his temper, would only cause further unpleasantness: best to leave it alone. Abruptly Linda said to Andrew "I'm sorry I was rude about your doll. I was mean."

"I was growing out of it anyway," Andrew said.

Oddly, they became less reluctant as they neared the school. They ran into the underpass eagerly enough, casting him a last glance as they went, flushed oval portraits in Balaclavas. He strolled to the bank, musing.

They couldn't have felt more reluctant to come out than he had. But now, away from the house, he felt no reluctance at all. At home they were all caught in a tight spiral of neuroses. Now he saw that, he knew how to free them. They must go away at the weekend, into the countryside. The fog stepped back before him, parting.

He enjoyed the day. He joked with those of his colleagues who seemed gloomily befogged, until their polite smiles broke into spontaneity. He'd cleared his desk of the convoluted cases that had been gathering, piling up against his mind. He rang Chris at work. She sounded happier, and said she liked the idea of a day out.

He felt affectionate towards everyone he saw or thought of. Almost everyone. He stole a look at the young industrial chemist's account. No salary cheque had been received this month, and the account was overdrawn. So that's why he sits around all day.

Walking home, Pears felt ashamed of his snooping. It hadn't even gained him anything. He hardly knew the man; he'd spoken to him only once, to ask him to subdue a howling guitar at midnight. These days the chemist's flat was usually silent—inert was more the word. As he reached his road, Pears saw the chemist driven away in a van by one of the friends who'd visited him last night. Pears couldn't help feeling glad to see him go.

At dinner the children cheered the proposal of a day out. "I did feel odd yesterday," Pears said. "And this morning too. It must have been something I ate. Didn't you feel odd, Chris?"

"You know I had a migraine. I don't know about anything else."

"What about you two?" But they didn't know what he meant any more than Chris seemed to, and when he remembered how he'd felt it seemed healthier to forget.

The next day was cold and bright. They drove into North

Wales. Slate hills were silver against pastel blue, white watery clouds streaked the horizons. They parked in a village whose name they stumbled over, laughing helplessly. The village seemed full of slim spires, of churches built of plump bricks of creamy dough around rose windows. They sat outside a pub, watching tractors pass, a market in the street opposite, a pony cantering by. "I wish I had a book about ponies," Linda said.

They bought her one, and *Watership Down* for Andrew. As they walked back to the car, Chris said "Do you think there's a hotel?" There was: two cottages knocked together, with a double room and a single free. "I bet you're called Mrs Jones," Linda told the landlady, who was. Andrew ran upstairs to read his book, and later they had to open the bedroom door to let the smell of dinner tempt him down.

After dinner they walked through the village. The streets were full of greetings and good-nights; distant windows came alight on the hills. An elderly couple said good night to them. They put the children to bed. Glancing through Andrew's book, Pears found a poem he thought was one of the most beautiful things he'd ever read. He read it aloud to them, letting himself go completely into the poem and into the children's eyes; by the end he was almost in tears. The children said good night quietly. Later Chris and he made love tenderly, unhurried, tranquil. They lay and felt the wide night calm around them.

"Now I think about it, you were right," Chris said. "I did feel strange on Thursday."

"In what way?"

She was asleep as soon as she'd said "I don't know why, I was jealous of you and Linda."

On Sunday Mrs Jones invited them to visit a friend's farm. The farmer's children were playing on a collapsed haystack. Andrew and Linda plunged into it shouting, pleading with their parents to join them. Urged on by Mrs Jones and her friends, Pears and Chris climbed the stack, pretending reluctance. At the top Linda began tickling Pears to make him roll down. Feeling her small fingers move over him, he froze for a moment. Then he retaliated, and while Andrew played with the other children—bringing him out of himself, Pears thought, good—he and Linda set about Chris. They rolled to the bottom entangled, laughing.

The farmer's wife insisted they stay for dinner. They drove home leisurely, through thin drifts of mist. The children slept in the back, nestling against Chris. Whenever he caught her eye in the mirror she smiled gently. Even Liverpool seemed refreshed by their outing; the long carriageway of Tuebrook was polished clean by frost and sodium light. The yellow paintwork of their house surged forward from the terrace to greet them. The flat next door was dark. Pears couldn't remember ever having been so pleased to return home.

On Monday evening he hurried home. Chris wouldn't be back for an hour, the children were staying late at school for recorder practice. He'd had enough of the rusty gate. The tin of paint nudged his thigh. Paint now, oil tomorrow. Fog unrolled the street like a carpet for him, yards ahead. A light appeared in the flat next door. He didn't bother looking.

He'd climbed to the loft in search of a paintbrush when the sound began. It was a low rumbling, almost inaudible; for a while he wasn't sure he heard it. Dust stirred wakefully in the dim charred light beneath the roof. The sound seemed to be deep in the walls; momentarily the uncoloured shapes around him in the loft appeared to be vibrating. Surely it couldn't be thunder. Of course, it was a plane approaching overhead.

He had just climbed down to the landing when he felt the sound inside him.

It was growing there. It was a huge rusty lump of metal, sharp-cornered and jagged, exploding slowly from the centre of his cranium, forcing its dull saw-toothed way out through his ears. He could taste it. His mouth tasted full of coins.

Don't let it be starting again! Please, no!

He rushed for the stairs. Downstairs he wouldn't be so close to the sound. He had to halt at the top, clutching at the banister, for he was plummeting towards the hall like a plane out of control. As he moved, his head had gone hurtling uncontrollably forward and down, as if on a cable. Within him metal rasped heavily.

By the time he reached the hall, gripping the banister and holding himself immobile on each step while his momentum subsided, the plane was fading. He sank gingerly into a chair in the living room. The sound drained lazily away, a murmur, a whisper, cold and rough in his head; he couldn't tell when it began to persist only in his imagination. He sat still. If he didn't move nothing else would happen. It would all fade, he would feel it go and know when it was safe to move. The walls held themselves still, almost trembling with the effort.

Soon he felt there was nothing wrong except the fog, which now had night on its side. The privet hedge was sliced thin by a block of grey. He stood up to draw the curtains, but fell back into his chair. There was something out there he must watch for, to be prepared when it came. Each time he looked the fog had inched more of his surroundings into itself.

Because the window was closed he didn't hear them coming. The fog within the gateway stirred. Two small forms were rising to the surface. They came slowly, like bodies floating up from grey mud. He heard the faint clang of the gate, and then they were rushing towards the house. They came to the window and peered in at him, mouthing. Then a key scrabbled at the front door.

He knew their names, Andrew and Linda. That didn't help. He struggled to grasp memories before they came in. Andrew was both younger and older than his age, prone to trip over his own feet, oversensitive. No use. Pears was coldly analysing a stranger, and every phrase was a cliché. And Linda—

Memory deluged him, one image smashing against him again and again. Oh my God. Oh my God. How could he have had such feelings about a ten-year-old child, his own daughter? Even worse, how could he have tried to ignore them, forget them, pretend he'd meant Chris all the time? What was he becoming? Or had this secret self been waiting within him all the time?

Linda ran in, flushed, excited. "Bet you can't guess what we did today," she said.

She was all freed hair and pink flesh, palpitating. He clenched his fists down the sides of his chair, gouging his palms, trying to lock in a threatened explosion of nausea. "Tell me, tell me later," he managed to say. "Go and play."

"But I wanted to tell you," she said, hurt.

"Not now." Each time he spoke another voice, muffled, joined him in chorus. It was his own. He tried to ignore it long enough to speak. "Go, go on," he stammered.

Their sounds in the playroom annoyed him like the bumbling of flies, but at least he'd avoided further speech. He stared emptily at the encroaching fog. He wasn't going mad, he wasn't, but he couldn't bear to think that what he'd been experiencing was real. Yet if he was going mad the horror was himself, dragging him deeper, saving its worst until all his defences were down—not yet even hinting at its worst. His thoughts slithered, eluding him. He wasn't mad, but there were states of mind similar to madness. Suddenly he knew he'd been drugged.

How? In food. The chemist next door— Nonsense. He had neither opportunity nor motive. Detectives always looked for those. But Pears had detected a drug in himself, however it had got there. Chris, experimenting on behalf of the hospital — Rubbish. It was temporary. Bearable. Drugs didn't drive sane people mad, drugs couldn't overcome a strong mind, a mind that wouldn't weaken, that was in control, they couldn't. Perhaps Chris could determine what drug it was, and the antidote. The wall of fog shifted forward, hanging dull and slack, leaving only a cramped strip of dark bedraggled lawn.

The children muttered in the playroom, blurred. Pears lay back gingerly; his head felt thin-shelled, rocking with liquid. He closed his eyes and let sounds pass him by: Andrew's toy train rattling on its cramped line, Linda's padding bare-socked footsteps, Linda's voice. His eyes sprang wide, glaring.

"I want the bunny." That was all she'd said. A frayed stuffed rabbit sat in the corner of the playroom, the children rarely bothered with it now, but Linda had just asked for it. She hadn't really said "He wants to fuck me."

Or perhaps she had. After all, she needn't have meant her father. Of course she hadn't meant him, Pears thought, his face burning. Then whom had she meant? God, surely nobody! She had just been trying out the word, as children do.

She could have meant Pears. Young girls were supposed to go through a period of sexual love for the father. But wasn't she too young? Perhaps not: perhaps hidden in her mind were pictures of her father pulling off her clothes, his huge hairy body pressing down on her, forcing her wider—

He leapt up snarling. His rage relieved him of nothing. He had to know. All he could hear now was what he thought she'd said. He strode into the hall, and baulked. What could he say? He couldn't accuse her directly, in case his mind had tricked him. Why should his mind play that particular trick? He stood, trying to force himself forward; his hands felt bloated, and spiky with sweat. Andrew's voice squeaked. The playroom door hung immobile, smugly threatening. Linda answered.

She'd said "We want to stick these blocks up here." She hadn't said—

Pears slammed the door wide. The children stared at him: startled? innocent? pretending? Some building blocks were scattered amid the clutter on the floor, but he demanded "What were you saying?"

When Linda gazed at him, perhaps without guile, and opened her mouth, he interrupted savagely "You know what I mean. Just now. What were you saying?"

She looked uneasy now. "I don't know. What was I saying?"

"Leave Andrew out of it, don't try and make him answer for you. Don't drag him into it, you little—"

Her eyes were wider, rimmed with moisture. In a minute she would run to him in tears. He couldn't bear to have her near him. If she touched him— "All right. All right. It doesn't matter," he stammered, to escape. "Just keep quiet," he said and slammed the door.

He couldn't shake off the suspicion that Linda had got the better of him. She had seduced him again: into silence. She was knowing, evil; her body was. It was taking over, possessing the little girl he'd loved. He mustn't think of her.

The fog had fitted to the windows like the backing of a mirror. A dull discoloured lump of flesh sat in his reflected armchair, staring at him. They were still gazing at each other when he heard Chris's key in the lock.

Fear burned through him. The children might tell her how he'd behaved. She'd know he was going wrong again. His eyes might betray him if she looked closely; drugs were supposed to show in the eyes. If her terror were added to his the onslaught would disintegrate him completely.

Wasn't he looking at it the wrong way? The inspiration lifted him to his feet. Being near her should help. It was exactly what he needed. He hurried after her, into the kitchen. "Hello," he said. "I was going to paint the gate but the fog came down. I'll do it tomorrow without fail. I'll make myself if I have to. Not that I'll have lost interest." He was saying too much, too fast, trying to outrun his muffled other voice. "Do you like that colour paint? Never mind, don't answer, you must be tired. Was your day all right?"

"It was all right." She sounded a little weary. "You can get your own drink, Andrew. Don't start nibbling, Linda, dinner won't be long."

He avoided looking at the children. "Can I help you at all? Have you a migraine?"

"No, not yet." But all of a sudden Pears had. Perhaps she was in fact suffering secretly, but he was experiencing it directly. Perhaps he was imagining what migraine felt like. All he knew was that open metallic sores were burning coldly through his scalp; his cranium felt like a raw wound. Yet somehow he wasn't yet feeling the pain. If he weren't with Chris it might fade. "You don't want me to do anything, do you?" he gabbled, hurrying away, his scalp corroding.

He'd managed to attune himself to the fog, to its untroubled colourless calm, when Chris called him to dinner. He walked down the hall, bearing his calm carefully. That telephone is red. That wall is yellow. No need to touch them with his mind.

In the dining-area he found he felt invulnerable. He smiled surreptitiously. The effect was wearing off. He raised a forkful of dinner to his mouth.

He couldn't taste it. He almost reached into his mouth with the fork to examine the food. Lamb chop, mint sauce, potatoes, sprouts; no taste of any of them, just solids moving in his mouth. It was all right. No need to strain. This was only reaction against what he'd been suffering, what did they call it, sensory overload.

He chewed. Linda was gazing towards him as she ate. He'd been chewing for hours. Linda gazed at him.

He chewed faster. Faster, faster. No use: he couldn't make

Linda move. His time was slowing to a halt. Each moment was only a fraction of the one before. They would never add up to the next; he was trapped in this moment forever. And Linda's pictures of him were creeping towards his mind. "What are you doing?" he shouted. "What do you think you're staring at?"

Linda gasped. "I was just thinking."

Oh no, she couldn't trick him again so easily. Her gaze had been slowing him down, as though time were amber. "Ah," he snarled triumphantly. "And just what were you thinking, eh? Would it have been about me?"

"I was just thinking about my recorder. I played a whole page today."

She was nearly crying, and Chris was staring at him. If he went on, she might suspect what had happened to him on Thursday night—when Linda had got the better of him. She mustn't know that, nobody must know, he must wipe it out of his mind. "All right," he told Linda abruptly. "It doesn't matter. Get on with your dinner."

Faces gazed at him. "I'm sorry," he said, to turn them away. "All right," he shouted. "I'm sorry. I am sorry," he said quietly. Maybe Linda had been telling the truth. At least he'd escaped the trap of the dwindling moment, though his time still felt more intolerably stretched than it had since his childhood. Perhaps that was how Linda's time felt too.

Having eaten all he could, he retreated to the living-room. He lay back in its stillness, letting its shapes and colours lie on his eyes. If he didn't move they would stay still. But they grew harsh, alert. Someone was coming down the hall.

He'd forgotten: he had to get through an entire evening with Chris and the children. Surely the effect would fade before then. He had only to keep still, calm.

Chris read while the children watched television. They were pretending. They knew something was wrong with him, they were watching covertly, until he betrayed himself, but he wasn't going to. Let them watch how calm he was. He closed his eyes.

Which sprang open. Rushing up from their depths there had been a doll whose head was cracked wetly like an egg of blood, a doll with Andrew's face. As Pears glared at Andrew, he glimpsed the cracks fading into the boy's hair.

Worse was waiting for his eyes to close. He stared at the television. Too hectic. He stared at the palely coffee-coloured wall. If he kept his eyes open the images would die away. His eyes twinged, smarting, and he blinked.

Linda sailed up, naked, posturing, ready to engulf him. He gasped, then tried to smile convincingly: he could just have woken from a doze, they couldn't prove anything. He blinked. Chris flashed out at him and was etched on his mind. All her nerves were laid bare; small sharp hooks like dentist's instruments plucked at them. Her head was a mass of buried razorblades.

He sprang from his chair and stumbled upstairs. If he couldn't see the three of them they wouldn't be able to provoke these nightmares. He lay on the bed. Ahead hung the window, a faint grey smudged rectangle. It was receding from him.

Instead of yielding more light to his eyes it grew fainter, dwindling. The bedroom was enormous and very dark. The floor was crowded with figures, creeping lopsidedly toward him on all fours. The heads of the foremost, grey blurred ovals, were peering at him over the edge of the bed. Little of his scream escaped between his fingers. His other hand groped for the light-switch, found something, switched it on. The room was defiantly bare. He examined that fact for a long time, until he felt it might be true. The depths of his mind waited for him. It was only a temporary lull. The tide would flood back soon. Each time it returned it was more overpowering.

He was descending the stairs, which felt still in the way a

boobytrap might, when a terrible certainty gripped him. The effects must wear off eventually, no drug could last for the rest of one's life; but his nightmares must be imprinted on the house. Exactly as if some dreadful tragedy had happened there, the house was haunted now.

His gaze was drawn to the hall wallpaper. It was faintly speckled with a brownish stain. Blood. That was the beginning of the nightmare, when he'd seen the accident victim. If he could wipe off the last of the blood perhaps it would erase the imprint of his terror. Sickly he felt that the walls were soft within, as if subtly corrupted from their core, by the haunting; but he bent closer.

Peering, he wasn't sure whether the spots were blood or shadow. He sniffed the wall. Still unsure, he touched the stain with his tongue. A faint metallic taste: blood. Before he knew what he intended he was supporting himself, palms flat against the wall, while he licked avidly, searching for the taste.

He threw himself back, but couldn't escape himself. Maybe, he thought in a desperate bid for distraction, that's what the dopey chemist thought I meant to do when he saw me in the hall. Now his fantasy's true.

Chris and the children looked up when he opened the door. His face froze. He didn't know what expression he wore, but dared not alter it in case his face betrayed his terror. A tight mask he'd never seen before was clamped on him. As he paced to his seat the mask tugged painfully at his face, determined to reshape itself. He sat down and had to pass his hand over his face, as if brushing away sweat, in order to change the mask.

"You don't feel well, do you," Chris said. He managed to shake his grinning head. "You ought to lie down," she said.

He realised fully how helpless and alone he was. "No," he shouted.

"You two had better go and play."

"I want them here." He wanted to keep an eye on Linda. "Stay here," he told them.

He seemed to have earned himself a lull. Someone was knocking and ringing the bell next door, but he could bear that. Now they were banging on the window of the ground-floor flat, several of them talking in low voices. "Come on," one said. "I can't stand this." Pears was glad to hear someone else feeling that, for a change. They were going; the gate clanked. He looked up, smiling emptily, and saw Linda gazing beyond him in horror.

He twisted about. A dark blotch was scuttering over the wall, hectic tendrils quivering. It was—it was a cranefly; its legs fluttered hysterically, as if in a dying paroxysm. Still the lull. It scuttled into a corner. "I'll get it," he told Chris. She usually dealt with intruding insects; this time he'd do it, to show that he could.

He had trapped the whirring fly, it was trembling violently yet feebly in his fist like an essence of terror, when he glimpsed Chris's expression. At once she was thrusting the poker deeper into the fire. He opened the window and released the fly, and then he gazed at the fog, trying to understand. She wasn't frightened of insects. Then he knew: he'd projected his own fading terror onto her face. His nightmare had lent her a mask. He sat down, smiling at her.

When he looked away her weak smile collapsed into naked terror.

This time her smile wasn't swift enough. He forced himself to look behind him at the corner towards which she'd been glaring. He wouldn't panic, he'd fought through, the effect was fading, vanquished. But as he turned, a faint smell of something like meat touched his nostrils.

The corner was bare. He felt weak with relief, yet uneasily baffled. Briefly he'd dreamed that he was infecting Chris. He must have been right before: he was simply imposing the last of his terror on his perception of her.

Mightn't that show that the terror was leaving him? He glanced at her.

She smiled at him. She smiled. She was almost convincing. But he knew what was happening, and reality parted beneath him. The smell filled his nostrils. She hadn't been looking at the corner, but at him. He had already smelled what she smelled: himself. Behind her smile her eyes were transfixed by slivers of growing horror. As if her eyes were mirrors he could see what she saw.

In his chair she saw an eyeless face of mottled bone, grinning at her through its gaping cheeks.

At last he managed to look down at his hand. He felt his neckbone creak. His hand was still flesh, but he could feel his corpse. It was inside him, slowly corroding its way to the surface, a core of numbness spreading outwards, reaching lazily for him. It was unhurried. It had as much time as he had.

He suppressed his scream, even though it would say he was still alive. There was worse to come, he realised almost dispassionately. He looked at Andrew and Linda, watching television, sitting still. Still as corpses.

Suddenly he knew, gazing at their immobile faces on which colours flickered lightly, that they were feeling rigor mortis stake its claim on them. Death was squeezing their windpipes experimentally, like a witch in a dream. There was no dream, for he could smell them. It must be terror that was fluttering trapped in their eyes.

All he could do was close his own. It no longer mattered what was waiting in there. Anything would be more bearable than the sight of his dead children. He closed them out.

Blank.

White.

Nothing.

When he opened his eyes, feeling purged and somehow released, he was in a room with three strangers.

There was a woman, and a small imitation of her: a girl, less haggard, pinker, more plump. There was a small boy who reminded him vaguely of someone. All three of them were pretending his presence in the room was natural—pretending that they knew who this man was. They didn't, any more than he did.

They were watching him surreptitiously. He had to get out before they moved on him, the stranger. But they would never let him reach the door unless he defended himself.

He caught sight of the poker. Half of it was buried in the fire and red-hot, but the handle was insulated. He stood up gingerly and began to move stealthily towards the fire. He felt the three of them pretending not to watch him. If he used the weapon he would have to close his eyes, though he wouldn't be able to close his ears.

He had to escape. He inched towards the poker, trying to seem casual, aimless. For a moment he was surrounded by the three; his held breath burned in him. But they didn't leap.

The presence of the young girl disturbed him most of all. She was his greatest danger. There was something in her he must destroy; her freshness was deceitful, her soft plumpness was a snare. She was like the walls of the house, whose corrupted cores oozed now, thick with evil. Her innocence was disgusting, intolerable, false. He'd make sure her body could never again lure anyone. He stooped to the fire. As the poker stirred, its nest of cinders fell open, brightening.

Something came howling towards the house.

He jerked and almost fell. He stumbled to the window, knocking the television askew. They'd trapped him in his room until the howling came for him. He shouldered the clinging curtains aside and wrenched up the sash. The howling growled into silence.

A blue glow pulsed through the fog. The fog's dead heart was beating. It took him minutes to discern a blue will-o'-the-wisp, flashing sluggishly. Uniformed men strode towards him out of the fog. No, they were heading for the next house.

He turned to watch, and came face to face with a pinched white almost fleshless mask, peering through the neighbouring window.

It was his own reflection. No: it was his enemy, the man who'd been trying to drive him mad. At last Pears had found him. Now he would make him suffer.

Pears was trying to remember where he'd put the poker when the uniformed men closed around his enemy. Pears snarled in frustration. The white mask was still as they lifted the body to its feet, but the body was breathing. They could have him, so long as they used the poker on him. Pears would give them his. He turned, but the ambulance had gone.

He was staring emptily at the fog when the chemist's friends returned. They were the three he'd seen on Thursday night. He could remember. He let memories drift back as they might, hoping he wouldn't remember anything he couldn't bear.

One of the young men hurried into the flat and rummaged in a rickety chest of drawers. He snatched out a piece of paper, and something else. He moved offstage, and Pears heard a toilet flushing.

As he emerged, one of his friends demanded "Have you got the formula?"

Pears tried to control himself, but already was screaming with laughter. The three glanced sharply at him. "I'm sorry," he gasped, weeping, and was hoarse with laughter again. He ran out, ashamed and spasmodically hilarious, to explain if he could.

One frowned at him from beneath a red mock-leather cap and edged away. "Don't get paranoid," said the one who'd entered the flat. "We aren't going to make this stuff. Neither is anyone else," and he tore up the piece of paper minutely. The fragments swarmed away on the hint of a wind.

"He'd freaked out completely, that guy in there," the third said, winding his long scarf tautly into his fists. "We had to call the ambulance."

"He'd synthesised a new trip," the man in the red cap chattered, released apparently from guilt into speech. "It was too much. It got worse every time you tripped. But he said it was worth learning how to control it."

"The last one was so bad we took him away for the weekend. We thought we'd persuaded him off it. But tonight he was even deeper into it."

"I never took any," said the man with the stretched scarf. "But I was picking up his trip while we were waiting. It was that powerful, being near him could turn you on even if you hadn't taken any. It was bad. We had to call the ambulance."

"I think you had," Pears reassured him, feeling his surroundings start the long slow fall back into familiarity. He remembered the face he'd seen carried away. The eyes had been sunken, passive, immobile, at the mercy of whatever passed before or within them. They had looked exactly like red cracked glass.

Weeks later he told Chris some of what had happened, and why. Perhaps she believed him. "Did you feel any of it?" he asked. "Anything at all?"

"I don't know."

"Anything you can describe?"

"No."

Perhaps she was telling the truth; he couldn't be sure. Had she forgotten her jealousy of Linda? If so, what should that convey to him? How should he react? Since his experience he seemed to be approaching decisions more and more gently and circuitously, and making fewer.

He carried the paint and brush down the hall. Today would be the rusty gate's last day. The children shouted in the playroom. Had they felt any of it? How could he find out? It would be better to let them forget. Besides, he seemed to have forgotten all he'd ever learned about how to talk to them.

"The shuttlecock's under the stairs," Linda said, muffled.

So it was, behind a tangle of nesting chairs. Andrew ran into the hall, bursting into brighter colour as he entered the path of sunlight. He stooped beneath the stairs, but shrank back at once. "I can't find it," he called, his voice unnaturally high.

What had the boy flinched from? "There it is, Andrew," Pears said, and handed him the shuttlecock.

When Andrew had gone Pears forced himself to stoop beneath the stairs again. Under his hand the wall felt thin, a crust over softness. He made himself look at what he'd glimpsed from the corner of his eye.

It was snarling silently from the dark corner where the underside of the stairs met the floor. It was pale and smooth, and had no eyes that he could see. A mat of grey hair like a lump of dust hung over most of the face. Its mouth was huge and red with an unbroken ring of teeth, gibbous with rage.

He managed to save the tin of paint before it fell, and saw at once what the face must be. Someone had wiped a splotch of red paint with a wad of paper. The matted hair was a tangle of dust.

But the corner was bare. There was no paper beneath the stairs, and the corner was clean of dust.

CALLING CARD

RAMSEY CAMPBELL

Dorothy Harris stepped off the pavement and into her hall. As she stooped groaning to pick up the envelopes the front door opened, opened, a yawn that wouldn't be suppressed. She wrestled it shut – she must ask Simon to see to it, though certainly not over Christmas – and then she began to open the cards.

Here was Father Christmas, and here he was again, apparently after dieting. Here was a robin like a rosy apple with a beak, and here was an envelope whose handwriting staggered: Simon's and Margery's children, perhaps?

The card showed a church on a snowy hill. The hill was bare except for a smudge of ink. Though the card was unsigned, there was writing within. A Very Happy Christmas And A Prosperous New Year, the message should have said – but now it said A Very Harried Christmas And No New Year. She turned back to the picture, her hands shaking. It wasn't just a smudge of ink; someone had drawn a smeary cross on the hill: a grave.

Though the name on the envelope was a watery blur, the address was certainly hers. Suddenly the house – the kitchen and living-room, the two bedrooms with her memories

349

stacked neatly against the walls – seemed far too large and dim. Without moving from the front door she phoned Margery.

"Is it Grandma?" Margery had to hush the children while she said "You come as soon as you like, mummy."

Lark Lane was deserted. An unsold Christmas tree loitered in a shop doorway, a gargoyle craned out from the police station. Once Margery had moved away, the nearness of the police had been reassuring – not that Dorothy was nervous, like some of the old folk these days – but the police station was only a community centre now.

The bus already sounded like a pub. She sat outside on the ferry, though the bench looked and felt like black ice. Lights fished in the Mersey, gulls drifted down like snowflakes from the muddy sky. A whitish object grabbed the rail, but of course it was only a gull. Nevertheless she was glad that Simon was waiting with the car at Woodside.

As soon as the children had been packed off to bed so that Father Christmas could get to work, she produced the card. It felt wet, almost slimy, though it hadn't before. Simon pointed out what she'd overlooked: the age of the stamp. "We weren't even living there then," Margery said. "You wouldn't think they would bother delivering it after sixty years."

"A touch of the Christmas spirit."

"I wish they hadn't bothered," Margery said. But her mother didn't mind now; the addressee must have died years ago. She turned the conversation to old times, to Margery's father. Later she gazed from her bedroom window, at the houses of Bebington sleeping in pairs. A man was creeping about the house, but it was only Simon, laden with presents.

In the morning the house was full of cries of delight, gleaming new toys, balls of wrapping paper big as cabbages. In the afternoon the adults, bulging with turkey and pudding, lolled in chairs. When Simon drove her home that night, Dorothy noticed that the unsold Christmas tree was still there, a scrawny glistening shape at the back of the shop doorway. As soon as Simon left she found herself thinking about the unpleasant card. She tore it up, then went determinedly to bed.

Boxing Day was her busiest time, what with Christmas dinner Mark II, and making sure the house was impeccable, and hiding small presents for the children to find. She wished she could see them more often, but they and their parents had their own lives to lead.

An insect clung to a tinsel globe on the tree. When she reached out to squash the insect it wasn't there, neither on the globe nor on the floor. Could it have been the reflection of someone thin outside the window? Nobody was there now.

She liked the house best when it was full of laughter, and it would be again soon: "We'll get a sitter," Margery promised, "and first-foot you on New Year's Eve." That reminded Dorothy to offer the children a holiday treat. Everything seemed fine, even when they went to the door to leave. "Grandma, someone's left you a present," little Denise cried.

Then she cried out, and dropped the package. Perhaps the wind had snatched it from her hands. As the package, which looked wet and mouldy, struck the kerb it broke open. Did its contents scuttle out and sidle away into the dark? Surely that was the play of the wind, which tumbled carton and wrapping away down the street.

Someone must have used her doorway for a waste-bin, that was all. Dorothy lay in bed, listening to the wind which groped around the windowless side of the house, that faced onto the alley. She kept thinking she was on the ferry, backing away from the rail, forgetting that the rail was also behind her. Her nervousness annoyed her – she was acting like an old fogey – which was why, next afternoon, she walked to Otterspool promenade.

Gulls and planes sailed over the Mersey, which was

deserted except for buoys. On the far bank, tiny towns and stalks of factory chimneys stood at the foot of an enormous frieze of clouds. Sunlight slipped through to Birkenhead and Wallasey, touching up the colours of microscopic streets; specks of windows glinted. She enjoyed none of this, for the slopping of water beneath the promenade seemed to be pacing her. Worse, she couldn't make herself go to the rail to prove that there was nothing.

Really, it was heartbreaking. One vicious card and she felt nervous in her own house. A blurred voice seemed to creep behind the carols on the radio, lowing out of tune. Next day she took her washing to Lark Lane, in search of distraction as much as anything.

The Westinghouse Laundromat was deserted. 000, the washing machines said emptily. There was only herself, and her dervishes of clothes, and a black plastic bag almost as tall as she was. If someone had abandoned it, whatever its lumpy contents were, she could see why, for it was leaking; she smelled stagnant water. It must be a draught that made it twitch feebly. Nevertheless, if she had been able to turn off her machine she might have fled.

She mustn't grow neurotic. She still had friends to visit. The following day she went to a friend whose flat overlooked Wavertree Park. It was all very convivial – a rainstorm outside made the mince pies more warming, the chat flowed as easily as the whisky – but she kept glancing at the thin figure who stood in the park, unmoved by the downpour. The trails of rain on the window must be lending him their colour, for his skin looked like a snail's.

Eventually the 68 bus, meandering like a drunkard's monologue, took her home to Aigburth. No, the man in the park hadn't really looked as though his clothes and his body had merged into a single greyish mass. Tomorrow she was taking the children for their treat, and that would clear her mind.

She took them to the aquarium. Piranhas sank stonily, their sides glittering like Christmas cards. Toads were bubbling lumps of tar. Finny humbugs swam, and darting fish wired with light. Had one of the tanks cracked? There seemed to be a stagnant smell.

In the museum everything was under glass: shrunken heads like sewn leathery handbags, a watchmaker's workshop, buses passing as though the windows were silent films. Here was a slum street, walled in by photographs of despair, real flagstones underfoot, overhung by streetlamps on brackets. She halted between a grid and a drinking fountain; she was trapped in the dimness between blind corners, and couldn't see either way. Why couldn't she get rid of the stagnant smell? Grey forlorn faces, pressed like specimens, peered out of the walls. "Come on, quickly," she said, pretending that only the children were nervous.

She was glad of the packed crowds in Church Street, even though the children kept letting go of her hands. But the stagnant smell was trailing her, and once, when she grabbed for little Denise's hand, she clutched someone else's, which felt soft and wet. It must have been nervousness which made her fingers seem to sink into the hand.

That night she returned to the aquarium and found she was locked in. Except for the glow of the tanks, the narrow room was oppressively dark. In the nearest tank a large dead fish floated towards her, out of weeds. Now she was in the tank, her nails scrabbling at the glass, and she saw that it wasn't a fish but a snail-coloured hand, which closed spongily on hers. When she woke, her scream made the house sound very empty.

At least it was New Year's Eve. After tonight she could stop worrying. Why had she thought that? It only made her more nervous. Even when Margery phoned to confirm they would first-foot her, that reminded her how many hours she would be on her own. As the night seeped into the house, the emptiness grew. '

A knock at the front door made her start, but it was only the Harveys, inviting her next door for sherry and sandwiches. While she dodged a sudden rainstorm Mr Harvey dragged at her front door, one hand through the letter-box, until the latch clicked.

After several sherries Dorothy remembered something she'd once heard. "The lady who lived next door before me – didn't she have trouble with her son?"

"He wasn't right in the head. He got so he'd go for anyone, even if he'd never met them before. She got so scared of him she locked him out one New Year's Eve. They say he threw himself in the river, though they never found the body."

Dorothy wished she hadn't asked. She thought of the body, rotting in the depths. She must go home, in case Simon and Margery arrived. The Harveys were next door if she needed them. \

The sherries had made her sleepy. Only the ticking of her clock, clipping away the seconds, kept her awake. Twenty past eleven. The splashing from the gutters sounded like wet footsteps pacing outside the window. She had never noticed she could smell the river in her house. She wished she had stayed longer with the Harveys; she would have been able to hear Simon's car.

Twenty to twelve. Surely they wouldn't wait until midnight. She switched on the radio for company. A compere was making people laugh; a man was laughing thickly, sounding waterlogged. Was he a drunk in the street? He wasn't on the radio. She mustn't brood; why, she hadn't put out the sherry glasses; that was something to do, to distract her from the intolerably measured counting of the clock, the silenced radio, the emptiness displaying her sounds –

Though the knock seemed enormously loud, she didn't

start. They were here at last, though she hadn't heard the car. It was New Year's Day. She ran, and had reached the front door when the phone shrilled. That startled her so badly that she snatched the door open before lifting the receiver.

Nobody was outside – only a distant uproar of cheers and bells and horns – and Margery was on the phone. "We've been held up, mummy. There was an accident in the tunnel. We'll be over as soon as we can."

Then who had knocked? It must have been a drunk; she heard him stumbling beside the house, thumping on her window. He'd better take himself off, or she would call Mr Harvey to deal with him. But she was still inside the doorway when she saw the object on her step.

Good God, was it a rat? No, just a shoe, so ancient that it looked stuffed with mould. It wasn't mould, only a rotten old sock. There was something in the sock, something that smelled of stagnant water and worse. She stooped to peer at it, and then she was struggling to close the door, fighting to make the latch click, no breath to spare for a scream. She'd had her first foot, and now – hobbling doggedly alongside the house, its hands slithering over the wall – here came the rest of the body.

ACKNOWLEDGMENTS

For this Encyclopocalypse Publications edition of Spook City, I would like to thank Steve Jones, who provided further contractual guidance and advice, and Peter Atkins who, over dinner in Musso & Frank, suggested that we dust off this dark guidebook and look to again revisit the haunted streets of our hometown.

COPYRIGHT NOTICE

Clive Barker

- "The Forbidden" © 1985. Originally published in *Fantasy Tales No.14*, Summer 1985.
- "Dread" © 1984. Originally published in *Clive Barker's Books of Blood Volume II*.
- "Coming to Grief" © 1988. Originally published in *Prime Evil*.

All are reprinted by permission of the author, and Little Brown.

<u>Ramsey Campbell</u>

- "Coming to Liverpool" © 2008. Previously unpublished.
- "The Man in the Underpass" © 1975. Originally published in *The Year's Best Horror Stories III*.
- "Mackintosh Willy" © 1979. Originally published in *Shadows 2*.
- "Concussion" © 1973. Originally published in *Demons by Daylight*.
- "Through the Walls" © 1985was originally published in *British Fantasy Society Booklet No.5*.
- "Calling Card" © 1981. Originally published in *Dark Companions*.

All are reprinted by permission of the author.